Draw Me In

Logan Meredith

RIPTIDE
PUBLISHING

Riptide Publishing
PO Box 1537
Burnsville, NC 28714
www.riptidepublishing.com

Draw Me In

Cover art: L.C. Chase, lcchase.com
Editor: Veronica Vega
Layout: L.C. Chase, lcchase.com

ISBN: 978-1-62649-974-4

First edition
October, 2022

Also available in ebook:
ISBN: 978-1-62649-975-1

Draw Me In

Logan Meredith

RIPTIDE
PUBLISHING

Table of Contents

Chapter One

Brick

I hoisted the lone remaining cardboard box to the kitchen table with the elation of a marathon runner crossing the finish line. The box cutter sliced through the multiple layers of tape as quickly as the first thousand. I inhaled and pushed out the breath slowly, pulled the flaps free, and peered inside. *Oh, wonderful!* Yet another mystery box my ex-wife, Jane, allowed the military to cart across the country for no reason other than she thought I should have helped unpack more when we were together. Cursing, I separated the copious amounts of paper from the contents—piece by piece, unwrapping old mail and the remains of a kitchen junk drawer from three addresses ago.

"It's outdated, but it has good bones." Zach Robinson, my oldest friend, strolled into the kitchen. He glanced around, apparently at the conclusion of his self-guided tour, displaying the same apprehensive expression I'd worn the first time I laid eyes on my new place.

I huffed. "Yeah, like us." The house was from an era not long after we were born, but the previous owners had updated it about fifteen years ago. It was bad, but not quite "avocado green appliances" bad.

"Speaking of old. What's with the gray?" I pointed to the salt-and-pepper hairs on his chin that had been reddish-brown when I'd last seen him a few months ago. I should have known he'd be one of the lucky bastards made more attractive by it.

"You don't like it?" He stroked his beard.

I shrugged without answering, but he flashed a toothy grin that said he knew he looked good. "This place is exactly what I need. It's turnkey, but chock-full of distractions. I've got a few projects planned before school starts."

"I hope that gold wallpaper and red paint in the master is on the list."

"Absolutely," I answered, shuffling through the mail and setting aside anything that appeared remotely Army-related. Then I dumped all the paper, inconsequential flyers, and junk back into the carton. "Just a second."

I made my way to the garage, sorted the contents between the recycling and trash container, broke down the box, and stacked it with the others. Exhaling a breath of relief, I surveyed the well-organized space. *There. Done.*

When I returned to the kitchen, Zach dangled a piece of junk mail I must have overlooked in front of me with a mischievous smile. "You missed one, Bainbridge," he chuffed, still as amused by my legal first name as the day he'd learned it.

I shot him a knock-it-off expression accompanied by my middle finger. "You're never allowed to call me that."

His smile broke into a laugh, and I was filled with a warm sense of nostalgia. It was going to be nice living near Zach again. He was one of the few people in my life who knew the real me, even if that meant he could use that information against me occasionally. Lifelong friendship came with those sort of privileges.

Zach dropped the letter on the stack, and then picked up the pile. "Toss these?"

"No. I'll shred them later. Want a beer?" I opened the fridge and placed a chilled bottle in Zach's outstretched hand, led him to the sliding door, and stepped out on the sun-drenched deck. The weather was warm, but not uncomfortably so for Texas in early May.

"Sit." I offered him a cushion for the new patio chairs. They cost a fortune, but I'd always loved outdoor living. One of the few vices Jane allowed me had been smoking a cigar on the patio in the evenings. It'd always been the best part of my day, even after my mother's lung cancer diagnosis caused me to quit smoking.

Zach plopped onto the lounge chair, toed off his shoes, and put his feet up. His pasty-white legs extending from khaki cargo shorts created quite the contrast to his tanned arms. "Finally, time to relax and kick back, eh? This is what I thought 'come over and see my place' would be all about. I arrived an hour too early."

Grabbing an extra pillow to support my back, I mirrored his position. "For the record, *this* was the plan." I gestured around the deck. Why the previous owners had chosen to add an outdoor kitchen and kick-ass sound system before updating the inside remained a mystery, but it sold the place for me, so I supposed their strategy had worked. "It took me forever to get that damn garage put together, and you've seen how I like my shit organized."

His brow peaked, and I knew he was thinking of the time he'd shown up unexpectedly at our place in Virginia about three years ago. It was a month after Jane and I had moved in. I'd been down at Fort Benning the week before and hadn't unpacked, let alone cleaned. "That was all Jane."

Zach laughed with a knowing smile. "Without you, that woman will end up on one of those hoarding shows."

I tilted my head back and cast an amused smile in Zach's direction. Jane was famously not a great housekeeper, which was a frequent source of aggravation in my life, but to the limited extent I'd had a "bash the ex" phase, it was over. I sipped my beer, imagining Jane's new life in Maine. She'd gotten herself a job at a retail shop and, true to form, had made a gaggle of new friends. "She'll be fine."

Zach didn't take the hint. He rehashed in Jane-like detail how unfair he thought our settlement was, particularly her share of my pension. Most of it was residual bitterness from his own divorce six years earlier, so I let him vent. There was no point trying to explain to him yet again that our situations were not the same. Zach's ex had done him dirty, ripping apart both his heart and bank account on her way to another man. Jane and I had both known my retirement would be the end of the road for us. Our physical and emotional relationship had ended long before our legal one.

We were, dare I say, friends? *Eh.* We were getting there.

I only knew we were both trying not to harbor any resentment. The woman could have authored a how-to book on being a perfect military spouse. She learned the lingo, became an expert at navigating bureaucracy, and never missed a chance to flatter my chain of command or offer support to other spouses. I owed it to her to stick it out until our twentieth anniversary so she'd keep her spousal benefits and, yeah, max out her split of my pension. As far as I was concerned, she'd earned them, same as me. I didn't begrudge her a fresh start. Our marriage was a little like that last box—we hauled it around from city to city because it was easier than offloading it, but I wouldn't miss it.

"So, what else do you have planned for your summer?"

I'd been hotly anticipating having the ability to meet someone, invite them back to mine, and see where things led, but Zach didn't need to know that. Gesturing to the vast empty lot behind the deck, I chuckled. "Definitely landscaping, and I have a few other minor projects here and there to keep me from losing my mind."

Zach's ears perked up. I knew that expression.

"Fuck. What?"

He took a swig, grinning roguishly around the head of his beer bottle. "So remember that whole debacle I told you about with Craig Nelms last month?"

"Is that the teacher that you fired? I thought you found someone to finish up the year."

Zach nodded, his lips pursed in disgust. "I hired a permanent sub to take his classes, but Craig wasn't only a history teacher, he coached the Academic Olympiad team, and since you're officially a—"

My hands shot up as though I could physically stop the words from leaving his mouth. "No way. I don't even know what that is, but I'm nervous about teaching JROTC enough already. Let me crawl before I walk."

Zach huffed. "But you'd be perfect for it, and it's actually a great program. The kids practically do all the work themselves. Jared Armstrong and Peter Lim would love you. Peter is JROTC battalion commander this year and applying to West Point. Jared is headed to the Ivy Leagues. He's been on the team all three years. These are some of the most self-motivated students at Northridge."

"If it's so easy, why doesn't an experienced teacher take over?"

Zach frowned. "Okay, I can't lie . . . it's intense. Most of my faculty have families or already have clubs or activities they sponsor. Craig didn't exactly play well with others, so no one was eager to help him. But Northridge High has gone to the State competition three times in the last ten years and once to Nationals. Trust me, the superintendent notices these things."

"Nationals?" I snorted. "So this is a whole thing?"

"Oh yeah. It's a big competition. Think National Spelling Bee-level pressure. Each team comprises six students, three girls and three boys. The kids that win State get $50,000 college scholarships."

I whistled. "Damn. But if these are the brightest kids in the school, don't they already get scholarships?"

"They aren't necessarily the smartest kids. They have academic weaknesses too. The rules say you have to have two students with no better than a B average and two kids with no better than a C average. I hope I can find someone to take over. Northridge isn't exactly an affluent community, and fifty grand would make a big difference to these kids . . ."

I launched a pointed stare at his aggressive sales pitch. He paused and flashed his boyish *Who me?* smile. The one that always ended with me getting in trouble, or him getting laid, or—in one particularly regretful night—both.

"Knock it off with the puppy-dog eyes. I said no."

"Okay." He took a gulp, trying to wait me out in silence. When I leveled a *this won't work* glare at him, he chuckled. "But is this the same no you gave me when I wanted to move the Virgin Mary statue into Father James' bed at St. Bartholomew?"

I cracked up with the memory of one of Zach's better pranks. "No."

He bobbed his head a few times, no doubt taking the time to plan his attack. Zach wasn't one to go down swinging, but that was only because he usually got his way without expending that much effort. Thankfully, his cocky smile didn't do shit for me anymore.

"So it's more like the no you gave me when I told you to get your teacher's license so you can head up the JROTC program and move your ass to Northridge, Texas."

I made a disagreeable noise, although he was right. I'd turned down Zach's suggestion initially, multiple times, but then Jane announced she was moving to Maine, and I realized I had no reason to stay in Virginia. "That smirk of yours will get you punched one day. No, this will not be another thing you talk me into."

"You offend my smirk. We've made it to forty-six without getting decked."

"What about Melissa Villanueva's dad?"

He tsked and rubbed his jaw with the memory. "That punch was because he caught me deflowering his daughter. The smirk came later when I was telling you and the guys all about it."

My laugh into the neck of my beer whistled back, and I shook my head. "Forty-six and still a punk."

"Hey, just because you married the girl you lost your virginity to . . . Oh shit." Zach sat upright suddenly and grabbed my forearm with a wide-eyed expression that gave me heartburn. "New summer project idea! We have to get you laid."

I choked on the rush of acid licking the back of my throat. "Um . . . No."

He angled toward me. "Come on, man. You gave Jane a respectable courtesy period. She's two thousand miles away. You've only been with one woman. It's my duty as your oldest friend."

"Zach . . ."

"C'mon. Brick. You're an attractive guy. Ladies of Northridge will be all over you."

"Zach." Any of my subordinates would have heard my tone as a warning to knock it off, but not Zach. He rambled on about all the women he could fix me up with. Unprepared to go into details, I tried saying nothing until I couldn't anymore.

"Zach," I spat out and heaved an irritated sigh. "I'm not looking for *ladies*."

He stared at me, his mouth gaping. I held his gaze for a few seconds to give him time to process, but it was clear his disbelief wasn't going anywhere. I rolled my eyes hard. "You, of all people, shouldn't be shocked."

"But you married Jane."

"Did you think it cured me from being bisexual?"

Zach stiffened. "No. I . . . I'm sorry. I assumed you had decided since you were into women too, you would . . . It was dumb. Sorry." He twisted, slung his feet up again, and leaned back. Arms behind his head, he fixed his eyes intently on the sky.

So, I guess I *was* going there. "It's fine. And I never mentioned it because of Jane, but it's not like I didn't explore that side of me for the last twenty years."

"You cheated on Jane?" Another audible intake of air reminded me of the reasons I'd never corrected his perceptions of my marriage. Understandably, Zach could be sensitive about that topic, given his ex's adultery. I should have eased him into this part, but what the hell? I was over being discreet, especially with my oldest friend.

"Jane and I had an arrangement."

He trained one skeptical eye on me. "What kind of arrangement?"

"The kind that left both of us free to get our physical needs met elsewhere."

"You both cheated!" He sat up again, judgment rolling off of him in waves, but I refused to feel bad. Any guilt or shame I had, I'd worked through years ago. An open relationship had worked best for both of us.

"No," I said calmly. "She wanted the flexibility to explore as much as I did, so after they ended DADT, we agreed on the rules, the most important being discretion."

"So you only—" he made a finger in hole gesture "—with men now."

"Look. I'm out of the closet. I'm not in the market for a second wife any more than a first husband. I want to enjoy the freedom to pursue whoever catches my eye, but lately my eyes have been heavily seeking men. That going to be a problem?"

"No, of course not." The words didn't match his rigid body language, but I knew he'd get there. Not unlike the first moment I'd come out to him, we sat there together, in uncomfortable silence. When he took a sip of his empty bottle, shifting nervously, I put him out of his misery.

"You get two questions to help wrap your head around this."

He smiled relief and without hesitation asked, "Are you still . . ." His pained expression was the only thing I needed to finish the sentence, but he gestured to himself anyway.

"Have I been hiding feelings for you for thirty years?" I released a hearty laugh. It was so like Zach to go there first. "Not even a little.

You may have been my first crush, but I'm definitely not interested in straight guys. Besides, you're not my type."

"First, fuck you. I'm everyone's type." We both laughed, and I appreciated he was trying to recover from his earlier awkwardness. He was good like that. "Second, what *is* your type?"

I bit my lip as I contemplated his question and tried to picture the guys that had drawn my attention of late, but a single image didn't come. The bars in a military town weren't a safe option, so I'd made an early decision to keep my explorations professional. Literally. No chance of broken hearts or misunderstandings. While escorts didn't offer ironclad guarantees of client confidentiality, it sure beat the odds of random hookups. Not that I wanted to explain any of that to Zach. "Is that *really* how you want to use your second question?"

"No." He snorted. "I guess I want to know how that works? Like you only want a guy now? Does that mean you're gay?"

"No. It means I'm still bisexual, but . . ." I stopped, pondering a Zach-friendly way to explain it. "Look. I married Jane because I loved her. Our issues had nothing to do with a lack of attraction. She was a beautiful woman. Still is. But on some subconscious level, I guess I proposed because I didn't want to deal with myself. Getting caught with a guy back then would have ended my career, and being married gave me a good reason to not think about it. We rushed in. Too different and too young to realize we didn't want the same things."

Zach nodded sympathetically. He knew Jane and I were totally different people. She hated exploring a new city, and anything remotely outdoorsy or cultural bored her to tears. She much preferred socializing with friends and shopping, which I loathed. As we neared my retirement, staying together had felt like a prison sentence neither of us had earned.

"Jane and I dealt with our arrangement as a sexual outlet. Since our divorce, I've realized it's bigger than that. At this point, I'd like to find someone I connect with and who turns me on to spend time with. That could be a woman, but I've always suspected I'd be happier with a man." I sighed heavily and found comfort in Zach's earnest expression. "I'm not straight and I don't want to look back at my entire life and regret not living that truth."

Zach's face split into a grin. "Dude, if Brick Hausman is going to talk about living his truth, I'm going to need another beer."

Chuckling, I retrieved another round and turned the conversation into something way less deep. We ordered a pizza and talked about the upcoming school year into the wee hours of the night. Zach was good like that. We'd been friends since we were teens, and he'd been a huge motivator in the second career I was about to embark on, but he wasn't the guy you poured your heart out to. Especially not a rainbow-colored heart. I wasn't trying to change the nature of our friendship after thirty-some years.

But after he'd left, I lay in bed staring at the truly horrendous wallpaper, thinking about what I wanted in this new stage of life. The evening had given my vague feelings of longing some clarity. I wanted to date a man. Jesus, that thought was overwhelming. I was forty-six years old and had dated no one since I'd met Jane. Where did I even begin?

Chapter Two

Jesse

"It's clear in the flyer. Students must submit at least four finished pieces before they can take my AP class. Zach acted like it was my fault registrations were messed up." Olivier Lesueur, one of the few coworkers I actually socialized with, nodded along as I ranted about our boss.

I grabbed the top rung of the ladder and stepped up, stretching my arm as far as it would go. Olivier fed me another section of the gorgeous three-dimensional floral panel I was installing to hide the institutional-gray paint.

"This is too heavy. Hand me that bigger fastener. I'll need to hook this part to the ceiling."

"Jesse," Olivier chastised me. "Nothing should go in the ceiling tiles. They covered that about a million times. Mr. Samuel had to repair six classroom ceilings last year."

Undeterred, I shook my hand at my desk until he handed it over. I was careful as I secured the installation and climbed down from the ladder. I took a moment to enjoy the flow of the piece and the way it obscured the drab portable wall that was better suited for inspiring arson than creativity. "Well, what do you think?"

Olivier stepped back, his eyes roaming critically. "*Magnifique*," he said with a perfect French accent. "But the second Mr. Samuel sees it, he will take it down, so I don't understand why you bother."

I growled. Ever since they'd exiled me to the portables, it had been one custodial conflict after the other. "Mr. Samuel hates me for no reason."

Olivier disagreed with a huff. "You bit his head off over the storage closet fiasco."

"I didn't bite his head off. How do they expect my students to do their best work with this prison motif they've sequestered us in?"

"Better find a way to deal with it, because we're definitely not getting any more space until the TRE passes. You think last year's budget cuts were bad? Next year will be a bloodbath."

I shuddered at the thought. The Tax Rate Election, or TRE, was to fund a new elementary school and a math and science building, in addition to critical building repairs and program support. It was going to the voters in November. "If Zach cuts electives again, I swear I'm changing careers. I'll work with Sierra at the Artsy Soul and give pottery lessons to preschoolers before I make one more concession. I am absolutely not combining the AP classes."

With a sympathetic quirk of his lip, Olivier took a seat at my desk. "I'm sure Sierra would love to have her best friend with her, but unless you're open to a volunteer position, I wouldn't bank on that plan. The Artsy Soul is barely covering her salary these days. I'm not exactly sitting pretty with these latest changes either. French enrollment dropped thirty-five percent across the district."

"I should have introduced her to a rich man," I quipped.

"Too late. She's mine." He wiggled his ring finger, showing off his gold wedding band. Olivier checked his watch and stood, feet angled toward the door. "We need to get a move on. Faculty meeting starts in ten minutes."

"Oh, good. Another tedious jeopardy game to see if we read the handbook."

As usual, Olivier didn't react to my sarcasm. He bumped the door with his hip and waited for me to wash my hands and grab my bag. On the way out, he gave me an uncharacteristically stern look. "You've made enemies of the principal, the custodian, and half the staff. Will you at least try to play nice this year? For me. *S'il te plaît.*"

My nose wrinkled. Despite my reputation, I never intended to be difficult, but my coworkers didn't make it easy. "I'll try to be nice, but I'm going to stand up for myself. Always."

In the six years Zach Robinson had been Northridge High principal, I'd come to hate faculty meetings. Actually, hate might be too kind. I loathed them.

My mood improved ever so slightly when Olivier and I ran into Monique, who taught foreign languages with Olivier, and Marie and Tessa, my art and music teammates. It was hard not to catch their infectious energy as we caught up from the Summer and found our seats. They were the sort of teachers that inspired me and reminded me of why I'd chosen my career. Their optimism even carried me for about thirty minutes into Zach's meeting when I heard the dreaded words.

"Don't forget we're here for the kids."

I couldn't recall a single faculty meeting where Zach hadn't uttered that phrase. This time the comment came after he'd finished outlining two new policies that, "we were basically already doing anyway," that we were absolutely not all doing.

Translation: Stop complaining.

It was such a belittling statement. My colleagues and I hadn't had a raise in three years. He was delusional if he thought anyone was here for a reason other than the kids.

My hand shot in the air, and Olivier served me a warning glance accompanied by a chorus of sighs from the entire English department.

Zach's head dipped to check his watch. "Yes, Mr. Berry."

I did my best to be reasonable. "I appreciate the concern about propping doors open, but could you make an exception for the art teachers because the paint fumes overwhelm the portables? We don't have the high ceilings like they do in the J building."

"Since your concern is limited to the art program, can we discuss this after the meeting?" Poorly controlled frustration dripped from Zach's tone.

I nodded, and Zach avoided my eye contact as he moved on in his agenda.

"Teachers, I realize you have a lot going on, but we had abysmal compliance with completing syllabus uploads by last Monday. We invested heavily in technology because it was the number one concern of our families. They asked us for better communication. When we issue deadlines, parents rely on those announcements." I glanced at Olivier and a few other faces, but everyone seemed to accept the lazy teacher narrative Zach loved to dish out. Well, not me. My hand returned to the air.

"Yes, Mr. Berry."

"The parent portal was down all weekend."

Zach's eyes started an upward track, but he caught himself before he fully rolled them at me. "Other teachers met the deadline."

I explained as calmly as I could how the outage had impacted us and detailed the process that was far from the simple task he'd represented. Murmurs of agreement ran through the crowd. Then there was another swell of dissent as the teachers that had been successful tried to assist those who hadn't.

Olivier raised his hand, casting a remorseful glance in my direction. "I finished mine. They told us in the training you have to remove the percent sign from all the averages. Enter everything as a decimal even though the field help text says to enter as a percent. Did you do that?"

I was still processing the tire tracks rolling over my back when an angel in the last row shouted, "They didn't cover that in my training. What training did you have, Olivier?"

The topic devolved into mass confusion as we realized some people got in-person training and others watched a video.

"Okay, everyone. Please." Zach's voice carried above the throng and quieted the frenzy, but his eyes zeroed in on me. Which, screw that. All I did was point out that he shouldn't be blaming teachers for things beyond our control. We had enough shit to deal with. "Please, guys. I will check into the training issue. Let's return to the agenda. Classes start in one week, and I have several clubs and extracurriculars that need faculty sponsors . . ."

A deep, low laugh rumbled behind me as Zach moved on. I shifted in my seat to catch a glimpse at the source. The guy was huge—tall and built like a statue of Zeus come to life. His shirt and tie amongst the jeans and T-shirt crowd screamed, *I'm from administration*. Whoever he was, he was new. There was no chance I hadn't noticed him last year.

Thick eyebrows jumped when he caught me glowering at him, but his expression registered more amusement than commiseration over our principal, so I returned my attention to the front of the room. His gaze weighed on the back of my neck as I tried and failed to keep my mouth closed. Whenever I said anything, I could hear his suppressed sounds of enjoyment, which I couldn't quite interpret. Was he laughing with me or at me? It was hard to tell, but he sure found the dull meeting hilarious. Unable to resist my curiosity, I snuck another glance over my shoulder, covertly taking in as many details as I could.

Who was he?

Brick

When my first faculty meeting concluded, Zach became engaged in what appeared to be a heated discussion with the art teachers. Figuring that he'd be tied up for a while, I refamiliarized myself with my new workplace.

Northridge High School was a sprawling campus of one- and two-story buildings, connected by covered walkways. A spattering of parking lots seemed to fill all the open spaces. Except for the lack of security, it appeared much the same as my old workplace, with aging buildings interspersed with newer ones.

The administration offices and cafeteria were in A building, which served as the main entrance and was original to the school. The letters progressed alphabetically as the buildings moved out from there, with some oddities thrown in to keep me from getting too confident. The J building, where my classroom was located, was across the large parking lot adjacent to the F building, a much-older two-story building that housed the math and science classrooms. Behind it was the school football field and a track. To the east was a row of portables labeled K through O on the map.

The midafternoon sun beat down on me as I crossed the blacktop. I rolled up my sleeves, cursing my decision to wear a shirt and tie, then adjusted the computer bag I'd slung over my shoulder. When I reached the J building, I checked my watch. Seven minutes at a good clip. Guess I wouldn't be using the teachers' lounge in the A building for my thirty-minute lunch breaks.

The JROTC classroom was large and flanked by a wall of south-facing windows. On the back wall were pictures of the President, Vice President, Secretary of Defense, and Secretary of Army. Sergeant Major Grant had left posters that emphasized good citizenship, uniform standards, and the various ribbons and awards handed out for students.

I took a seat at my desk and mindlessly opened the drawers. The only contents were a stack of postcard-size laminated cards printed with the Cadet Creed. I ran my fingers over the smooth edges and read it.

I am an Army Junior ROTC Cadet.

I will always conduct myself to bring credit to my family, country, school and the Corps of Cadets.

I am loyal and patriotic.

I am the future of the United States of America.

My brain tripped over that one line, transporting me back to high school, when thoughts of joining the Army filled me with all the good feelings. Every value in that creed had spoken to my younger self—honesty, integrity, good citizenship, accountability, patriotism, hard work, and leadership. I was the kid that fell asleep staring at a Be All You Can Be poster and not only because it had a picture of a hot guy on it.

May God grant me the strength to always live by this creed.

Something hit me sharply in the chest, shrapnel from the near lifetime of memories that had exploded into my consciousness. Forcing my brain to relive all the hope, anticipation, fear, and disappointment from my career all at once.

I'd bought the complete package. I wasn't regretful about my career, exactly. Or cynical, even. While life as a soldier hadn't lived up to all the "Mom and apple pie" dreams I'd once had, the Army had given me a lot and taken from me far less than I'd been willing to sacrifice for it. I'd had a good, rewarding career, and I'd retired with my mind and body intact. The Army was still giving to me now—a second career. A chance to mentor kids.

Emotions flooded into my psyche like they were pouring out of an open faucet. I took a few wet, deep breaths and tried to get my shit together. These kids *were* the future, and somehow Zach and the Army thought it'd be a good idea for me to prepare them. To instill in them a value system that had served our country well for generations.

This was real.

I mopped up my wet eyes and summoned the same level of enthusiasm and confidence I'd had when I accepted my ROTC scholarship. I put aside all my reservations and focused on my mission.

I got moving, organizing tables and moving flags to the back of the room near the door so they'd be more convenient for the color guard to take outside for drills. I worked on my seating charts and made a list of tasks for the cadet commander's addressing, starting with the charlie foxtrot going on in the small office next to my classroom.

Zach had warned me I'd be in for a major reorganization, and he wasn't kidding. The room had barely any shelving. Boxes of all sizes were precariously stacked on the floor and desk like a nearly over Jenga game. I'd be hard-pressed to locate anything, let alone safely remove it. The whole structure would collapse.

I looked around for something on-hand that might aid organization, unsure of the protocol for acquisitions. Given the temperament of the faculty meeting, I didn't think the Army standard practice of acquiring whatever your fellow soldiers left unattended would go over well. I tabled that decision in favor of rearranging a few other things to make the classroom feel more mine. Since I walked when I talked, I made an aisle for pacing and moved the pictures of current officeholders out of my line of sight.

"Settling in?" Zach asked from the doorway, loosening his tie, clearly amused by my intensity. His suit jacket was off, but he wasn't nearly as disheveled as I was.

"Attempting to," I said, straightening and stretching my back. "Hey. Who is in charge of acquisitions and logistics? Is that you?"

Zach's lips pursed, and he smacked them like he did when he was thinking. "What for?"

"Come with me." I walked to the small office and attempted to fling open the door, which was immediately met with the boxes on the other side and swung back. I shot out my hand to stop it, and Zach and I slid into the opening.

"This will not work." I pointed to the pile of supplies I had no room for that had grown with my other reorganization efforts. "I need shelves and storage space."

"Well, first, I'd suggest talking to Jesse Berry about the shared closet space. It's honestly where most of this stuff should be. Sergeant Major Grant found it easier to give up his office than fight Berry over the space after a skirmish last year. There is a district surplus area you have to check before you can order anything, but if you're nice to Mr. Samuel, he can keep an eye out for something that might work."

I nodded, laughing softly. "Berry? That's the guy who had the vein bulging on your forehead, right?"

Zach nodded curtly. "The same. Talented teacher. Royal pain in my ass."

"Now, now, Zach. Don't forget we're here for the kids." I did my best impression of his condescending tone.

Zach pursed his lips. "I don't sound like that."

I slapped him on the shoulder. "You kind of do, my friend. I was reading the room, and I got to say it went over about as well as telling a bunch of corporals to 'be all they can be' when I needed them to dig latrines."

Zach's unamused expression was enough for me to back off. It would take adjustment to remember he wasn't simply a friend anymore, but my actual boss. "C'mon." I lassoed my arm around his shoulder. "You promised me a drink."

I followed Zach outside and caught sight of Jesse Berry on the ramp between two portables, talking animatedly with a tall, dark-skinned man I recognized from the meeting. It appeared Jesse was giving him a piece of his mind too. Awfully intense facial expressions for a minor disagreement. I elbowed Zach. "Does he fight with everyone like that?"

Zach peeked up and when the other man noticed him, he waved and smiled. "That's Olivier Lesueur." Zach returned his wave.

"Olivier? As in Sir Laurence Olivier?"

Zach nodded, cringing. "Yeah. And definitely not a fan of being called Oliver, trust me. He teaches French. Good guy. Strong teacher. He and Berry are friends, so I imagine it isn't fighting. Berry can be . . .

passionate about certain topics. As you could undoubtedly tell from the meeting, he's my resident shit-stirrer."

Interesting. So Jesse was a hothead of sorts. My attention was drawn to his constantly moving hands. Since I'd been seated behind him during the meeting, other than the vague exchange of smiles, I hadn't gotten a good look. I could see him clearly now as we walked toward the car.

He was handsome, if not conventionally so. On the shorter side with an average build. His facial features were sharp and way too intense for his bohemian style. Kind of like seeing one of the generals dressed up as a hippie for Halloween. It didn't quite fit. He wasn't someone that typically caught my eye, but there was something about him I found oddly captivating. Perhaps it was his passion or his outspokenness. Jane was no shirking violet, that was for sure.

The way Jesse dealt with Zach had gotten a small laugh out of me a few times. But watching him now, there was more to my interest than the way Jesse got that vein in Zach's forehead bulging. Something about him made me want to see if I could redirect some of that passion toward me.

"You'll want to buddy up to him when he gets to food week. You don't want to miss the crêpes. It's usually the week before fall break."

I tuned back into Zach. "Sorry, what?"

"His students make crêpes as part of their French cultural studies."

I shook my head to remove the rogue thoughts of Jesse Berry. The last thing I needed was to develop a crush on a coworker. Even if everything about him was totally working for me, it was a risky idea. If I'd learned anything from Jane's insistence on discretion, it was you don't shit where you eat.

Chapter Three

Jesse

Technically, the entire week before classes started were faculty workdays, but other than Zach's welcome back faculty meeting and a few continuing education seminars, the schedule was pretty loose.

I cruised into the near-empty parking lot and secured my favorite spot—immediately outside my old classroom, under a large shade tree, and close to the handicap ramp. Full of enthusiasm, I used the handcart to wheel my summer accumulation of bargain finds and discounted bulk purchases from the Artsy Soul's vendors to restock my closet.

Key in hand, I entered the J building, then proceeded to my storage area. Humming gently to myself, I stuck the key in the lock and . . . *nothing.* My heart sped up as I briefly considered someone had tampered with it again. My mind raced forward to a nightmare scenario where I couldn't get in and was behind from the very first week. The lock appeared fine, so I tried again. "Damn it," I muttered, turning the key as hard as I could without breaking it.

"That won't work."

"Oh, Jesus fuck," I screamed, twisting to see the owner of the voice who had startled me. Disappointment hit me hard. First, because the body I'd been fantasizing about for days was draped in a military uniform, and second, because the dimple I'd spent an hour trying to capture from memory was on his right cheek instead of his left.

Hand still covering my racing heart, I glanced to both sides, grateful no one was around to overhear me swearing. I pulled myself together with an exhaled, "Sorry. I didn't realize anyone else was in the building."

"Didn't mean to scare you. We haven't met. I'm Lieutenant Colonel Hausman, the new JROTC instructor." He extended a hand for me to shake, which I did. His face relaxed a bit. Damn, I'd got his eyebrows wrong too. They were much thicker and darker than I remembered and way more expressive than I'd done justice to.

"Jesse Berry. I teach the AP Studio Art Program. Welcome to Northridge."

"May I . . ." He gestured to the door and without waiting for my response, stepped his imposing form in front of me.

I shuffled backward to make room, narrowly tripping over my handcart. "Oh. Um. I need to find the custodian. Someone changed my lock."

"That was me. I understand you had issues with my predecessor."

I nodded, although with his back to me he couldn't have seen, and before I could get a word in, he continued, "I spoke to Mr. Samuel and attempted to get shelves for my office to store our supplies. Unfortunately, we could not because of the fire code." He produced a key from his pocket and unlocked the door. Pushing it open, he gestured for me to enter first. "Since this was the only space allotted for our use and neither Mr. Samuel nor I had a key, I had your lock replaced."

From outside the door, I could see the entire closet had been rearranged and brand-new shelves installed. I entered cautiously, trying to sort through my confusion among the meticulously arranged cubbies and boxes. "Is that a table?"

His lip quirked, and I couldn't tell what about this gave him so much enjoyment. "Yes. Not only does this provide extra workspace, but it also serves as a neutral zone buffer. I have placed this sign here." He flipped over the plastic stand so I could see it.

"No JROTC behind this table," I read. My eyes whipped around the room, outrage growing as I noticed shiny white cards were under each section, half of which had neatly printed black labels and the other half messy handwritten scrawling I recognized as my old labels taped on top of new cards.

"Honestly, there was a lot of opportunity to maximize space. I don't get what Sergeant Major Grant was thinking when he ordered those shelves."

Offended, I huffed. "I ordered the original shelves. And I was thinking about what I needed for the art classes."

"Noted. May I?" He gestured to my handcart and rolled it all the way into the room, lifting the boxes onto the table like they were full of feathers. The uniform didn't show off his physique, but the effortless way he moved, after I'd broken a sweat loading it, gave my imagination plenty to work with.

"I'm sure you'll agree that this is far more optimized. The label maker is here." He pointed to a small plastic bin. "Feel free to use it."

He glanced up and smiled. A knowing smile with twinkling eyes that reminded me of Zach's. He expected to get his way. He totally thought I'd be putty in his rather large hands. Well, no sir. I opened my mouth to tell him exactly what he could do with his label maker when he kept talking, leaving me standing with my mouth gaped.

"There were some half-open boxes of the same thing, so we combined what we could and—"

The absolute nerve of this guy. "You moved my stuff? You cut off my lock, and you moved my stuff. Do I have that right?"

"I'm—"

"Listen Sergeant Major Hausman—" I paused when he physically winced. "Hallman?" I guessed.

"Um . . . Hausman is correct, but you took away my commission. It's Lieutenant Colonel Hausman."

"Your what?"

"My commission. I'm an O-5 . . . You know what? Never mind. You can actually call me Brick." I swore his smile existed only to fluster me.

"Brick?" I repeated. "Did your parents not like you or something?"

Brick barked out a laugh, and I closed my eyes to get my bearings. It was rare to get laughter when I was about to explode. Not to brag, but most of the time, my colleagues tried not to piss me off. Why should he be immune?

"Seventh-grade football coach. Nickname stuck. So, did you want my help to reorganize or label?" He held up the label maker like he was showing me his favorite toy.

I drew up as straight as I could, still inches short of coming eye-to-eye. "Brick, as you can imagine art requires a lot of supplies. My colleagues and I need this entire space for our students. I'm sorry, but this will not work. Now, then. Where are the rest of our things?"

Brick cringed, glancing behind me at the shelves. "This is everything."

"No." I gestured to the room. "This entire closet was full of art supplies. So, if your stuff is taking half—"

"We have exactly forty percent of the room, which is what the space survey the custodian gave me showed."

"You measured the room?"

Brick nodded proudly. "The replacement storage system has two extra shelves. We put the flatter, lighter stuff on top and the smaller stuff here." He pointed to a cabinet with shoebox-sized bins. "Mr. Samuel was very clear that we can't have stuff stacked to the ceiling because of the fire—"

"You moved my stuff." A sullen teenage voice escaped my mouth. "Sorry." I cleared my throat and restored my normal speaking voice. "I don't think you're appropriately reacting to the fact that you did all this without consulting me."

Brick stiffened, but his tone didn't shift to match his posture. "I organized *our* closet. You're free to move your stuff around. I gave you this side so my students would not have reason to be near your area. I would have consulted you, but I didn't have your number, and well, it's not even the first day of school. It was practical and fair."

Fair? He wanted to talk about fair? No fucking way. His calm, *I'm logical and you're being irrational* attitude sent my blood pressure through the roof. "Glitter!" I shouted.

"Excuse me?" he chuckled.

"Last year. The JROTC made some posters for a fundraiser and spilled an entire bottle. There was glitter everywhere, and Mr. Samuel blamed me. Plus, I lost nearly two hundred dollars in supplies to other teachers who didn't want to walk to the main supply building because JROTC students forgot to lock the room. I pay for much of this out of a different budget, Major Hausman. This will not work. Last year, teachers were treating this closet like a Hobby Lobby, and I'm not here to monitor it since—"

Brick held up a finger. He appeared genuinely upset. Perhaps I was finally getting through. "What?"

"Just, it's Brick or Lieutenant Colonel Hausman. Major is actually a . . ."

I clutched the box, knowing if it wasn't so heavy, it'd be hurling at his head right now.

His eyes widened, and I recognized the moment he decided to stop being a dick. "Never mind. I mean, it's a demotion, but . . . Yeah. Not important."

"So, you can have your students clear this out by, say, tomorrow end of day?"

"No. I'm afraid I already spoke to the custodian and the principal, and there aren't other alternatives. Tell you what. I hear your concerns. This is what I can do. I promise controlled access to the closet and a rotation of daily inspections from my most reliable students. I'll even put an inspection sheet here." He tapped the wall. "Anything you're concerned about, let me know, and we will check it as frequently as it needs to be. As for the lost supplies." His eyes drifted up, and he tapped a finger to his ridiculously chiseled jawline. "Perhaps an inventory system is necessary? But if we leave the closet unattended or unlocked and you lose supplies because of our error, I will reimburse you for the lost materials. How does that sound?"

Completely fucking reasonable.

But I was far too worked up to negotiate rationally. "I must consult with my team. You can't expect us to share a single key," I said flatly buying more time. Tessa and Marie would back me up; it'd be three against one.

"I already provided them their keys. Tessa and I met yesterday. She was such a help. I'm afraid my art knowledge is rather limited. I like it though. Art, that is. I got to go to the Louvre once. I was on leave and my wife met me in Paris. It was a little overwhelming, but the history—"

"*Louvre*," I repeated, pronouncing the name of the museum correctly instead of a homophone for lover.

He blushed. An actual rosy tint to his cheeks that was almost enough to erase the disappointment of learning he was straight. It so fucking figured. All those faculty meeting looks *were* him laughing at me. He had this entire thing already planned. Damn it.

"Right. The Louvre," he repeated perfectly.

"I'm sure your wife appreciated you taking her."

"Actually, she didn't. She wanted to shop." He huffed a laugh and trained his gaze on me, all dimples and sparking eyes, like he wanted to commiserate on the shopping proclivities of the fairer sex. Which was so not going to happen.

"I love to shop. Course, you know us gays . . ." I camped with a full limp-wrist to chest move to see if I could throw him off his cocky stance. It worked, but there was a slight head shake of confusion too, like he wasn't sure he heard me correctly, followed by a heated stare. So his whole reaction was far less satisfying and way more arousing than it should have been. "Well, since it's clear the only opinion that matters to you is yours, I guess we're done here."

"Hey—" He objected, and for second, I considered not storming off, but in for a penny and all that. He had to understand just because I was gay and wasn't built like a tank, no one pushed me around.

Brick

My head was spinning with thoughts of Jesse when I met Zach for lunch. I couldn't pinpoint why him being worked up over the closet had me worked up in a very different way. That sort of thing had never been a turn-on for me before.

We took a seat at a sports bar close to the school. I finished answering Zach's question about my latest attempt to meet men, this time a gay men's hiking Meetup group.

"So no hot guys there?" Zach's disappointment still felt like he was rooting for me to get laid rather than actually meet someone, but I knew he'd come around. I was tempted to ask him a few more questions about Mr. Berry, but given what he'd already told me, I decided against it. I wasn't sure why I was so drawn to Jesse, but I didn't want Zach ruining it before I'd figured it out.

"Sadly, there were only six men, four of whom were already dating each other. The fifth guy spent the entire hike on his phone, and the sixth guy zoned in on this." I lifted my shirt sleeve and flashed my ill-advised, much regretted Army tattoo I'd gotten when I returned from Afghanistan. "He seemed determined to educate me on American Imperialism. I tried to correct his understanding, but my degree in history and political science was no match for his degree in Google."

Zach laughed. "Was it at least a pleasant hike?"

"Yeah. Ridgemont is a decent park, but it was basically a flat three-mile walk through the woods. If that was a moderate hike, I'd hate to see what they call easy."

"A walk around the block?"

I chuckled. "Yeah. Probably. It was good to get out, I guess, but I don't see myself making friends, let alone a more personal connection with any of those guys. What's good here?"

After reviewing the menu, Zach and I ordered and spent the wait talking about my latest home improvement efforts. When we finished with our meals, I sighed and patted my full stomach. "After all this eating out, I'm going to have to let out my uniforms."

"Better hurry. Classes start Monday. I'm kind of surprised you're not freaking out. You're taking all the change well. Aren't you?" Zach punctuated his question with a concerned expression—friendship shorthand for *You'd tell me if you're not doing okay, right?*

I held his gaze for a beat, debating how much I wanted to share. I wasn't one to spill my guts usually, but it was Zach—he was the last guy to make me talk about feelings. There wasn't any point in denying the transition was tough. "There was a moment in the classroom that hit me hard a few days ago."

Concern washed over Zach's face. "You okay?"

"Yeah. There was just a moment." I paused, trying to come up with an explanation for the feeling. "You ever have this weird thing happen after a major event in your life? Something that requires a lot of planning. There's all this anticipation and build up. You think you're ready for it, but then the day arrives and it kind of knocks you on your ass. A flash bang goes off and it's not something you're planning anymore, it's finally real?"

Zach's nose wrinkled. "I don't think so. After finishing college—a little, I guess. Or my wedding," he added wistfully. "Although Catherine did all the planning."

"Same thing happened to me when I touched down in Afghanistan for my first tour: there was this moment when my brain caught up to everything. These last few months I've been so wrapped up in getting my teachers certification, retiring, the divorce, moving—it's all been kind of building, but it sort of hit me that my life has completely changed. I'm not in the Army anymore. I'm not married. I'm living in the future I'd been planning for. It's wild."

"Does it feel good?"

"Yeah. Overwhelming, for sure. But I think so. I can't thank you enough, Zach. You've been a real friend to me through all this, and I haven't exactly returned the favor." I regretted not being around for him after Catherine left, but we'd been preparing for the troop surge, and since I was denying leave for everyone else, taking leave to help my brokenhearted buddy wouldn't have been possible.

Zach dismissed my concern with a wave of his hand. "I'm just glad you're finally here. I've missed you, man. It's going to be a blast having you around. Just like old times. I'm only sorry I don't know more bisexual or gay men to introduce you to. It's opened my eyes a bit. My crowd is a little . . ."

"Straight?" I laughed and Zach nodded. "It's okay. I've been thinking maybe I should get established in my new normal before I try to meet people anyway. Focus on teaching and getting the house spruced up." *Figure out if my type is art teachers with attitude problems.*

"I realize it isn't what you're looking for, but we're still searching for players on that recreational basketball team I told you about. It's low-key, so I think your neck will be fine. You sure I can't change your mind?"

"You know what? Sure. I need to stay physically active. It sounds fun."

Zach grinned widely and did this weird wiggle thing with his eyebrows that spelled trouble. "Is there a chance you'd reconsider Academic Olympiad too, because I'll admit I'm desperate."

I shook my head at my buddy whose presence in my life seemed to be the only thing that hadn't changed. A warm swell of appreciation accompanied a flood of shared memories—including some of my most cherished moments that began with me giving into Zach's wiggling eyebrows and boyish grin.

"What the hell. Yeah, I'll do it."

Chapter Four

Jesse

The door chime played as I entered the Artsy Soul. Since she was closed, I locked it behind me and headed back to Sierra's private studio. I found her perched on her stool, paint brush in hand, working on her latest piece.

"Is that Attorney General Barr transmogrified into a boar?"

She twisted toward me and strands of her lavender-silver hair flowed over her right shoulder in a wave.

"Yes." She appraised her work thoughtfully, face registering a rare smile of approval and nodded. "You like it? It's going on Instagram and my website soon."

I proceeded to get a closer look. Sierra was an amazing painter. Back in college, her portraits were the envy of our class. "It's interesting. I love the snout and mouth. How did you get it to seem like he's exhaling?"

"The important part was the shapes of the shadows. I added more color under the glasses and eyes, used Alizarin Crimson for this thin shadow here." She walked me through her technique, and I wished I could borrow the concept for my portrait section. I'd love to see what the kids would come up with if I asked them to convert other famous political faces to animals, but mixing politics, a new technique, and an untested lesson plan was a recipe for disaster.

I grabbed the stool tucked into the corner and took a seat next to her. "Where's Olivier?"

"At home enjoying the last weekend of summer."

"Is he still mad at me?"

Sierra gathered her brushes and started cleaning them with a nervous energy that didn't fit her laid-back demeanor. "Not exactly mad."

"You can tell him I had a perfectly productive conversation with Zach the other day. He made an exception for us to air out our rooms. Olivier was acting like I'd demanded something unreasonable. I can't believe he threw me under the bus like that."

Sierra's head shot up. "He didn't . . . He's worried about us." She winced like she hadn't meant to say anything, before dropping her gaze to her brushes.

I studied her a minute while attempting to interpret her comment. "Did Olivier hear something more about the budget cuts?"

"No. But if the TRE doesn't pass . . ." She shuddered, and we both understood what a catastrophe that would be.

She stepped to the sink and cleaned her brushes. She wasn't acting right—too in her head about something. Combined with the changes in Olivier, my concern grew. "Hey," I said to get her attention. "What's going on with you two?"

Her harried expression provided no assurances. Sierra viewed all experiences, even bad ones, as valuable tools to draw upon as an artist. She'd never been one to worry about things. My stomach dropped, a spur of panic roiled in my gut. Something was wrong. Like *I have three weeks to live* wrong. My eyes widened and my mouth fell open. Oh god. Thoughts of my mother came rushing back. "You have cancer."

"What? No—"

"Does Olivier? Who is sick? Do you need a kidney or blood? Shit! I can't donate blood. Damn homophobic asshole government. What can I do? Tell me. How can I help?" I'd spun myself into a frenzy, guessing what calamity had befallen my dearest friend, when she finally clamped her palm over my mouth.

"No one is sick or dying. No one needs an organ. Calm down." She gave me a pointed stare, and when I nodded, she dropped her hand. Her eyes welled red, enough that the ache of fear didn't entirely subside.

"Then what?" I grabbed her hand, bracing for some horrible thing I hadn't considered.

"I'm pregnant."

"Oh my god!" I screamed, leaping to wrap her in a hug, jumping as much as her stiff body would allow. "You fucking scared the shit out of me." I exhaled, letting the terror give way to relief, but when I pulled back, her face hadn't changed. "Wait? Are we not happy about this?"

"Well," she said, drawing out the word. "We're not *not* happy about it. We're still figuring out how it will work with a baby and the shop and Olivier's teaching. I don't want to lose my studio space, but I bought this building thinking I could live upstairs, you know, but then we decided to keep Olivier's place after the wedding because it was bigger. We're in over our heads financially with two mortgages. I can't . . . Anyway, we're still thinking through what will be best for our—" she swallowed hard "—family. The only thing we're certain about is nothing works if Olivier isn't employed. We need his income and the insurance, so—"

All the missing blanks filled in at once. Olivier's sudden transformation from partner in crime to hard-ass rule-follower made a lot more sense. "So, he's trying to not make waves with admin right now."

She nodded, and I felt terrible for accusing him of being disloyal. He adored Sierra and had to be crazy anxious about making sure she could keep the Artsy Soul going. "Tell Olivier he can distance himself from all work-related initiatives if he needs to. No hard feelings." I hugged my friend tightly. "I can't believe you and Olivier are having a baby. That's so awesome."

A brief flutter of excitement crossed her face. "It's still early days, so keep it to yourself. My parents don't know yet. He doesn't want to distance from you or make you feel bad, but yeah . . . he needs to fly under the radar right now. And I know we talked about going shopping, but since getting knocked up, I'm so tired. Like all the time. This kid is basically an energy vampire. Can I get a raincheck?"

"Yeah. Sure. Do you mind if I use the studio? I could use some creative time."

Sierra patted my shoulder affectionately. "Gonna draw Mr. Perfect again?"

"Maybe." I sighed. "I can't help it. He's always the image that comes to mind."

"I know this guy was part of your sexual awakening or whatever, but I still say it's a weird obsession."

I didn't disagree. How could I? I hadn't seen Ryan Johnson since I'd left home at eighteen, but whenever I thought about my dream guy, it was his face and the way he doted on his family that I always pictured. I wanted a very gay, very single, and thirtysomething-year-old version of him to be the other father to my future child. Why was that so hard? "It's sort of my version of pre-gaming for my date tonight. Eye on the prize, right?"

"I forgot you had a date. This the guy from Plenty of Fish?"

I nodded with another sigh. "It's only a meet and greet. I'm not investing in full dates anymore." So far, I'd been on five meet and greets and exactly zero dates this summer. The new strategy was working well. The way I saw it, I'd had five cups of coffee I was going to have anyway and saved myself about fifteen hours of aggravation.

Because I knew she'd be curious, I whipped out my phone and showed her the profile picture of the guy I'd been chatting with. His name was Ken, and he was cute although a little more buttoned-up than I remembered Ryan being. Based on his rapid message response turnaround times, I didn't hold much hope for him passing my relationship-potential screening system. "He's always on his phone. I doubt he'll make it through a thirty-minute coffee."

"Good to see you're keeping an open mind. That's the spirit." She served up her sarcasm with a supportive pat on my shoulder. "I'll lock the front door. Set the alarm and head out the back when you're done. You need anything?"

"I locked the front already, and I might need some paint. I think I've still got a few canvases stashed in my nook."

"You know where I keep everything. Help yourself."

After Sierra left, I pulled out my easel and supplies, and set up near the window. Perched atop my stool, I closed my eyes to let my mind wander.

Sierra was pregnant.

A wave of bitterness crashed over me. She wasn't even trying. Planned. Unplanned. Why did straight people seem to fall in love and have babies without any effort whatsoever? Sure, some babies, like Sierra and Olivier's, won the parent lottery, but others . . . like me. They got told how much they weren't wanted every day. I pushed thoughts of my father aside. I needed something inspiring, not soul-crushing, to focus on before my date. *Someone other than Ryan for a change.*

The image hit me faster than I'd expected—the body of a mythological deity only with a square face, closely cropped wheat-colored hair, and fine lines that radiated from his honey-brown eyes, the kind that came from habitual facial expressions like smirking.

Brick Hausman. Interesting.

Anyone on the faculty would make for a terrible sample subject, so I couldn't use it for my classes. Nevertheless, my muse had arrived, and my fingers were already searching for the quinacridone rose and hansa yellow deep to mix for his skin tone. Work would have to wait.

My imagination was in the driver's seat.

I met Ken at a small coffee shop near my house. While I wasn't optimistic about the date, I'd put effort into my appearance and made sure I was smiling when I opened the door. The place was small and quiet, the perfect setting to assess any actual chemistry between us.

I located him right away, sitting at a back booth, staring at his phone screen. Even with him sitting, I knew his claim of being six foot and one eighty had been an exaggeration. Oh well, it wasn't the worst thing in the world to fudge a little on your dating profile stats. I sort of expected it. His lean legs stuck out of marina blue linen shorts. He had on a crisp white shirt, sleeves rolled up to show off impressive forearms. He said he worked at a bar, and every bartender I'd ever met had great arms, so maybe he'd been honest about that.

Unnoticed, I crossed the café toward him. I was practically at the table before he glanced up from his phone with a smile, baring blinding-white teeth that definitely weren't acquainted with coffee. A pair of sunglasses rested on his head, nestled in heavily styled sandy-blond hair. That's when it hit me. He fucking looked like a Ken doll. I stifled a laugh and lowered my expectations.

"Jesse?" he asked.

"Yep." I extended my hand, and he shook it with a barely there grip. I lifted my messenger bag off my shoulder and set it on an empty chair. "Thanks for meeting me. I'm going to grab a coffee. Can I get you something?"

"A chai tea."

"Sure, be right back."

I walked up to the counter and ordered, returning quickly with our drinks. When I got there, he was on his phone again, too distracted to take the cup I was handing him. I set it on the table with a sigh and tried to keep an open mind as I took my seat.

Finally, he put his phone down, screen up. "So, how's your day going so far?"

I drew a sip of my coffee. "Good, actually. Found out my best friend is having a baby. Total surprise." I explained how I'd introduced Olivier and Sierra and how excited I was by their news since they'd be my first close friends to have a baby.

"You like kids?" Ken asked as though we were talking about flesh-eating bacteria instead of children. His phone lit up, and he snuck a glance at the screen, chuckling and clearing the text alert with one hand.

I forced my shoulders down and breathed. "It's sort of a job requirement for teachers. I take it you don't?"

He shook his head, his nose wrinkling like he'd smelled a fart. I was sure even my low expectations wouldn't be met.

"That's right. You said you were a teacher. I thought you meant like on the side or whatnot cause you said you're an artist too. I'm from L.A., so half the bartenders are actors, you know?"

"Well, teaching art was actually what I studied to do. I like to create, painting especially, but I love teaching. What brought you to Texas?"

He frowned, but I wasn't sure if it was at my question or the text that had lit up his phone screen a second time. "My ex Jason. We met in L.A. when he was trying to be a model, but he's from this area and wanted to move back. We signed a lease, but then he got a modeling job in South Korea and left me here."

He had mentioned he'd been in a long-term relationship, which was one of reasons I'd agreed to meet him, since that was what I was in the market for. "I'm sorry," I said, searching for a way to pivot the conversation to his interests, but before I could, he picked up his phone.

He swiped a few times, then typed what was likely a response to a text or a tweet based on the brevity. "You want to see a picture of him?"

My brows jumped. Did I need to see a picture of his model ex? "Um, not really." I took another three sips of my coffee in quick succession, wishing I'd gotten a small instead of a large. Seriously, why did crazy never come out via chat?

"This is him." He held up a picture of what might have been the most plastic man I'd ever seen.

I coughed to cover my laugh. "How long ago did this happen?"

"About three months now." Ken turned the phone toward himself. "My friends keeping pushing me to meet other people, but have you ever been through a nasty breakup?"

"Um . . . not like that. Were you together long?" I took a larger swallow, wishing it wasn't too hot to down.

"Yes, like almost six months."

Six months? Coffee droplets came flying out of my mouth, landing on his white shirt. The way he'd been talking on the app, I'd thought they'd been together for years. "Oh my god." I covered my mouth, trying to stifle my amusement. He grabbed a napkin and started dabbing at it. I forced a cough, to avoid laughing aloud. "I'm so sorry."

"It's okay. I'm sure it will come out."

"If you need to go . . ."

"No," he said. "You're here. Might as well get to know each other."

"Oh, um . . ." I hedged, eyeing the door longingly. "Sure."

"So what kind of things are you into?"

A pivot finally. Excellent. "My job keeps me busy during the year, but besides painting, I enjoy reading, films, museums, anything that challenges me to think. I'm active politically. I volunteered for a few local campaigns and helped organize a protest to keep them from building a landfill like five miles from the elementary school. Have you heard of Powered by People? We did a bunch of voter registration drives. Really successful. Are you registered to vote in Texas?"

He cringed. "I meant like in bed. Your profile didn't specify your preferences, but you're giving me a lot of bottom energy."

I swallowed hard and glared at him while reaching for my bag, no longer bothering to hide my annoyance. What a waste of time. "I think I'm gonna go."

"What? Why?" Frown lines deepened on his forehead. "Are you a top?"

"I'm just . . . Yeah, I'm going to go. Nothing personal, but we're not a suitable match. Enjoy your tea. Sorry about your shirt."

I made it to my car before the disappointment forced my eyes closed. *Why was this so difficult?* When meeting people in organic ways failed, I figured I had nothing to lose by trying a few dating sites and apps. Except the more I leaned on technology to meet quality guys, the more pathetic my dating life had become. If a man wanted to learn my sexual preferences before my last name, it wasn't going to end with wedding bells.

Someday I would belong to a family like the one in my head. I would find a husband who wanted to create a house full of love, we'd hang our kids' paintings on the fridge, read bedtime stories together, and build a backyard swing set. All of it.

But it was time to admit that guy wasn't on a website or an app. I reread Ken's profile, looking for signs of what I'd missed before deleting the Plenty of Fish app and the four others just like it.

I needed a break.

Chapter Five

Brick

I flipped through the thick packet of information Zach had handed over, still unsure how he'd suckered me into coaching a thing I had zero experience in. The Academic Olympiad had more rules than most sports, and any of them could be used to disqualify our team. Most were common sense—and could be summed up as *don't cheat*, but the three pages dedicated to validating GPAs was giving me serious flashbacks to my early days in the Army when I didn't quite know the lingo.

I reread the information three times, deciphering which classes counted, which didn't, how to handle honors and advanced placement credits. I pulled out the worksheets and surveyed the six transcripts Zach had given me. Five for the returning students and one for a rising freshman whom Nelms had selected to replace a matriculated senior. I rechecked my math and got the same result.

I dialed Zach's number, unsurprised he answered on the first ring.

"We have a problem."

"Problem? What problem?"

"You told me this team was set, but I have three students with an A average. And according to this encyclopedia of a rule book, you can fill an A spot with a B student or a B spot with a C student, but I can't compete with three A students. The maximum is two."

"That can't be right. Jared Armstrong and Peter Lim have been our A students for the past three years. Who is the third?"

I checked the paper for the student's name. "Natalie Sanchez. The rules say you have to use the fall semester from the previous year, but when I check what Craig Nelms put together here, he didn't. I redid the worksheet with all the kids, but hers is the only one that changed. She got a 4.0 last fall and took a couple of honors classes. Her cumulative GPA is 3.75 on the nose, which, according to this sheet, makes her an A student." Since I could tell that Zach didn't want to believe me, I took a picture of the worksheet and sent it to him. A few minutes later, he swore under his breath and confirmed my math was correct.

"I can't believe Nelms pulled this shit too . . . Fuck that guy. It'll take time to organize a new tryout. We're already behind. Maybe we should forfeit."

I sighed. Zach may have been quick to cut-and-run, but I sure as hell wasn't. "Hold on. It's not that dire. There's nothing in the rules about competing with five kids, but which kid do I cut? Of the three, Natalie has the lowest GPA, but her scores in last year's competition are better than Jared's. Wait, didn't you say there were tryouts? Is it feasible to use the runner-up? Is the next highest score from a male or a female? Cause we can only have three each, so that could be the rationale we use to cut either Jared or Natalie. Peter has the highest scores and the highest GPA, so I'd say he's definitely the keeper."

"No." Never had a single utterance been more loaded with a backstory, but after a beat of silence, it was clear Zach had no intention of giving it to me.

"Why not?"

"It's . . . Shit. It's fucking complicated. That's why."

"Zach. C'mon, man. You urged me to do this. Don't ask me to lead something, then tie my hands behind my back. Tell me what's up or find another guy to unfuck this mess."

Zach sighed. "The next highest scoring student was Em Delacroix."

"Okay." I shuffled through the file to locate the tryout test scores and found the listing for Emmett Delacroix. "So, is Emmett an A student too?"

"No. Definitely be a solid B student."

"Okay, great, so Emmett takes the B spot, and we cut Jared. Actually, that's kind of perfect because it's a male and female student at each grade level spot."

"Because . . . it's not that simple. The Armstrongs are not a family I'm interested in having on my bad side. I doubt Em would even still want to do it. We should cut either Peter, Jared, and Natalie, then compete with five."

"But if Emmett can improve the team, why—"

"Zach, you know that saying about going to war with the army you have?"

"Are you honestly quoting Donald Rumsfeld to me?"

"Trust me. Did you send the kids the practice schedule yet?"

"No."

"Okay, good. Ask the three to meet you in your classroom after the last bell tomorrow. I'll come over, and we can talk to them together. It's not ideal, but they drop the lowest two scores in each subject; if we are down a student, then we only get to drop one. You should keep the two with the strongest overall performance."

"Well, according to these files, Peter is a whiz at history, Jared had a perfect score on his Math SATs, but Natalie excels in social science and while none of them were strong in fine arts, she is the strongest. So, how do you suggest we determine that?"

"Give them a mock test. There are some in the packet." His decision didn't leave much opening for debate. "It's the most fair."

"Yeah. Okay. I'll set it up."

"Thanks. Did you ever connect with Jesse Berry on that storage room?"

"No, but I sorted it."

"You sorted it? I hope that doesn't mean what I think it means."

"What do you think it means?"

"That you basically do what you always do and decide you know best without consulting anyone."

"I took care of it. Why does it matter how it got done?"

"Brick." Zach sighed. "You're not in the Army anymore, my friend. You can't simply pull rank on other teachers. You have to work collaboratively."

"I held battalion-level, multi-functional logistics commands, Zach. I think I can handle the simple task of installing some shelves."

"Trust me, when it comes to Jesse Berry, there is no such thing as a simple task."

Zach's warning was like a well-placed knock on the side of a jammed vending machine. Something fell into place. *That's why I couldn't stop thinking about the guy.* Jesse was the furthest thing from the men I'd worked with or the escorts I'd hired. He didn't care one iota about my rank, and he wasn't eager to please. He was a complete puzzle, and I loved the thought of trying to solve him.

The Northridge High final bell chime was the most welcomed sound I'd ever heard. I couldn't contain my smile as students shot up, gathered their belongings, and got the hell out of my classroom. Not that I didn't enjoy teaching, because I did. Once I'd gotten over my nerves, I'd loved it.

But there were a ton of them. And they all had questions. I was used to fielding questions. Making tough decisions, sometimes with life and death consequences, was a big part of the job. But nothing had prepared me for teenagers finding inconsistencies and ambiguities in a syllabus. It was exhausting. And the excuses, *Lord save me from the excuses.*

I'd somehow forgotten there were about a hundred people in the Army who buffered me from repetitive, basic *read the fucking manual* and *I just said that* type questions. Now there was no buffer. Not yet. I needed to shake out a few kinks, instill a renewed respect for the command structure, empower my level IIs and IIIs to take more leadership positions, and basically unfuck several years of bad habits. My predecessor had done these kids no favors. Judging by the mass confusion about promotion-board procedures alone, I couldn't be sure cadet rank translated to demonstrated competency. Thankfully, Peter Lim had been a strong pick as Battalion Commander. The XO and some company commanders, on the other hand, had me concerned.

The classroom emptied, and I took my place in the doorway, listening to lockers slam and students laughing and joking as they flowed out of the building. Zach had said to be present, wave, and give pointed looks to anyone who wasn't making adequate progress at getting to where they needed to be. No one needed any encouragement. The building emptied in short order, giving me a chance to check the storage room before Peter, Natalie, and Jared arrived at 1530.

I grabbed the key and crossed the hallway. The outer door to the building opened, and I glanced up to catch Jesse and Marie struggling to navigate a large cart loaded up with small baskets and packages of canvases.

I don't know what came over me, but I ducked behind the row of lockers as their laughter and voices filled the air.

"Thanks again for helping me, Jesse."

"Of course. Oh, watch it." I peeked around the corner as Jesse's arm shot out to steady the stack of canvases.

"Aye," Marie cried and exhaled a breath as they worked together to right the tower.

"It's no bother." He unlocked the closet, and they disappeared inside. I exhaled relief, then realized how ridiculous I must look hiding from my crush like I was back in high school again. Resting my head on the metal of the locker, I huffed a laugh.

I was just about to return to my classroom, when I heard Marie's accented voice say, "The new JROTC instructor did an outstanding job, didn't he? Did you meet him yet? He's so handsome, don't you think?"

I froze and held my breath, waiting for his response.

"If you like muscles," Jesse said flippantly. Too flippantly, like he was trying to convince her he didn't find me attractive. *Well, well. This was going to be interesting.*

I turned on my heel, moving closer to hear more, but he'd moved on to recounting his eye-opening side of our initial conversation. Although I did detect a begrudging acceptance that the closet was better organized.

"I'm so optimistic for this year. It sounds like Brick is going to respect our needs. Grant would never have offered to reimburse you. The portables aren't perfect, and they took getting used to, but I kind of like being away from the main part of campus. Plus, your floral walls are amazing."

"Thanks. They turned out well. If you and Tessa don't want me to push the closet issue, I won't."

"We appreciate you standing up for us last year, but this is way better than before. It'll be nice to be able to find things again."

"Yeah. I guess."

"What are you doing?" I whipped around to find Zach staring at me curiously. Before I could answer, Marie and Jesse stepped into the hallway. Zach's face flashed surprise, but I was too busy melting under Jesse's glare. *Busted. So busted.*

"Um. Hi, Zach. No, I was coming to check the closet. Marie, Jesse, I didn't realize you were there. Everything okay?"

"Oh, yes. I was just telling Jesse it's great. Thanks again, Brick."

Zach shuffled past me and peeked inside. "Wow. So this is what you meant by sorted, huh? Looks great." He clapped a hand to my shoulder, and Jesse muttered a noise of disapproval.

"What brings you out this way?" Jesse asked, eyeing the friendly way Zach had left his hand resting on my shoulder with suspicion.

"We're meeting with the Academic Olympiad kids," Zach responded, unbothered or unaware of the way Jesse was scrutinizing us. "Brick is going to be the new coach."

"Oh, that's nice. Jazmin and Natalie both took my Art History class last year. Smart girls," Marie said.

"Good to know. We're sorting out an issue," I explained. "May have to open up tryouts again, unfortunately."

"Oh! Why's that?" Jesse asked, and I heard Zach gulp.

"Well, there is a bit of snafu with our A-level students. Seems my predecessor messed up some math, and we have three, which is against the rules. But we have room for another B—"

"Um, Brick, the students are here. We should go." Zach tugged on my arm.

I stole a quick glance over my shoulder as Peter and two other students walked through the J building door. When I turned back, Jesse's eyes were trained on Zach like he was summoning a superpower that could vaporize him. I glanced between them with a growing sense of unease. I didn't fully comprehend what was going on, but Jesse's body language had crossed from riled to pissed, and Zach had clearly expected his reaction. Zach leaving me in the dark didn't sit right with me, but Marie was clearly concerned about the approaching students, so whatever it was, it likely didn't need to get hashed out with an audience. "Yeah, okay." I straightened my jacket, gave Jesse an apologetic smile, and followed Zach toward my classroom.

As soon as he and I had a second alone, I was going to have a few words with my new boss.

Chapter Six

Jesse

My email inbox remained stubbornly empty. I sat at my desk, tapping my pen and trying to reassure myself that the plan to give Zach one more day to respond to my demands for an explanation was a good one.

The portable door creaked open, cutting off the mental monologue I'd been rehearsing to deliver to Zach if he didn't respond. I checked the clock on my computer, worried I'd stewed away my entire pre-school prep time.

"Emily, you're about an hour early. Everything okay?"

Emily fidgeted with her phone, slid it into the back pocket of her jeans, and fussed with the loose brown curls hanging an inch past her shoulders.

"Yeah. Um, I know we're supposed to make an appointment, but I wanted to talk about my, um, my AP portfolio. I think I have an idea for concentration pieces."

I motioned for her to sit down, and she swung her bag forward, unzipped it, and lifted her ever-present sketchbook with thin fingers.

"Cute!" I motioned to the black-and-white designs on her bag meant to look like panda faces.

"Thanks," she said, looking at them with a reserved smile.

"So tell me about your idea."

She flipped open her sketch pad. I laughed as her shy demeanor took a back seat to make room for the enthusiasm she had to discuss her artistic vision.

"I shouldn't be surprised you're already thinking ahead." The AP Studio Art Program at Northridge comprised three classes: Drawing, 2D Art, and 3D Art. I spent the first month teaching the design principles and helping them develop their concentration ideas. I rarely started vetting project themes until mid-September.

"You warned me if I took both drawing and 2D not to get behind. I promised myself I'd stay on track and finish both portfolios." Students were given college credit based on portfolios submitted in the spring. Each portfolio had two sections. The first was sustained investigation, or concentration pieces, where students submitted around fifteen pieces linked with a common theme, and the second portion was five selected works. The college board didn't allow crossover pieces, so it was rare for a student to try to do more than one class at a time, but Emily wasn't an average art student.

"So let's hear it."

She took a deep breath, eyelids fluttering as she handed me her sketch pad. She tucked her bottom lip between her teeth as she waited eagerly for me to examine the image.

Emily had drawn . . .. herself, face forward, her chest hidden behind the length of her forearm. The image was beautiful and largely realistic until I came to where she'd drawn the area between her hips and knees, distorted and draped in grotesque folds of skin. It was provocative, as all Emily's work was. "The style reminds me of Egon Schiele. Tell me more."

"I thought for my drawing concentration I would do a series around body dysphoria, an evolution of my transition in a series of self-portraits. Document how I see myself. I did this one last year before I started hormones."

I smiled warmly. Emily had changed drastically since then, both in body and mind. It was hard to remember the person who sat in the back of my class and wouldn't speak during freshman year, but Olivier's warning about playing nice with Zach was ringing loud in my head and this was the exact sort of thing he'd lose his mind over. I wasn't even sure her concept was workable for a class assignment.

"Emily, first, this is brilliant." I lifted her sketch pad and handed it to her. She smiled widely with my approval. I paused, giving myself a minute to enjoy her pride. I'd taught several talented students over my career, but Emily was different. I'd learned as much from her vulnerability and authenticity as she'd learned from me. Her technique was advanced but not out of the norm for high school, but her eye was something else entirely. The way she saw the world—she brought a sophistication to her art, beyond even my own abilities. With every piece, she bared a piece of her soul. I'd had to dig deeper as a teacher and an artist to get on her level. It often terrified me that my limitations would stifle her development. "However, part of your grade is peer review, and while I love the concept, you wouldn't be allowed to show your classmates nude self-images. I wouldn't want you to sacrifice the integrity of your investigation based on that."

She slumped back in her seat, crossed her arms, and frowned. "Peer reviews?"

"I know. I'll tell you what we'll do. Keep at it. I think you have something great here, but I have to confess I'm concerned that it's so incredibly personal. Why don't you brainstorm on how you might make it work, taking into account the peer reviews and nudity issues? We can talk again next week when I've had time to digest it."

"Who was the artist you mentioned before?"

"Egon Schiele. He studied under Gustav Klimt."

Emily scribbled the name in her notebook and sighed.

"I'm sorry. I appreciate this isn't the news you wanted to hear, but I'm not saying it can't work. We may have to think it through a bit."

"Thanks. I'll do more research. Schiele might give me some new ideas."

"It's an excellent start. Was there anything else? Any thoughts on your 2D portfolio?"

"I've been experimenting with a mixed-media series."

My ears perked up. "Mixed media?"

"I'm still playing around, but I have this one picture." She fished her phone out of her pocket and flipped to the picture. The image was of a toy aisle sign labeled for boys. Behind it was neat rows of action figures, trucks, and toy guns. Then she flipped to another page of her sketch pad where she'd enlarged the image and cropped it so the shelves were pasted to either side, curved inward, and looming menacingly over the aisle. In the center, she'd drawn a small child holding a toy gun aimed at his own head. The pain she'd captured on the child's face was gut wrenching. I released a stuttering exhale to relieve the rush of emotions before clasping a hand to my mouth.

"Oh, Emily." I closed my eyes, attempting to regain my composure. Tears bubbled, held back only by pure willpower. "I'm in awe of this. This is so powerful."

"It's supposed to represent how societal expectations about gender hurt trans people. I wanted to try it on canvas through," she mumbled. "I wasn't sure how I feel about sharing it yet."

I handed it back to her. "I'm honored you let me see it. If you don't make it a focus of your concentration, it should be in your college portfolio. Honestly, one of your best pieces. You continue to amaze me, young lady."

"Thanks, Mr. Berry." She turned and tucked the pad back into her bag. I reached for a tissue to dry my eyes. When she turned back, her emotions were shining in her eyes. We stared at each other, overtaken by the moment. "I'm not . . ." She gestured to her bag. "You don't need to worry. I'm doing much better since I started hormones. I asked my mom to keep you updated."

I smiled. Wishing like hell times were different because I really wanted to give her a huge hug. Instead, I settled for squeezing her hand. "She did. I understand the end of last year was tough for you with school, and the new laws, and your dad moving to Los Angeles after the divorce."

Her lips twisted into a pained grimace and she shrugged, resigned. Texas had made it increasingly more difficult to access gender-affirming healthcare, particularly for minors. Emily's father relocating to California for work had been hard on her, but there was an unspoken relief for the safety net it provided too. "Mr. Nelms is gone at least."

"He is." I nodded. "I worked with your counselor to make sure you have more supportive teachers this year. We meet with your mom next month, but you can always come to me if there is a problem."

"It's okay. Some other kids dislike the new teacher. They gave me a hard time about it."

"You're not to blame for Mr. Nelms losing his job. Teachers are required to respect all of our students. His constant misgendering of you and refusal to use your name got him fired. That and your fabulous mother who loves you so much she raised holy hell. He had a choice to be transphobic. You did not have a choice about who you are. One thing I've learned when I came out is you can't control how people feel about you, but I refuse to take any blame or guilt for being me, and neither should you."

"Thanks, Mr. B. That helps. I've been trying to not let it get to me." She stood and hesitated a few breaths before she added, "My mom bought me this cute skirt for back to school, but I chickened out. Do you think if I tried to wear it sometime, I might leave class a few minutes early to change if I get scared again?"

"Of course. The same dress code rules apply for you as they do for all the other girls. And like last year, you are welcome to come in before school anytime. I'm usually here early, any day except Thursdays, when I have my planning meetings. We still have about thirty minutes before first bell. You can stay now if you'd like, but I have some stuff I need to take care of."

She nodded and moved her stuff to her normal seat. Then pulled out her sketch pad and placed her headphones. With shoulders hunched in concentration, she drew.

I checked my emails again. No response. I wished I could march her latest piece down to Zach's office and show him how his fence riding last year had impacted her. Yes, he eventually fired Craig, but only after ignoring months of complaints from her mother. It shouldn't have taken Savannah recording his transphobic rants and threatening a lawsuit to get results. I couldn't prove it, but I knew something was up with the AO tryouts too. Emily had been confident in her tryout test, and she'd needed that win so bad. Knowing that Craig had messed up the GPA calculations renewed all my suspicions.

A loud knock at the door startled me out of my thoughts. I glanced to Emily, whose music might have been too loud for her to hear. "Come in," I called, expecting another student who didn't want to wait outside in the heat. Instead, a behemoth of a man with a lopsided smile and one irritatingly charming dimple strolled in like he owned the place.

Brick

"Can I help you?" Jesse's greeting was not exactly warm, but he didn't appear ready to cut my balls off any longer. The cooling-off period Zach suggested I give him seemed to have worked.

"Zach sent me your email about the Academic team. I have a proposition about—"

Jesse released a spasming cough and pounded his fist to the desk, cutting off my words. I frowned, until a head popped out from behind an easel and removed her headphones. I knew immediately I was looking at Emily. Thank goodness Jesse had stopped me from putting my foot in my mouth.

"You okay, Mr. B?" She asked, eyes growing wide as she noticed me. "Oh, wow. You're giant. How tall are you?"

I smiled at the familiar reaction. "I'm six feet, six inches."

Jesse frowned. I hadn't the slightest idea why, but he didn't seem to like me breathing, so it wasn't something I worried about. "I'm going to step outside for a minute and talk to, um, Col—"

"Lieutenant Colonel Hausman. Pleased to meet you. I'm the new JROTC instructor." I stepped toward Emily and shook her hand, then turned to Jesse. "Sorry, I can come back after school. I didn't realize you were with a student." I began backing up toward the door.

"Emily hangs out here in the mornings." Jesse locked his computer, stood, then said to Emily, "I'll be right back."

"Sure thing, Mr. B." Apparently unbothered, Emily replaced her headphones and returned to her drawing. Jesse beelined toward me and grabbed my sleeve in what appeared to be an attempt to strong-arm me out the door.

I wasn't used to being physically manhandled by anyone. Normally such a move would piss me off, but the sight of Jesse, who was at least eight inches shorter and a hundred pounds lighter than me, rebounding backward like a bungee cord that'd run out of stretch was amusing as hell.

"Come with me," he seethed between tight lips.

I made a careful glance toward Emily, who was still bobbing her head and drawing, before challenging him with a raised eyebrow to first let go of my sleeve.

He rolled his eyes and dropped his hold, allowing me to walk on my own volition. I didn't fight my smile as I took a step toward the door and pushed it open, gesturing for him to move ahead. When he stormed out, I released a full-belly laugh. Like a toddler staring down a panel of unlit numbers in an elevator, my hands itched to run the gamut. I hoped to light up all of Jesse's buttons.

Jesse rushed down the ramp toward the parking lot and turned around, looking aghast that I was still one step outside the door. An animated "come here" arm wave and a sharp foot stomp to boot. Okay, he was fricking adorable.

I took my time descending the ramp, strutting all the way because I knew it would get a reaction. I hadn't felt this drawn to a person in forever. Surely, a *little* teasing couldn't hurt. Only enough button-pushing to satisfy my curiosity.

"What do you want?"

"Good morning," I said plainly. "How is the supply closet working out?"

"How's the eavesdropping working out?" he shot back.

Another chuckle escaped. Excellent. In better times, Jane used to banter with me too. "It needs work, apparently."

Jesse's lips twitched at the corners, which was all the encouragement I needed. My mission that morning might have been to secure his help, but now I was determined to make him laugh too.

He rolled his eyes, which were the exact bluish-gray hue of storm clouds, but my focus narrowed to his freckled nose. I toyed with asking him if the slight crook had anything to do with how often his nose got bent out of shape but decided against it.

"You said something about a proposition?" He tapped a foot impatiently with enough sass to set off gaydars four towns over. I loved that. Confidence was sexy in any gender, and Jesse oozed it. Ever since that shopping comment on the first day of school, I knew he put his sexuality on blast to get a reaction from me. But I wasn't sure I had the kind he'd been expecting. Unless he'd planned to star in some of my better fantasies. *Okay, Mr. Berry. You have my attention, but why did you want it?* I cocked my head and tried to determine if there was anything flirtatious underlying the way he said *proposition*.

His eyes narrowed menacingly.

Nope? Okay. Just me.

I drew a deep breath and put away my crush to focus on my reason for the visit. "I spoke to Zach last evening. He forwarded your email to me and asked to deal with it. To be clear, I didn't have a clue about what happened with Nelms and Emily until recently."

"So, Zach sent you instead of dealing with the problem. Some leader . . ." he grumbled.

The way he dramatized his every annoyance with his hands mesmerized me, but I was nothing if not loyal, so I felt duty bound to defend my friend. "In this case, I think Zach delegating to the coach is an excellent example of leadership."

"I've worked with the man for years. I know him better than you."

A delighted noise escaped my lips, which only turned Jesse's face redder, which only put *me* back in the elevator staring down more buttons. He was so easy to rile.

"Do you want to tell me what it is about me you find so god damn amusing all the time?"

I swallowed hard. He tickled the hell out of me, but I had no intention of crossing any lines. "Why do you assume it's about you?"

"Uh, because you're smirking and no one else is around. I'll have you know, most people find me intimidating."

I wanted to say his scowl was about as ferocious as a Yorkie puppy, but I willed myself to be professional. "Zach—"

"I've worked for the man for six years," he continued.

Do not look at his arms crossed over his chest. Do not look. You do not find his irritation cute. "Six years, huh? Well, I guess that is plenty of time to get a read on him. So tell me, why do you think he delegated this to me?"

"Because he's—no offense—a straight, cis guy who is uncomfortable talking about LBGT issues. I don't want to say he's transphobic or homophobic or anything."

"Good, because he's not."

Jesse gawked. "You don't even know him."

"Zach has many flaws, and I'll give you a pass on the uncomfortable part. He'd be the first to admit to not being as versed on these issues as he could be, but he's not homophobic or transphobic. Any insinuation otherwise is—"

"Are you seriously coming in after a few days and defending Zach?"

"Look, maybe I should have mentioned that we went to high school together, and I was the best man at his wedding. That was why I laughed, but fun and games aside, Zach is a good guy, and I can't stand by and let you malign his character."

"You're..." Jesse opened and closed his mouth, but I was sufficiently disappointed by the turn in the conversation that I couldn't appreciate the fact I'd stunned him into silence.

"So, about this situation we have on the Academic Olympiad team. Peter, Natalie, and Jared are going to retake the tryout test for our two A-student spots. That frees up one B-student spot that Natalie can no longer fill. Emily had the next highest score in the B-students range on the tryout test from last year."

"She's on the team?"

"Well, that depends. I still need to speak with her, obviously."

"So ..." He gestured up the ramp. "Get to it."

Frowning, I debated aborting the mission right then, but what the hell ... *Here goes nothing.* "The rules specify each team must have three girls and three boys."

Jesse groaned. "So, Emily can only take part if Natalie has the lowest score."

"No." I cringed. "Actually, according to the rules, Emily can only participate if Peter or Jared—"

"Emily *is* a girl!"

"I know." I held my hands up as if that might give me a fighting chance to explain. I'd have to get used to being interrupted when I was speaking. "I'm not disputing that. Unfortunately, we have to submit students' official records, and Emily is officially identified as male, so—"

"But that's because the school uses her birth certificate, and Texas won't issue an amended certificate ..." Jesse continued on, lecturing me on everything from his dislike of the governor and misconceptions about gender binaries to a rather convoluted explanation of trans women participating in women's sports—hormone levels and testosterone.

Zach warned me there'd be a negative reaction, but I had to admit as far as verbal tongue lashings went, Jesse rivaled a few of the tougher generals I'd served under. I kept my cool, and yeah, I didn't follow all of it, but damn, Zach's warnings aside, I'd come to the right person. I knew Jesse would be educated on this stuff, and more importantly, I could tell from his impassioned email he cared. That made him perfect.

When students started drifting across the parking lot, I realized I'd underestimated his stamina to rage. I still needed to explain my proposal, so I waited for him to take a rare breath, then interrupted him. "I'm glad you're so passionate about this. That's good. Exactly what I need in an assistant coach."

His jaw snapped shut, and I couldn't contain my laugh because yeah, that was precisely how I'd envisioned this moment.

"There is no way . . . Are you insane?"

"No. Our team needs to brush up on fine arts, and you—" I mimicked his flamboyant gesture up the ramp to his classroom. "—are the team lead for the art program."

"Yes, which means I already have my hands full. Why would I get involved to help you? I'm not even sure I like you."

I arched an eyebrow at him because it was fairly clear he didn't. "Then do it for Emily."

"Emily might not be on the team, and this has nothing to do with me. Besides, there is no way her mother lets her compete as a boy, not after what she endured to get the right to use her name and pronouns. They wouldn't risk a setback like that."

"She wouldn't be competing as a boy. It doesn't require her to change her appearance. All the kids wear the same team T-shirts and jeans. It's only paperwork and only until—"

"Other schools would challenge her." He lowered his voice as a few students marched up the ramp behind me. "Do you know how stressful it would be to her if she had to explain why there are four girls on stage? You know why she spends every morning in my classroom? Bullies, Brick."

"If you could stop interrupting me, I would explain."

Jesse tossed his hands up. "Fine. Explain this brilliant plan of yours."

"I'm going to change the rules, and I want you to help me."

Chapter Seven

Jesse

I flung open the door of the J building, anger still rushing through me like wildfire. The long wait of the school day had done nothing to quench my rage after finding out Brick had spoken to Emily when I'd specifically told him not to. I'd made myself more than clear, his plan was unworkable.

The words formed in my mouth, exploding as soon as I opened the classroom door. "How dare you?"

A handful of heads turned to me. Peter Lim, a student I recognized as a popular senior, glanced up from the front of the class. "Uh. Hi, Mr. Berry. Is there something wrong with the supply closet? I did the inventory and status check this afternoon myself."

"No. Sorry. It's fine. I don't. Where's, um, Major, no, um, Col . . . Where's your teacher?"

"Lieutenant Colonel Hausman is in his office." He motioned behind him. "Did you want me to get—"

The office door on the opposite side of the room opened. "No need. I'm here." Brick appeared in the doorway and glared at me. I swallowed hard, second guessing my approach. He didn't seem happy to see me, and while the weird way he found amusement in my every word didn't thrill me, it was far better than whatever was happening here. "Carry on with your battalion command meeting, Lim. Here is the drill-meet schedule I need distributed. Mr. Berry, this way, please."

"Yes, sir," Peter said.

I crossed the room toward Brick, absolutely not staring at his ridiculously firm ass on the way. *High and tight, indeed.* We crowded into the small space, which had originally been the art prep room, but was now his office. When he brushed close to me to shut the door, my nose tickled at the smell of a sweet, fruity odor I couldn't place.

Exhibiting zero sense of urgency, Brick took a seat at his desk with a frustrating, insouciant calm that made me want to come out of my skin. He motioned for me to sit too.

"I'll stand." I gripped the chair back in front of me.

He let out a long-suffering sigh and rolled his eyes. "Suit yourself. What can I do for you, Mr. Berry?"

"Emily told some kids in class during first period that she was on the Academic Olympiad team." His eyebrow rose, but he said nothing, so I continued. "You told her she could compete. Do you know how difficult transitioning is for a sixteen-year-old? What she's been through? Of course you don't. No offense, but you and Zach have a lot in common. It's all about the simple path. Doesn't matter who gets hurt." I glared at him, hoping to see any level of remorse, but he sat there rubbing the back of his neck, a borderline scowl forming on his tight lips. "Well? Say something."

"Oh. Were you done ranting at me? I wasn't sure."

"This is not ranting. This is communicating."

He huffed, but the slight movement sent his face into a concerning contortion. He opened the drawer to his desk and took out a tube of cream. Smearing some on his fingers, he rubbed his neck. I got a glimpse of the label when he replaced the lid. Topical pain relief. Well, that at least explained the subdued mood and odd smell. "What's wrong with your neck?"

"Nothing serious. Would you please sit?"

I plopped down into the wooden chair across from him, determined to not let my rage soften because of sympathy he didn't deserve. "Well? What do you have to say for yourself?"

He sighed, rolled his head from side-to-side slowly, then wiped off his fingers on a tissue. "I spoke to Emily because there was a spot available for her to fill."

"But you sent me an email that Natalie had the lowest score. I thought this entire issue was dead." Unless we did the rule change route, something I was admittedly not thrilled to do, since the odds of succeeding before the first competition were slim. Now she was all excited about it . . . and fuck. I would have to help if for no other reason than that I didn't trust Brick to protect her.

Brick sighed. "You mean the email you didn't respond to? Natalie had the lowest score, but I've since had to replace Jared Armstrong, so Natalie is taking his spot. There was an opening for a male student with a B average, which Emily qualifies for on paper. I spoke to her and her mother about my plan to petition for a rule change, explained my thinking—well, actually, your thinking—and they were game for it. The more I thought about it, the more I agree that the entire gender aspect of this is crazy, so I decided it was worth the effort to do myself. Filling this team of six has been a greater pain in the ass than managing logistics for an entire battalion. So no, Mr. Berry, I have nothing to explain to you about it. If you don't like the way I'm running the team, then take over, but since you couldn't even be bothered to help . . ."

Take over? I huffed out a laugh. *Maybe he had a small point about returning his emails, but let's not get carried away.* "You're being awfully melodramatic. I think I liked you better before." He glanced up, with what might have been an attempt to smile. And Jesus, I felt sorry for the guy. He seemed miserable. "It's your posture," I said, motioning to his hunched shoulders and crappy ergonomic desk setup. "You need to raise your monitor and . . . when you teach and grade papers, you look down a lot, so you need to stretch regularly. It's easy to get into bad habits."

My advice was met with a blank stare.

"Okay, then," I muttered. Back to the topic at hand. "So what happened with Jared?"

Brick's forehead creased as a mixture of anger and annoyance filled his eyes. "Apparently, the Armstrongs were big fans of Nelms, and he never would have asked Jared to retake a tryout test. Thought I should fudge Natalie's grades to keep Nelms's team intact. I told them if they didn't like the way I was doing things, perhaps Jared shouldn't take part, and now he's not."

I puffed out a sarcastic "Welcome to teaching." We'd all been on the receiving side of parental tirades. Although suggesting a teacher *lower* a kid's grade for eligibility reasons had to be a new one.

He nodded, unamused. "Was there anything else?" It wasn't so much a question as a dismissal.

"So, you still want my help?" I asked. His eyebrows shot up, and I shrugged off his unspoken question. "You already got her hopes up about changing the rules. I need to make sure it gets done. Emily should have an advocate."

Brick made a disgruntled noise, so I explained. "You don't understand what it's like to be LGBT, and I don't want you saying something that will set back her progress. No offense, I'm a little better prepared to deal with any situation that may come up. Have you ever met a trans person?"

Brick blinked at me slowly as if I had spoken in a foreign language, then frowned. "Has anyone ever told you that you have an irritating habit of making assumptions?"

"Whatever. You know I'm right. If you choose to work with me, you'll learn that I'm very vocal about things I believe in. If we encounter a judge or coach or another student that treats Emily unfairly, I will say something."

He let loose an aggravated sigh, and I let myself believe it had to do with his neck and not me.

"No doubt. But if *you* want to work with *me*, then you should recognize that saying 'no offense' after you say something offensive doesn't fly. You can't keep going around making ignorant assumptions. Nor will I tolerate the way you stormed in my classroom ready to chew me out without knowing the complete story. It's not how I behave, and it damn sure isn't the behavior I want to be modeled to my students."

I guffawed. "What ignorant assumptions? If you think Emily's going to interact with coaches and kids from all over the state and not have one shot taken at her because of who she is, then you're the one who is ignorant." What was it about this guy? First, everything I did made him laugh. Now, he seemed determined to be pissed off at me.

Brick rolled his eyes. "Look, I may not know her like you do, but we should get one thing out in the open—"

A hard knock cut off his words. "Enter," Brick barked.

The door opened, and Peter Lim's stoic face appeared. "Excuse me, sir. I wanted to inform you the battalion command meeting has concluded."

"That issue with Bravo company get resolved?" Brick asked.

"Yes, sir. Cadet Sergeant Gomez will submit absentee reports to the XO first thing tomorrow. Apologies for the oversight, sir."

"It's only the first month. We'll get there. I appreciate your taking over the leadership of the meeting. Any other concerns raised?"

Peter continued to give Brick a rundown of the meeting with a sufficient barrage of terms and titles I didn't even try to decipher. I worked hard to foster a relaxed, friendly rapport with my students, so the formality between them caught me off guard. It felt like I was sitting front row for a play. Peter brought a lot of *you can't handle the truth* intensity to his words. Brick's chiseled features, buzz cut, broad chest, and bulging muscles were basically central casting for hot military porn. A fleeting thought about calling Brick *sir* in a far less professional setting had me squirming in my seat. Brick's eyes trained on me, and for a brief, horrifying second, I wondered if I'd inadvertently verbalized that thought.

Peter gave a curt nod and said a quick "You're welcome, sir," before turning on his heel and walking out, shutting the door behind him.

"You have something else to say?"

My cheeks heated. "Isn't he supposed to salute you or something?"

The edges of Brick's lips tugged upward. "No."

He said it succinctly, but there was a heat behind his honey-brown eyes, tempting me to engage in a more playful exchange.

I bit my lip at the weird shift in energy. It was almost as though . . . No. That couldn't be. He was married, I reminded myself. As an artist, I could appreciate the way Brick looked, but I absolutely drew the line at entertaining fantasies or flirting with straight guys. Particularly hypermasculine straight coworkers who appeared capable of crushing me and were best buds with my boss.

"So, you were saying something about me being ignorant?" I tried to keep my tone businesslike, but damn it, a playful "*sir*" slipped out under my breath.

His smirk said he'd heard me. And he was getting way too much enjoyment out of it. "Well, for starters, there were trans men and women under my command during both the Obama and Trump administrations, so I've had plenty of sensitive conversations about trans-related issues. I only spoke with Emily and her mother once, but

I can tell Emily isn't quite the delicate flower you portrayed her to be. Savannah thought she was up for the challenge. She only asked that I do my best to change the rules and keep an eye on her, and I will, as I plan to do for all my students."

Brick stopped, catching me in what I'm sure was a scowl, judging by how pleased he looked with himself. I licked my dry lips, and Brick raised his brows, practically daring me to admit I'd been wrong. Which okay. I was an adult. Emily had gotten stronger, and I probably needed to remember that I couldn't protect her from all the bad people in the world, but Brick hadn't seen what she'd gone through. There were a lot of nights last year I genuinely feared she wasn't going to be able to hold on.

I could admit to making a snap judgment, but it damn sure would not be while staring up at him. I had my pride. I rose to my feet and paused with my hand on the doorknob, signaling that I was done with the conversation. "I apologize for saying a straight, cis man couldn't be a good ally to a trans person. Happy?" I opened the door and crossed the threshold, hoping to make a quick getaway.

Brick spat out a disbelieving, "There you go again."

I turned without thinking. The single reaction, combined with the incredulous stare, undermined my entire exit strategy. "You're starting to piss me off."

He stepped out from behind his desk and leaned in the doorway, bulging arms crossed over his chest. "Starting to?" He laughed dismissively. "Seems like I haven't been able to stop. I am kind of surprised, though. I thought LGBT advocates were anti-heteronormative assumptions."

So damn cocky. He was fucking with me and enjoying it. "You said you had a wife."

"Exactly. *Had*. I never said I was straight."

The potential of a not-straight Brick sent a zing of awareness directly to my cock. I had to remind myself that I hated guys that played games. My feet felt trapped in cement, anchored to the floor, preventing me from leaving until I understood what he meant to accomplish with his little word puzzle. But he stood there mute, leaning in the doorway like a goddamn wet dream, grin aimed at me like he was locking in the coordinates for a missile strike.

"Let me guess, you just up and came out as gay at forty-whatever-you-are, left your wife, and now you're single." I laughed at how preposterous the idea was. "And you think, what? Hmm. Oh, I know, you think all gay men can't resist you because you're all hard muscle and—"— His grin grew bigger, and I tossed my arms up in disgust. "Why are you doing this? I already told you I'd help you coach the AO team."

"Wow." There was a playful heat in his voice. "You are *really* bad at this, huh? Tell you what . . . I'm feeling generous, so I'll give you partial credit for the one thing you got right. See you at the first practice, Coach Berry." Then he turned back into his office and shut the door.

"So he shut the door? That's it. No explanation." Thank God for Sierra. I took the broom and swept up the ceramics area of the Artsy Soul for lack of anything better to do with my hands. Saturday afternoons were a terrible time to pop by, since she was usually knee-deep in birthday parties, but I had to talk to her.

"Yes." I stabbed the concrete floor with the broom. "I said, 'You want me to believe you're a gay man' and he gave me this incredulous 'You're such a dumbass' attitude and shut the door. I was gobsmacked. Like honestly, completely, gobsmacked. He's so . . . ugh. I just . . . I should help him with the paperwork or whatever and let him handle the actual coaching, right? Emily will be fine."

I glanced up to see her wide smile. "Oh my god." It came out in a slow, nasally, high-pitched voice like a Canadian version of Janice's catchphrase from *Friends*. It was an old joke between us, but Sierra's face brightened. Voice laced with accusation, as she singsonged, "You like him."

"What?" Protests crowded out each other in my head so none of them could break through. "No, I don't. I loathe him."

Her smile cracked further, full on laughing at me as she clucked her tongue. She was lucky she was with child or I might have hit her with the broom. "That's why you're freaking out, because it may be true. He might be gay, and then you'll have to admit it."

My skin prickled under the scrutiny. "Admit what? I admit nothing. Besides, if he's gay and I was only right about one thing, then he's taken, and it's not like it does me any good, does it?" I somehow kept my voice mild, not about to feed into her delusions. "And you act like I'm commitment phobic or something. I date men specifically because they are looking for a commitment."

"Eh. You nitpick dating profiles and insist on these 'meet and greet' pre-dating interviews. It's nonsense, and you use it to guarantee you'll never connect with anyone."

I scowled, purposely omitting my recent decision to take a break from dating. "I'll have you know my 'meet and greet' process is highly effective."

Or it would be if I were still doing it.

I continued, "Do I have to remind you about Paul, the guy who smelled like chicken soup, or Trent, the Fox News junkie, or the Ken doll with the South Korean model boyfriend?"

She shook her head. "Brick snuck up on you and that's what has you—"

I cut her off with a warning noise as the front bell chimed. "Your pregnancy hormones need to be checked, woman."

"Uh-huh," she said.

"What's wrong?" Olivier's voice spiked with concern as he crossed the room and walked directly to his pregnant wife. He stroked her flat belly, his forehead creased with worry. "Is something wrong with the baby?"

"*Non mon amour*," Sierra said, rising to her toes to kiss him. "Jesse *est amoureux*."

I rolled my eyes. "Christ Almighty."

"You're in love?" Olivier laughed. "With whom? Please not the Ken doll. He sounded boring."

I shook my head vigorously, dread filling my chest as Sierra caught Olivier up on my run-in with Brick using far more French than I could reasonably fact-check. Not that I didn't trust him, but gossip about a teacher romance at Northridge was the last thing I needed. Besides, Sierra was wrong. I did not have a crush on Brick; it was a fleeting attraction, and he wasn't even ga—

"So, bisexual," Olivier said plainly.

I scrubbed at my hair. "Huh?"

"Brick." He paused as if waiting for a translator to catch me up. "He *had* a wife, and he's not straight, but only one of either recently out as gay, or single. So he's openly bisexual? Or pan or whatever. But single, that's good. So you like him?" He stared at us expectantly, then clearly losing patience, gestured in a winding motion as if his hands could move us there faster.

Sierra met my gaze as the obvious explanation struck us simultaneously. "We are complete idiots."

"But . . . No." I sensed what was coming next and bit my lip, because holy hell, that—

Sierra head bobbed up and down, cementing my place as the world's biggest dumbass. "Makes total sense to me. He's not an ally, he's bisexual."

I revisited all my accusations. As much as my brain tried to form a staunch defense, all of Brick's puzzling comments about hetero-normative assumptions and his funny, borderline heated looks fell into place. "I'm such an asshole."

Olivier nodded in agreement, letting out a loud *oomph* when Sierra elbowed him in the chest.

"I told him he didn't understand what it was like to be LGBT! I accused his best friend of being homophobic. Ugh. I said he had hard muscles. What am I going to do?" I planted my palm on my forehead.

Olivier stole a glance at Sierra, who shrugged unhelpfully. "You told him his best friend was homophobic? Why would you do that? Who's his best friend?"

I groaned, angst slicing through my chest as I dragged my hand down my face. My behavior horrified me. I'd fed into every stereotype there was. Super masculine men in uniform could never be gay, or bi, or just . . . Fuck. "Zach," I said meekly. "He was the best man at his wedding, or maybe Zach was the best man at his. I don't remember."

"Brick and Zach are best friends? And you . . ." Olivier gasped, then muttered, "*Tête de noeud*," under his breath. Based on the unhappy face Sierra made, it was surely some creative French insult. "So, that lie-low pep talk I gave you? That's going well then, huh?"

"What do I do?" I asked Sierra because Olivier was already showing himself out of the room.

She gritted her teeth, cringing so hard I didn't hold out much hope for a solution.

"Well. You do make a mean chocolate chip cookie."

Chapter Eight

Brick

*B*efore my divorce, I usually spent Sunday tackling the honey-do list Jane was fond of keeping on the fridge and decluttering any hoarding hotspots in the house. Now, I stretched out in my recliner, drank beer before noon, ate food without consideration of my next mandatory fitness test, and watched football on my giant-ass television in a tidy home.

I'd been living life so wrong for so long.

Thanks to Zach's basketball league, today's football game would also be attended by a hot water bottle, but who cared? As lonely as I found living by myself in a new town, this? This was pure heaven.

The Ravens had scored on the Texans, when the doorbell rang. I lowered the footrest of my recliner and plodded, bare feet, wearing boxers and an open robe to the door, one eye trained on the attempted two-point conversion.

"Yes," I screamed at the killer block. I cinched my robe around me before reaching for the knob, mouth already salivating in anticipation of my hot wings delivery. Extra spicy with blue cheese. I'd spent twenty years getting mild sauce with ranch because of Jane, but now *my* opinion was the only one that mattered. Zach was right. A man could get used to this.

The door swung open, but instead of a uniformed delivery man with a plastic bag, Jesse stood gripping a small metal box of some sort.

I coughed, hands fumbling to fasten the belt around my robe. "What the hell are you doing here?"

"We got off on the wrong foot. I made you cookies." He thrust his container at me. "May I come in?" He peered around the doorway, undoubtedly looking for a woman.

I glanced over at my recliner and mourned the rest of my game. "Yeah, sure. Let me get dressed." I stepped aside, and he tiptoed cautiously over the threshold, a far cry from the way he'd stormed into my classroom the Friday before. "Came to meet my wife, did ya?"

His eyes shot to me and he frowned. "Is there a—" He swallowed as though the next part were painful for him. "—a significant other of any gender?"

I suspected that was as close to admission of error as I would get and answered his implied question as a reward. "No, I'm recently single. Divorce finalized about six months ago."

He nodded.

"You?"

He smiled sheepishly. "Single. Never married."

"Well, look at us. Communicating." I smirked and shut the door behind him. "Take a seat. I'll be back in a second." I left him standing in the foyer while I hurried down the hall to my bedroom. In the safety of my room, I let myself have a moment of optimism about what his visit meant. He'd come over to my house. With cookies. To apologize. Well, maybe not apologize, but definitely showing up with treats qualified as a mea culpa. I'd been so disappointed when he'd shown no interest and yeah, embarrassed that I'd made such a stink to Zach about having him be an assistant coach. Strike three for my flirting attempts too.

I dressed quickly, selecting faded jeans and an Army T-shirt that I knew showed off the biceps Jesse seemed to admire between tongue lashings, then brushed my teeth. When I returned, he was hovering around my built-in bookshelves that lined the wall behind my couch, his back toward me. I watched him finger the spines of a few rows. *Snooping. It figured.*

"Find anything interesting?"

"Jesus." Jesse jumped and clutched his chest, drawing a small laugh from me. "You scared me. You have a lot of books. I was curious what a man like you reads."

My eyebrow peaked. *A man like you* was doing some heavy lifting in that sentence. I could only imagine what other assumptions he'd made. After butchering the name of the Louvre and admitting the source of my nickname, dumb, uncultured jock seemed apropos. "And was your curiosity satisfied?"

I knew a smart comment was coming when his eyes sparkled and his lips pulled at the corners. He'd done that the first time I'd noticed him with Zach, like the mere thought of getting a zinger out made him giddy. "Well, you interrupted my snooping. I'd only gotten through what looks to be an impressive collection of military strategy, biographies and . . ." He picked up a small pamphlet I'd gotten at the meetup and read, "Northridge hiking trails."

He huffed disgust, and I had to agree. I'd tried a few and was not impressed.

"Could you leave and come back?" His hands moved in dramatic flourishes as he spoke. I smiled at the return of the exact move that'd caught my eye in the first place.

"Pity I didn't know you were coming, or I could have taken a hike. I guess you'll have to satisfy your curiosity by asking me questions like a civilized adult."

He thumbed through the thin book, feigning nonchalant perusal. "If you like hiking, there are way better options about two hours from here."

His breath caught as I took the book and replaced it on my shelf. When I stepped back, there was no mistaking the interest in his gaze. When he realized I noticed his reaction, his lips pursed and he glanced away.

I left him standing there, fidgeting with his clothes, and made my way around the couch to the recliner, checking the score before using the remote to turn off the game. "Do you enjoy hiking? Or do you prefer shopping to outdoor activities?"

He shrugged. "I like painting and photography. It lends itself to being outdoors occasionally. It's no shopping trip to Paris, but I've been hiking several times. I enjoy it."

"Me too." I smiled. "So, I don't recall telling you where I live."

"I . . ." He peered up at me, nostrils flared and cheeks growing pinker by the second. "Your class website mentioned you had recently moved here, your neighborhood, and that you were looking forward to working on your house. Real estate transaction data is public. Your last name isn't that common. Bainbridge, huh? Yikes." He cringed, then shrugged as if to say that his explanation was a perfectly appropriate way to get a coworker's address.

Too impressed with his brazen admission to be creeped out, I laughed. "So if the teacher thing doesn't work out, you've got a bright future as a stalker."

His nose crinkled, but he didn't disagree. "Since we'll be doing this Academic Olympiad thing together, I thought we should clear the air before any students pick up on . . . tension. I would have waited until Monday to arrange a time, but practice is before school. Let's not get distracted by the details and who did what to whom and figure out a game plan."

I nodded, trying to keep a straight face. It potentially said something about me that I enjoyed this so much, but I didn't care. "Interesting," I said.

His eyes lifted to me, a question in his expression. "What is?"

"Oh, I sort of agonized over putting my cell number on the practice schedule I sent out to all the kids and emailed to you Friday evening. It never even occurred to me that someone could figure out where I lived if they wanted to talk to me." I shrugged.

He opened and closed his mouth a few times. It was worth every bit of aggravation to see him speechless.

"Do you want me to go?"

"No," I said. "You wanted to clear the air, and you did *sort of* acknowledge being wrong. How could I refuse this olive branch?"

"Does . . . Can we start over? I know I've been kind of a dick to you."

"And . . ." I prompted. "Come on. You'll feel so much better. It'll be cathartic, I promise."

His lips tightened up. "And I apologize." The words finally tumbled from his mouth like he was spitting out sour milk. I wanted to fist pump it was so glorious.

When the doorbell rang, I didn't miss a beat. "Time for my bisexual support group."

Jesse's eyes widened comically.

"Let me get rid of them. Don't worry, we're used to being erased." I grabbed my wallet to tip the delivery driver and left Jesse standing dumbfounded in the middle of my family room.

I blocked his view with the door and waved. "We'll try it again next time, Bob," I yelled at the delivery driver when he was backing out of my drive. Laughing to myself, I took the food order into the kitchen and inclined my head to indicate Jesse should follow. As much fun as I was having, sheepish and contrite didn't look right on him at all. I considered maybe it was time to stop clowning around and deal with the work stuff.

"Listen," Jesse said, "I'm realizing how much of a line I crossed showing up here, so I'm going to go now." He turned to leave, face all defeated. A wave of regret swept through me. I didn't tease him to knock the confidence out of him. I did it to have him dish it right back.

"Jesse." I called as he moved toward my front door.

"Yeah?" He turned back to me, and his gaze dropped to my lips before his focus returned to my eyes.

"You like hot wings?"

He smiled weakly. "Yeah."

"Blue cheese or ranch?"

"Um. Blue cheese." He stepped toward me, peaking at the packages on the counter. "Not a fan of ranch."

"Good man. Here take this." I motioned to my fridge. "I'll grab us some beers."

There was no way to eat wings gracefully, but Brick didn't even try. He attacked his food like a vulture, ripping the meat off and sticking the bone in his mouth to strip it clean. It wasn't a good look, but I'd basically accused him of being a poor queer advocate while simultaneously forgetting an entire letter of the LGBT family existed, then shown up unannounced like an idiot, so the least I could do is let the man eat his wings in peace. It wasn't like we were on a date. *Stop staring at his lips. Clean up your mess and try not to make another*, I chastised myself as I took a delicate bite.

The heat in my mouth steadily rose to a million degrees. "What kind of sauce is this?" I took a sip of the beer, my mouth puckering at the bitter flavor. It wasn't doing much to cool my tongue, but damn if I would admit to being fussy. I could only imagine what he'd do with *that* information.

"Habanero." Brick took another messy bite of his wings and chased it with a swig of his beer, all very bro-ish. If I hadn't already been taken to task for stereotyping, I would have asked for proof he was into dudes.

We were sitting on the deck in the late-summer heat at a brand-new teak table, and Brick had amassed a healthy pile of bones and soiled napkins.

I slapped at a mosquito, the third one that'd taken a snip out of me, and wondered if this was a test. A river of sweat dripped down my back, and the moisture had caused my shirt to cling. "Are you enjoying our lovely Texas weather?" I asked.

Brick laughed, licking his fingers one by one while squinting at the sun high in the sky. "It is balmy."

I chuckled, pulling my shirt away from my skin. "Yeah. Don't you love feeling all sticky?"

His brow shot up, and it was only after I noticed the slight blush on his cheeks that I realized there might have been a hint of innuendo in my words. Brick cocked his head, forgiving me with another smirk that should not have been as cute as it was. He'd all but admitted to purposely teasing me, so I rolled with it to show him I could laugh at myself as much as the next guy.

"In certain circumstances. Sure. Sticky can be fun." He winked.

Oh boy. Flirtatious winking would not be good for me. I diverted my gaze. "Hell of a place you have here." I gestured to the lack of landscaping. The builder had clearly done the front, since most of the houses on the street had a similar aesthetic, but the back had been cleared and offered no privacy from the neighbors.

"You like landscaping? I could use help."

"I'd suggest trees and . . . grass," I joked, but an image struck me. I'd spent many a day staring at Ryan throwing the ball to his son on the perfectly manicured yard. It had been lined on either side with white flowering shrubs to divide it from their neighbors. "Perhaps some blackhaw if you don't mind the berries. They're pretty in the spring and the flowers attract birds, if you like that sort of thing."

Brick gnawed through another wing and tossed the bone in a cardboard boat he'd been using to collect trash. He did his finger-licking ritual again.

"Do you think after you're done eating, we could move inside to experience the joys of air-conditioning?"

"You said you enjoyed being outdoors. We can move in now if you want. I'm pretty well done."

He was absolutely not done, but I was not built for ninety-degree picnics without sunscreen. "I would not be opposed to it."

Brick rolled his neck in a way that reminded me of his earlier pain, and he used his non-wing-eating fingers to rub it.

"Neck better?" I asked as I stood and helped him gather trash.

"Yeah. Nothing an evening with a TENS unit can't cure."

He had a TENS unit? I froze mid cleanup. "It had nothing to do with your posture, did it?"

Brick peeked up at me; a wide face-splitting grin answered my question. "I'm sure it didn't help, but no. It's an old injury that likes to remind me I'm too old to play basketball once in a while, but I'm blaming the stress of being yelled at by infuriated coworkers."

"Is there anything I've said to you since we've met that doesn't make me sound like a jackass?"

Brick stared at me, silence stretching out over a long minute. He peered up to the sky, like he was thinking hard.

"Never mind," I grumbled, slightly mortified.

He flashed a wolfish smile. "Wait. I got one."

I rolled my eyes. "Don't hurt yourself."

"You said you loved my hard muscles."

That he misremembers. "I said you had hard muscles. Not that I liked them."

He pouted playfully, but I wouldn't indulge a solicited compliment, not when he already had the upper hand on me.

"Stop it." I held up my hands full of trash and jutted my head in the house's direction. "Why don't you use those muscles to open this sliding door. I'm melting here."

Chuckling, he grabbed the necks of our beer bottles between his fingers and the remaining boat of wings, then hurried to comply. Our banter continued as I helped him put the food away and clean up. I stuck the extra blue cheese in his fridge, noticing the package of steaks. Filet mignons. My favorite. "Should have held out for dinner," I teased.

Brick peered over my shoulder. "There is extra, but not sure one tin of cookies and a half-ass apology are quite filet worthy."

I grinned. "What if I said I *do* like your muscles?"

"Nah." He leaned against his counter, arms crossed over his broad chest. My eyes zoomed to the bulge of his biceps before I caught myself. When I met his gaze, he winked at me. "I already know you do. You weren't as sly with those looks in the faculty meeting as you think you were."

I swallowed and turned around, shoving the Styrofoam container over to one side and shuffled it with other items to give my blush time to fade. "Just as well, judging by the way you inhale wings, you probably eat your steak well done or some other atrocity. Let me guess, with French fries and ketchup." I closed the fridge. When I turned around, he was eating one of my cookies and dumping out the nearly full contents of my drink. "Hey," I protested, although I hadn't the faintest idea why. It tasted vile.

He rolled his eyes. "The only way to eat a steak is with a loaded baked potato."

"Agreed."

He set the bottle in the recycling bin under the sink. "Now then. What do you *actually* like to drink?"

"Water," I admitted. "Or coffee drinks."

"No alcohol?"

"I'll have red wine or vodka on occasion, but no, I'm not a big drinker."

Brick nodded as though committing that information to memory. It was conceivable that Sierra had been right about me being too quick to judge. If I'd seen a man from a dating app eat wings like Brick had, I would have undoubtedly found a reason to leave. Then I might have missed his kind offer to move inside or his noticing I didn't like beer. Brick was observant. It made me wonder how many of my meet and greets would have paid close attention to how I ordered my coffee? I couldn't say. Maybe I—

"Lime?"

"Huh?" I gave my head a shake and focused on Brick.

"Stay with me, Jesse. Remember, I say some words, then you say words back. All nice and civil."

On reflex, I flipped him off like I'd done many times to Sierra. As soon as I done it, I regretted it, but Brick smiled wider and laughed, so I mirrored his reaction.

"Oh. So close. We'll keep practicing. Let's try again. I asked if you want tap water or sparkling water with lime?" When taken in the spirit he'd intended it, his teasing was slightly endearing. And damn it, he was getting to me. I laughed, which only encouraged him.

"Sparkling water is great, thanks."

Brick retrieved a can from the fridge and poured it over ice before handing it to me.

"So you ready to talk about the Academic Olympiad team?"

"Yes, finally. What I came here for."

He called me out for the stalking again, but it was all in fun. We talked for a long time, not only about work but other things too. A documentary about art forgery we'd both recently watched and the places the Army had taken him to. I hadn't had the chance to travel much, but I found Brick's stories fascinating. By the end of the night, I knew we were behaving like my students did when they were crushing hard, but what could I say? I liked that he asked me questions and cared about the answers. That he deferred to my teaching experience and took my opinions about how to make Academic Olympiad a wonderful experience for *all* the kids seriously. He noticed things about me, even if only so he could tease me about them later.

I didn't get schoolboy crushes often. But there was something about Brick that made me laugh at myself and relax more than usual. As far as evenings went, I didn't hate it.

Chapter Nine

Brick

"Hello. My name is Lieutenant Colonel Hausman, and my pronouns are he and him." I surveyed the room, ignoring the surprised expression on Peter Lim's face. "I'll be your Academic Olympiad coach this year. As I said in my letter last week, we have some major catching up to do before the start of competition." A few of the older kids nodded along, but no one seemed overly concerned, so I didn't dwell on the lost time. "The first round is general knowledge, so there isn't much we can target to study, but we will take a practice test next time to assess where we are. Mr. Berry is passing out the study guides and the schedule for you. We'll meet three times a week before school and rotate through math, science, history, economics, geography, art, music, and literature."

I nodded to Jesse, who finished passing out the packets I'd put together. "Thanks, Lieutenant Colonel Hausman. Hi, everyone. I'm Mr. Berry. My pronouns are also he and him. Welcome to our first team meeting. In your packet, you'll find the topics that might be covered in competition. The theme this year is The Birth of America, which will be used in all rounds beyond the initial qualifying test. So, for example, the art test could cover artists that worked in America during the Revolutionary War, but it could also cover later works that portray the founding fathers, such as Leutze's *Washington Crossing the Delaware*. All fair game. Given our limited time, we have taken a divide-and-conquer approach. Each of you has specific things to research, and you will present that information during team practices for the group's benefit." He returned to his seat and smiled. "Now, I know a few of you, but why don't we start with introductions? Please introduce yourself with your name, pronouns, grade, and favorite subjects. Emily, would you like to start?"

"Um. Sure." Emily glanced around nervously, picking imaginary lint off her black skirt. "I'm Emily Delacroix. My pronouns are she and her. I'm a junior and my favorite subject is art, but I also like science." Emily spoke fast, almost too fast to be understood. We'd have to work on that for the quiz competition. She settled her gaze on the short, chubby Latina with dark flowing hair, who sat up straighter in her chair.

"Hi, everyone. I'm glad to be back this year. I'm Natalie Sanchez, and I'm . . . uh. I'm a girl." She giggled. "I'm in tenth grade and my favorite subject is science and math."

"Great, thanks, Natalie," Jesse said. "Peter?"

"Yeah. Um. Peter Lim. Senior. My favorite subject is history and JROTC. I'm decent at straight memorization, so I'm good with things like geography."

"And your pronouns?" I prompted.

"Oh, sorry." Peter peeked at Emily, who blushed. "He."

I cast a glance at Jesse, worried that the pronoun thing wasn't working out as well as he hoped. The last thing I wanted to do was shine a spotlight on Emily by calling attention to the fact that she was the only one whose pronouns might be in question, but he gave me a smile and slight nod as reassurance.

"Great." I turned to the next girl, a tiny thing with a thick spattering of freckles across her nose, a multi-colored pixie cut, and dark eyeliner. "Want to go next?"

"Sure. I'm Jazmin Lee. Sophomore." She waved, and her arm full of dangling bracelets clattered with the movement. "My pronouns are she and her. I want to say, one of my cousins is nonbinary, so I think it's cool that you asked because they are always correcting people." She smiled brightly. "My favorite subject is English. I love to read, and I checked this list and I've got all these covered, so if anyone wants to take my math concepts, I'll do your literature."

"Sweet." The group focused on the Black kid with a head full of short, twisted curls and a strong New Orleans accent sitting next to

Jazmin. He had sharp cheekbones and pierced ears. "Uh. Hi, y'all. I'm Nate Hamilton. Freshman. Pronouns are he and him. I hate to read, so I'm gonna take you up on that offer, Jazmin. My favorite subject is music, but I do a'ight in pretty much everything."

The group laughed, and my shoulders dropped a few inches.

"Well, I guess I'm last, then. I'm Blake Wyatt. I'm a Junior. A girl, obviously." She motioned down her bright red dress clinging to her ample curves. "But since I have a boy name, I get tired of correcting people. She and her, please. My favorite subject is French, but I'm good at math too."

Jesse clapped his hands. "All right. We have a good mix of interests, so that will make things a fair amount easier. Are there questions?"

Peter cast an apprehensive glance around the team, then between Jesse and me before raising his hand. "Are we sure our team is appropriately, um, balanced?"

I jumped in, cutting Jesse off before he could get more than the first part of an unspecified syllable out. By the glare he gave me, this did not go unnoticed. "Yes, Mr. Lim. I appreciate your concern, but Mr. Berry and I will ensure our team is eligible as constituted."

Peter nodded, but the worry lines on his forehead didn't quite relax. We fielded a few additional questions from the team and reviewed the study guide in greater detail. The kids broke off into pairs after that, tackling the first part of their research, which was art and music. Jesse flitted from student to student, checking in and answering questions while I stuck to the head of the room and waited for students to come to me or call for my attention.

Jesse was in a full squat, eye level with Nate in the back of the room when he sprung up like a jack-in-the-box between the rows. "Brick, can I use your projector?" He rushed forward before I could get out of his way. He leaned over me, fingers flying over my keyboard, but his scent distracted me too much to see what it was— damn, he smelled amazing. Some spiced, lemony aftershave that drove me wild.

He clicked the button to share the screen, and an image appeared for the class to see. Just as quickly as he was in my space, he'd left.

"Y'all, look at this." He motioned to the screen like Vanna White. "This is on your study guide, but I want you to see it because it'll be easy to remember this one. George Washington, Gilbert Charles Stuart. Bet you've seen this before?"

"Yeah, you're right. That's the same picture on the one-dollar bill," Nate volunteered.

"Exactly," Jesse said proudly. "It's one of the most recognized images of Washington and one of the most reproduced images ever. It's unfinished because he died before its completion."

I smiled because I loved history. And Jesse's enthusiasm. My confidence soared as I realized I could contribute something on this one. "The Athenaeum Portrait," I remarked.

Jesse nodded approvingly. "That's right. It's also referred to as The Athenaeum Portrait because Stuart painted many portraits of Washington in his lifetime. After Stuart's death, the painting was given to the Boston Athenaeum."

Blake chimed in, reading from her laptop. "It says here, Martha Washington commissioned this portrait intending to have one of herself done as well, but he never started hers."

"What's *Athenaeum* mean?" Peter asked. "That could be a good test question."

"It's a synonym for library, right?" Natalie asked.

"That's a good way to remember it," I confirmed. "But it would include more than books; it could contain art, artifacts, periodicals. Think anthology as the root."

The group's energy gelled as they dug deeper, researching other artists and works central to the theme and sharing potential sources of test questions. No matter how engrossed I was with a student, my eyes kept finding Jesse, thoughts drifting back to the few hours we'd spent together. We had a surprising amount of similar interests.

I had never been one to jerk off excessively, but when Jesse had left my place, I quickly discovered yet another advantage to living alone. My hand had been on my dick almost before he was out of the driveway, and I'd still gone to bed horny. I'd tried to convince myself that it was mostly the novelty of him. Having someone to flirt with, who flirted back—and we had definitely turned that corner. But watching him teach, I knew that wasn't all it was. He was . . . impressive. Patient. Encouraging. Kind. It was a whole different side of him and—

"You okay, Mr. Hausman?" Jazmin asked.

I lifted my gaze from my desk. "Uh, sure. Why?"

"You looked kind of moony. Like how my dad gets when my mom makes him cheesecake."

"Oh. Yeah. Just tired."

Jesse's eyes zipped toward me, and he cracked a knowing smile before he checked his watch. "Y'all did great today. Why don't you pack it up?"

I wasn't sure she believed me, but Jesse clearly didn't. Thankfully, the first bell rang.

Jesse

"That went better than expected," I said to Brick, grateful that Peter had forgotten something in his locker and had left us alone in the JROTC room.

Brick nodded, stood, and joined me on the other side of his classroom desk. He eased back gingerly, testing the integrity of it before giving it his full weight. When he was situated, I realized we were finally eye to eye. A fact that made it difficult to avoid looking at him or pretend not to notice him looking at me. The temptation to step between his knees was intense, but in a classroom minutes before the bell was neither the time nor the place. Still, I took a step closer.

"We make a good team," Brick said in a softer and sweeter tone than he'd previously spoken to me.

"We do." I nodded, biting my lip as he apprised me and brushed the outside of my arm with his hand.

"You have plans after school?"

That was . . . well, I couldn't say unexpected. After Sunday, it was clear we were both feeling that spark of awareness between us. Not that it was explicitly acknowledged. Was this a good idea? "Um . . ." I hedged, but it was too late to stop the little seed from blossoming. After so many crappy dates, I kind of really wanted to.

He straightened his spine. "We still need to discuss strategy for the rule change. I have an idea."

"Oh, yeah … of course." I worked hard to keep the disappointment off my face and shift gears back to work.

"I have drill team practice until five thirty. I'll need to stick around until everyone is picked up."

"We could, um. We could get dinner. You know. If you want?" I cast my eyes up to him, peering at him through my lashes, blinking more rapidly than was normal. He smiled at me. Like wow . . . pure sunshine. My hands grew sweaty. What even was this feeling? "I need to prep for tomorrow, but I'll be in the supply closet setting up kits or in my classroom. Come find me when you're done?"

One expressive eyebrow raised. "Yeah. That sounds good. You owe me a meal after all the shit you pulled." He slouched again, bringing our eyes back into alignment. They were intensely warm, and the color reminded me of gingerbread. I was growing way too enamored with the little lines that radiated from them when he teased me.

"Oh?" I took a small step forward to chuck him playfully on the shoulder. "So, I'm paying too?"

He caught my fist, holding on to it for a second and swinging it back and forth a few times before reluctantly letting it go, heat blazing from his eyes. I rested a palm lightly on his thigh, noticing the way his fingers were clenching the edge of the desk, the whites of his knuckles facing me.

"All right," I said seriously. "My treat."

His mouth gaped, and I had no doubt he was going to say something else equally flirtatious, but the door opened, and Peter Lim stepped into the room. A heartbeat later, Brick pushed off the desk so hard it scraped across the floor. I stumbled back, giving the impression we'd been doing something we had absolutely not been doing. Brick cleared his throat and fidgeted with his already straight tie. All the reasons this was a bad idea collided in one perfect image. "Thanks, Mr. Berry. I'll see you later. Have a good day."

Peter's eyes shifted between us, and well, he was a smart kid. Brick and I had been standing less than arm's length apart, our bodies, though not pressed against each other, had been angled intimately. I struggled to regain my composure and grabbed my bag, checking the large clock above the door. "You too. Bye, Peter."

I wasn't sure if Brick had intended to come out to his students, but one glance at the expression dawning on Peter Lim's face as I walked past told me he had.

On the way back to the portables, I refused to indulge in romantic thoughts. So what if he was gorgeous and drooled over me like I was dessert? Brick had recently gotten divorced and we worked together. A little flirting and dinner wouldn't harm anything, but I needed to keep my wits about me.

Brick

Jesse Berry was trouble. The kind of trouble that had me daydreaming in the middle of class and drawing funny looks from my students all day.

Those blue eyes, his cologne, the electric way my skin tingled when he touched me. Every time I thought of his hand on my thigh, my dick stirred. I'd clamped down on my bottom lip to get hold of myself so many times that I now had a small cut. It was a fucking problem.

When the last bell rang, I fought to push Jesse out of my mind and give the drill team an hour and a half of my unadulterated focus.

I entered the gymnasium ready to go. "Cadet commander," I called to Peter. Although they weren't in uniform, this would be the first time I could assess the fourteen-member unarmed drill team in action. Zach had briefed me on their lackluster meet showings under my predecessor. I'd always enjoyed drill team in ROTC—the pageantry and ceremony were both inspiring and challenging. One of my top objectives was to help them improve, and I intended to follow through.

I wasted no time reviewing the agenda for the practice before turning things over to Peter.

"Pretend I'm the judge. Make sure you're centering on me."

"Yes, sir."

I took my place and watched Peter call the platoon to attention and fall in. Mostly the lines were good. There were minor precision issues and one kid whose half step was making too much noise. All of that would be worked out with practice.

With a crisp movement, Lim executed the report in with a clear voice and saluted me as he would the head judge, then requested permission to conduct the unarmed platoon basic drill.

"Permission granted," I answered, using my well-perfected Army voice for the first time in a long time.

"Thank you, sir." Lim about-faced, then yelled the command to "Dress Right Dress." Alignment good, he proceeded through the drill while I noted issues as I saw them on the clip board I'd brought with me.

When they finished, I had them do the entire routine again and reviewed my notes with Peter. "You're rushing. I need at least five seconds after Platoon Halt, and we need to work on column left. Spacing is way off."

"Yes, sir."

"Let's run it again."

For the next hour and half I worked with the team. We ran through the basic drill a third time and began working on an exhibition drill, which to put it kindly was a hot mess. The lines fell apart, and we had major spacing issues on several rotations, but the kids kept at it and I was impressed by the sustained effort.

The practice did me good. It reminded me I had a job to do and kids that were counting on their instructor to be engaged. By the end, I'd almost forgotten my plans with Jesse.

Almost.

When the last student left, I stopped off to lock up the classroom and cleaned myself up a bit. On the way out, I checked the supply closet. It was empty, but I smiled like a fool because it was still in pristine order and someone—and I had no means of knowing who— had generously used my label maker.

I strolled across the parking lot toward the portables, forcing myself to walk at a normal pace. Anything more would definitely fall under the "too eager" category. On the odd chance Jesse was watching from the window, I didn't want him to know exactly how much I was looking forward to spending time alone with him.

I didn't want to play games, but his early rejections had messed with my confidence. My goal was to proceed cautiously and ignore the way my heart raced and mouth watered at the sight of him. Let whatever was building build at its own pace without scaring him off or getting in over my head.

"Hey," Jesse greeted me when I stepped inside his classroom, but his attention remained focused on his computer. Then he glanced up and smiled, and all my good intentions were lost. "How was drill team?"

"Eh." I teetered my hand back and forth. "We have work to do still. How was your day?"

"Hectic," he responded. "I'm almost ready."

Since there was no way I would fit in a student desk, I nodded and paced the classroom. I stopped to admire the students' art.

"This is amazing." I moved to get a closer look at the elaborate floor-to-ceiling display of paper crepe flowers. I thought they were maybe each done by a student and just artfully arranged, but it appeared they were connected to a mesh backing and it was all one piece.

"Thank you," Jesse said proudly.

"Did you do this?"

He nodded.

"I'm impressed." I took in the details of each petal before Jesse stuck some papers in his bag and locked his computer.

"I'm ready. Where did you want to go?"

"I'm easy," I said.

There was a brief pause as he likely decided what to do with my obvious double entendre. "We'll see about that." Jesse winked, slung his bag over his shoulder, and ushered me out of his classroom, key in hand.

He filled me in on his day as we walked to our cars, debating where to go and if we should take one car or two. We agreed to drive separately to a steakhouse near his place. It was a short walk and a benign discussion, but being next to him, listening to him, had my mind running ahead to the outcome of the evening.

In the openness of the parking lot, his body language was a far cry from before, friendly still, but guarded. I slowed when we reach my car, fiddling with the fob. "Okay, so I'll see you there?"

Jesse stopped in front of me, eyes cast up, which only called my attention to the tendons in his neck. I salivated with the thought of kissing my way along them.

"Brick, before we go—" He bit his lip, our eyes meeting as whatever he'd planned to say evaporated.

"Yeah?" I prompted, swallowing hard as he peered at me through long lashes. I took a step closer, my tongue peeking out to moisten my dry lips, unable to resist the pull I felt toward him.

"I'm—" His mouth twitched, but this time neither of us laughed or smirked or teased. Instead, I cupped my free hand to the back of his neck. His hair against my fingers was exactly as soft as I'd imagined. He gasped, his sweet blue eyes blazing longingly into mine and the desire on his face obvious. He wanted me, and I wanted him.

"Brick," Jesse breathed.

"Yeah?"

He laid a hand over my heart and shifted his gaze to the building behind us. "This isn't a good idea."

I stumbled back quickly as a wave of regret and embarrassment rushed in. My cheeks heated. "God. I'm so sorry."

"No," Jesse cried, reaching for my arm to keep me from moving back farther. "I meant not here. Not at school."

"Oh." I swallowed. "Yeah. Sorry. You're right."

"It's just, I don't want any students or other faculty or, um, Zach . . ." He shrugged, glancing nervously up at the windows in the surrounding buildings. "This morning I think Peter might have thought we were . . ." His comment died, but the mention of how close we'd been turned his cheeks pink.

"Really?"

"Yeah. I assumed you weren't planning to advertise your sexuality to students. Why don't we go? Let's get some dinner and we can talk."

There was an edge of accusation to his words, like he expected me to be concerned about being seen with him when that was the furthest thing from the truth—dating men openly was my goal. "I'm out. I don't . . ." I stammered a bit, suddenly feeling self-conscious. Should I not have outed myself to a student? Did I care? I wanted to be free to pursue who caught my eye, but pursuing a coworker? Was there a protocol for that? Would we have to hide it? Discreet was the last thing I wanted.

"Do your students realize you're gay?" I raked my fingers through my hair and laughed at myself. I felt way too old to be this clueless. "I'm not sure what I'm doing, actually."

A small smile played on Jesse's lips and his eyes gleamed. "It's called communication, Brick. You know, I say a few words, you say a few words. Don't worry, we can keep practicing. And yes, I think it's fair to assume everyone at Northridge knows I'm gay, but we need to have a leg to stand on when we tell kids what level of PDA is appropriate on campus, so we should take this conversation elsewhere." He laughed gently and stroked a comforting hand over my biceps before squeezing it. When my eyes met his, I knew he wasn't so much saying it wasn't a good idea, only that it warranted a conversation. He was trying to look out for me. For both of us.

"Yeah. That's probably for the best. We should talk."

He smirked. "If you prefer, I can make all kinds of assumptions about what you're thinking."

I relaxed my shoulders, shaking my head with the same goofy grin Jesse kept inspiring. I would love to know what that might be, but based on his cocky expression, it wasn't likely to make keeping my hands off him in public any easier. "That isn't a good idea."

"Uh-huh. I thought as much. Come on, big guy. I'm going to need food for this conversation."

Bynum's Steakhouse was one of the nicer places in Northridge. The ambiance slanted toward the romantic side without the white linens and candlelight that made me feel like I should be wearing a suit. It was a favorite date place of mine, though I hadn't been here in years.

Brick and I followed the host to a small booth for two tucked in the back corner. As soon as I sized up the table, I worried about Brick's long legs. I shot a glance over my shoulder at him as the host set the menus down. "Would you prefer a different table?"

"No." Brick's mischievous smile set my teeth on edge. Now what was he planning? "This is fine," he said to the host.

He settled across from me, and it only took a second to discover there was no arrangement that kept our legs from touching. Based on the way he kept my knee pressed between his thick thighs, this had definitely been part of the plan.

"So." I laughed as I tried to move my foot without starting a game of footsie. "You want to try words first or should I make another of my stunningly brilliant assumptions?"

Brick chuckled. "I'd love to hear an assumption."

I made a show of thinking about it before saying one of the first fears to cross my mind. "This is all an elaborate scam to get me back for being a jackass."

Brick tsked. "Wrong again. I told you I accepted your proposal for a fresh start. Besides, I kind of like the look on your face when you're apologizing."

I rolled my eyes. "Don't get used to it."

"Guess again? Or should we try words?"

"Words work," I deadpanned.

"I'm incredibly attracted to you."

"Well." I gulped. "That was . . . honest."

"Would you prefer I lie?" He smiled and his shoulders relaxed. "I was planning to play this much cooler, but then with what happened in the parking lot, I decided on the drive over here I don't really want to. We work together, so if you're not interested, then I'd rather hear that now, so I don't keep sexually harassing you."

"You're *sexually* harassing me? All I felt was harassed." I kept my tone playful, but I might as well have waved a red flag in front of a bull with the way Brick's eyes heated.

The corner of his bottom lip slipped through the bite of his teeth, and he swallowed hard. "I want to make sure that when I harass you—sexually or otherwise—it's mutually enjoyable."

"So, you want my permission to torment me?"

"I don't think it's unnoticed that I enjoy pushing your buttons, which admittedly is kind of a new discovery of mine. But, first and foremost, I respect the word no. If you're not into it, say so, because

I'd like to know this will not end up in a very awkward conversation with my boss."

"How *new* of a discovery is this?" I asked cautiously. As strong as the attraction was between us, I couldn't ignore that he'd been recently married to a woman. Brick had all but confessed earlier he wasn't sure what he was doing. It'd be good to know if I was dealing with a man who got aroused watching some gay porn once or if he'd actually acted on his attraction to men.

Brick's face fell, and I took his hesitation as confirmation that my fears were valid. "Perhaps this would be a good time to practice using a few more words."

"I've dated bi-curious men before. It doesn't always end well."

At that, Brick laughed. "I'm not curious, I promise. And I can be flexible on the dating part if you want."

"So you've . . ." I gestured.

"Words, Jesse."

I huffed because communication was one thing, but . . . *What the hell*, maybe I did need to spell it out. I had to guard against magical thinking. The image of my dream guy loomed large in my brain, and I'd already learned enough about Brick to be wary. "Look, I'm sort of particular. I don't really like casual hookups. I'm—for lack of a better way to describe it—interested." His eyes widened as I confirmed what he had to have realized already. "But," I hedged, and his lips twisted like he was already planning a response, "you're divorced from a woman and we work together. I'm thirty-three, and I have goals for relationship stuff. I not interested in wasting my time being anyone's big gay experiment. Have you ever been in a relationship with a man?"

"That's not fair. I've only been in one serious relationship. I got married young."

"But is it something you even want?" I lowered my voice because *oh, shit*, a fresh fear popped into my head. "Have you been with a man at all? You haven't, have you?"

His shoulders tensed and his hand cupped the back of his neck, rubbing vigorously. "I don't want to keep reassuring you I'm attracted to you, you're going to have to trust me. I know myself. I'm bisexual." He chewed on his bottom lip, clearly not pleased with my latest assumption. "I've been with men before. Multiple times. Multiple ways. I came out to several of my friends in high school. The last few years, my attraction toward men has far outweighed my attraction to women, but it's always been more about the person than the parts for me. If you keep questioning that, we might be done here."

I grimaced and shook my head, memories of various exes surfaced as I attempted to explain. "I'm sorry. This is coming out wrong. I know bisexuality exists and if that's your label, great. It's . . . You were married to a woman, and you've never been in a relationship with a man. I've dated bi men before who were fine with men as partners for sex, but not necessarily for romantic partners. Some didn't want to be in a committed relationship with a man for social reasons or because it's more difficult to have a family, which fine, bisexual men have options I don't, but it makes me nervous, so in the spirit of communication, I thought I'd get it out there."

"Look. I hear your concern about being an experiment, but I can't promise. I *am* recently divorced, so it wouldn't be fair to misrepresent where I'm at or to guarantee you some outcome. We seem to have things in common and, like I said before, I would like to pursue this attraction between us. See where it goes. That's what I'm talking about."

"See where it goes?" I asked incredulously. Those were not the words of a man looking for a serious relationship. All my instincts were screaming at me to abort, but Brick's massive biceps were making a valiant argument for throwing my goals out the window.

"Yeah, and to be clear, my interest isn't only sexual, I like you. I enjoyed watching how passionate you are about teaching. The way you stand up for what you want. I like that you don't put up with bullshit. Even this conversation. I like that you're willing to put your demands out there. I'll give you the same level of honesty back. I'm not saying there are no circumstances where I'd settle down again; if that were true, I'd be up front about it. I promise. But it's not an active goal of mine either, if that makes sense."

His confession smothered the hell out of my instincts, rendering them, and me, speechless.

"You, um, like . . ." My heart raced as I processed what he was saying. "Most people find my candor obnoxious."

"Yeah," he laughed. "I do. The first time I saw you in the faculty meeting giving Zach shit, I liked it. Even when you were tearing my head off, it made me a little hot. I have no idea if this will work, but I want to get to know you and, yeah, a big part of the fun of that for me would be mapping out all the things that make you tick."

He was on the rebound. He wanted a little fling, something fun and flirty, the exact opposite of what I wanted. But then again, I'd already decided to temporarily suspend my true love search, and we *would* be spending a bunch of time together. Maybe it wouldn't be the worst idea in the world if I used my brief break from dating to see where all this sexual tension could lead. As long as we kept whatever this was simple and discreet.

"Zach," I said plainly.

Brick laughed. "What about him?"

"He's your friend, our boss, and he infuriates me. Is that going to be an issue?"

"He doesn't even have to know."

"If you try to kiss me at school, he will."

He shrugged. "Then I won't try to kiss you at school."

"Simple as that, huh?"

"It can be as simple as you need it to be. We're adults. I don't ask my boss or my friends for permission about who I spend time with, and it's not like this Academic Olympiad thing doesn't give us plenty of cover."

I bit my lip. Brick had a point. Coaching would make it impossible to date anyone else anyway. A little fling wouldn't kill me—a palate cleanser. As soon as Academic Olympiad was over, I would restart my search for Mr. Right.

"Okay. Then as long as we keep the school out of this, I'm open to seeing where things go."

We stared at each other, and I could tell the exact moment he accepted my condition.

"Okay, good. Do you want to order food now or should we see if I'm better at making assumptions than you?" He lifted his hand to call the server over. When she arrived, I gave Brick an amused nod. Even a bad meal would be enjoyable if I finally got to tease him about his mistakes for a change.

He perused the menu and ordered a bottle of red wine, two nine-ounce filets, medium rare, with loaded baked potatoes.

"And dressing for the salads?"

"Blue cheese," Brick answered with a wink. He took my menu from me and returned them to the server. "He's not a fan of ranch."

Oh, he was good.

Chapter Ten

Brick

There was a rhythm to my new schedule, and once I found it, I enjoyed being busy again. Between classes, faculty meetings, Academic Olympiad, drill team, basketball, and Jesse, my days were long, but rewarding.

I was in my office finishing up my review of the recent practice scores from the Academic Olympiad team when Zach's head popped into view. "Hey, am I disturbing you?"

"Not at all." I motioned for him to take a seat. "What brings you out to the boonies?"

"I wanted to check in, see how it's going. Haven't heard from you since our last scrimmage."

"It's good. Really good. Been busy. Actually, you saved me a trip." I pulled out the folder containing the paperwork requesting the rule change to the Academic Olympiad governing body. "Here. I need your signature on this."

Zach opened it, glanced at the top page, and closed the folder without comment. "Yeah, the first part of school is like that. I saw the drill team meet end well."

"Yep. Great inspection scores. Kids all knew their stuff. Exhibition drill still needs a lot of work. You need a pen?"

"I'll need to review this," he said, lifting the folder. I nodded an acknowledgment, with a low-key sense of concern. Probably wanted to cross t's and dot i's, but Jesse had done his homework. It was an incredibly thought-out and well-reasoned argument.

"How's the Academic Olympiad team going? Jesse behaving?"

I frowned, the loyalty gene kicking in hard. "He's not a child, Zach. He's been a big help. Things are going well."

"Trust me, with that one you can't get too comfortable. He's always looking for a way to push his agenda."

"Should you be talking smack about teachers with other teachers?"

It might have been the slight jump in my voice that Jesse inspired, but Zach was acting suspiciously, and I didn't need him digging.

Zach put his hands up. "So that's how it's going to be, huh? You're one of *them* now?" He stood abruptly, but his facetious tone revealed the whole thing to be an act. "All right, I will leave because you have a small point. Can't go talking shop with the likes of you anymore." He might have been teasing, but disappointment seeped into his body language. Like he was finally realizing that we weren't only friends and he *did* need to adjust what he shared.

"You know where to find me if I'm needed. It'd be nice to see your face once in a while. I swear I see you less now than I did before school started."

"Yeah, good thing I'm able to use a compass. Might be a challenge to find your ivory tower." I kept the wisecracks going about our new reality, so he would know I still had his back and wasn't turning in our friendship card just yet. But all joking aside, I was relieved when Zach left, because I did feel guilty that I'd been avoiding him.

I meant what I'd said to Jesse. I was comfortable keeping secrets. As far as I was concerned, Zach could remain as blissfully unaware about my dating Jesse as he had been about my open marriage to Jane. I had years of experience doling out information on a "need to know" basis, and right now, Jesse and I were still feeling things out. Something I hoped to do more of tonight.

I returned to what I'd been doing: killing time until Jesse finished up for the day. I knew it wouldn't be long, because I had heard him and Tessa in the supply closet setting up materials for the next day's lesson. Making good use of my table, I noted.

"Hey."

Jesse's *hey* had become like the bell to Pavlov's dogs. I was salivating before I even had eyes on him. When I glanced up from my computer, there he was—looking pretty much how he had that morning at AO practice. Only now he had little flecks of blue paint on his cheek and messier hair that'd had fingers running through it all day. Not mine, though, because he forbid me to touch him at school. Apparently, I had no chill.

"Hey, yourself. I finished reviewing the practice scores and turned in the paperwork to Zach."

Jesse made a funny face at the mention of our boss. "Hope you didn't tell him I had anything to do with it. How did they do? Nate was so discouraged. He's worried about bringing down the team."

"Zach knows you helped. I advocated for you to be assistant coach, remember?" He returned my smile, and I flipped my screen around so he could see the spreadsheet I'd put together to track the team's progress. "Our lowest overall scores were Nate and Blake. But Nate scored the highest on the music section, so that should make him feel better. As expected, Jazmin did poorly in math, but had the highest score in literature. Peter was near perfect on geography, science, and history. Honestly, when I look at the top four scores, we're very competitive in every subject except art. Emily did amazing, but the top-four average was low."

"We'll keep working. What about economics?"

Northridge didn't teach economics until senior year, so none of the kids had taken it. "Peter and Natalie did well, but we may want to spend an extra session or two on it. How comfortable are you with the subject?"

"On economics?" Jesse chuckled. "I can balance my checkbook, does that help?"

"Probably not. It's been a while, but I at least took it in college. Let me see what I can do. Who is the best economics teacher? Can you talk to them? Is there a chance they can help us?"

Jesse slouched in his chair and made a show of sliding to the floor like he was trying to melt into it.

I stood and peered over my desk at him, laughing. "If you're going to crawl under my desk, I have a suggestion about what you can do when you get there."

He cracked up and stood, growing suddenly serious as he dusted himself off as though he were too dignified for such antics. He took a seat, crossing his legs like a debutante and fanning himself. "Well,

Colonel Hausman. I never." Fuck, he was cute, almost cute enough to ignore his disregard for my rank.

"It's—"

"I know. I know, Lieutenant Colonel, but it doesn't roll off the tongue nearly as well. You couldn't stick it out for a few extra years?"

I chuckled. "Sorry my lack of advancement potential spoiled your performance. Now, what did you do to the economics teacher?"

"I may or may not have accused her of maliciously having my car towed three years ago."

"And *did* she have your car towed three years ago?"

"Yes," Jesse said definitively.

I frowned at his quick answer, which was clearly evading the real story. "Was it malicious?"

"Um, not exactly."

"Jesse." I found his coy smile far more adorable than it should be. "This might be one of those rare times when communication would be a lot easier if we skipped all my words and just focused on yours."

"I usually park in that spot right outside."

I nodded, now familiar with his preference for the spot under the shade tree.

"That morning there was a car parked in my spot because I was running late and, in my haste, I accidently parked in the spot next to it."

"The handicap spot?"

"No, the spot with the yellow lines next to the handicap spot. When I got out of school, I'd forgotten that I parked there and . . . Look, it's not a great story for me, so I'm going to fast-forward to the point. I'm not the person you want talking to Mrs. Gipson if you expect help on something."

"Oh. No. I need to hear this." I sat back and settled in for a story that didn't disappoint, even if I needed a crowbar to pry out the relevant details. "So, poor Mrs. Gipson's wheelchair-using husband shows up at school to surprise her with coffee and breakfast for their anniversary, parks in a designated spot, and comes out to find your car blocking the space he needs for his ramp. Do I have that right so far?"

Jesse slunk down again, face a crimson red. "What have I told you about tormenting me?"

"You said I couldn't touch you at school because I was being too obvious. There was no rule established for torment."

"Yes, okay. I assumed I parked legally as I always do, and the tow request was personal because I'd disagreed with her about having a morning Bible study for students. I may have insinuated she should study the Bible a little harder and called her a shitty Christian."

"Oh my god." I wasn't proud of my unmanly cackle. "Do you ever stop to think before you accuse people? If you did that in the Army, you'd have met with a few knuckle sandwiches for those kinds of mistakes. How did you get so paranoid, anyway?"

Jesse winced like he was in physical pain, sobering me quickly.

"What's the matter?"

"Um . . . I know we have this whole teasing thing going on, and you mean nothing by it, but you should know I didn't have the easiest upbringing."

"I didn't . . . I'm sorry for the wisecrack. If you faced abuse at all—"

"No. I didn't face a knuckle sandwich, but my dad is an alcoholic. The man could hold a grudge like nobody's business. If I came home and something important to me was fucked up or missing, it was on purpose, but always done so he could deny responsibility. My mom wouldn't have tolerated physical abuse, so when he was pissed, he'd fuck with me in more subtle ways—let the air out of my tires when I was late for work, 'accidentally' leave stuff out so I'd trip and fall, spill soda on an assignment the morning it was due, that kind of thing. It got worse after my mom died, but I left before he put his hands on me."

"That's awful. I'm sorry."

"Thanks." He flashed a weak half smile that spoke to how uncomfortable he was with the subject. "Listen, I don't want to get into my childhood or make you think I can't laugh at myself or that you shouldn't tease me. I thought if we're doing this . . . whatever, it's something you should be aware of. I have an unpleasant habit of jumping to the worst-possible explanation for things, but that's because in my house, that was often true. You said you like that I stand up for myself, which honestly meant a lot to me because it's something I don't think I could change if I tried. It took effort to get to the point where I could, but then it was like I couldn't turn it off. It's always been a bit of an issue for me, but I don't want you to think I'm not embarrassed when I accuse people in error or that I don't try to learn from my mistakes."

My heart ached for him. I stood and walked over to shut the door to my windowless office, although I was confident the building was empty. "Thank you for telling me." I pulled him to his feet and tugged him to me. Even if it wasn't the way I'd envisioned wrapping him in my arms for the first time, it felt right to comfort him. I slid my arm up his back and caressed his nape until unexpectedly he shifted his weight, exhaling softly as he returned my embrace. My chest swelled and, instinctively, I squeezed him tighter.

When we'd met, I'd wanted to push his buttons. To light up the fighter inside of him that amused the hell out of me and captured my attention. Now, knowing about his father, something shifted inside me. I wanted to find his broken buttons—the ones that no matter how many times you pushed them, didn't light up—and I wanted to try to fix them.

When he pulled away, his mouth was smiling even if his eyes were still liquid. "You hungry?" he asked.

"Starving," I admitted. I picked flecks of paint from his skin, only to have a reason not to let him go. "Did you get in a fight with a paintbrush?" I joked, and it worked. He relaxed a little more. "I went to the store last night. You want to go to my place? I'll make you dinner."

"Yeah," Jesse said. "That sounds good."

"Dinner was amazing. Thank you." I dabbed my napkin over my mouth and took the last sip of my water. My nerves still clattered from how much I'd put myself out there earlier. It'd been a long while since I cared about what a guy thought of me, and I wasn't sure why it'd happened with Brick when this was supposed to be casual.

"Hard to screw up spaghetti with sauce from a jar, frozen bread, and salad from a bag, but I'm glad you liked it. I browned the meat and boiled water. Everything else was open and pour."

"Take compliments where you can get them, Bainbridge."

He grimaced as he snatched the plates from the table and carried them into the kitchen to wash. "You will have to do a lot more than compliment my cooking if you choose to use that name."

"Oh, yeah? What exactly would I have to do?" I picked up a dishtowel, leaned my back against the counter, and dried what Brick handed me.

"Considering only my mother called me that, we're looking at birthing an eleven-pound baby. Think you're tough enough?"

"Eleven pounds?" I laughed, almost dropping the salad bowl I was wiping down.

Brick nodded, taking the bowl and stashing it in the cabinet, before moving on to the skillet. We worked together to load the dishwasher and wash the few pots and pans he'd used.

"I'm not really surprised. I'm not sure if birth weight translates to adult size, but it's hard to imagine a guy your size as small."

Brick wagged his eyebrows. "No one has ever accused me of being small."

I rolled my eyes hard, ignoring his attempt to distract me with that image. "At the risk of bringing up parents again. That was the first time you mentioned yours. Anything deeply personal you'd like to share inappropriately early in the relationship to even things out?"

Brick laughed. "No childhood trauma to report, but if you're hoping for a man with longevity in his genes, you'll be disappointed. They're both gone now. My dad died the year I turned thirty from a heart attack, my mother five years later from lung cancer. I had a younger brother who died shortly after he was born from SIDS when I was two."

"I lost my mom to cancer too. I'm so sorry. Were you close to your parents?"

"Yes and no. My parents were proud of my service, and we got along all right, mostly. I regret that I never came out to them. They didn't like Jane so much, so there was always this tightrope of *Who do you love more?* that I had to walk around them."

"What didn't they like about Jane?" I didn't want to be curious about Brick's ex-wife, but my neck prickled at the mention of her name. Sometimes I could tell when he actively stopped himself from badmouthing her. I respected his restraint, and it was nice to know he wasn't the type of man who harped on the past, but it left me without much of a mental image of someone who'd been such a big part of his life.

Brick rinsed the sink, thinking carefully. I noticed he did that with students too. He always had thoughtful pauses when he was trying to formulate how he wanted to answer questions or explain something. I liked that for all his teasing, he was careful when he thought his words would be important.

"My mom was a very traditional homemaker. She used to say 'My home and my boys, that's all I need.' It drove Jane up the wall because we moved around too much for her to go to college or really have a career of her own. She'd babysit when she felt like it or if she wanted something extra, since we didn't need the money, but it never fulfilled her like it did my mother. But the real riff came when Jane decided she didn't want children. Oh lord, my mother could not deal with that."

"So Jane didn't want kids, but you did?" I tried to keep my tone nonchalant. It didn't really matter since we were keeping things light, but I leaned in for his answer.

Brick shrugged. "I didn't *not* want them, but I respected her choice. How could I not? She'd be the one to get pregnant, give birth, do most of the day-to-day stuff. When you're in the service, there's always a chance you'll be deployed or . . . well, we all know what we signed up for. It's not like I could assure her she'd always have my help."

It felt risky to keep pushing, but my heart began thumping hard and demanded an answer. I kept my demeanor on the outside as calm as I possibly could. My tone was even and light, as though I had zero investment in the answer. "Did you wish you had some?"

A smile split his face, and I knew there was a crack in there somewhere about being willing to knock me up, or something similarly suggestive forming on his lips, but for whatever reason he held back. "It's cooled off a little by now. Want to sit outside or in the family room?"

"I'd prefer inside if you don't mind. My outdoor mode doesn't activate until October." It was for the best my heart didn't get an answer, since it had no business making demands in this situation anyway.

Brick laughed. "I'll plan a hike to celebrate."

"Sounds good. Perhaps over fall break."

Brick refilled my water and handed it to me before leading me to the couch. We took a seat on opposite ends, facing each other. His hand wrapped around his second soda of the night. Which was the first time I connected what I'd told him earlier and the fact that he had a fridge full of beer he wasn't drinking.

"Just so we're clear, it doesn't bother me if you drink." A puzzled expression took over his face until I pointed to his soda. "If you would prefer beer, don't stop on my account."

"That's good to know, but I had a long day, beer makes me tired, and I'd prefer not to fall asleep on you."

Ah, of course. My cheeks heated. Why would he abstain for me? That was all kinds of presumptuous for what we were doing. My casual dating skills were clearly rusty. "I see."

"So, you were asking about kids. Does that mean you want them or don't want them?"

Brick didn't need to know how much I wanted a family of my own, so I shrugged and downplayed my desire. "I guess it would depend. My best friend, Sierra, is actually pregnant, so I'm excited about that. More excited than she is, I suspect, since I don't have to worry about affording the little one. Sierra is married to a Northridge teacher—Olivier Lesueur?"

Brick smiled. "French, right?"

I nodded.

"Well, children are expensive, that's for sure."

Okay, time for a subject change. If Brick and I were keeping things casual, we needed fun, flirty conversation topics. No more family traumas and life goals. "Enough deep subjects: you got to hear my embarrassing story, I demand you tell me one of yours."

"Demand?" Brick's eyebrow lifted as he took a drink. "What's in it for me?"

"What do you want?"

"I want to kiss you, but since I'm a very fair negotiator, I'll also consider allowing you to kiss me."

I bit my lip. This was more like it. God, I loved how direct he was. "You sure? There was a bunch of garlic in that sauce."

"I'll risk it."

"Okay, impress me with an embarrassing story and I'll come to the negotiating table. I'm sure I can accommodate one of your fair offers."

Brick bared his teeth in an over-the-top cringe. "I have to impress you, hmm. That's a little tougher. You're clearly very experienced at embarrassing yourself."

"Ha. Ha," I deadpanned.

"I think I have one that will suit." Brick's perfect white teeth scraped his full lower lip, and by the sheer happiness on his face, I knew it would be good. "When I was sixteen, I had this friend. I knew he was trouble. Kind of like you, actually, because when I was around him, I wanted to do reckless things to get his attention—"

"What—" My hand rose to interrupt him, but he caught it and used it to yank me closer. Unprepared for the strength in his pull, I flew across the cushion and landed right next to him, still a little surprised and breathless when his finger covered my mouth.

"Shh. You asked for the story, so listen." He repositioned us, slanting his body toward me and draping my legs over his lap, then cupped his hand under my thigh. I sighed contentedly, not at all unhappy with the new, highly intimate position.

"So this friend went to great lengths to tell me about this place he'd heard about from his brother—a secluded spot where the older kids went to make out. He asked me if I wanted to check it out. So, of course, as any hot-blooded, American teen would, I immediately agreed."

I snorted and rolled my eyes. "Obviously."

"I snuck out of my parents' house and got my dad's car out of the garage. Made it a few blocks to the parking lot where I'm supposed to pick up my friend. I'm crazy nervous driving over there and my heart is pounding. At this point, I still had done nothing other than a brief peck, so mind you, I'm expecting this to be a completely life-changing night. When I pull into the lot, the headlights whip around and my dick gets hard the second I see him. But then he motions to someone and a girl steps out of the shadows. Not any girl either. It's Sandra Young, who had quite a reputation, if you know what I mean. I was devastated."

"Oh no," I cried, imagining the heartache of baby Brick. "What did you do?"

"What could I do? I drove him to the make-out spot and walked around a bunch of cars with fogged up windows while my friend lost his virginity. But that's not even the worst part. Not only did I have to chauffeur Zach's hookup—"

"Oh my god. Zach. Our principal? You had a crush on Zach?" I howled with the image.

He tapped me gently on the side of my ass and mock scolded me. "Shush. I'm earning a very, very good kiss right now. Don't interrupt."

I made the *lip zipping and throw away the key* gesture. Brick beamed at me and his wide grin curled around my heart.

"I walked into this wooded area, but there was nothing but the soundtrack of sex all around me and I'd been thinking about it most of the day. I was beyond horny. I can barely see myself, so I figure it was safe." His eyes flicked down to his zipper and he blushed.

"Scandalous."

His cheeks deepened to fuchsia as he continued. "I lower my pants and lean back on this tree trunk and the damn thing must have been covered in fire ants."

"Nope. No way! I call bullshit," I cried and clamped a hand over my mouth.

Brick barked out an incredulous laugh. "Why would I make this up?" He could barely get the story finished, because I was in hysterics as Brick described his ordeal. "My skin is on fire and I'm jumping around like a crazy person smacking my own ass. Only I didn't get them all. On the way home, I felt more. So, I'm swerving all over the road, and Zach and his girl are making out in the back seat again. I had to ride home with my ass and junk swollen and these little fuckers crawling up my pant leg, stinging me while listening to my crush make out with his new girlfriend. When I pulled into the drive, my dad was standing in the garage wondering where the hell his car was. I had to sit for another hour while my mom yelled at me because there was no way I could explain why I literally had ants in my pants." He imitated his younger self wiggling around, laughing uncontrollably. "Hands down the worst night of my life, and I saw combat. I couldn't sit comfortably for weeks."

"Holy hell." I exhaled and pressed my hand to my chest as I tried and failed to catch my breath. "Okay, you win. I don't even care if it's true. Bonus points for including Zach." I clutched at my sides. "*That* is the most embarrassing story I've ever heard."

"So . . ." Brick grew serious, ogling me with a mixture of hunger and curiosity.

My laughter fell silent with the heady way he looked at me. "So . . ." I breathed.

His hand slid around my thigh and scooped under the curve of my butt, lifting me slightly. Warmth slid down my spine as he eased me closer to him. When his eyes softened and his chin tilted, he leaned in closer and whispered, "About that negotiation."

I licked my bottom lip, then used it to coat the top one, wetting them in anticipation of meeting the full pair inching toward me. "Yeah," I murmured and mimicked his head tilt, leaning in as he closed the distance between us, bringing our lips together for the first time. My nose flooded with the smell of him, something vaguely vanilla and oak that reminded me of a perfect autumn day.

He retreated slightly, our eyes meeting as something heavy passed between us. A final negotiation. The tip of his nose nudged mine. "This okay?" he whispered, and his breath, tinged with garlic, onion, and tomato, rushed over my skin, but he was right: I didn't care. He tasted amazing.

I was all in, struggling to stay in his reach as the weight of him pushed me backward, until my legs blocked him from following me down. His kiss was perfect. Firm but soft. Slow but insistent. He licked at the seam of my lips, and I opened for him, his tongue sliding inside and dancing with my own. I wanted it to go on much longer, but I didn't have the core strength to stay in my position.

I fell back, abs burning with the prolonged curl. Brick's lips twitched like he was trying hard not to tease me about it. Instead, he gently removed my legs from his lap and lowered them until my feet touched the floor. He brushed a hand over my cheek and kissed me again—a little chaser to accentuate the strength of the one before.

In one sure movement, he repositioned us again, rotating our lower bodies until we were angled the same way and draping his arm around my shoulder. Following his lead, I eased my back against his side and cupped his hand where it rested over my stomach, playing with his fingers until he interlaced them with mine. We stayed like that for a while, his thumb stroking the sensitive skin along the inside of my wrist. I could feel his heart pounding, still a little shell-shocked by the abrupt ending and drowning in the unexplored desire heavy in the air between us. I glanced back and studied his earnest expression.

His other fist clenched near the substantial tent in his pants, and I knew why he'd turned me the way he had. Why we weren't touching. He was calming himself down because all he had negotiated was a kiss.

Loyalty. Respect. Honor. Integrity. They weren't only words to a man like Brick. He'd internalized the Army values that hung on the wall of his classroom. I suspected they were an indelible part of who he was. Suddenly, I didn't mind the abrupt ending to our kiss so much.

"So, was the story true?" I asked softly and stroked his hand.

Brick gazed down at me and squeezed my fingers. "I never negotiate in bad faith."

"So, Zach, huh?"

He chuckled. "It was a long time ago and he's very straight."

I loved how his face was still flushed from arousal. From me. I had this sexy man practically biting his fist to calm down from a kiss. It gave me such a thrill to have that power and eased that little niggle of doubt in my mind about his sexuality. There was absolutely no way he could have kissed me like that otherwise. "But you're not."

"No." He made a show of adjusting his diminished, but still present, erection. "I'm most definitely not."

"I'm really glad . . ." I began, but guilt hit me as the words left my mouth. It pained me to realize how much I'd needed physical proof of his attraction to me. Why? I knew sexuality existed on a spectrum, but maybe I'd been a little insecure about my ability to hold the attention of guy whose spectrum had nearly limitless options. Ugh. Not sure if that made me biphobic, pathetic, or both. "That you're bisexual."

Another conversation passed between our eyeballs as he brushed my hair from my cheek and kissed my temple. I hoped he understood what I was trying to say. *I'm sorry I doubted you. I'm glad we met. I'm glad you saw me. I'm glad you didn't let me get in my own way.* But on the chance he didn't, I clarified: "I'm really happy we're doing this."

He grinned. "Me too, Jesse. Me too."

He stroked my hair for a few seconds, a rhythmic combing that felt so good I closed my eyes to focus on the sensations. Lulled into a near meditative state.

After what felt like no time at all, I startled at the sound of Brick laughing and the sensation of dry contacts stuck to my eyeballs. The television was on but muted. "Did I fall asleep?" I sat up and Brick immediately flexed his arm and shook his hand to restore the blood flow. I must have been out. Really out. "What time is it?" I asked, stretching my arms over my head.

"It's almost eleven. You're welcome to stay," Brick offered, "but I understand if you don't."

I yawned. "I should go. Last practice before our first competition. I can't believe I fell asleep on you. I don't do that usually." What was it about him that made me feel so comfortable?

Brick nodded, rising, and pulling me up into a hug. "It's okay. I kind of liked it. You're cute when you sleep. I'll walk you out."

We strolled to the door, and the closer I got, the less I wanted to leave.

"Can I see you after school tomorrow?" Brick asked, and I fought back my immediate instinct to say yes. It was crazy how much I liked being around him. *Crazy and dangerous.*

"I'd love that."

Chapter Eleven

Jesse

The Academic Olympiad competition kicked off on Saturday morning with a qualifying round of the eight teams within our local area. Northridge would be competing against Northcreek High, the other school from our district; John Coker, James Bowie, and Emily Morgan High Schools, which were all part of the neighboring Oakmont School District; as well as nearby Parochial schools, St. Brigid's and Lutheran High. Only the top fifteen schools in the six local competitions across the North-Central region would be invited to take part in the next round of the competition.

Given the small size of our team and the nearness of the location, we instructed the kids to meet at seven thirty at Bowie High School, our host site. I arrived at seven fifteen, unsurprised to see Brick already there, wearing our team T-shirt with jeans and pacing nervously in front of the school fountain. I pulled into a spot a few rows back and smiled to myself as he immediately recognized my arrival and approached my car.

With one hand, I cracked the door and lifted his coffee to him. "Here," I said. "One Splenda and a splash of half and half so light I'm not sure why you bother." I grabbed my refillable travel mug and bag and stood from my vehicle. "Hey," I said softly, flashing my brows and brushing his hand, hoping he'd know how hard it was for me not to greet him with a kiss.

"Hey, yourself. You didn't have to. I feel like you're spending a small fortune on these coffees for me."

I waved him off. It had started as a whim, but admittedly I'd gotten a little too attached to the ritual ever since he'd joked that no one else, not even his ex-wife, had managed to perfect his coffee order. I tried to downplay the gesture as we started off toward the event. "Please. I haven't paid for coffee in years. One of my first students was Micah Phillips. Had him all four years. His mother owns a bunch of franchises. She gave me two-hundred-dollar gift cards for Christmas and as a thank-you at the end of each year. Every time I think I'll finally run out, I get another Phillips sibling and the gift cards keep coming. Half the time, they don't charge me. I've never added it up, but I might be set until retirement."

Brick's face shone with amusement, and he took a careful sip. "Okay, well it's appreciated, please let me know if I can contribute." We reached the school entrance, and Brick opened the door for me. Not a minute after registration, Jazmin, Nate, Natalie, and Blake showed up at seven thirty on the nose, and much to Brick's irritation, Peter and Emily ten minutes later. I couldn't tell if it was being off schedule or simply his competition-day vibe, but once check-in was over, Brick grew intensely focused.

"Relax," I whispered to Brick as he double-timed it to our assigned room. "We have plenty of time. Some of us aren't over six feet."

He grumbled under his breath but slowed down to allow Jazmin and Blake a chance to catch up.

"Okay, ladies and gentlemen. Huddle up. Here we are, Room 218E. Mr. Berry and I will be right here after the first two subjects, which are math and science."

Jazmin groaned, and he patted her on the back.

"Look at it this way: you're getting the hard part over first," I said, and she nodded, renewed determination dawning on her face. "Everyone have their calculators and scratch paper?" I asked. "Remember, you must turn in the scratch paper at the end. Once you're inside the room, any cell phone out will be an immediate disqualification, even if the test is already turned in, so for goodness sakes . . ."

"Mr. Nelms collected our phones," Natalie said. "Just to be sure."

Brick surveyed the group like he hadn't considered that as an option. "Do I need to collect your phones or can you handle leaving them in a pocket or jacket?"

Nate was the first to pull his out. "Dude, I'm not gonna be the one to get us disqualified. That thing dings, and I can't concentrate until I check it."

"Turn it off, then," Peter said.

"Nope. I'll be distracted wondering what I'm not getting. I'm saying, if it's a choice, I'm handing mine over."

"I'll take it." I laughed, accepting Nate's phone and sliding it into my pocket. "Anyone else?" Blake was the only other taker, for pretty much the same reason.

When the Lutheran High team filed into the room, Brick checked his watch. "All right, everyone. It's time. You've prepared extremely hard for this. I'm proud of you. Remember there are no penalties for wrong answers this round, so answer every question."

Once the test door closed and the competition began, the coaches were mainly useless, so we proceeded to the cafeteria to wait.

Brick and I made small talk with a few other coaches, but it wasn't long until we'd isolated ourselves in a corner, in our own little world, joking and jumping from subject to subject.

"I'm glad you're here. This would be very boring without you," Brick said.

"Well, I'm always happy to entertain you."

He glanced around before drawing a pinky up the outside of my arm. Goose bumps formed on my skin. "You do, you know?"

"What?"

"Entertain me. It's been a long time since I enjoyed someone's company so much."

I grinned, cheeks heating. Oh, he was too good. "It's been a long time for me too."

"Excuse me, are you the Northridge coach?" We ripped our eyes from each other and toward the woman who'd snuck up behind us.

"Yes, I'm Jesse Berry."

"The exam proctor raised a question about your team."

"Emily," I gasped, casting a worried expression at Brick.

He patted my hand. "What seems to be the problem?"

She frowned. "Would one of you come with me?"

"I'm going." I rose to my feet, but Brick grabbed my arm.

"Jesse," he hedged, then to the official he asked, "Can we have a minute?"

She nodded, turned on her heel, and returned to the official's table.

"I knew this would happen," I seethed at Brick. "I knew it was going too smoothly."

"Hey, look at me." Brick placed a crooked finger under my chin and pulled my attention to him.

My eyes bugged out at the intimate touch, and I quickly scanned the room. "Not here."

He frowned before dropping his hands from me. "Okay, but we've done nothing wrong. You need to calm down. Let me see what's up and then if I need your help to resolve it, I'll come get you."

"Calm down? Calm down?"

Brick squeezed the outside of my arms tightly. It might have been the closest he could give me to a hug without taking me into his arms. "Repeating 'calm down' at me as you work yourself into a frenzy isn't convincing me you should be the one to deal with this. It could be something unrelated to Emily."

I guffawed. "They said it was about Emily."

"No, they said they had a question. You assumed it has to do with her. Let me find out what's going on, okay?"

"Fine. But don't let them check her ID in front of people. That's happened to her before. And don't let them misgender her."

"Okay. I'm going to go see what's up."

"Brick," I said as he hurried away. When he immediately turned, I froze at his concerned gaze.

That's when I realized I hadn't actually expected him to stop. I'd only said his name because I needed that one last beat of control, and the way he looked at me now, with this mixture of reassurance and patience and affection. He *knew* it. I wanted to ask him how. How did he understand things about me that no one else ever seemed to get? I racked my brain for something to say that didn't sound ridiculous.

"I got it," he said calmly with another squeeze to my arm.

I nodded. "Don't tell me to calm down, it never works. Do that arm thing."

He laughed. "Noted."

Brick was gone, speaking in hushed voices out of my earshot on the other side of the cafeteria double doors. My brain kept running forward to all the ways this could end in disaster. What if they disqualified the team? The kids would be so upset, and Peter—he'd specifically asked about it, and Brick had assured him we had it covered. We did not have it covered. What if this set Emily back? I should call Savannah. I fished out my phone, but the unlock wouldn't work. "God damn phone," I mumbled as the screen shook at me with an invalid passcode notice for the fifth time.

"Jesse." Brick was standing over me with an amused smile. "That's Blake's phone."

My eyes flicked to my hands and the phone I was holding, which, sure enough, was identical to mine except for one of those selfie pop-up buttons. I released a noise, half-laugh, half-frustrated sigh, before Brick took a seat and grabbed the phone from my hand. "Everything is fine."

"Was it about Emily?"

"Yes. It was. The proctor only had the event's official registration list, where Emily's dead name was listed with her driver's license picture, which has her correct name but wrong gender. The proctor handled it well. Emily began her test with everyone else and the proctor said nothing directly to her about it. She brought it to the judges' attention. They let me know her results might come back in the system with the wrong name."

"How did they get her dead name?"

"I guess when Emily tried out for the team last year, her student number was linked to her old name. It sounded like an honest mistake, Jesse."

"But she changed her name over Christmas break last year. The tryouts were in the Spring."

"Perhaps when Nelms created the accounts, he used the wrong name intentionally. Based on what Zach told me, I wouldn't be surprised. But I think the people here made an honest mistake. The important thing is Emily is fine, and the team is being allowed to compete. The woman was actually very sympathetic to the situation."

"Okay. If you're sure it's fixed. I hope they change the rule soon, though."

"Me too. I need to check with Zach and make sure he turned the paperwork in."

"You didn't turn in the packet?"

"No. I told you I gave it to him to sign. He said he needed to review it. I'll check with him on Monday."

I nodded, but for the rest of the day, I couldn't shake the feeling that I should have taken care of the petition myself. I knew Brick and Zach were good friends, but Zach had a way of screwing me over. I made a few offers to reinsert myself into the process, but I could tell Brick wasn't interested, and since I didn't want him to think I didn't trust him, I let it drop.

Brick seemed less inclined to keep me to himself afterward. He suggested we join the other coaches and get to know them, so I tagged along, trying not to beat myself up over how I'd overreacted yet again.

The St. Brigid's coach noticed Brick's tattoo, and as soon as Brick learned he was a former Army chaplain, they struck up a conversation about their overlapping time in Afghanistan and being educated in Catholic schools. So, in addition to everything else, I learned that Brick had a tattoo I'd never seen, had lost a friend in Afghanistan I'd never heard of, and came from a religious background I had a lot of concerns about. It was a helpful reminder that Brick was my break from serious dating. Whatever comfort I felt with Brick. No matter how much we enjoyed each other's company. That I could fix his coffee or relax him when he was stressed. That he instinctively knew how to calm me down. It wasn't because I knew the guy. I'd barely known him a month, and I'd spent a part of that not liking him.

After the competition, we made sure everyone got off okay, then Brick walked me to my car. The mood between us was a bit subdued. Seeing as how we'd spent part of the day stowed away together almost like we were on a date, then the rest of the time acting like coworkers, I wasn't quite sure what to expect when we got to my car.

"Hey, what are you doing next weekend?"

"Nothing. Why?" I fished my keys from my pocket.

He smiled and stepped toward me so I was in between him and my parked car, grabbing my hand low and close to our bodies, out of view. All the sensible reminders I'd spent the afternoon fortifying myself with crumbled at his touch. "JROTC has a drill meet. I know it's probably not your thing, but you should come."

"To the drill meet?"

"Yeah. It's open to spectators."

It was obvious he wanted me there, which, even if we weren't dating, was nice. Outside of art, there wasn't a lot of requests for my attendance at school functions, and since I didn't get along well with my colleagues, I didn't always feel welcomed. Still, I couldn't help teasing him a little. "I mean, I guess I could go to support Peter. He's a great kid."

Brick raised his brow at me, but issued a charming grin before he responded. "You want to support Peter, huh?"

"Yeah. Why else would I go?" I deadpanned.

"Certainly not to support your secret boyfriend." There was a moment's pause after he said the word, long enough for me to detect the moment he doubted himself. Where he obviously considered if I heard the word *boyfriend*, albeit said teasingly, that I might get the wrong idea. His smirk was another reminder of what this was to him. He liked the chase for sure, but I would not give him any satisfaction of acting like I took the title seriously.

"God no. Why would I want to do anything like that? After all, what would be in it for me?" I made a horrified face but couldn't hold it without smiling.

He stepped closer and looked around at the deserted parking lot before resting his chin on my forehead, but I could hear the amusement in his voice as he cleared his throat. "I see. Another negotiation, then. What is it you want?"

I went for broke. If he wanted to throw words like *boyfriend* around . . . fair was fair. "There's a new exhibit at the McNay I've been dying to see. Sierra was supposed to go with me, but she's having all-day morning sickness."

He pulled back, slanted his head, and raised a brow as if to say *Is that all?* "Okay. You come to the drill meet Saturday *for me* and throw in dinner and at least another chance to kiss you. Then, since I already told you I like art, I will happily take you to see your exhibit on Sunday afternoon. How's that sound?"

For a second, I thought he was teasing, but no. Oh, this was perfect. Finally, I had a little leg up on him. "Awesome. I'm looking forward to it." I caressed his broad chest and aimed for a seductive look as I batted my eyelashes and drew a finger down his arm. "But, uh, you've never heard of the McNay, have you?"

He cocked his head, obviously leery of my change in body language. He ran his fingers through my hair and smiled. "No. Why?"

"Because, um, The McNay Museum . . ." I chuckled, drawing out the end to see him panic. Even a little. "It's in San Antonio."

"San Ant—" The lines around his eyes flared as he tossed his head back and laughed. "All right. You got me." He sighed, but I could tell he really wasn't annoyed. "A deal is a deal. Looks like we're taking a road trip." He wagged his eyebrows.

"Looks like it," I agreed, but then had my own moment of doubt to contend with.

When we'd decided to "see where this goes," I already knew our destination. We'd end up in bed, where we'd have sex, hopefully multiple times. I figured the thrill of the chase would be over for Brick about the time the Academic Olympiad excuse ran dry, and by then, I'd be ready to leave this sexy side trip and get back to dating serious contenders.

I just hoped our little getaway wouldn't rush that timeline too much.

Brick

The second Jesse stood from his car in my driveway, I had him in my arms. I'd seen him across campus a few times and could tell from his body language he wasn't having a good day. "Ugh. I've been wanting to do that all day." I shook his hips back and forth, trying to literally shake a smile out of him. "Don't tell me you're upset about a second-place finish?"

With the mention of the outcome of the qualifying round, Jesse lifted his chin, meeting my eyes and managing a dim smile. That was better. We'd gotten the results at the end of the day. Of the eight schools we'd tested with, Northridge had come in second and advanced to one of the regional competitions in the state. They ranked us sixth of fifteen in our region going into the competition next month in Dallas. It wasn't as well as previous Northridge teams, but given our late start, two brand-new team members, and novice coaches, I was proud of us.

"No. of course not. I had a rough day. I'm so proud of Nate, too. Tenth overall in music for a freshman is impressive. And Blake, I know she said she was good at math, but highest score on the team and fifteenth overall? I didn't expect that."

"Jazmin brought her math score up six points too. Emily was third overall in art and what? Eighth in science, I think, or at least top ten. Peter had a near perfect score on the history section. Natalie came out of nowhere on the economics portion too—she really must have done a ton of independent research. They all did great. We only lost to St. Brigid's team by nine points."

"It was a good showing. Hopefully the JROTC will impress tomorrow as well."

I nodded. "I hope so. They've worked hard. Now come inside with me. I need to change." We had regular inspection days each week now, so I still had my uniform on and needed to wear it the next day.

After changing, I started dinner while Jesse mulled about, his mood unusually subdued.

I was nearly finished prepping our meal when the patio door slid open and shut.

"You have grass!" Jesse gasped from the direction of the family room. I chuckled at his enthusiasm, and I knew he'd gone out on the deck to see the completed project. He'd made many surprisingly detailed suggestions for how to layout the flowerbeds and what plants would be best for the space over the last few weeks. It was way more than I could tackle, but his ideas were solid, so I'd hired a landscaping company to execute the plan.

When dinner was finally in the oven, I poured him a drink and grabbed myself a beer, then went to check on him, but he wasn't outside or in the family room.

I found him in my guest room slash office. He'd gotten more comfortable now, so his snooping range had expanded to any room in the house except my bedroom. Usually, I was protective of my personal space. Probably because there was so little of it in the service, but I didn't mind. His back was to me, so I took a few seconds to check him out as he checked out my things. His shoulders were lower—less tense—and his ass . . . I closed my eyes and pictured what it would be like to finally get him naked.

Jesus. I need to stop acting like a horny teenager.

"Finding anything interesting?" I asked and handed him a vodka tonic. "Since you had a rough day, I thought you could use this."

"Thanks," he said, but when he took a small sip right away to be polite, I knew he wouldn't drink it. No biggie. I'd get him water with dinner.

"What did you think of the yard?"

"I love it," he said, a wistfulness to his tone that evaporated quickly with a smile. "What's the story here?" He gestured to a novelty plaque on my wall with the words *World's Greatest Fisherman* on it. Above it was a picture of me, soaking wet, holding a giant walleye.

I grinned. Jesse did that a lot. He'd pick up or point out something of mine and ask me to tell him about it. Such a Jesse way of getting to know me better.

"Some buddies and I tried to get an annual fishing trip going up in Minnesota for a while. I joined them about three years before they informally discouraged me from attending. This was my parting 'no hard feelings' gift. It's a fake. Or the fish was real, but they photoshopped it. Everyone was taking pictures with their catch, so I posed with my arms out like that as a goof because I hadn't caught anything. Made it easy for them to photoshop it, though."

"Why were you wet?"

"I was joking around and fell off the boat."

"Weren't you upset about being excluded?"

"Nah. Not really. I like fishing, but these guys were next level. Jane's cousin, Phyllis, owned a lake house. We used to meet up with Jane's family there. We called them our annual family fishing trips, but it was primarily drinking and bonding, with occasional fishing. These guys had fishing all day, every day in mind. They still go as far as I know, but days on days of not showering and no cell service wasn't a hardship for me to give up, plus Jane gave me grief for it."

Jesse's nose wrinkled, and I laughed, trying to imagine him on one of those trips.

"Do your Army friends know you're bi?"

"Not those friends." When the timer beeped, I added, "Dinner's ready."

Jesse followed me to the kitchen and set the table while I dished up our plates. We sat, chatting some more about the competition and strategizing how to improve our overall team score. The remaining rounds would be on the theme, so that was when all the preparation would really start to pay off.

"Did you talk to Zach about the rule petition?" Jesse asked as I took a bite.

I accelerated my chewing to answer him. "I did." I wiped my mouth with my napkin. It was probably more accurate to say that I tried, but there was no need to upset Jesse any more than he already was. "He promised to take a look this week."

Jesse frowned, and I changed the subject to happier topics. "So I was thinking about the McNay. I know we talked about—"

"We don't have to go. It's fine. It was like the secret boyfriend thing, you know. More of joke anyway."

"Jesse." I sighed, shaking my head. I had perhaps tossed out the term a little more frivolously than I'd intended. And I would be lying if there wasn't like a millisecond of panic on my part until it was clear Jesse hadn't taken the label too seriously. A weekend getaway was a tad more couple-like than I had in mind, but I wanted to find someone who I enjoyed doing things with that turned me on, and Jesse checked all the right boxes. As long as I'd been honest about my situation, I didn't see any reason why we couldn't do his museum visit. "I was going to ask what you think about leaving right after the meet on Saturday? We'd have more time in San Antonio. I haven't been there since, gosh, I don't remember. Spent time at Fort Sam for something or another, but I've never really explored the city, and I enjoy that sort of thing. The Riverwalk is supposed to be nice."

"Oh, um . . ." Jesse hedged.

"Tell me how I can help?"

"Huh? Why? With what? I didn't say I needed help."

It gutted me that maybe he'd had no one in his life offer to help him before. "Look, I'm a fixer by nature. Clearly fixing you a drink for whatever is on your mind wasn't the answer, which makes sense, but it's going to kill me to sit here and do nothing if I see you struggle. Do you need to step back from AO practice?"

Jesse's face tightened. "No way. I'm committed to those kids."

"Okay. Well, trust me, you're going to want to come up with a way for me to help or I'm going to drive you crazy offering." I left him at the table while I refilled my drink and got him water since he'd still not drank but a few sips of his vodka tonic. When I returned, he'd grown serious.

"I don't trust Zach and I'm trying to not think the worst of him, but it would help if you could push him a little and maybe get the packet and mail it yourself?"

I beamed. *Was it really that simple?* "Amazing," I mumbled. My affection for Jesse grew exponentially.

"What?" Jesse asked. "Why are you smiling like that?"

"It's just so refreshing. You actually gave me something I could do. Jane used to insist she only wanted me to listen to her complain. She actually expected me to let her struggle, even when the problem could be solved. I'll take care of it first thing Monday. Anything else?"

"Since we've been spending most of our evenings together, I haven't carved out any creative time for myself since the start of the year."

"I don't want to monopolize your time."

"Oh, I know. I enjoy being over here with you, but maybe we could hang out at my place sometime, or I could at least leave supplies over here, that way I can draw while you watch television or whatever."

"Of course. Either is fine."

"I have a pad and pencils in my car. Would you mind if I drew you?"

I snorted. "You want to draw me like one of your French girls, Jack?"

Finally, an actual genuine smile and laugh escaped from his mouth. "I mean, if you're offering. I'll take it, Rose."

"Sure." I shrugged, then followed up with my most flirtatious grin. "Have to admit drawing wasn't exactly what I had in mind when I thought about getting naked with you, though."

Ignoring my hint, Jesse hopped off the chair, moving so fast to the door I didn't have time to reconsider my offer. "Great! I'll get my stuff."

When he returned, he was so enthusiastic about the idea, I decided to roll with it. "How do you want me?"

"Strip down to whatever level you're comfortable and find a position where you won't need to move a lot. You don't have to be naked if you don't want to be. Um, do you have dog tags though? I kind of want you to wear them if you don't mind."

I laughed, shaking my head. I'd already guessed Jesse had a bit of a military fetish. "Yeah, somewhere. Let me find them. Come on, there's a chair in my room; you can sit there, and I'll lay on the bed."

"Are you sure you don't mind?"

"If it's helping, I don't mind."

"It is. I've been dying to draw you since we met. I tried once from memory, but it didn't go well."

"You know what they say: take a picture, it'll last longer."

"I'll bring my camera next time." Jesse winked.

I slipped off my shirt and pulled my tags over my head. He let out a little moan, and I turned toward him while I unbuttoned my pants and pulled them down.

"Don't suppose you like to draw while naked, huh?"

Grinning, Jesse shook his head, adjusted the light from the blinds, and situated himself in the chair in the corner of my room. I lay on the bed in the nude in the same position I always fell asleep in—legs stretched out and slightly parted with my hands tucked under my head. The realization hit me almost immediately. Jesse was the first man whose opinion I actually cared about to see me naked. I was in good shape, but I also liked to eat, so I've always had a belly. While I've never been self-conscious about it, maybe Jesse would prefer someone with less body fat.

"Are you sucking in your gut?" Jesse asked, a hint of amusement on his face.

"Maybe," I choked out because it was hard to talk while sucking in your gut.

"Don't."

I exhaled and pushed out my belly as far as it would go to get a laugh. "Better?"

He tsked. "Act normal. It'll be hard to hold any other way. Also, stick another pillow under your head so I can see your face. Feel free to switch on the television if you're bored."

I did what he asked, and because I thought he'd find it funny, I found Titanic on my streaming service and hit Play.

When the score started playing, he rolled his eyes and didn't spare a glance at the screen. He was already off to the races. His pencil flew over the page. I attempted to watch the opening scene, but the silence from him was getting to me. Plenty of men *told* me I looked good, but since I'd paid them, they weren't exactly honest brokers. It was shallow, but I couldn't help myself. "How's my dick look?"

Jesse peeked up from his drawing. "I haven't gotten there yet," he deadpanned as he returned to his work. "But I'm getting very close," he added, still looking down at his pad. I could see his tooth digging into his bottom lip as he tried to contain his smile.

It took a minute for his words to register, but if I kept thinking about what that might entail, he was going to have a hugely different drawing on his hand. We'd made out quite a bit, but there was no comparison between using an escort's services and the natural progression of intimacy without an hourly rate to consider. I'd been enjoying the slow build, particularly since I'd learned Jesse didn't take sex casually, but we'd be sharing a hotel in San Antonio. Was sex implied or should I ask? With a woman, a guy could feel it out in the moment, make sure he had consent, wrap it up, and go for it. But with a man, there were preparations—at least there would be if I were bottoming. I wasn't even sure of Jesse's preferences or routine in that regard. Maybe he didn't need much prep. He may very well be used to dicks way bigger than mine? That thought sent me down a rabbit hole of uncertainty and spurred an intense curiosity to know how I stacked up to his other lovers.

I watched Jesse, doing my best to stay still and let him work, but I couldn't let it go. "Do you think when you *do* get there, you'll find it pleasing? You know, aesthetically. In your professional experience as an artist. Does it stand out?"

He chuckled without looking up, hand still moving over the page in smooth strokes. "Brick, do you need me to confirm for you your dick is big?"

I could feel the heat rising in my cheeks. What was it about his brutal honesty I found so fucking sexy? "I mean, it wouldn't be a terrible thing to hear. Only if you want to. And, you know, if you could say it honestly."

He faked an annoyed sigh, stared at my crotch blatantly for a few seconds, and went back to drawing. *Little shit.*

"Hey." I pouted.

He was laughing when he glanced up again. "From what I can tell of you soft, you have a nice cock, Brick. I'm sure it will be a pleasure to . . . draw."

And now I was horny again. "Without trying to hurry along your . . . artistic process . . . did you have thoughts on when that might be?"

He paused again, looking earnestly at me. "I don't exactly have a date circled in my calendar, but if things head that way, you don't need to stop at a certain point. Now, if you want to help, lay there and don't move so I can work." He cracked an amused smile. "Trust me, this will be the *only* circumstances in which I make that request."

"Thank you for humoring me. And so you know, I like doing the work more than letting the work be done to me, but I'm open to either."

Jesse resumed drawing.

"But, also, like a little notice is appreciated if you want to, um, work one night."

Jesse huffed a laugh but said nothing as his pencil moved over the page.

"And I may or may not be orally fixated."

Jesse dropped his pad to his lap and chastised me with a look. "I understand why your friends disinvited you from the fishing trip." He shook his head. "All your preferences are noted. Now, feel free to talk, but I want to concentrate, so I'm going to be ignoring these blatant attempts to distract me."

"Oh, it's my turn to rant uninterrupted, huh? Well give me a topic at least."

"Fine, since you clearly have sex on the brain, tell me about your first time with a guy. You must have been young since you've been with Jane for so long."

Chapter Twelve

Jesse

So what if Brick hired male prostitutes while married to his wife? That shouldn't bother me if it didn't bother her. I knew going in he wasn't my forever guy. Although he was apparently the guy for whom I sat on hard bleachers of a strange school gymnasium watching uniformed students march back and forth and shout things in unison.

On one hand, his explanation and the arrangement he'd had with Jane made total sense. I got it. For him, it was a security measure. Escorts ensured discretion and removed any risk of developing feelings. It surprised me, though. Brick was all about honesty and loyalty and blah, blah. But, on the other hand, those two things didn't seem to reconcile. It made me question what I thought I knew about the man.

I was deep in my thoughts when a familiar face drew my attention. I spied her on the other side of the bleachers, sketchbook open. Emily's hair was curled and pulled half-up in an elaborate braid secured with a ribbon. She was wearing more jewelry than usual, and her skirt and mid-thigh heeled boots, while cute, did not look like something she'd wear on a casual Saturday. She had the distinct look of a girl who had absolutely dressed to impress someone, and I spent the better part of the next performance trying to figure out exactly who that was.

As soon as he stepped onto the floor, she came to attention.

"Well, I'll be damned," I said under my breath. Emily had the hots for Peter Lim. But he couldn't break decorum by waving or acknowledging anyone in the crowd. No way to tell if the feeling was mutual or if he knew she was there. Until that moment, I'd not seen Emily show a romantic interest in anyone, not even through her art.

If she was feeling freer to do normal teenage things like get crushes, that was a hopeful sign. Emily's attraction to Peter didn't surprise me in the slightest. Like Emily, he was a serious, hard-working, and introspective kid. Although he was handsome and socially adept enough to hang with the popular clique, he always seemed to be observing the in-crowd rather than truly embracing them.

As I watched her, face lit up with intrigue by the performance, I stewed about something other than Brick's confession. What if Peter didn't return her feelings? Would she be able to handle it? I'd never witnessed Peter be unkind, but teenage boys weren't exactly known for their sensitivity either.

I'd seen many of my students go through the highs and lows of first loves. Art teachers got to see the flourishing strokes of new love as often as the dark, bitter, thick black lines of the aftermath more than most. I knew better than to become invested in the dating lives of American teenagers, but I couldn't help but worry for Emily. Dating could be a minefield for adult trans women, but combined with the emotional upheaval and fear of rejection all teens went through, I didn't envy her or her parents. It made my predicament with Brick feel all the more trivial. It was casual. I needed to quit overthinking every new piece of information I learned about the man.

When the meet concluded, I waited for Brick to wrap up whatever he needed to do. I'd already packed for San Antonio, but he needed to ride back to the school on the bus to let the color guard store the flags, so I'd planned to meet him at his house. That way he could change, and we'd be on our way. I wasn't in a hurry to leave anymore; the little telenovela playing out on the far side of the bleachers had me captivated.

Peter definitely knew Emily was there. And, lord, did I get sucked in by seeing that smile on her face. The hushed exchanges, laughing and touching that appeared to be mutual to me. It was doing my little queer heart so much good to watch. I'd have never been so openly flirtatious at their age. Times really had changed.

"You let her fuck you with her dick, Pete?"

My head whipped around to see a large crowd of Northridge students, many of whom I recognized but couldn't name, several wearing JROTC uniforms. Emily's face turned white as a ghost.

"Hey," I yelled. They didn't hear me over the group's continued laughter. I took the bleachers two at a time, the metal clattering under my heavy steps. A few of the kids noticed me and took off, but four remained.

I marched up to them and straightened as tall as I could, using my most authoritative voice. "I want to know who said that right now or you're all getting referrals."

"You can't do that. We're not even on campus."

"Watch me. Sit down! All of you." I pointed to the bleachers, drawing the attention of a few adults. I glanced up at Emily, whose obvious embarrassment was making me think twice about my approach. I probably could have been a bit more discreet to protect her privacy. I took note of our growing audience and assessed the best ways to minimize the damage. At the very least, I should get them out of the spotlight and make sure they weren't subjected to any additional slurs if these clowns decided to double down with a show of their bigotry. "Emily and Peter, the event is over, you need to take your conversation outside." They nodded sharply, but I noticed Peter didn't exactly wait for Emily to get her stuff before taking off.

I focused my attention on the row of teen boys in front of me. "Now, who said it, or is everyone going to visit with their vice principal on Monday?"

Silence.

"Okay, well the uniforms will come in handy. Mr. Rodriquez, Mathers, Abbott," I read their nametags. "I will let Lieutenant Colonel Hausman know you find lewd comments hysterical."

The uniformed boys flashed synchronous pleading looks toward the non-uniformed boy in the group. He scowled. "Fine. It was me. And everyone knows that Emmett's a tranny, so I don't know what the big deal is." I glared at the kid who spoke up. "The rest of you need to go immediately to the bus." They scattered like cockroaches.

"What's your name?"

"Sean Abbott. Two *b*'s. Two *t*'s." He flashed a cocky smirk. "And I don't go to Northridge anymore. My parents make me cart my little brother around. So, I'm not sure what you think you're gonna do, *Jesse.*"

My jaw tightened, but bigger assholes had tested my patience far worse than this kid. "Well, Mr. Abbott. The first thing we're going to do is educate you starting with your use of an incredibly offensive slur, then if I don't feel you are sufficiently learning from your mistake, we'll see about getting you banned from school events. I suppose your parents might have an opinion on your being unable to assist with transportation for your younger brother."

That, at least, wiped the smirk from his face.

Brick

"Can I talk to you a minute, sir?"

After what Jesse told me he'd witnessed, I was surprised by Peter's interruption. He must have been laying low, waiting for all the other kids to leave. I saved my unfinished correspondence, still dissatisfied with the options for reprimanding the three JROTC students who'd taken part in harassing Peter and Emily. They were off my competitive drill team, that was for sure.

"Sure, Lim. Have a seat. Nice job today."

"Thank you, sir." Peter slumped into the chair across from mine, looking very much like someone had removed his usually perfectly functional spine. "Can I . . . Can I just talk? I mean, can we pretend you're not my teacher?"

"We can talk freely, but there are certain things I can't keep confidential."

"Like what?" His eyes bugged, and he shifted forward.

I extended a hand, ready to slow him if he bolted. "Hey. Calm down. There are legal reporting requirements for teachers. Like if you told me you were thinking of hurting yourself or someone else or were being abused in any way, I couldn't keep that between me and you, but I would try to get you help."

Peter relaxed, and I said a brief prayer of thanks. Not only for him. I didn't feel ready to handle something as serious as a suicidal or abused student. "That makes sense. I'm not being abused or anything."

"I'm extremely glad to hear that. So what's up?"

"Um . . . Don't be offended or anything, but I know you and Mr. Berry are kind of into each other."

My brow arched. "Is that so?"

"Yeah, well, everyone knows Mr. Berry's gay, and I walked in on you about to kiss that one time. Sorry for that, by the way. When he showed up at the drill meet, I figured it wasn't a big secret or anything, but if it is, you should probably try not to touch him so much. Even Nate says you're mad obvious and he's a freshman." He shrugged.

"So I've been told," I said with a little chuckle. "And while I will not talk to you about Mr. Berry, suffice it to say, I'm not offended."

"So you're gay?"

"Is that relevant to the conversation you want to have with me?"

"Yeah, kind of need to talk to someone who understands these things."

I nodded. "I understand these things."

Peter flashed a grateful smile, rising a little taller in his seat. "I'm supposed to go to West Point. Already have my nomination and started my application the day my class opened."

"You should be enormously proud. It's an amazing place from what I hear."

"For gay men?"

"There are plenty of gay soldiers, Peter, if that's what you're worried about. While not everyone you encounter will be supportive or an ally to the community, that's true in all walks of life. I wouldn't let that dissuade you from pursuing a goal."

"I just . . . Emily told me how they kicked out transgender soldiers, and it's messing with my head. It's making me doubt . . . But I've always wanted to do this. My grandfather was born in China. He always talked to me about how great America is. How special it is to have the freedoms he didn't have growing up. I guess I wanted to hear if you think I should?"

I nodded to show I understood his question, then paused to reflect on how best to respond. "Peter, I'm not here to recruit you to the military. Going to one of the service academies is a privilege, and I agree with your grandfather. We enjoy many freedoms in this country because of people willing to fight to protect them, but joining the military is a very serious commitment and there are plenty of other ways to serve your country without enlisting. Even if you knew emphatically that the military was right for you, I guarantee there will be many days where you'll doubt your decision. It's normal to have doubts, but that doesn't mean you shouldn't listen to them or talk with the people who care about you about them."

"I guess I wish . . . I wish I knew . . . Do you think Emily is a girl?"

I swallowed hard, uncomfortable with the stark turn in the conversation. "If you're asking if I think trans women are women, then yes, I do. But I'm not sure I follow your train of thought. It would be helpful if you told me what you wished you knew."

His eyes turned a little uncertain. "I figured Mr. Berry told you what happened. Emily and I have . . . We've been hanging out a bunch with the Academic Olympiad stuff. I didn't really know her before, you know, like last year when she wasn't . . . when she was still a boy."

"I see. I think you mean to say you didn't know her when she presented as a boy. Inside, she's always been who she is. Now she's let everyone else know who that is. Does that make sense?"

His lip quirked. "Yeah. I can see why she thought I should talk to you. That sounded like how she explained it. I'm trying, really, I am. Emily is super patient with me. When we first started hanging out, I didn't think about it that much. I knew she'd transitioned, but it's not like I looked at her and thought she's a boy dressed up like a girl, I just see *her* and we have fun hanging out. We like a lot of the same things and, well, she's funny and smart."

"I'm sure Emily really appreciates that about you."

"Yeah, until I freaked out on her today. After the drill meet, she kind of told me she liked me as more than a friend, and I guess I realized she . . . She wasn't wrong to think I liked her too, but then Abbott said what he said and . . . I didn't know what to say or do because I'm not . . . Like, I know there's nothing wrong with being gay, but I really didn't think I was."

"Peter, are you concerned that admitting you're attracted to Emily makes you gay?"

"Um. I mean, I don't know how it works, but if she still has the same equipment that I have and it works like mine does when you kiss and stuff, I think that would feel pretty gay."

I took a deep breath. I had no way of knowing if Emily had undergone gender confirmation surgery and wasn't knowledgeable about any potential impacts of puberty blockers and hormone therapy. I couldn't speak to if that would be an issue for them. Regardless, talking one-on-one with a student about erections, even with the best of intentions, felt highly inappropriate.

"Okay, so I think it's important that you understand someone's sexuality isn't etched in stone. Labels can be good for some things, but they can also be really unhelpful. For instance, I had a soldier in my command who came out as trans. He was married to a woman and they stayed together. He and his wife had always identified as lesbians before that. Does that mean he's now straight and his wife is no longer a lesbian? I don't know, and I guess my point is, does it really matter? Remember how in the command meeting, we talked about talented leaders knowing how to ask the right questions?"

"Yeah?"

"Well, let's take a step back. The first thing you need to ask yourself is if you like Emily for who she is as a person. Do you think about her a lot? Want to make her laugh? Are you attracted to her? Maybe want to kiss her?"

"Uh, yeah. I kind of . . . Um, it was after the AO competition, and we were sitting . . . She smelled great." He cleared his throat and turned flaming red. "I . . ."

"A yes or no will suffice."

He exhaled. "Oh. Yeah. Um. Then, yes."

I smiled. "Okay. That's good. You like Emily and she likes you. Congratulations. The next thing you have to ask yourself, and this will probably take a little more reflection on your part. Do you think you can be good for her? That might mean supporting her through challenges she faces both physically and emotionally, having her back when people say hateful things. But it also means that you may have cruel things like what Abbott said directed at you."

"Um . . ."

"You don't have to answer me. It's tough stuff. But you need to ask yourself if you're willing to take that on. If being with her is worth that, because unfortunately it's unlikely to go away entirely."

"What if I don't want to? Does that make me a bad person?"

"No, but it makes you the wrong person for Emily. She deserves someone who thinks she's worth it. Someone who won't walk away and leave her alone to face that kind of bigotry."

He nodded. "So if I decide I want that, then doesn't that make me gay?"

"You will feel attracted to lots of people in your lifetime. Have you ever felt about a boy the way you feel about Emily?"

"No," he said, with a little exhale of relief. "Not at all."

"Then most likely that's your answer. Look, Peter, I believe we're attracted to who we're attracted to. Human sexuality is far more nuanced than gay and straight. It's okay to not know exactly where your preferences fall, particularly at your age. I get that it's confusing. It was for me too, but I'd encourage you to figure out what you want to do with your attraction to Emily. She's a special person with some big challenges in her life, and she's made herself vulnerable to you by admitting her feelings, so while you don't owe her a relationship, you owe it to her to be respectful of her feelings and honest with her about your own. If you're not up for it, then don't take the good stuff you want and leave all the awful stuff for her to deal with alone. You have plenty of time to decide if you prefer to use a different label for your own sexuality than the one assigned to us by default."

"Yeah. Okay. I get it. I don't want to hurt her; she's kind of amazing."

"Well, speaking from experience, finding someone you think is amazing and thinks you're amazing back is rare, so think hard before you give that up. As for the military, talk to your parents if you're having second thoughts. No matter what your sexuality, military service is a life-changing decision. If you're not sure, you can always go to a regular college and do ROTC for a few more years. If you do decide to pursue admission to West Point, and later determine it's not for you, you can change your mind. It's okay. Either path, you won't have to commit to enlisting for two years, so you have the time to think it through."

Peter chewed on his thin lips. I had no idea if I was getting through to him, but he seemed slightly more at ease than when he sat down. "Thanks. This was helpful, sir. Do you think you can keep this between me and you? Mr. Berry is nice and all, but he's really protective of Emily and I don't want him to think I'm a jerk."

I nodded. "My door is always open. You can trust me to keep this confidential."

I walked Peter out and returned to my car. I started the ignition and turned it off, taking a minute to gather my thoughts about the conversation. Peter's doubts about his sexuality were such a time machine to my own adolescence. I could recall with absolute clarity the anxiety of not knowing what my attraction to boys said about me. Even after I learned the word *bisexual* . . . Even after I'd used that word when I came out to Zach, I'd still had this sense that what I was feeling wasn't really me. Some days I'd been convinced it might be a phase I would grow out of or that my feelings for Zach were some aberration. Other days I'd worried I was gay and that I was somehow faking my attraction to women.

Then I met Jane and I knew there was an attraction. No doubt about it. I'd had such a profound sense of relief that something finally felt real, I hadn't stopped to consider if Jane was right for me or if I was right for her. Falling for her meant I didn't have to figure the rest out. I didn't have to come out to my parents. I didn't need to change my career plans. So, that's what I did.

Maybe if I'd had a trusted adult in my life to confide in, I could have saved us both a lot of heartache.

Brick was stupidly adorable on our road trip to San Antonio, still riding some kind of high and saying cryptic things like "days like today are why I wanted to work with kids," then refusing to elaborate.

I'd still been flexed about the incident with Emily when Brick got back to his place, but he said that he'd spoken to Peter and that he seemed okay. When I'd given Savannah a covert heads up, I learned Emily had made it home, seemed fine, and was in her happy place, which I knew to be the small studio her parents had created for her the year before. I figured I should at least be coping better than the people who'd actually been harassed and try to enjoy my weekend.

Brick turned down the stereo he'd been singing along to. "There's the Space Needle."

"The Space Needle is in Seattle, you dope. That's the Tower of the Americas."

"Oh, yeah."

I groaned as the downtown traffic thickened and we slowed to a crawl. "Are you sure you don't want the GPS?"

"I didn't need it for 'drive south,' but now that there might be actual turns involved, directions may be helpful."

Excitement growing, I pulled up my GPS app and searched for the Riverwalk hotel we were staying at. "I haven't been here in so long. This city gets bigger every time I see it."

He reached over and patted my knee. "So, um, Jesse?"

I glanced over, alarmed by his serious tone. "Yeah?"

"I didn't want to assume, but did you need me to stop, so we can, um, get supplies?"

I burst out laughing. "Are you thinking sodas and water for the room or are you asking me if you're finally getting laid tonight?"

Brick flushed crimson. "Um, well, I was thinking lube and condoms, but now I'm worried we should get drinks too." He smiled nervously. "I know we kind of talked about it, but after I explained the whole sex-workers thing, I didn't know if you changed your mind."

"Got us covered." I went back to entering our destination into the GPS app on my phone, then muttered, "I packed a small cooler of drinks." I kept my head down, grinning to myself, but Brick released a pained noise that made me want to put him out of his misery. Well, almost. "It's kind of insulting, you know. If you want to fuck me, you better be getting the good lube, not some KY from CVS." I gave him another minute to regret his lack of preparation before easing the lines entrenched on his forehead. "Don't worry. I brought lube and condoms, although they are regular sized, so if that will upset your delicate ego, we'll need to find Magnums."

Brick's nostrils flared as his eyebrows did their own happy dance. "My ego knows better than to cockblock me. I'm good with whatever you brought. Was that a right or a left?"

I grinned, stupidly, I'm sure, and we stopped talking so Brick could follow the navigation instructions. When he turned into the hotel driveway, I finally caught a glimpse of the sheer excitement on his face. Like he'd be seeing a concert of his favorite band or, I don't know, going to the Super Bowl or something. It was sort of intoxicating to be the object of that much anticipation. "You must really want to see the Alamo," I teased.

"Uh-huh," he said.

He kissed my hand before letting it go so we could grab our stuff and turn his car over to the valet. After checking in, we cleaned up a bit and went to explore. We stepped out of the hotel at river level, taking in the sights and smells of the bars and restaurants that stretched on both sides of the riverside path. The crowds were dense as we strolled past diners crowded around colorful umbrella-covered tables but thinned considerably as we reached the less touristy area, where the towering canopy of cypress trees, winding stone paths, and romantic bridges helped you forget you were in the middle of the city.

A few times Brick brushed his fingers next to mine like he might be considering how to grab it, but the hand-holding felt dangerous. I was already concerned about the energy between us. The more Brick acted like my boyfriend, the harder it was to keep my imagination in check. "It's hard to hold your hand," I said, noting the difference in our arm lengths.

Undeterred, Brick pulled me closer to him by the shoulder. Every once in a while, he'd kiss my temple, until finally he wore me down. It'd been so long since I'd had an actual boyfriend, and Brick was so persistent. Just for the weekend, I could let myself pretend. "You're remarkably comfortable with PDA," I observed.

Brick stopped short, concern clouding his face. "Does it bother you?"

"No," I said. "It's nice, actually."

He exhaled. "Good. Cause I hate not touching you when I want to at school. FYI, Peter informed me that all the AO kids are onto us."

I smiled at him because I was well-aware of that. No matter how much I wanted to keep things quiet, the unresolved sexual tension had made it impossible to completely hide our attraction for each other. Even the innocent looks he gave me when I walked into the J building made me flush.

It was still hot, but the breeze helped as we popped up to the street level and walked toward Hemisphere Park.

We strolled leisurely around downtown, eventually navigating toward the Alamo, which took a long time because Brick read every single word of every sign and plaque we passed.

When we arrived at the famous facade, Brick let go of me and veered left to the courtyard, then stopped in front of the giant live oak tree that dominated the space. I wandered around, taking in the historic grounds dotted with statues and information about the Battle of the Alamo and the people who'd died there.

When Brick found me, he wrapped me up from behind and turned me, so I was staring at the massive tree truck with low, sloping branches spanning at least thirty feet. He kissed the top of my head and rested his chin there. "Did you know they moved it here in 1912 when it was already forty years old. Think about what that must have taken. They moved it with four mules." He huffed out a disbelieving laugh, and when I shifted to see his face, it looked like he was playing out the scene in his mind. I liked how affectionate he was, but I *loved* his intellectual side. I was almost looking forward to seeing his reaction to the special exhibit as I was to see it myself.

"If I had any artistic talent, I would draw this," Brick said.

"That's how I feel about you." The words left my mouth without thought. Brick cast a curious glance my way, a small smile playing out on his face as he pulled me back against his body. "You do have artistic talent."

"That's not what I meant. I meant when I look at you, I feel this need to draw you, but I get frustrated that I can't do you justice."

"That might be the nicest thing you've ever said to me."

"Even better than saying you have a nice dick?"

"Way better." He kissed my forehead. "You getting hungry?"

"I could eat. Sierra suggested we go to Mi Tierra."

He nodded, pulling out his phone to look up directions. "We should get an Uber. When do I get to meet this Sierra?"

"You want to meet Sierra?" I asked, surprised.

"As much as you talk about her? Sure. She seems important to you. I'd introduce you to my friends too, except the only one that lives in Texas you know and don't like."

I frowned, not really wanting to get into a prolonged conversation about our boss when we were having such a great time. Brick grabbed my hand and led me out of the gated courtyard toward the street. "Come on. The car is on the way and I'm starving."

By the time we got back to the hotel, I was full on swooning. Dinner had been delicious, and the atmosphere festive with mariachis and colorful accents. We'd each had two margaritas, which was enough to feel more relaxed and floaty around Brick than I usually did.

As soon as we were inside our room, Brick claimed my mouth like he'd been craving it, the full force of the evening's pent-up urges released in one blistering-hot kiss. I didn't object as his persistent lips pressed against mine and his hands started groping my ass. I ran the tip of my tongue over Brick's bottom lip, pushing for him to let me in, striving to give as much as I took, but it didn't take long to figure out that Brick planned to drive tonight. Retreating briefly, all Brick said was, "Bed," before he was moving me and drawing his every breath from my body. I hit the mattress with a bounce, with Brick following. The movement sent my knee upward, nearly grazing Brick in a most inopportune place.

"Gah. Sorry," I said, or maybe I sort of panted it because Brick was doing something to my neck that made my heart race. Still giddy from alcohol and anticipation, I tried a few times to apologize but couldn't be sure if anything left my mouth other than moans.

Brick lifted off me, appraising me for a second with a wide smile. "You don't have to injure me to get me to stop."

It felt right that he teased me. It felt like us, but I wasn't interested in being teased at that exact moment.

"Don't want to stop. Want you to fuck me." I grabbed a fistful of his shirt and yanked him down. His nostrils flared, and I could see the relief in his face that we were on the same page. He stroked over my torso, lifting my shirt to caress my skin.

I curled up to kiss him, hands reaching for his buckle. Needing to be free to explore the magnificent body I knew was under there. "Want me to kiss it better?"

"Not yet," he said in a way that definitely put sucking his cock on the agenda but had my hands exploring the strong planes of his back instead. He kissed me again, but our frantic pace slowed considerably. Each press of our lips turned into a leisurely exploration until finally, the temperature dialed down to a simmer and he brushed his hand over my cheek. The contemplative expression of his face and the intensity of his gaze sent a shiver down my spine. The look of a man who wanted to get laid replaced by one who was about to share something with me, something far more meaningful than I think he'd prepared for.

"You okay?" I raked my hands through his hair and waited for an explanation, silently praying he wasn't experiencing some postdivorce remorse. I'd been the rebound fuck enough times to know ex-related emotional landmines sometimes detonated at very inopportune moments.

"Yeah." Brick swallowed. He caressed my temple with his thumb and set my heart adrift into a sea of feelings with one touch. It sloshed around in my chest completely untethered to reality. "We have all night. I've never . . ." His voice cracked, and I couldn't look away from the longing in his eyes. "I've been with men, but never like this."

"I know." I nodded, granting him permission to do what he needed. It wasn't difficult for me to cede Brick the lead. I'd always been more passive in the bedroom than out of it. He'd never gotten to take his time, do intimate things like cuddle and tease. Be the playful lover he wanted to be and know that I was with him because I wanted him. Not a paycheck. Even if the change in temperature made it difficult to remember this wasn't making love, I wanted to give him that experience.

When he moved us so I was lying on my back and he on his side against me, I wasn't surprised. From that position, he could touch and kiss and gaze into my eyes as much as he wanted, and he did all three for what felt like hours. I closed my eyes, pretending this was what it felt like. That his lips belonged to the man I'd been searching for, that all his whispered sweet nothings and gentle kisses were lovemaking. My chest ached as my fantasies sent me careening into a dangerous place. I knew I had to bring myself back from the edge. I reached up to stroke over his cheek, needing to reset. Needing my heart to have an anchor again. Lust, lust I could handle. "You're so sexy."

"You are too. Jesse, I . . . You drive me crazy."

"Good. The feeling is mutual." I snaked an arm between us and rubbed over his cock.

His eyes widened and he bit his lip, then tossed me a look that said he'd gotten the message. "Tell me what you love, okay? Teach me how to love you."

"You like instruction?" I laughed softly, gently running my hands through his soft, prickly hair.

Brick blushed. "I want to map every inch of your body, and I appreciate instantaneous feedback."

Lifting my arms and folding them behind my head, I smirked. "Well, the teacher is in. Explore away."

Smile blossoming on his face, he scrambled to his knees. "Oh, you are in so much trouble." He grabbed my wrist and pulled me until I was sitting, then stripped my shirt off in one fluid motion. I fell back to the bed, laughing, biting my lips as I attempted to be as seductive.

"Slower," I whispered, testing to see if he'd really take instruction.

"Yeah?" Delight bloomed on his face.

"Yeah."

He pressed against me and dropped a sweet kiss to my forehead. "You got it, baby."

His hand fluttered over my chest, a light pressure that had me arching from the bed to get more. His muscles bunched and released as he repositioned himself. He smiled down at me before turning my chin to the side, exposing my neck. He nipped at my earlobe then started an exquisitely slow descent down my neck. I keened, opening my mouth in a low moan.

"That's what I want," Brick whispered against my skin as he traversed my chest. "Let me hear you."

"I love my nipples played with."

Brick chuckled against my skin, cooling the wet swath his tongue was traveling. Tingles ignited everywhere. When he arrived at his destination, the press of his mouth over the hard bud had me cupping the back of his head, wishing he had more hair to grab. "Fuck, yes," I groaned, my cock filling. "Kiss me," I demanded shamelessly. "Please."

Brick's face was the picture of joy when he rocked up to meet my request. Sealing his mouth over mine, he kissed me hard. I grabbed on to him, unable to get him close enough to satisfy the deep ache I had for him.

He returned to my chest, taking the other nipple in his mouth, testing out pressure and sensitivity. Each change dialed in the exact setting to drive me out of my mind. I was so hard I hurt, crying out with relief when he finally rubbed a heavy palm over my swollen member, then unbuttoned and unzipped my shorts.

"Take it out," I panted, curling up to see him.

He reached for my waistband, gripping both my shorts and my underwear roughly. "Lift," he demanded, then guided the fabric down and tossed it off the bed. "Fuck, baby. You're beautiful."

"I want you naked . . ." I reached for the hem of his shirt and tugged. Even though I'd sketched him and stared at the lines and curves of his muscle for hours, I hadn't seen him like this. From under him, I could look up at his imposing form, feel the weight and power of him looming large. There was no better view for his slow striptease. I shook my head, breathless from his beauty.

Brick stood from the bed, pressing his thick, clothed thighs against the side of the mattress out of my reach. He unbuttoned his pants. "Take them off me. I want you to see how hard I am for you."

I scrambled to get to him, sliding the fabric of his pants and cotton briefs down his meaty ass and legs with one determined push. His cock standing proudly before me, I licked my lips and cast my eyes up to him before stroking it. It was much thicker and longer than I'd expected. "I may have done you a disservice with the word 'nice.'"

He hooked a finger under my chin and lifted. "You can apologize to it later."

Nodding, I swore under my breath. "I want. I want so much."

Brick smacked my ass with a filthy grin. "On your back, baby."

Before I could comply, Brick flipped me around and went back to exploring. He kissed every inch of my body, mapping out erogenous zones I hadn't even realized I had, sucking along my hip bones and biting my inner thighs. When he finally took my cock in his mouth, the warm, wet cavern sliding down my shaft, his tongue probed my slit and catapulted me to the heights of ecstasy with almost no warning. "Fuck, stop," I yelped, hand stilling him. "I don't want to come yet. Let me suck you."

"Yeah," Brick groaned, while still kissing the tip and caressing my balls.

"Brick." I twisted to urge him to stop. When he reluctantly did, I beckoned him toward me with a crooked finger. "My turn."

He knee-walked up the mattress and brought his leaking cock to my mouth. "This okay?" he asked, rubbing himself over my lips. I opened for him, and he slid slowly inside.

"Jes— Fuck," was all Brick managed, listing forward to grab one-handed onto the bed frame and fist the other in my hair. I licked and slurped, sucking what he gave me, eyes watering to keep up with the thrust of his hips. "Fuck, fuck," he chanted, spurring me on. I guided him deeper by the globes of his ass until I gagged.

He eased back, concerned, but I kept him from retreating completely. It was exactly what I needed to keep my head right—a hot and filthy release of sexual tension.

"I like it. You can fuck my throat." I looked up, waiting, straining to get more of him. He thrust his hips, groaning and cursing in low, breathy tones. He'd occasionally slow, peering down with heavy-lidded eyes to praise the way my mouth stretched to accommodate him. After a particularly long set of punishing deep strokes, he pulled out, saliva and pre-come smearing across my chin with his withdrawal. Brick swiped his thumb over the mess and bent down to kiss me. "I'm getting too close. Tell me what you need, Jesse. I want you to come so hard you see stars. It doesn't matter to me how."

I nodded, rocketing up until I was sitting and pressing him back with a palm to his chest. "I want to ride you."

He allowed himself to be moved, and while he settled himself on his back, fingers jacking over his thick, swollen shaft, I retrieved the supplies. I tossed him a condom and slicked myself while he suited up. "It's been a long time for me."

Brick nodded sharply. "You'll have to tell me what you need prep wise. Haven't . . ."

"I'll teach you." With an eager confidence, I straddled him and guided his hand around behind me. He was a quick learner, teasing my hole open like it was a part of the fun and not a precursor to it. Taking him inside was a slow process. It was hot and intimate, silly and sexy. There were enough false starts to frustrate both of us, but when it finally happened, it was perfect. He was perfect, guiding my hips as I lowered myself on his cock and moved gingerly, testing angles until I found one that turned my pants to gasps. When the pleasure-pain liquefied my bones, he took over, lifting me up and down on his shaft, pushing into me until I was dizzy with the need to climax.

"G-gonna . . . Oh fuck . . ." He forced himself as deep as possible and my body sparked with pleasure. My eyes squeezed shut, I moaned, long and low, and when he took my cock in his fist, the entire galaxy appeared. My come splashed onto his abs.

Brick kept thrusting, body flailing as he gripped my hips until his rhythm faltered, and with a euphoric sigh and persistent trembles, he came. A sweat-slicked arm wrapped around my waist, anchored me to his chest, and rolled me over onto my back. He kissed his breath into me. "Oh my God."

"Uh-huh." I kissed the base of his neck and snuggled against him.

Brick grinned down at me and kissed me softly. "So, stars?"

"The Milky Way."

Brick fist-pumped proudly. Laughing, I pulled his arm back around me and tried to ignore all the sweet, tender feelings bubbling inside. Maybe the sex had moved my head back to the right side of the tightrope I was walking, but my heart hadn't budged.

Chapter Thirteen

Brick

I was smitten—a few drinks away from tattooing his name on my chest surrounded by little rainbow hearts—smitten. While people might say this overwhelming swell of emotion was lust and a manifestation of my sex-addled brain, I didn't care. It was a fucking delight.

If I wasn't sure after Saturday, I'd confirmed it Sunday morning when I woke up with Jesse asleep in my arms and I felt this sense of total contentment. Like he was exactly what I'd imagined when I told Zach I wanted to be in a relationship with a man.

We enjoyed so many of the same things—food, hobbies, movies, television shows, music. Whether we were goofing around or talking about how much it sucked to lose your mom to cancer, I felt like I could be myself around him. And the sex was . . . I mean, I didn't think I'd ever had truly bad sex before, but I was wrong. There was nothing mechanical about the way Jesse fucked; he was generous and vocal and revved my engine like no one else ever had. The chemistry between us was crazy good.

It wasn't until we were at the museum that I realized the weird swell in my chest and unerasable grin Jesse inspired wasn't only from a strong sexual attraction or the novelty of a new relationship. Something much deeper had taken root. There wasn't a moment of our day I didn't want to listen to what he had to say and learn what interested him and, as always, see him riled. Even if that led to a dissertation on the shift of modern painting from Paris to New York after World

War II that lasted nearly the entire drive home. Mental note: abstract expressionism is not the result of leaving kindergarteners alone too long with access to paint.

Monday morning, I cruised into the administration building like I'd just won the Academy Award, the Powerball, and the World Series all in one weekend. I tried to think about any number of miserable things to get my smile down to a "Happy Monday" level, but it wasn't working.

Zach sat up rigidly, his eyebrows drawn together. "You look weird."

"Weird? What kind of way is that to greet your best friend?"

He tsked, clearing the papers off his desk as he waved me in. I shut the door to his office and took a seat across from him. Zach retrieved a folder from his desk drawer and lifted it. "I see you had an eventful drill meet judging by these four discipline referrals I walked in to find."

We spoke a little about what happened, and Zach, while not happy, didn't seem overly concerned. "Kids say dumb things, Brick. Was it an asshole thing to do? Sure. But I think this might be another case of overreaction."

"I don't think Jesse overreacted."

His brow furrowed as he reread the referral. "The teacher mentioned here is Jesse Berry?"

I nodded.

He studied me skeptically. "Is there something going on with you and Jesse?"

"Why do you ask that?"

"Jesse is not a teacher I see at school functions unrelated to his position. Why would he go to your drill meet?"

"Seems like a question for you to ask him."

"Uh-huh. Well, I let the vice principals handle discipline, but since all they did was laugh, I don't think we can do much."

"Do what you got to do, but I'm removing them from the drill team."

Zach furrowed his brows. "You're not allowed to make discipline decisions, Brick. You make referrals and administration decides appropriate punishment and that includes participation in extracurriculars."

"Well, I issue demerits, and eligibility to take part in JROTC events is contingent on standing. They insulted and used lewd language in front of their commander, a teacher, and a young lady while in uniform. That can't go unaddressed."

Zach exhaled a long breath through his nose. "According to this report, all they did was laugh. Looks like a former student took responsibility for using the language. You're not in the Army anymore. Is that really a fair punishment?"

"I didn't send them to the clink or reduce their rations, Zach. It's not up for debate."

"Okay, fine. If that is what you choose to do, but I hope you're prepared to hear from angry parents."

"I can handle angry parents."

He nodded, leveling an unimpressed expression at me. "Fine. The vice principal for each student will talk to them today. Was that all you wanted to talk to me about?"

"No, I wanted to check in on that Academic Olympiad rule-change petition. I need to get that in."

"You're still pursuing that?"

"Yes. I gave you the paperwork to review, and we talked about it last week. Don't you remember?"

"But Emily is on the team. Things went fine at the qualifying round. Why rock the boat?"

"Because she's registered as a male member of the team, which is ridiculous. Jesse made a very thoughtful argument. Did you know four teams competed last year with five students because they could not find a third male student to participate? So they created a rule to avoid schools excluding girls, but those teams had potentially interested female students who couldn't compete. The rule functions counter to the original goal. It's also antiquated to use gender binary for coed teams. We're asking that they remove the requirement for gender entirely. That way the six best-qualified students can take part."

"Brick, this is . . . Look, I was expecting an exception request for Emily to take part. I always want to advocate for our students. But after what happened with Nelms?" He cringed, shaking his head. "It blew up the superintendent's phones. The entire school board was getting harassed from the community. Jesse should really know better than this, and you need to be careful listening to him. He doesn't think about the bigger picture. He's reckless. Northridge is a conservative place. Parents don't enjoy seeing their local schools in the paper, particularly not for controversial topics. I don't think I can allow you to move forward with this."

My coffee and bagel turned to cement in my stomach. "Allow me?" I repeated. "Zach, I made a commitment to this student. You asked me to do this."

"Let sleeping dogs lie for now. She's on the team. It's a win for her. I'm sorry, but I have to tread carefully. Pissed-off taxpayers could take it out on us in the election in November. It's feasible to reevaluate the situation after the TRE passes." Zach stood up, straightened his tie, and walked to his office door, opening it in a ham-handed way of dismissing me.

I stared at him, puzzled by his behavior. Would he really do this to me? "Zach, you can't ask me to let this go. I gave my word to people based on our conversations. Based on your assurances."

"I'm sorry, Brick, but there's a big difference in getting an exception request for one student and trying to change the entire system. It'll attract unwanted attention. This one is my decision. And, to use your words, it's not up for debate."

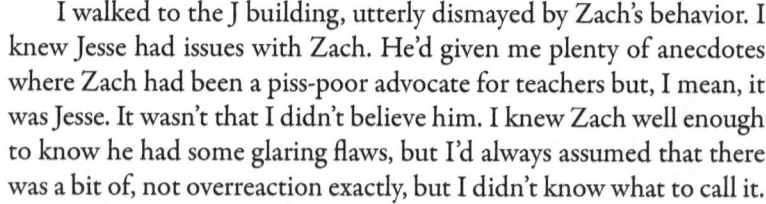

I walked to the J building, utterly dismayed by Zach's behavior. I knew Jesse had issues with Zach. He'd given me plenty of anecdotes where Zach had been a piss-poor advocate for teachers but, I mean, it was Jesse. It wasn't that I didn't believe him. I knew Zach well enough to know he had some glaring flaws, but I'd always assumed that there was a bit of, not overreaction exactly, but I didn't know what to call it. A bit of *Jesse* in those stories.

Never in a million years did I think he'd be spot-on. I felt bad that I hadn't believed him, but telling him? I couldn't imagine what good would come from that. Jesse and Zach already disliked each other, and I didn't relish the thought of being in the middle. At some point, I'd hoped to be able to hang out with them together.

As if my thoughts manifested him, I heard Jesse's voice calling to me. "Hey, General Hausman."

Jesse was standing at his car, talking to Olivier and waving at me. The big grin on his face and the way my mood changed because of it told me two things: his cavalier misuse of my military rank was now a permanent inside joke, and I wasn't going to ruin his good mood with my problem.

I slowed and detoured to the parking lot, quickly deciding that I wouldn't mention my conversation with Zach to him. At least not until I had a solution. Even if things hadn't gone according to plan, I'd told Jesse that I'd take care of it, and that was what I intended to do. Zach had a legitimate concern about the referendum. If it didn't pass, there would be more cuts, drastic ones. There had to be a way to change the rule without risking other people getting hurt.

"Hey," I said as I neared, wishing I could at least kiss him on the cheek, but settled for a slight brush of my hand on his lower back while I extended the other to Olivier. "We haven't formally met. I'm Brick."

"Olivier." We shook hands. Olivier and Jesse exchanged a look then grinned at me like I was a zoo animal on display. Oh, he definitely knew. Jesse was telling other teachers; this was good. Hopefully he was getting more comfortable with people knowing about us.

"So, Brick," Jesse began. "Olivier and Sierra invited us for dinner this week. Are you free Friday?"

"Oh!" I said a little too enthusiastically as my brain made the connection. "That's right. You're Sierra's husband. Sorry, I forgot she was married to a fellow teacher. Congrats on the baby. I hope Sierra's feeling better."

"Thank you. I'm a lucky guy. Sierra's finally over her morning sickness. We think." He raised his hand and showed us his crossed fingers. "Anyway, we'd love to have you. The Artsy Soul closes at seven. How does seven thirty work?"

Jesse stared at me expectantly, and I nodded. "Sure. Thank you. I look forward to it."

"Awesome. Well, I have to run," Olivier said, turning toward the portables and leaving Jesse and me in the parking lot in front of my building.

"Where are you headed?" I asked.

"Supply closet, needed to grab a few things. I have student portfolio meetings in a few. I really hope Emily has figured out her concentration. She's falling behind. Academic Olympiad must stretch her thin."

"Sure, probably nothing to do with her boyfriend, right?" I gestured for him to walk ahead and accompanied him into the building, hanging out in the doorway to the supply closet while he gathered what he needed. When he finished, he pulled me by the tie into the closet and shut the door.

"Hey," he said shyly as he crowded into me. "I'll need a kiss to get through my morning. It's going to be a long day."

I pressed a quick one to his lips, growing more confident in my decision to not burden him with Zach's nonsense. I would figure it out; he had enough on his plate. "Rule-breaker," I teased.

"I know. I wish I had more time."

"Have a good day, babe." I opened the door, and we walked out together, hands touching. Jesse turned right to the exit, and I left toward my classroom, until a loud throat clearing turned my attention to the hallway straight ahead. Peter Lim was standing there and shaking his head with an amused expression.

I glanced towards Jesse, who shrugged, then sighed resolve. Busted. No sense in pretending otherwise. "Good morning, Lim. You're in early today."

"Good morning, Lieutenant Colonel Hausman. Mr. Berry. Hope you had a pleasant weekend."

"We did. Thank you. You?"

"It was . . . good. Emily and I went to the movies. Emily is in the art room, Mr. Berry. She's excited to talk about her concentration project with you."

"I'm on my way," Jesse called over his shoulder.

"C'mon, Lim. Is the XO here? There are packets to assemble."

"Uh, sir. I wanted to thank you for the advice you gave me. I appreciate that you didn't just tell me what to do, too, because it made me really think about what I wanted."

I smiled, recalling the number of times Jane had informed me, rather angrily, that I needed to stop thinking I had all the answers.

"That's nice to hear. I'm glad it helped. A wise woman once told me you don't help people when you give them the fish, you help them by . . ." I paused, the solution that eluded me earlier dawning in one brilliant stroke of genius—Jane's cousin, Phyllis.

"Teach them to fish, sir?"

"What?"

"The saying you were referencing, it's 'Give a man a fish, he eats for the day; teach a man to fish, he eats for a lifetime.'"

"Oh, yeah. Hey, sorry. The packets are on my desk. Do you mind finding the XO and organizing them for me? I need to make a quick phone call."

I hurried outside, phone already dialing the familiar number.

"Hello." Jane's voice was her usual chipper self.

"Hi, Janie. I need a favor."

She laughed. "I already gave you the best years of my life, but sure, what's one more?"

"Your cousin Phyllis. Does she still teach at that all-girls school?"

Olivier and Sierra lived in a small condo close to the Artsy Soul and my apartment. Brick picked me up at seven sharp, seemingly a little less overwhelmed than he'd been all week. He'd still been his usual affectionate, infuriating self that I had grown to lo— think fondly of, but something had distracted him. The few times I hinted that he could talk to me about it, he'd changed the subject.

"Why are you dressed for a job interview?"

Brick's gaze skimmed down his long body at the khaki pants ironed within an inch of their life and a medium-blue oxford shirt and tie. "It's a dinner party, right?"

"Yeah, but with my best friend and her husband, not the Queen of England."

"Damn it, Jesse. I had on jeans and a T-shirt, but Jane thought it was too casual, and then I changed into a polo and couldn't decide tucked in or not. Shit . . . This was the only good thing about uniforms.

It literally says on the invite which fucking one to wear. Let me go home and change."

"It's fine," I said laughing, pulling him by the belt buckle into my apartment. "Come in. I'm almost ready." He took a seat at my table while I roamed around searching for socks and shoes. "Did you say you talked to Jane? Your ex-wife, Jane?" I asked as casually as I could from my bedroom. I only had a one-bedroom, and the walls were paper-thin, so there wasn't anywhere he couldn't hear me.

"Yeah. Is that a problem?"

Biting my lip, I slipped on my shoes. Was it? It kind of bothered me, but I couldn't really explain why. When I rejoined him in the family room, I tried to smile. "No. I guess I didn't realize you kept in touch."

"Oh, well we don't talk every day or anything, but our divorce was amicable. We check in as things come up. Her folks even invited me to Thanksgiving."

I winced. Okay, spending the holidays with an ex when there were no children? That was weird. I was nearly sure of it. The sudden flare of irritation felt suspiciously like jealousy, which was a major deduction in the mental gymnastics I was doing to keep my feelings for Brick from getting out of control. "Are you going?"

"I don't know, babe. It's not quite October. I figured we'd discuss it, eventually. Can we focus on my attire?"

"Take off your tie, unbutton the top button, and roll up your sleeves."

He did as I asked, staring at me while I appraised him. What I wanted to do was unstarch his pants until they resembled his usual style, but time was limited, and I tried to push aside worries about his ex-wife and focus on the fact that he cared about impressing my friends. I'd always wanted to double date with Sierra, and Brick was the first guy who I'd had the chance to since she'd married Olivier. "Okay, perfect."

"I can go home to change if it will embarrass you."

Relaxing, I smiled for real. "It's cute you think that's why I'd be embarrassed when you trivialized Willem de Kooning's entire body of work."

"I seem to remember my opinion of abstract impressionist changing at a rest stop north of Austin." He gave me a smug grin and winked.

My face heated at the memory. One of the most reckless and scorching-hot things I'd ever agreed to. Brick's exasperated declaration that he'd changed his mind hadn't rung true. So I kept going to drive home my points. He started rubbing high on my thigh, hand dipping between my legs in a blatant attempt to distract me. Admittedly, it got out of control in Austin's sluggish traffic. I kept talking to win our very ill-defined game, but at some point, forgot why I cared. When he declared it his new favorite way to shut me up, I suggested a better way and asked him to pull over. What had I been thinking? "I told you that was a onetime deal. You ready? I want to stop to get a bottle of wine."

"Is that a good idea?"

"Yeah. Sierra loves wine."

"Last I heard pregnant women don't generally drink wine."

"Oh, shit. That's right. I'll pick up dessert instead."

Brick drove us to a nearby bakery and, cupcakes in hand, we arrived at Sierra and Olivier's place. I knocked and, as I was accustomed to doing, let myself in. "Sierra," I explained with a shrug. "She never remembers to lock her door when she's home."

"Hello," I called from the entry. Sierra was on the couch, her feet up, hand resting over her bump. "Hey, Mama." I leaned over the couch cushion to kiss her forehead. "Feeling bad again?"

She nodded her head. "Exhausted all the time. It's brutal."

"She's got low iron." Olivier appeared out of the kitchen, wearing a crisp white apron embroidered with the French flag and the words *Heaven is where all chefs are French*.

I laughed, pointing to the apron. "Student gift?" I guessed and handed him the cupcakes.

"Sierra's mother." Olivier smiled patiently. "Welcome. Brick, can I get you a drink? I have soda, wine, and beer."

"Uh, sure. Beer, thanks."

"Jesse, you want your usual?"

I nodded and Sierra went to lower her legs from their perch so she could greet Brick. "Oh, don't," Brick said, rushing toward her. "Stay comfortable." He stuck his hand out, which Sierra shook.

She grinned at me. "He passes."

Brick chuckled, and I clapped his shoulder and took a seat next to Sierra, so Brick could have the chair. We made small talk at first: Sierra asked Brick where he'd moved from and how long he'd been in town, which led to questions about his military service. Then they started to talk about European travel, which always made me a little bitter about the trip I'd never been able to take.

"So, Brick. Jesse hasn't told me where you're from originally."

"I grew up in Indiana. Lived there until I went to college in Bloomington. Jesse told me you two met in art school."

"Yeah, did he tell you how?" The delight on her face was a warning sign. Surely, she wouldn't tell—

"Nope," Brick quipped.

"We need not get into this," I interjected.

Brick cast an amused glance at me and rubbed his palms together. "Oh, I think we should."

"Wait for me. I love this story." Olivier brought a makeshift tray of four drinks into the family room and distributed them before dragging a chair from the dining room to sit on. "Okay."

Sierra laughed and took a sip of her sparkling water. "It was at the end of our freshman year. I had to get an extension on my last projects because I'd been in a nasty car accident the month before. So, I'd made special arrangements with the dean to use a model for my life drawing class. I'd spent all day working on it, but it was done. All that was standing between me and my Habs were the finishing touches on one last painting." Sierra paused to take another drink, so I gave Brick additional context.

"Sierra is from Montreal. *Huge* hockey fan."

Sierra nodded enthusiastically. "So, I have my drawing in hand and head to the art studio where my painting was, and when I get into the studio, there's Jesse."

"And we became best friends. The end."

Brick shook his head, eyes full of amusement, and nursed another sip from his beer bottle. "Go on, Sierra."

I exhaled loudly, but they ignored me.

"Jesse is carrying this gigantic box piled up to here." She cut her hand over her forehead.

"It was the last day to clear out our lockers. I had a studio apartment and no car. I stored a ton of stuff there all semester."

Sierra shot me a dismissive look. "He's in and out of the studio taking trips to his place and getting rid of the rest. I'm painting in my own world, headphones on. Then I notice it's getting late and the playoffs are on, so I hurry to clean my brushes. When I come back and start getting ready to leave, I cannot find my drawing. It's vanished. I mean, I looked everywhere. I'm panicking because it's not like I can redo it since I'd used a live model. Finally, I notice that Jesse had been sorting his stuff on the same table where I'd placed it. So I asked him if he took my drawing and he gets . . . well, you know him. Now I'm Canadian, mind you, and that was my first-year spending any extended amount of time in the States."

"There you go again. She always thinks American and French are rude, but all Canadians are polite, ay?" Olivier laughed, stressing his wife's accent.

She flipped him off playfully. "No. I'm saying my bar for decorum was much higher before I married you."

"Back to Jesse." Brick laughed, leaning forward in his seat.

"Oh, yeah. I calmed him down and apologized profusely, although I didn't think I said anything offensive. Until, finally he accepts my apology and offers to help me look. I explain what I'm missing and he goes so still, and his eyes are like this big." Sierra used her fingers to show a saucer-sized circle, and everyone was laughing at me, even me.

"Apparently, he came across a drawing he hadn't remembered doing that semester and had *thrown it away*." She slapped her thigh and tossed her head back in laughter.

My face heated as I scrambled to wipe the look of outrage off Brick's face. "I thought it'd been a mix-up. There was no name on it and the semester *was* over."

Sierra waved me off. "We found it in the Dumpster, but other people had cleaned out their lockers on top of it, so it was ruined. Anyway, I joke that was the day I became an American, because I've never yelled at anyone, but I screamed at him."

"In French. She's much scarier in French," I clarified.

"Oh. My. God." Brick imitated my Janice from Friends voice I frequently used, and Sierra shot me a look before absolutely falling into hysterics.

"Yes, exactly. That's where our inside joke came from."

"Tell him the part where I saved the day."

"Oh, yeah. Jesse here became my replacement model."

"So did you miss the game?" Brick asked.

Olivier went to the other room and returned with a picture frame and an enormous smile. "Brick, say hello to *Hockey Fan.*"

Brick took in the life drawing that Sierra had done of me standing nude in front of the television, the light from the game perfectly reflected on my skin, holding a vintage Roy jersey by one finger over my shoulder. "This is incredible."

"Thanks," Sierra said. "I got an A and the Habs won Game 3, but we lost the series 4-1." She frowned, clearly still bitter. Brick and Sierra continued to bond, having more fun at my expense until Olivier excused himself to check on the timer.

"Dinner's ready," Olivier called from the kitchen. "Hope you like cassoulet."

"It's pork, sausage, and duck," I whispered to Brick. "Olivier is such an amazing chef. I never gave French food a chance until I met him."

"Smells delicious," Brick said as he pulled out my seat and then Sierra's while Olivier was preparing to serve the meal.

After we got situated, Olivier and Sierra exchanged a look and she slipped a paper out from under the credenza that sat behind their table. "So, Jesse. We have some news." She handed me the black-and-white photo. Olivier slipped his hand over his wife's shoulder, and Sierra lifted hers to hold it.

"Is this the baby? Why is it labeled Baby B? Is it a boy?"

Brick peeked over my shoulder. "Oh my," Brick exclaimed. "Wow, guys. Congrats." Sierra, Olivier, and Brick shared this entire moment I felt excluded from.

"What am I missing?"

Brick pointed. "That's Baby A and this is Baby B. They're having twins."

"Twins," I shrieked, jumping up to my feet as Sierra and I both said, "Oh. My. God," in complete harmony.

We laughed and talked about the babies for way longer than it took to eat. My heart soared hearing Sierra finally sound excited about the pregnancy. She said the ultrasound had made it more real for both of them.

"I can't believe you guys are having twins. I'm so jealous."

Brick raised an eyebrow at me and chuckled. "Have you spent much time around babies? Twins seem like a ton of work to me."

"Oh, it will be," Sierra confirmed. "But fun too."

"Do you have kids, Brick?" Olivier asked, sitting back from the table and rubbing Sierra's back as he spoke.

Brick shook his head. "No. My ex didn't want children."

Sierra's eyes widened, and she glanced at me before insisting a little too strongly, "Well, still plenty of time. It's not like there's an age limit on having kids for men. Elton John was what? Sixty-five, I think when he became a father. And Alec Baldwin and George Lucas, they were in their sixties too."

Brick chuckled. "Well, if I had their kind of money, then maybe, but I think that ship has probably sailed for me."

Every muscle in my body tensed, but the only one who noticed was Sierra, who deftly changed the subject.

While Brick continued talking to Olivier about potential family cars, Sierra leaned over to me and whispered, "Don't overthink that. He makes you happy."

But it was too late. Because yeah, Brick made me happy. Too happy. So happy I got turned on from objectionable art opinions. "I'm not. It's just a fling," I whispered back, then tried to rejoin the conversation. But I wasn't sure who I was trying to convince, because while Olivier and Sierra peppered Brick with questions about safety ratings, my brain rushed ahead to the end of the collision course I'd strapped myself to. Every day I spent with Brick was a day further from being where Sierra was—happily married and planning for a family.

After Sierra yawned, Brick clamped my shoulder. "I think we should let you get to bed. You ready, babe?"

"Sure," I said, rising to my feet. "Thanks for dinner."

While Brick helped Olivier clear the last few dishes to the kitchen, Sierra tugged me close to her. "He didn't say he never wanted kids. You always look for what's wrong, and if you don't find it, you assume you're missing it. Sometimes you can't find something wrong because there *is* nothing wrong. Give this one a real chance. He's great. Let it be great."

I didn't have a chance to respond before Brick and Olivier returned. We repeated another round of goodbyes, congratulations, and thanks before heading out.

When we got to the car, Brick opened my car door. "What's the matter? Did I not pass the best friend test? I thought that went well."

"You did. You passed with flying colors." I forced a smile for Brick, then tucked myself into the passenger seat, swallowing hard to hold back the clamor of disappointment aching to come out in very undignified ways. Sure, I could try to do what Sierra suggested. Brick was great and I could let it be great. After San Antonio, I had no doubt that I could absolutely fall head over heels in love with him. *But then what?*

He didn't want to get married again and he didn't want children. So was I supposed to toss away my goals? Or worse? Maybe Brick agrees, then something happened to me? I could be responsible for another kid growing up with someone who never wanted them. I could never do that.

No. Letting it be great now meant eventually our relationship would become a series of sacrifices and compromises until we'd resent each other.

I needed to stick to the plan—as soon as Academic Olympiad was over, we'd have no reason to be hanging out as much as we did. I could enjoy it while it lasted, then have the time to focus on what I really wanted.

Chapter Fourteen

Brick

The Regional Academic Olympiad competition was on the outskirts of Dallas, about two hours from Northridge. It was district policy that travel of that distance be done via school-provided means, so after a somewhat chaotic morning, Jesse and I arrived via a shared car to meet the kids at the bus. He was worked up about the quiz component and the potential for issues if the makeup of our team was questioned. While I appreciated his concerns, life in the military had shown me how useless ruminating on potential negative outcomes could be. Unfortunately, sharing my perspective only seemed to worsen his anxiety, so now I was biting my tongue.

"Did you hear back about the rule change?" Jesse snapped. "I should call them and ask for a status update."

I swallowed. I'd expected we'd have an answer by now, but I still hadn't heard anything from Phyllis. "We should hear soon, before State. It'll be fine. I'll handle it if there's a problem."

I could tell Jesse wasn't convinced, but thankfully Peter and Emily arrived, also in a shared vehicle. The small squeal of excitement from Jesse, which not only signaled a better mood but also a change of subject, let me exhale.

My shoulders lowered, reminding me of the tension I'd once carried day in and day out trying not to start a fight with Jane. God, I didn't miss that.

I glanced at him, reassuring myself that we were still in the getting-to-know-each-other phase where his little idiosyncrasies were cute. He noticed me looking and grinned at me in a way that implied he assumed my thoughts were inappropriate. With one wink, they actually were. Yep, we were all good.

"Stop it." He laughed. "It's kind of romantic." He gestured to Emily and Peter. "Don't you think it's romantic?"

"I thought you were worried about her falling behind. Shouldn't you be anti-distraction?"

"Ah, some things are more important than college credits. I'm thrilled she is so happy right now. She settled on her concentration theme. It's an investigation of gender fluidity. She's drawing a series of body parts from people of all genders, sort of put together chaotically. The composition is so cool." Peter and Emily emerged from their car and started toward the bus. "I mean look at that." Jesse swooned as Peter reached for Emily's hand. "How can you not root for them?"

"Blake and Natalie are here," I said instead as they both emerged from their respective cars. "And I think that's Nate's mom pulling in now."

Jesse opened his car door, and we met the kids at the bus. In short order, Jazmin arrived, then we were on our way.

"Hey, team," I said above the excited energy. "I wanted to say a few things on our way. Nate, can you take out your headphones?" I pulled at my ear, and when he didn't see me, Jazmin, who was sitting behind him, swatted him on the head for me.

"Ouch." Nate ripped out his headphones and twisted toward Jazmin. "Why you hitting me?"

Jazmin pointed to me and rolled her eyes, but at least I had Nate's attention.

"So, let's review the agenda for today one more time. We will do our wildcard round first. The top three schools were St. Brigid's, Dallas International Academy, and Lamar Alexander High, so they're guaranteed to advance. We need to be in the top three after the wildcard to join them in the Super Quiz."

"We know," Natalie said. "You've told us about a billion times, LTC."

"Natalie, what have I told you about calling me LTC?"

"It's an abbreviation for writing and not supposed to be used when we talk to you, but c'mon, it's a mouthful. You need a nickname."

Jesse laughed, and I shot him a warning look. The last thing I needed was for Jesse to make a suggestion.

"How about you call me Mr. Hausman, then? Since you have such a splendid memory and this isn't your first rodeo, perhaps you can help the team by reminding us of the Super Quiz rules."

Natalie straightened. "Well, as you were saying, only the top six teams get to Super Quiz, and you face off by placing. The first ranked team against the sixth-ranked team, etcetera. The first round is ten questions each. They ask the question to the team in an alternating fashion, and if your team gets it wrong, the other team can answer for a steal. After all six teams go through round one, the top three advance to round two, the speed round. The questions in this round are not asked directly to the school. When you know the answer, you buzz in. Wrong answers lose a point, so you don't buzz in before you hear enough of the question to answer it. After that, the top two teams advance."

"And if there's a tie?"

"Then the wildcard scores are the tiebreakers, which is why all teams take the test during the wildcard round, even those guaranteed a spot in the Super Quiz."

Peter added, "That was us last year. We were top two going into regionals, but we tied for second after Super Quiz. Luckily, our wildcard scores were ten points better and we beat out Lee High to go to State."

Natalie groaned. "Don't remind me. We did so bad at State. Nelms was livid."

"Well, Mr. Berry and I want you to try your best. You worked hard to get here. It would be amazing to make it to State again, but let's take it one step at a time."

"Should we run some practice drills? Nate, you want to start with music?"

Reaching for his bag, Nate extracted an enormous stack of blue index cards the team had amassed in the last few weeks. We had a color-coding system for each subject and anytime someone stumbled across a good test question, they captured the potential question and the answer on a card and added it to the stack.

"What is the name of the British Army surgeon who penned 'Yankee Doodle' during the French and Indian War to make fun of colonial soldiers?"

"Richard Shuckburgh," Emily said.

"That's right."

"Name the song and composer who is attributed for the phrase 'United we stand, divided we fall'?"

"'The Liberty Song' by, um . . ." Jazmin guessed. "Oh shoot. James Dixon?"

"No, John Dickerson," Peter corrected. "Don't buzz in if you don't know the complete answer. There are no partial points on multi-point questions, and you give other teams an edge."

"Yep," Emily said to a chorus of other nods.

The kids rotated through quizzing each other with the more experienced students helping the newer ones for the remainder of the ride. Jesse was working on a PowerPoint for his class, so I used the time to respond to emails. I carefully constructed yet another response to the parents of Seth Abbott, who still didn't quite get why Seth had gotten in trouble for Sean's words. Then reviewed more condescending reminders from Zach that had gone to the entire teaching staff about keeping the grade system up-to-date for the end of the first grading period. I saw an incoming message flash on the screen and my heart jumped. Finally, Phyllis!

I clicked on the email, skimming the body to confirm it meant what I thought it meant.

"We're here," Blake exclaimed, and the kids spurred into action, storing their flashcards and gathering their belongings. By the time we reached the bus parking lot, the kids were confident in their preparation and rearing to go.

I navigated the team through the crowds of students to our designated area while Jesse waited in line to check-in and turn over the required paperwork. The morning session was just the wildcard exam, and if we made the Super Quiz, we'd stay for the afternoon. The break was nice because the kids' parents had time to make it if they wanted to.

They held the wildcard test in the auditorium for all students to take together. Unlike the qualifying round, test questions were presented on a large screen and had a limited response time. There was no returning to former questions, so if a student didn't know the answer when it was presented, they either guessed or missed it. They allowed coaches to stand in the back, and a glance at their respective faces gave me a feel for who felt good about their team's chance to make the Super Quiz.

The first section was math, followed by science and economics. A few coaches looked worried, but I wasn't overly concerned. We'd covered all the concepts and subject areas in our review.

The announcer took to the microphone to start the art portion. Jesse stood up to get a better view of the screen and cast a big smile back toward me when the first image appeared. It was The Athenaeum Portrait.

"Question one. This portrait of George Washington is commonly referred to by what name?"

"Question two. Name the artist."

Jazmin's head whipped around to find Jesse. They exchanged smiles, and she made a subtle gesture of patting herself on the back since she'd been the one to remind everyone on the bus. Question after question we got "tells" from at least a few team members. Blake wiggled in her seat doing brief victory shakes each time she had one. Peter and Emily would look at each other. Nate tapped his pencil three times if he wasn't sure, and Natalie flicked hers on the side of her cheek when she was. We had covered nearly every question asked, not that all six remembered the answers to each, but still, Jesse and I were optimistic.

The energy built steadily through the music portion, but we'd yet to hit the geography and history questions, so I knew better than to get too cocky. Peter was strong in both, but the other kids struggled a bit. When it was clear we needed to narrow the scope to master the material, we'd gambled on the Revolutionary War battles, the Declaration of Independence, and the Constitutional Convention for history. The round started off strong with several questions from the Battle of Yorktown, then the Articles of Confederation, which I was reasonably sure we'd covered, but the remaining questions focused on the lesser-known founding fathers that we had studied little.

Jesse leaned over to me midway through the round and pushed his clipboard toward me. I read the question he'd scribbled.

Who was the lone Catholic to sign the Constitution? Did we cover that?

Frowning, I scribbled, *No. Carroll?* because I wasn't sure either, then added *or George Mason?*

Jesse shrugged, then wrote, *Is he the one who refused to sign?*

I nodded my head. Jesse exhaled and drew a sad face.

The geography portion was about two-thirds historical landmarks and battle sites, which we'd hit hard, and the rest were a potpourri from the original colonies. When the timer expired, we waited while the kids turned in their tests.

"I think I did well," Emily said first. "I was keeping track, and I think I'm somewhere in the ninety to one hundred range."

"That's great, Em. I'm about there too." Peter patted her on the shoulder.

"The highest possible team score is five hundred, right?" Nate asked.

"No. Four eighty," Peter corrected. "Top four students are scored in each category."

"Oh, that's right. Eight subjects and fifteen questions for each subject, so a single student score maximum is one hundred twenty." Jazmin rolled her eyes as Blake rattled off the math.

"Okay, everyone, get your stuff. We can get a snack while we wait."

Jesse

It was more than an hour before they announced the results. Brick was a nervous wreck as we waited. When a thin woman with straw-blonde hair and a smart tan pantsuit took the stage, a hush fell over the crowd.

"Good afternoon, Academic Olympiad students. I'm Lara McCombs, regional coordinator for today's competition. I want to congratulate you for your hard work and dedication to make it this far. As you know, only six teams can advance to tonight's Super Quiz. However, before we get to our results, I'm incredibly pleased to announce that our governing body has recently approved significant changes to our program for next year."

Brick clamped a hand to my shoulder, shaking me excitedly like he knew exactly what this was about.

"The Academic Olympiad seeks to include everyone who wishes to take part; therefore, beginning next year, we are introducing a small school and large school division. Small schools will be categorized as those with a total enrollment under five hundred students in grades 9-12. In addition, to allow greater participation, we will expand the large school division teams to nine students. To make fielding teams easier and to allow participation of our all-boys and all-girls schools, teams will no longer be required to conform to a specified gender mix."

A rousing round of applause broke out, and Brick was beaming. I leaned into him, my heart soaring with pride, and asked, "You knew, didn't you?"

Brick winked. "Got the email on the bus ride over. Wanted you to be surprised. I told you there was nothing to worry about. Everything went according to plan."

His words were so close to Sierra's, my heart jumped. *Was I worried for nothing? Maybe we could work out?* I smiled at Brick, allowing the seed of that possibility to take root.

We returned our attention to Lara as she recognized the kids who'd received perfect overall scores. Then perfect scores in six and seven categories. There were three, none of which were on our team.

"Now, we want to recognize students who received perfect scores in five subject areas. In today's competition, five students qualified for this ribbon. Marisa Zapata, Dallas International Academy; Patrick Smith, Desert Valley High School; Celeste Bowers, St. Brigid's High School; Madison Krueger, Rudder High School; and Peter Lim, Northridge High School."

"Peter, oh my god. Way to go." The team all reached to high-five and pat him on the shoulders as he walked to the stage to receive his medal. It was adorable how Emily kept gleaming at him and showing rapt interest in his award. The ceremony continued to recognize achievement in three or four subject areas.

Lara once again took the microphone. "Now for our team scores. Dallas International Academy, St. Brigid Catholic School, and Lamar Alexander High School were guaranteed Super Quiz spots by nature of their qualifying scores. They will be joined by our top three finishers today. With four hundred and two points is Desert Valley High School. With three hundred and ninety-eight points is Northridge High School. And with three hundred and seventy points is Rudder High School. Congratulations to all our teams." Raucous applause broke out. Forgetting myself, I threw my arms around Brick and gave him an enormous hug. If it shocked the kids, they didn't let on. They were too busy jumping up and down and hugging each other.

It was so loud we had to strain to hear Lara's final words. "Coaches for our six competing teams, please see the registration desk for your Super Quiz instructions."

"I'll go," Brick said. He held my gaze in the noisy gym. His tongue peeked out and traced his upper lip, his desire to do more than hug me written in his expression. "We make a good team."

My heart clenched as I squeezed his biceps. "Yeah, we do."

"Just kiss him already. We all know your boyfriends," Jazmin said with her signature eye roll. Blake and Emily sighed.

Playfully, I swatted her arm and mentally prepared to laugh off her comment with some vague response. While it was nice to see their attitudes about two men dating, it wouldn't have been appropriate in front of students, but before I could respond, a strangled sound came from Brick. My gaze whipped to him, and in short order, Brick's startled expression recovered to a sheepish grin.

The entire team had witnessed his response, and a full complement of uncomfortable stares turned to me seeking an explanation for the six-foot six-inch man who appeared seconds away from sprinting out of the room and changing his phone number.

I shook my head to erase the image, but it didn't work. All thoughts of a potential future I'd been entertaining came to a screeching halt. *This is why it can't work.* I pushed aside my foolishness and focused on my job. "All right, everyone, that's enough, back to the bus. We need to get lunch before the quiz. Whose parents are coming to the show?" All six kids raised their hands. "Let's go."

I gestured for the kids to walk and followed behind, leaving Brick standing to process whatever it was that was going through his head.

"Jesse . . ." he called. "Wait."

But I didn't stop, because while I couldn't explain his reaction to our students, I did know that look. Pretty well in fact. And there wasn't much to be done about it. It was one of those inevitable conversations that usually ended in a man telling you they "needed to be alone for a while" or "were feeling restless." Not that it mattered since I'd already decided to end things as soon as AO ended. It didn't affect me.

Nope, that look shouldn't be affecting me at all. Brick was a good guy, but he wasn't *the guy*. I knew this. I had a plan. I needed to stick to it.

Brick

The wildcard rankings were used to determine placement; since we'd finished in fifth place, we would face off against the second-place team, St. Brigid's, in the first round. In alternating fashion, Lara asked each team a question. After round seven, they tied us 6-6, both teams having each missed one question and failed to steal.

"Northridge, question eight. On what date did Cornwallis surrender to Washington at Yorktown?"

Peter beamed. "October 19, 1781."

"That's correct."

"St. Brigid's, question eight. In 1775, the American Post Office was established. Who served as the first Postmaster General?"

The St. Brigid's team discussed the question briefly before they answered. "Ben Franklin."

Lara smiled. "Yes. That is correct. After eight rounds, the score is tied 7-7."

"Northridge, question nine. Samuel Hopkins was issued this by General Washington on July 31, 1790. An American first."

Jesse mirrored my cringe. Who the hell was Samuel Hopkins? The kids discussed it for a long time before Peter hesitantly answered. "A patent?"

When Lara announced, "That's correct," Jesse squeezed my biceps so tightly it hurt. With a hopeful expression, I patted his thigh. I'd always loved competition, but the level of investment I felt toward this outcome rivaled the Super Bowl. I wanted the kids to win because I cared about the kids. And Jesse did too. He might have started off taking part because of Emily, but he'd grown fond of all of them, and seeing him interact with the team did something to me. It inspired me to want to be a better teacher.

"St. Brigid's, question nine. What book by William Hill Brown is widely considered to be the first American novel?"

The St. Brigid team looked utterly defeated. When time expired, they did not offer an answer, which gave us a chance to steal. Jesse was on the edge of his seat, vibrating with anticipation.

Peter, our spokesperson, looked to Jazmin, our resident literature genius, but I could tell by her anxious hair twirling she didn't know. Time expired, and the round ended with neither team getting a point.

"After nine rounds, Northridge is in the lead 8-7. This is the final round."

"Northridge, question ten. This painter known for his portraits, also painted four battle scenes of Lexington and Concord that were made into pro-revolutionary propaganda prints."

Peter looked to Emily, who stared back with enough horror on her face I knew she didn't know. The kids shook their heads, all six expressions wash with disappointment. "Philip Dawe?"

"No, I'm sorry, That is not correct. St. Brigid's for the steal?"

A small girl with large oval glasses cheerfully leaned into the microphone and said, "Ralph Earl."

Lara grinned proudly. "That is correct. The score is now 8-8. This is St. Brigid's final question. If you get this correct, you will advance to the next round. If you get this wrong, Northridge will have a chance to steal for the win. St. Brigid's, your last question." She cleared her throat and read the card with purposeful annunciation. "Dr. Richard Shuckburgh penned the lyrics to what well-known American song?"

Nate drew in a sharp breath as he looked to his teammates with wide eyes. Jazmin grabbed Blake's hand, practically vibrating out of her seat. St. Brigid's team knew our kids had the answer. They took all the allotted time to discuss it.

"St. Brigid's," Lara called for the answer.

A confident, well-groomed boy with Harry Potter glasses leaned toward the St. Brigid's spokesperson, who then answered clearly into the microphone. "'Yankee Doodle.'"

The room fell silent, our kids deflated before my very eyes, and my chest ached.

"That is correct. St. Brigid's advances to the second round. Ladies and gentlemen, please join me in acknowledging Northridge High. Congratulations, St. Brigid's. Well done."

The last-minute defeat sucked all the air out of their sails as they shuffled to their feet and shook hands with the other team. All that hard work, hours of studying, and it was over. I was heartsick for them. I tapped Jesse, who looked to still be processing the loss. "Let's go congratulate Jim."

"Hold on a minute," Jesse said, then summoned the kids into a group. "You all did amazing and should be really proud of yourselves."

"I can't believe we lost," Jazmin bemoaned. "Who the hell is William Brown Hill? I didn't even have a notecard on it."

"They didn't know either, Jaz," Nate offered with a clamp to her shoulder. "It's not your fault."

"It's no one's fault," I interjected. "We're a first-year team with new coaches. We did pretty well if you consider our late start. Jesse's right. You should all be proud of yourselves and each other. We're certainly proud of you."

"And Peter got an award!" Emily offered, which kicked off a fresh round of congratulations and a very red-faced Peter.

We let the kids have a few more moments to commiserate, and while they left to find their parents, I was surprised by how upset Jesse looked.

On stage, the Super Quiz continued with the next two schools. "Should we go say congrats to the St. Brigid's coach?"

Jesse nodded, and we set off to find Jim. Since it was the first time we'd had a moment alone, I wanted to talk to him about what had happened. Jesse wanted to keep our relationship discreet and he'd clearly been upset. "Hey, about earlier—"

"It's fine," Jesse said, but in a way that kind of made me think it wasn't.

"You sure? I didn't want the kids—"

"Of course. It's what we agreed to. Look, there's Jim." Jesse darted away from me and headed toward him.

"Jesse—" I called, but he didn't wait. That cleared up any doubt I had about the source of his irritation. Clearly, I'd messed up. If he'd stop running away from me, I could talk to him and explain. Or at least I could attempt to. I wasn't entirely sure I *could* explain my reaction, because I was still trying to figure out why the hell I'd reacted the way I had. It wasn't a surprise the team knew about us, but I think it was the way Jesse had laughed. When he looked at me like Jazmin had declared we were both teachers or adults or something else equally indisputable instead of boyfriends. My heart started pounding. My palms started sweating. Then the kids were staring at us, and I know I didn't respond the way he wanted. It caught me off guard is all. Were we boyfriends? Did *he* think that's what we were? Did it matter? I liked where we were. Why didn't I just kiss him? I knew how concerned he was about my bisexuality. A little peck on the cheek would have given the kids the confirmation they were looking for and avoided Jesse getting upset. I had no problems with people knowing Jesse and I were seeing each other.

"Northridge had a good run," Jim remarked as I caught up to him and Jesse. He shook our hands and accepted our congratulations. "We lucked out. Our whole team returned this year, and we have four seniors. You'll give us a run for our money next year for sure."

"You can count on it," I said, glancing sidelong at Jesse, who kept his eyes glued to Jim. Testing my theory, I tossed an arm over Jesse's shoulder. Jim eyebrows jumped as Jesse stepped to the side, sending my arm crashing down, and gave me a *what the hell are you doing* glare. Okay, maybe *he* still had a problem with people knowing we were seeing each other.

Tension crawled up my neck, and I rubbed it, doing my best to covertly apologize and pretend I hadn't embarrassed us both in front of the competition.

Jesse turned to Jim, whose lopsided smile and easy demeanor said he'd been more surprised than offended. "Best of luck at State." He turned to me, concern entrenched on his face. "I'm going to find the kids."

Before I could respond, Jesse turned on his heels and walked away, leaving me to make excuses with Jim. "Good luck, coach. We'll see you next year."

I hurried to the lobby to find Jesse with our team and their parents. Emily was sobbing in her mother's arms, and Peter was nowhere.

"Emily, what's the matter?" Jesse asked, but she couldn't be consoled. The other kids looked just as upset. Jazmin was the first to offer an explanation.

"Peter's parents dragged him out of here by the arm. I don't think he's coming back on the bus."

Savannah glanced up, looking wrecked by her inability to calm her daughter down. "The Lims saw Peter and Emily kiss. They didn't know." It was clear by her barely contained rage that the Lims' problem was not Peter kissing a girl, but rather Peter kissing a girl like Emily.

Jesse gave me a helpless look, but I didn't have the first clue how to make this better.

Chapter Fifteen

Jesse

Friday evening, I sat on my couch, sketch pad open on my lap, mind racing. Between what had happened between Emily and Peter, disappointment over our loss, and having no idea what to do about Brick, the entire week had sucked.

I finished the shading on Ryan's face with a sigh. I still wasn't happy with the proportion of his son's hands holding the football, but I needed the reminder. Eye on the prize and all that.

The previous four pages were all pictures I'd drawn of Brick, starting with him on his bed wearing nothing but dog tags. I closed my eyes, remembering the sex-charged conversation that ended in him telling me he used male prostitutes. There couldn't be a bigger contrast.

I closed my sketch pad and tossed it on the coffee table with a frustrated sigh.

I thought we'd have more time, but Academic Olympiad was over. I thought the chemistry would have waned by now, but it most definitely hadn't. I thought Brick would have ended things, but instead he apologized and was bending over backward to help smooth things over for Peter and Emily. All week, I'd been comforting Brick and letting him comfort me, alternating between indulging in my fantasy and trying to convince myself that eventually, when everything calmed down, things between us would come to a natural end.

A car door slammed, followed by the familiar beep of Brick's car alarm.

I rose from the couch and opened the door to see Brick ascending the stairs to my apartment with deep frown lines etched on his handsome face.

"Oh shit," I murmured.

The worry I'd been carrying in the pit of my stomach turned into a lump of concrete. We'd both been a nervous wreck for the meeting Zach had called at the Lims' request. The meeting Zach expressly said I was not welcome to attend. By the looks of him, Brick could have used the backup.

"Come here." I pulled him into my arms. His arms closed around me, and he sighed like he'd been waiting for my embrace to exhale. I squeezed him tighter and rubbed the knots at the base of his neck and shoulders. We stayed like that until my thoughts drifted into dangerous territory. How good he felt in my arms. How nice it was to have someone to hold me after a bad day and to feel him relax under my touch.

"I'm afraid to ask, but how'd it go?" I ushered him inside and closed the door, then helped him remove his jacket.

Brick slipped off his shoes and practically collapsed on my couch, tugging me down with him. "The Lims think I attempted to talk Peter out of going to West Point." He grabbed a throw pillow and situated it on my lap, then rested his head there. Staring up at me, his eyes slightly unfocused, he pinched the bridge of his nose. "My neck is killing me."

"I should have been there." I stroked my fingers on his scalp, scratching his head gently.

Brick scrunched his nose in disagreement. "They wanted Zach to remove him from JROTC and ensure he's not near Emily."

"Did Zach go along?"

"No, thankfully. Zach said it was improbable for the school to monitor contact between two students simply because the parents requested it. When they threatened to pull him from the school, he convinced them it would be a detriment to Peter's chances of West Point if he dropped JROTC or changed schools now. But I'm not to discuss personal information or give him any advice. I have to refer him to his school counselor for all matters outside of JROTC."

"I'm sorry, Brick." I tapped him so I could stand and grabbed the ibuprofen, a heating pad, and a glass of water. "Here." I handed him the pills and the drink, then plugged in the pad. Once he seemed more comfortable, I sat at the other end of the couch and rubbed his feet while he continued to vent about how terrible he felt.

"You should have heard Peter's father. I can't imagine what he said to Em—" He stopped suddenly with a remorseful purse of his lips and sat up, rubbing at the obvious twinge in his neck. "Damn. I've been going on and on about the meeting and I didn't stop to ask. How was Emily today? Any better?"

"No," I said sadly. I drew a deep breath in and exhaled. "Still pretty glum. She's been withdrawn and didn't take part at all in peer review. Marie said a few of her students were talking about it today. She heard the Lims are close with one of the school board members. They're trying to resurface Nelms's firing again. I left a message with Savannah to let me know if she needs any support, but she hasn't responded."

"That explains why Zach is so bent out of shape."

"It'll die down."

"I feel terrible. Do you think I did the wrong thing? Zach thinks I got too personal and that I should've never agreed to keep our conversation confidential."

"Of course not. Peter came to you. He trusted you, and you gave him advice on how to think about the problem, not specific dating advice. You encouraged him to talk to his parents about his college plans and doubts. You established appropriate boundaries when discussing sex and your own sexuality. I don't understand how they think teachers can function like this. We have to be trusted to make judgment calls."

"Thanks."

"No problem. I know we talked about going out for dinner tonight, but do you want to stay in? I can order food. We can just chill."

"Yeah, that sounds perfect, actually.

I moved a pillow to replace my lap under his feet. "Just relax. I'll get the takeout menus."

"Thanks, babe."

I stiffened upon hearing the term of endearment, my heart speeding up at the domesticity of the evening. It was precisely the sort of thing I should be avoiding, but I couldn't help myself. I liked taking care of Brick too much. I needed someone to share the burden of a heavy week, and it was nice to not only have him there, but have him understand my frustrations on a personal level.

I brought a stack of menus from the junk drawer in the kitchen, and we ended up ordering Thai food. Without asking, I switched on ESPN for Brick and carved out a small space between him and the back of the couch, sort of half on top of him, but careful of his neck.

He kissed my forehead and ran a hand down my back. "This is nice."

I nodded, yawning as his fingers inched a little lower and rested on my ass.

"Kiss me," he commanded.

I peered up, a small smile creeping in. Why did he have to be so adorable? "What happened to you being tired and having a sore neck?"

"It's better, and I'm never too tired to make out with you."

Using my toes on the couch end for leverage, I pushed up until I could reach his lips, and his hand immediately settled on my ass, squeezing gently. A warmth flowed through me.

Brick's body felt so good under mine, warm and solid. I vibrated with need from the kissing alone. It was all I could do to keep from begging him to take me into the bedroom.

"Hey—" I rolled away at the vibration against my upper thigh, and Brick laughed as he fished the cell phone from his front pocket.

"It's Jane."

I tried to keep my face neutral as I pushed to get up, but his heavy arm came around me and kept me anchored to him.

Brick propped the phone between his shoulder and ear. "Hello," he answered as he stuck his hand down the back of my pants, fingers inching toward my hole. I snorted, squirming on top of him until he chastised me with a little swat. Okay, apparently, I was supposed to lie here and be fingered while he talked to his ex-wife. That was normal, right?

"Oh. Cool. Yeah. I'd love to see you. Dinner?"

I stiffened against Brick's body. I knew he and Jane spoke, but I hadn't actually witnessed how they communicated and wasn't sure I wanted to.

Brick pulled his hand out, and I moved to get off him again, but he pushed two fingers into his mouth, sucked them, and went right back to teasing me.

"Yeah, that works," he said into the phone.

I squirmed, cock growing hard as I pressed my hips down. He smiled at me and shifted his leg a bit to give me a better angle to ride his thigh.

"I don't know, I'll have to ask." He glanced up. "You okay having dinner with Jane next month?"

He thrust two fingers into my hole as I responded, so my surprised "Huh?" came out more like a choked sob against his shoulder.

"Yeah, Jane. No. Jesse's very excited. Oh yeah, he's dying to come." He winked at me and continued to piston his fingers inside me. "Uh-huh. Thanks."

I bit his shirt and zoned out the remainder of the conversation as Brick continued to toy with me. I humped his leg shamelessly, nearing the point of no return.

"That's it, baby." Brick moaned, warm and sensual in my ear. "Make yourself feel good."

"Fuck." I struggled to remember my own name, let alone who he'd been talking to. "Jane?" I choked out.

"You want to fuck Jane?" He laughed.

I glared at him, but any protest died when his fingertip pressed against my prostate. "Fuck," I seethed. "I need to— Fuck. Need." The thoughts were obliterated by pleasure. I needed a hand on my cock, but the pressure building in my balls made me think maybe I didn't. If I gave it a few more seconds, it might be enough. I pushed my hips into his thigh, frantically humping to get the friction where I needed it. "Fuck. Fuck. Pants. I can't."

Brick chuckled at my predicament and removed his fingers long enough to smack my ass. "Get naked. Hurry, the food will be here soon."

I struggled to sit up, then shuffled off my pants while Brick yanked my shirt over my head. He scooted his uniform pants down, enough to free himself and stroked himself hard before motioning me to get back on his lap. "C'mere."

I followed his lead, and soon Brick had one hand wrapped around our cocks and his other pulling my ass toward him. "Get us off, baby." He kissed me, wet and wild as we writhed together.

I rocked my hips, sliding my cock along his, gasping at how good it felt. There was no better feeling than his skin on mine. I ripped my mouth away from his. "Jesus, Brick." I grasped his shoulders as his hand pulsed around me.

"Faster, Jesse. Yeah. Like that. Fuck."

"God, this feels good," I moaned.

"Yeah, you do. Want to see you go, Jes. C'mon, beautiful." He pushed two fingers back inside my ass and squeezed our cocks with his other hand. "Fuck yourself on my fingers. You're so hot. Love how you grip me."

The warring sensations of his fingers filling me and that perfect upward twist of his strokes were too much to take. Just one more— *Finally.* My head listed back and I moaned as my balls drew up tight, my internal muscles spasming in quick pulses. "I'm gonna come."

"Yeah, baby. Do it. I'm right there too. Gonna blow as soon as you do."

I cried out, arching up into Brick's fist and sending a thick ribbon of semen over his belly. The tension released from my entire body like an unleashed coil, eradicating my ability to stay upright. I slumped forward as Brick gasped and made a mess of his hand, then trembled through aftershocks.

He held me with one arm, our chests heaving against each other. As our heart rates returned to normal and breaths evened, he made no attempt to move. I leaned against him, straddling his lap, come smeared between us. The silence grew with each breath and the stillness became saturated with what wasn't being said.

I could feel the rise and fall of his chest. Hear his heart beating. His breath on my neck. My chest expanded until it ached, but I couldn't bring myself to look at him.

Because I knew.

Even when the sex was frantic and dirty, it was there. The need I had to take care of him and make him happy. Wanting him with me at the end of the day. It wasn't going to fade. It was only going to get stronger.

I was in love with him.

My head lowered, I pressed back against his hold until his arm slacked and I dropped my foot to the floor. Standing, I mumbled, "I'm gonna take a quick shower."

"Jesse, wait." Brick reached for me. I forgot myself at the touch of his hand. The look on his face was so intense, I was almost afraid to hear what he had to say, but I couldn't not know. He guided me down, and I settled my weight against his knees again, leaving daylight between us. He brushed my hair back from my eyes.

"Hey," Brick said and gently lifted my chin with a finger. "I got distracted and didn't get to tell you something earlier."

"Yeah?" I bit my lip, finding it hard to breathe. *Oh my god.* It was all over his face. *The L word.* If he loved me too, maybe this could work? No man had ever told me they loved me before. I closed my eyes, swept up with anticipation and fear. And hope. So much hope. I struggled to keep my breaths even.

He stroked a hand over my cheek and left his palm there. "You took real good care of me when I got here, baby. That means a lot to me. More than you know."

I felt strapped into one of those crash test cars, waiting to discover if my heart would come out okay or completely fly apart after impact. *This is good. Let it be good.*

"I'm starting to understand how your brain works, so I don't want there to be any misunderstanding about me talking to my ex. I told her I've met someone special, and she was going to be in town on a long layover. You should never feel you need to leave the room when we talk."

I nodded, drawing in an erratic breath. *This was good. Let it be good.*

"I need to clean up a bit and wash this shirt. Would you be okay if I left a few things over here? You can leave stuff at my place too. You look cute in my shirts, but we're really not the same size."

I cupped my hand over his, my body flying toward the wall now at breakneck speed. *I love him. And he loves me back.* "Yeah." My voice cracked. "Um, you can leave whatever you need."

"Okay, good. Because I love"—as Brick began speaking, my mind rushed ahead. My response formed in my mouth. *I love you. I want to be with you*—"your couch. It's so comfortable."

He hauled me down and kissed me, but I was too stunned to respond. "You okay?" he asked when he released me. I nodded dumbly, still reeling from the impact.

He lifted me from his lap to set me gently on the cushion next to him and walked into the bathroom like he hadn't even noticed my heart slamming into a brick wall and shattering into a million pieces.

He returned from the restroom with a wet washcloth and handed it to me. "Here." He jutted his chin toward my semen-covered stomach.

"Uh. Thanks," I said, wiping up the mess. "I'm going to grab a shower."

I rushed to the bathroom before he could respond, and locked the door behind me, still fighting to catch my breath. My chest clenched uncomfortably tight. When the doorbell rang, I turned on the water and waited for it to warm.

Brick knocked at the door. "Foods here."

"I'll be right out." I lifted my head to the spout, rubbing at my eyes, then relived the entire moment in the shaving mirror suctioned to the shower wall. "You're not in love with him," I told myself. *He's not the guy.*

No matter what Sierra had said, I didn't need to let it be great, I needed to let it be over. I bargained with myself, reviewing how I could proceed without giving up what I wanted. The problem was I wanted Brick and I wanted a family and I didn't know how to choose.

I decided not to. At least not yet.

January.

In many ways, it was my original plan. I told myself I'd end it when AO ended, and if we'd gone to State, AO would have ended in January. Surely, by then we'd both be ready to move on. What better time to start over than in the New Year?

I climbed out of the shower and dried off, then pulled on clean sweats. Repeated pep talks cycled through my brain, but none of them made my plan sound any wiser. If I had half a brain, I'd end it now, but I wasn't going to. I'd keep digging this hole because in the back of my mind, what I really wanted was Brick to tell me I didn't have to choose. I couldn't help myself from hoping that maybe, with enough time, he'd what? *Fall in love with me?* Maybe. *Want all the same things I did?* Doubtful. *Break my heart?* Likely.

Taking a deep breath, I stepped into the living room to find cartons of Thai food spread out on the coffee table and Brick on the couch, thumbing through my sketch pad.

"What are you doing?"

"Checking out your art. The picture of me definitely does me justice. I don't know why you were worried." He wiggled his eyebrows at me. "Hey, who is this guy?" Brick held up a picture of Ryan's face.

"No one." I marched up to him, took the pad, and set it aside. "Just a guy from a dream."

"He's cute. Must have been a hot dream."

Brick

When I first reviewed the school schedule, I thought the concept of fall break was a little silly, but I was wrong. So, so wrong. After all that had happened, Jesse and I both needed a vacation, and the timing couldn't be better.

We were happy, I thought. The sex was fantastic, and Jesse seemed content with how things were. Still, knowing he was dreaming about other guys was a reminder of one of the realities of single life I'd forgotten. I had competition. I wasn't the jealous type, but I also wasn't oblivious to the fact that while Jesse checked all of my boxes, I didn't necessarily check all of his. So when it came time to plan our hiking trip, I figured upping my game for a full weekend getaway couldn't hurt. I didn't want him shopping around in his spare time.

The final hours before the much-needed five-day weekend lasted forever, but the last bell had rung over an hour ago. I'd used the quiet time to catch up on paperwork, update midterm grades, and confirm the weather conditions for the cabin. Jesse had had AP portfolio meetings before and after school for the last few weeks, which meant he was doing lesson plan prep in the evenings. But the weather was cooling off and there was no lesson planning to be done for at least a few days.

I shut down my computer, eager to get off campus and surprise him.

I was locking my office when a noise came from the direction of the supply closet. Scanning the hallway, I could see the building was clean and trash emptied. Mr. Samuel had been through already. "Jesse," I called to the empty hallway, but there was no answer. Then I remembered he'd already left. The noise came again, faint, but unmistakable.

With a heavy sigh, I traversed the hallway, mentally preparing myself to find a teacher since students were all long gone. Peter had been so distracted, I wouldn't be surprised if he'd forgotten to lock it.

When I arrived outside the closet, the door was closed, the sounds of shuffling inside. I hung my head and pushed the door open, one horrified gasp met with a flurry of activity as I found the switch and turned on the light. Peter tried to yank Emily from her knees and cover himself at the same time. I inhaled sharply, face on fire, and turned away, covering my eyes to give them a modicum of privacy to cover themselves.

"Are you both decent?" I asked, peeking through my fingers on the hand shielding my eyes.

"Um...yes, sir." I identified the noise I'd heard as him dragging the table his bare ass had been leaning on back to its correct orientation. Peter's voice trembled as he stammered an explanation. Good. He should be afraid. "I'm sorry, sir. I know this was inappropriate."

Oh, this was a hundred levels beyond inappropriate. "What in the world were you two thinking?"

"It's my fault," Emily cried. Peter's eyes whipped to her, and he shook his head in protest. Their eyeballs held a silent exchange that was only subtle if you were a busted teenager trying to get your story straight. I'd seen much the same on newbies after they'd fucked up countless times.

With a new soldier, I'd use this sort of thing to put the fear of God into them and send them on their way, but in essence, they'd already had their warning. *Damn it.* They weren't only breaking the school's rules; Peter had crossed his parents and used his access to the supply closet—a privilege I'd entrusted him with—to make out with his girlfriend. Not to mention he'd landed us all in a difficult and uncomfortable situation. Hormones were no excuse. Peter wasn't a kid anymore; he was eighteen. The same age as kids this country sent to war. He should know better.

"Seems to me you were both here by choice. Do I have that correct?"

Emily's gaze dropped to the ground, but Peter looked me in the eye, jaw rigid, as they both nodded.

"Please, Lieutenant Colonel Hausman, Peter will get in so much trouble if his parents find out. We only wanted to be together. He's the only thing that makes me happy. The only thing. Without him, I'm nothing." Emily was actively crying now, her blue eyes surrounded by a halo of red, and her skin splotchy.

"Emily." I softened my Army voice into something closer to fatherly. "That's not true. You're a very talented artist and an excellent student. You have plenty of things going for you besides a boyfriend. Now, I understand that this is difficult, but rules are rules."

"Sir, would you consider keeping Emily out of this? I'll take the punishment."

God Bless them. Noble sacrifices all around. I shook my head, almost sucked in by how smitten they were. Not that I was tempted to let them off, because lord knows if it were any other two students, I wouldn't have considered it. If the Lims found out I knew and said nothing, I couldn't even imagine what hell would rain down on the school. As far as letting one off and not the other? Well, I knew what the discipline referral form asked, and I wasn't about to lie about who was present at the time of infraction.

First things first. I knew administration was gone, because Zach had texted me a reminder about basketball practice that evening and been irritated when I'd blown it off. "Look, it's fall break. Administration is gone for the day. The buses are all gone. Emily, how were you getting home?"

"Um . . . Peter takes me. He drops me off on the corner of my street."

I sighed. That meant it wasn't likely this was their first time and Savannah probably didn't know they were still seeing each other either. "Call your mother. Ask her to pick you up or if she is okay with me giving you a lift home. Peter, you have your car?"

He nodded and hid his face away. I couldn't be sure if he was hiding his fear from me or from his girlfriend, but I wasn't about to send the kid home if he were in danger. "Answer me honestly, son. If your parents find out about this, are you at risk of physical harm?"

He bit his lip and, after what looked like a painful swallow, he returned a stoic gaze to me and shook his head. "No, sir. My parents aren't like that."

"Okay." I exhaled a long breath through my mouth. "Where are your keys?"

Peter shoved his hand into his pocket, his movements growing frenzied as he searched them and found them empty. I spied his key ring under the table, approximately where they might have fallen had someone shoved their pants down a little too hurriedly. *Jesus.* I palmed my forehead. "Under the table." I pointed to them.

Peter blushed. "Oh. Um. Sorry, sir. Thank you." He swooped to pick them up and Emily's phone dinged with an incoming text.

I extended my hand. "I'll need your keys to the closet and to the classroom. I'm not sure how the battalion commander can function without access, but I clearly can't trust you to keep them. Suffice it to say any inconvenience I experience because you proved yourself untrustworthy will be revisited to you tenfold."

Peter's hand shook as he removed the two keys from his key ring and handed them over. I'd give them back after a few weeks, but it would be good for him to think about how his actions impact others. Every time the drill team or color guard had to stand outside the building and wait for me to show up to let them in, he'd remember. If he had to traipse across campus to find Mr. Samuel when I was unavailable, and then wait for our septuagenarian custodian to make his way to the back lot with his keys, all the better.

"Emily." I motioned to the phone in her hand. "Did you get ahold of your mother?"

She wiped the wet streaks from her cheeks. "I texted her. She's on her way."

I had been hoping to hear the conversation to confirm she was in fact contacting Savannah. Not that I didn't believe her, but . . . Okay, yeah, I needed to be sure. Everything with these two was going to be *trust but verify* for a long while. "Can you show me that message?"

Emily handed her cell phone over and, as I'd suspected, Emily hadn't been truthful. "Missed the bus, huh?"

She cringed. "I did, um, miss it."

"Listen, you two. I know you care about each other, and I'm sorry that it's difficult for you to find appropriate places to be together. If you ask me, you should be going to the movies and doing whatever kids your age do, but that's between you and your parents. It's not my place to challenge their rules any more than it's my place to police what you tell them. But choosing to do this on school grounds, well after school hours, was plain dumb." I held back the commentary I had about the multitude of places this little make-out session could have gone down with far less risk. Peter had a car. Weren't there make-out spots in Northridge?

"We know," they said in unison.

I sighed, finding a modicum of respect in the fact that they didn't try to make excuses. "Fair warning, there is a referral going in after fall break and it's going to say you were together in a place you shouldn't have been. I will not mention what you were doing, because I really don't think that's important and I'm not trying to embarrass you, but you were in a supply closet, after school hours, and without permission or legitimate purpose. Presumably, your parents aren't stupid. I'd suggest you talk to them and explain the situation before they get a call from your vice principals, because if they ask for details, I'm also not going to lie. Do you understand?"

They both nodded, and though they stared at me like I was the murderer of love, the tiny brush of their fingers made me want to throw them some kind of bone. "You're probably looking at detention, both of you."

With that, Emily's chin rose. "Together?" Her voice lifted in optimism.

Fuck. I hated this. I nodded. "There's only one detention."

She smiled, a little quirk of her mouth, and cast longing eyes toward Peter. And God help me, my chest ached, and I had to suppress the urge to find this even a tiny bit romantic. "All right, lovebirds. Let's go."

I had a romance of my own to tend to.

Chapter Sixteen

Jesse

"How long have you had this planned?" I was still processing Brick's announcement that he'd booked a cabin a few hours away and wanted to spend fall break hiking. "You want me to leave with you, like, right now?"

"We talked about hiking in the fall, but not much. I thought we could use a break after AO ended. And yes, pack and let's go. I was hoping to get here earlier, but the day got away from me, then I had to deal with an issue at school."

The hairs on my neck stood up. "What issue?"

"Don't worry about it. Now, seriously, go pack what you need. I have everything else covered. I want to get on the road so we get there before dark."

I didn't have time to process the million reasons why this was a terrible idea, so I settled on the two most obvious—no guy had ever planned a surprise trip for me, and I was so not a last-minute kind of packer. Before I could talk myself out of it, I flew into action. Hauling my suitcase out of my closet, I set it on my bed and started throwing things into it while Brick read on the couch.

"Do you think the cabin will have towels?" I dropped a stack on my bed and went into the living room.

Brick glanced up from his Jackson Pollock biography and smiled indulgently.

"Yes," he said. "The cabin will be well-stocked. Bring hiking clothes and personal items. I have the food and everything else covered."

I returned the towels to the closet and spied my beach bag. That reminded me. I peeked around the doorjamb. "What about a swimsuit? There's a hot tub, right?"

Brick winked. "The hot tub is on a private deck. You won't need a swimsuit."

"Bug spray?" I called from my bathroom.

"Got it," Brick yelled back.

This was getting ridiculous, I just needed to tell him I couldn't go. It was like that damn supply closet all over again. He thought if he made things all organized and perfect, I couldn't resist. I could resist. I should resist. *Shouldn't I?*

That's what he'd been doing this whole time. He cooked, he was tidy, he paid attention to what I said and did. I mean, I'd doodled a silly take of *Squares with Concentric Circles* one night while he was watching football, and the man turned off the game to talk about Kandinsky. Who does that? No one. That's who. He made it impossible not to fall in love with him.

What if this trip helped him realize he wanted this too?

"Condoms?"

He aimed a pointed stare in my direction. Of course, that would have been the first thing he packed. "Jesse, I have what we need other than your personal hygiene items and clothing. When I said I planned a trip, I meant it. I planned the trip. Now please, can you finish up so we can get on the road?"

I pouted for a moment because *gah*. Every time he touched me, I had to fight the words back, but after my brief stint as a crash test dummy, I knew I needed to keep my expectations in check. I banished all the thoughts that threatened to make this weekend harder than it needed to be. No one had ever done anything remotely this sweet for me before, and no matter what it meant, I wanted to enjoy it.

"If you really don't need me to do anything else, I guess I'm as ready as I'll ever be."

Brick

"Come on, you got it." I tried to stay upbeat and encourage Jesse as he scrambled up the steep inclined trail. He was filthy, and not in the way I preferred. Still wasn't sure how he'd managed to fall off that perfectly stable flat stepping stone when crossing the small stream, but he had, and he'd fallen forward into mud, so besides wet feet, both hands, one knee, and most of his shirt were caked in mud.

"Yeah. Yeah." He lifted, catching his breath for a few minutes as he assessed the exposed roots and wet rocks for the best path around a fallen branch.

"If you put your hand there—" I pointed, but he ignored me. With a hand braced on the trunk, he planted one foot and swung his other leg over, then scowled at my extended hand. He grabbed onto the branch and lifted himself up the last bit to the small observation deck that overlooked the forest valley. "Oh, wow. This is gorgeous."

I smiled in relief, thankful for the healthy dose of autumn colors painting the treetops. I wrapped an arm around his waist and positioned him in front of me against the wooden railing. Leaning down, I kissed his neck, the taste of his sweat salty on my tongue. He ran his fingers through my hair, scratching over my scalp, but the gesture felt a little placating. "Worth the climb?"

Jesse huffed, looking down at his soaked hiking shoes. "I still think the moderate three-mile paved trail sounded better . . . and drier."

I had pushed for the more strenuous hike because the paved trail was loaded with families and I wanted Jesse to myself even if he was a little too winded to carry a conversation for most of the hike.

"This is a romantic spot you have to admit." I pushed my dick against his ass, teasing him. The trail wasn't quite *that* isolated, but I'd been trying to cajole him out of the odd mood he'd been in all day. It was fucking with my head.

I really thought things were going well between us, but now . . . I didn't know. He'd been full of energy on the drive up. But as soon as I began explaining what I had planned, he started acting weird.

"Yeah"—Jesse didn't face me, but I could hear the eye roll—"so romantic."

While I usually loved his quick sarcasm, there was an undercurrent of real annoyance coming from him I wasn't sure what to do with. I knew Jesse didn't have a problem with romance, so was it me?

"Hey," I said and swiveled him around. "What's wrong?"

"Nothing." He wiped his hands on his shorts and reached for the water in his pack. Unscrewing the top, he took a long drink and went back to checking out the view.

"Are you sure?"

"Of course. You ready to go back?"

I frowned. "You want to go back already?"

"Yeah. I'm muddy and my shoe is wet." He lifted his foot up and shook it.

I had hoped to spend a little time at the summit enjoying the view, but he didn't wait for me to reply before he headed back down the trail. "Okay," I muttered with a sigh and followed.

For the next two hours, Jesse and I scrambled over rocks, around trees, ascended rickety stairs, and descended slippery mud-slicked trails, but nothing got me any closer to learning what was going on inside his head. That was until we reached the creek he'd fallen into and it finally dawned on me. *Because he didn't like wet feet.* A detail he'd strongly hinted at multiple times when suggesting we take the easier paved trail.

After that, I paid closer attention and it became clear, beyond the creek and streams we crossed, this entire hike wasn't his idea of a good time. So at least I gained some of the context I'd been missing for Jesse's "so romantic" quip.

"Got it?" I asked as he approached a particularly steep incline.

Jesse stretched and wiped his muddy hand off on his shorts to get a better grip on a tree branch. "Yeah." His determined eyes met mine before he navigated around the exposed roots with grace and agility.

My pulse revved faster as I watched him, sun glinting off his blond hair.

"Need help?" I asked, extending a hand to him.

"No, thanks," he said with a defiant edge and lifted himself, then scrambled over a series of boulders with an unexpected look of pure determination and grit on his face. Maybe this hike wasn't what he had in mind, but it absolutely wasn't above his skill level. God, he was kind of amazing. Whatever he did, he went all in. When Jesse made it to the top, I met him, grinning. He brushed off his hands, a small lip curl of disgust for the mud still caked under his fingers, and met my gaze. I grabbed him by the waist and gave him a fast, hard kiss.

"What was that for?"

"I feel sorry for anyone that ever underestimates you."

Jesse beamed, a genuine smile that renewed my optimism for the weekend. "You should, Major Hausman." He playfully shoved me out of his way and led me back to the trailhead.

While Jesse finished getting ready, I stuck the candles I'd purchased back into the bag and the steaks from the cooler into the freezer. So much for the candlelit dinner I'd planned, but Jesse had been pretty adamant about going out, and I did feel bad about the hike.

Jesse surfaced from the bedroom wearing jeans and an oversized hoodie. I stopped what I was doing to drink him in, regretful that we wouldn't be staying in as I had planned. My well-exerted body could definitely have used a night by the fire, and Jesse looked snuggly.

"You're going to love their bratwurst. These little German towns have the best food." He went on to describe the place he wanted to go.

"You want me to drive?" he asked as we walked to the car. "Since I know where we're headed. I can drive home too, in case you want to drink."

"Sure," I mumbled and tossed him my keys, feeling less and less enthusiastic by the minute.

We arrived at the lively outdoor biergarten full of Oktoberfest decor and a brass band playing German oompa music and were seated at picnic tables made for below-average-height men. Servers dressed in lederhosen and dirndl carried traditional beer mugs to mostly drunk revelers. The air smelled of cabbage and caraway. Not exactly the romantic theme I'd been going for this weekend.

"This is fun," Jesse said, surveying the crowded space before giving the menu his full attention. For someone who didn't drink, he sure seemed enthralled by the beer list. "I like the lights."

"I'm glad you're enjoying it," I yelled over the music, shifting over to avoid the elbow of the random man next to me. It was like the place had been created from my nightmares.

"I think I'm going to order the Würstl with bacon and sauerkraut. Do you want to share some pretzels?"

"Jesse, I—"

"Or maybe some potato salad. Do you like the mustard kind?"

I sighed, forcing myself to not be a downer on the evening. He'd done the hike for me, and I'd suffered through plenty of crowded events for Jane. I could do it for Jesse too. "Yeah. Sure. Order whatever you want. We can share some things."

Jesse ordered, and by the time the food arrived, the beer had helped me relax. We shared some great food, and Jesse seemed to like the band and the atmosphere and since I liked Jesse, I tried to stay focused on that.

I also wasn't ready to completely abandon the romance plan, but I was running out of time. "Tomorrow, I was thinking we could sleep in, try another hike, then maybe test out that two-person hammock or the hot tub?"

"You wanted to go hiking again? I was actually hoping to draw a little tomorrow, so maybe you can hike while I do that?"

"Do you want to draw me again?" I asked optimistically, thinking a repeat of our first session could be fun. Our heads turned as a child let loose an ear-piercing scream at the next table over. I shook my head. "God. Who would bring kids to a place like this?"

Jesse frowned. "I'd kind of like to walk down to the pond and draw some landscapes. You don't mind, do you? Maybe we could get up early and have time to do both?"

I gave up. "No. That's fine."

When we finished eating, I reached out to touch his hand, but he instantly pulled it back, then retrieved the lip balm from his pocket.

I sighed, a bit exasperated and a whole lot concerned. "Are you sure nothing's bothering you?"

Jesse took a sip of his water, smeared the balm over his lips, and replaced the lid. "I don't know what you mean. I'm having a good time. This was fun, right?"

I worked hard to keep the frown off my face. The more Jesse stressed the word *fun*, the more glaring it became that he seemed to be actively avoiding my romantic overtures. "That's like the third time you've pulled away from me today."

He shrugged, then turned to watch the band for a minute, before answering me. "You're paranoid. I'm fine. I wasn't prepared for such a strenuous hike. My thighs are burning. I hope you weren't expecting anything too wild tonight."

My years of marriage allowed me to easily translate his meaning. Jane had a million ways of announcing "there will be no sex tonight," but they all came with the virtually identical tone that Jesse was serving me now. Which was fine, it's not like I thought he owed me sex, but I couldn't figure out why in addition to no sex, Jesse's body language was telling me there wasn't going to be a connection of any kind happening on this trip.

"If your legs are sore, I can massage them," I offered.

Jesse's half smile disappeared as quickly as it arrived, and then he laughed. "Sorry. I was just thinking of the last time I had a massage. The therapist kept touching my ass, and I thought he was coming on to me. Turns out, I checked *glutes* on the form they gave me as a problem area. I can still see the panic on his face when I accused him of being unprofessional. Humiliating."

"Well, when I massage your glutes, there won't be any confusion about what I want."

Jesse pursed his lips. "Yeah. Trust me. I'm not confused about that. You've made your intentions very clear." There was a teasing tilt to his voice that at least alleviated any concerns that Jesse was doubting my sexuality again. I did my best to focus on being with him. That was what the weekend was all about. Enjoying each other's company. It shouldn't matter how, but as the evening continued, I kept wishing it felt more like it had when we were in San Antonio. I wanted to hold his hand and touch him. I wanted to feel closer to him, and I didn't understand what had changed, but I couldn't help wondering if it had something to do with the guy in his drawings.

On the way back to the car, Jesse pointed across the street where a row of stores were selling a range of German-themed knickknacks and crafts. "Would you mind if I pop into those little shops? They always have such cute things."

"Shopping? Really? Your thighs hurt too much to have sex, but you want to shop?" In my sluggish brain, the words had formed as a joke, but the second they left my mouth, I wished I could claw them back.

Jesse froze, glaring at me as though he couldn't believe I'd said what I said. As much as I didn't want to go shopping, I wanted an argument even less. "Sorry. Maybe I had a little too much beer. Let's go."

"Never mind," he mumbled.

Oh Jesus. If he was anything like Jane, now the entire weekend would be ruined. "It's fine. I had to do it for Jane all the time."

"Luckily, you don't *have* to do anything for me." Jesse sped up, and I struggled to keep pace.

"Jesse—"

"Let's go, Brick." He held the car fob out, lifted it, and pressed the button. I shook my head, reminded exactly of the no-win situations I'd spent the last few years of marriage trying to avoid.

I lowered myself into the car and leaned over the dash to stop Jesse from starting it. "Hey, I'm sorry. If you want to go in the shops, we can."

"It's not a big deal. As usual, I overreacted."

I slumped back in my seat. "Jane used to say things weren't a big deal and then hold it against me for days."

Jesse glared at me. His voice was low, but the irritation unmistakable. "Let's get one thing clear. I'm *not* your ex-wife."

"Really?" I laughed, intoxicated enough to have lost my usual filter. "'Cause acting like this, but refusing to let me fix it is right out of Jane's playbook. I'd rather go shopping than have the entire weekend ruined because I made a bad joke."

Yup. Two decades of marriage had taught me exactly nothing about when to shut up. Jesse recoiled, and his jaw hardened. He said nothing for a long enough period that I regretted not renting a cabin with a better couch, since I'd clearly be sleeping on it tonight. This weekend was turning into a complete disaster. I thought I'd planned this surprise romantic getaway for Jesse. But if that were true, why was I the one bothered by the lack of romance on this trip?

Fighting to keep an even tone, I reached over and squeezed his hand. "Is this honestly about shopping? I . . . Did you not want to come this weekend? Should I not have planned this? Because I can't help feeling like I messed up and it had nothing to do with that joke. Was it the hike?"

Jesse gave me a crooked grin that didn't change his sad eyes. "I kicked ass on that hike."

I smiled, grateful for the levity. "Yeah. You did. But that doesn't answer my question. Do you want to be here with me?"

Jesse sighed, tone edging toward defeated. "Brick, I wouldn't be here if I didn't. I don't do things I don't want to do, and I'm not the type of person who guilts people into doing something they don't want to do either."

I got the distinct impression we weren't talking about shopping any longer. "Okay. So did I guilt you into coming?"

"No. The surprise was nice. I appreciate it, I do, but I kind of feel like maybe the schedule was missing in my welcome packet. Creative time is important to me. Is there any time for me to draw?"

"No, because I didn't really think I needed to reserve time for that. God. I'm sorry. I don't want you to feel like I'm dictating an agenda. If you want to draw tomorrow, you should. I guess I thought this weekend would feel more like it did in San Antonio."

Jesse's eyes narrowed, and his brow furrowed in concern. "How so?"

"I don't know. We'd have fun together, talk for hours, and fuck our brains out. At least, I wouldn't be worried if my neck would survive a night on the couch."

Jesse frowned. "I wouldn't make you sleep on the couch. Are you not having fun?"

"I did on the hike today, which I realize you did for me, but honestly, I hate these kinds of places. Crowds. Lots of kids." I shuddered.

"In San Antonio we were doing stuff we both liked instead of taking turns doing things only one of us enjoyed."

"Yeah. Maybe that's why the shopping kind of triggered me. Jane used to force me to go shopping all the time. I guess that's one of the things I like best about you, you never try to force me to do things I don't want to do."

Jesse exhaled a long breath and started the car. "No. No, I won't."

Jesse

He just needs more time. He can change. I know it.

I used to think that was the mantra of every person in a miserable relationship. It was my mother's for sure. She died believing my father was a day away from sobriety. I never understood how she kept faith. I'd asked her how long could you wait for someone to change when they'd never given any indication they intend to. It turns out when you're in love, the answer is a long damn time.

I knew if I let it, that could be me. Forget January. I could see myself turning forty, justifying to everyone who knew me that yes, of course I still planned to have a family, Brick only needed one more year. But Brick wasn't anything like my father; he was kind and decent and right. I'd never force him to choose, which meant he never would.

That night as I waited in bed for Brick, I tried to focus on the here and now. The light of the fireplace flickered around the darkened room. The buzz of Brick's electric toothbrush cut off, and the water ran as he rinsed his mouth.

He stood in the doorway wearing nothing but a pair of black briefs instead of his usual boxers. "Hey," he whispered, turning off the bathroom light.

"Hi." I flipped open the comforter to make a space for him.

He slid next to me, and I gave in to my urge to cuddle beside him. He pulled me tighter, like he couldn't get me close enough, and began stroking down my side and up my back, shifting his legs until they were entwined with mine.

His minty breath warm on my cheek, he kissed me. Then retreated far enough to study my face, like he was trying hard to follow my signals for where I might want this to go.

"More," I demanded, pulling Brick toward me and claiming another kiss, this one full of enough hunger to silence all the reasons this was a terrible idea. But I didn't care. If we were on borrowed time, I wanted to make the most of it.

"Damn. You . . . I want you, Jesse." Brick stroked through my hair.

"Same," I said, my eyes fluttered shut as he mouthed along my jaw. I welcomed every bit of his aggressiveness. Met him kiss for kiss. Moan for moan. Anything to keep the energy level frantic enough so I didn't think about what came next.

Brick snaked a hand between us and wrapped it around my cock, stroking me until I was achingly hard. "I know your legs hurt. Want me to suck you?"

I felt the finesse of his stroke everywhere in my body. "Yeah."

He moved purposefully, but lightly, his warm mouth dropping barely there kisses over my chest and abs. When he'd finally settled between my legs, Brick celebrated by licking the underside of my cock and flicking his tongue at my head until I shuddered.

"Like that?" His eyes were molten, burning up at me.

I smiled, raking fingers through his hair, delighting in his earnest need for feedback when it came to sex. He'd never stopped wanting to learn my body. Mapping what turned me on. "You're killing me. Don't stop. It's so good."

Finally, he swallowed me down, sucking me into his wet heat, wicked tongue making me groan. His desire to please and ability to take feedback had proven a highly effective combination. "Yeah." I sighed, giving over to the pleasure.

My hips lifted, and he sucked me harder. I didn't hold back. I let lust take over, chasing the irresistible pressure until my balls were pulling tight. "Brick, I'm close."

His fingers found my hole, teasing my entrance. "Do it. Come for me," Brick urged, then took me deeper still. Milking my dick with his throat sent shockwaves up my spine.

"Fuck," I groaned as I came, barely through my last convulsion before my moans were drowned out by the frantic wet sounds of Brick bringing himself off.

"So hot, babe. Love how responsive you are." Brick repositioned himself and tugged my head down so he could kiss me as he continued to stroke himself.

"Come on me," I whispered, pulse surging, watching the straining cords of his neck muscles.

Brick scrambled to his knees and, eyes blazing down at me, released a long groan and came all over my abs. "Wow. That was—" He gave his weight to one arm and lowered to kiss me.

"On the agenda?" I supplied, hands rising to cup his cheeks. Eyes dancing with amusement, he laughed and lifted from the bed before retreating to the bathroom to clean himself up.

When he returned, he handed over a washcloth. "Sex was always on the agenda, but that was my kind of fun." He winked before climbing back into bed. He wrestled me into his arms, and it wasn't long before he was snoring softly in my ear.

In the dark, my thoughts replayed the events of our evening. *San Antonio. Of course, he wanted San Antonio.*

If I were in Brick's position and someone offered me a chance to have boyfriend-quality sex with none of the hard work or expectations of being in an actual relationship . . . My gut twisted. Anyone in Brick's position would want that. He hadn't noticed the difference between that and the kind of sex we had tonight. I wasn't sure if that made me feel more or less hopeless about our chances.

Because sooner or later, I was going to need him to make love to me. To hear him tell me he loved me and to be able to say it back.

I was going to need him to show up for me, even if there were crowds or small children or other things he'd rather be doing.

Eventually, during those long talks he loved so much, we'd cover our childhood stories and college memories and a list of all our favorites things. Until the only conversation left to have is what we wanted for our futures.

Then what?

What happened when we started to unpack the reality of our situation?

Chapter Seventeen

Brick

Zach opened the door for me like he hadn't just twisted my arm into grabbing a drink after the game. I was still in my basketball clothes and a lot sweaty, while he'd changed and, by the smell of him, reapplied deodorant. I waited impatiently as he chatted up the pretty ladies at the end of the bar. It hadn't been a great game since one of the guys on the other team, Kevin, decided to throw an elbow into my neck, then call me a fag. Mouthy bastard was lucky he didn't get punched.

"One drink," I reminded myself, yanking on his arm to get his attention when the bartender approached.

"Two Shiners," I ordered. When they arrived, I shoved his drink into his hand and tilted my head toward an open booth.

A few minutes ticked away, when he finally wrapped up his conversation and joined me, sliding into the booth across from me. "Christina and Jennifer would like to join us. I call dibs on the brunette."

"Zach," I warned.

"Fine. You can have first choice."

I rolled my eyes. "Not interested."

"Well at least come chat up her friend, so I can—"

"I'm tired, and I'm not in the mood to be your wingman."

"Relax. Jesus," he said with his signature boyish grin. He cast a longing glance at them and went to make his excuses, buying them each another round.

When he slid back across from me, he was pouting. "I told them I had to catch up with my grumpy recently-divorced, war-hero friend first. I feel like I haven't seen you outside of work in weeks."

I sighed. He wasn't wrong, but it wasn't like I could explain to him I'd spent all my free time with Jesse. "Sorry, it's been busy."

"So I heard."

I raised an eyebrow.

"An odd time for a referral for Peter. Sheila wanted to know if given the previous issues with the Lims, I wanted to handle it."

I nodded, relieved he hadn't been referencing Jesse. Sheila Benton was Peter's vice principal. "I heard Emily got a detention, so I assume Peter did as well."

"No, he didn't. I'm meeting with him tomorrow and, if he is sufficiently remorseful, plan to give him a warning."

I cocked my head and took a swig of my beer, formulating a response that wouldn't sound defensive. "That doesn't seem fair."

"Peter had legitimate access to the closet, Emily had no reason to be in the building."

I pursed my lips, biting back all the challenges flooding into my brain about that flawed logic. I didn't want to see Peter or Emily unfairly punished, but to my way of thinking, Peter had violated the trust instilled in him and bore more responsibility, not less. "I see."

Zach frowned, and I had no doubt he expected me to argue with him, although he'd made it clear it wasn't my place to issue discipline. That was the thing I'd never noticed about Zach until I worked for him. On the surface, he conveyed a large and in-charge attitude, but it often covered up a lack of confidence. I'd met plenty of military officers with the same issue: he wanted me to question his decision so he'd have a chance to explain his thinking. Not because he was interested in making a better one, but because he calculated that as his subordinate, I would agree, and he needed the validation. There would not be anything gained by getting into it for me. We engaged in a brief standoff before he accepted I wouldn't participate and moved the conversation to a different topic.

"Did you vote yet? Early voting for the TRE started last week."

I shook my head. "I didn't update my voter registration in time," I confessed. I'd voted absentee in my home state of Indiana throughout my military career. My voting record was fairly limited to presidential election years, so it hadn't really occurred to me to care about local politics again. Jesse had reminded me several times, but when I went to do it, I'd missed the deadline. "How's it looking?"

"Polling is tied, but we got word there's canvassing against the initiative." Zach's face scrunched up. "It has to pass. If it doesn't, the budget meeting is going to be a bloodbath."

"Who'd come out against school improvements? Even people without kids benefit from higher property values, right?"

"I keep telling you, Northridge is ultra-political. All it takes is one influential family to decide they don't like a decision I make, and every Bible study, book club, and country club is stirred up."

I blinked at Zach. "Are you referring to hiring me?"

"Well, you're not helping. The Armstrongs are pissed about Nelms and about Jared being removed from the AO team. There was that issue with Seth and Sean Abbott from the drill meet. Now, the Lims think you tried to talk Peter out of West Point."

"So, you think if you punish Peter, the Lims will blame me?"

"I'm saying I can't take a chance that the Lims will find out you allowed Peter and Emily to make out in a closet after they expressly told us they did not approve."

"I didn't fucking *let* them do anything, Zach. I sent a referral. When did you become such a coward? You can't be suggesting kids with influential parents get a pass?"

He puckered his lips like he'd eaten a lemon. "Just teach, let me handle the rest. I already have one pot-stirrer on my staff. I don't need another."

There was no doubt he was talking about Jesse. My hackles went up, much as they had when Jesse had spoken poorly about Zach. "He's one of the best teachers on your staff. He's passionate and caring and—" Zach's jaw slacked, and I forced my voice into a less outraged tone. "You should be more supportive."

It was too late. Zach fixed a pointed stare at me. "You're fucking him, aren't you? That's why I haven't seen you." He shook his head.

I opened and closed my mouth a few times, unsure of what to say. I promised Jesse that I would keep our relationship on the down-low, but I really didn't want to lie to Zach. "We've gotten to know each other through Academic Olympiad."

"Yeah," he huffed. "In the biblical sense."

"Zach, I'm not talking with you about my personal life."

He rolled his eyes. "That's a yes. You had no issues telling me about dating attempts all summer. It all makes sense now. Why I haven't seen you much and why you've changed."

"I haven't changed."

"Yes, you have. You're touchy like Jesse now, all politically correct about everything. Like that thing with Kevin tonight. You never used to get riled about some taunting."

"Homophobic slurs are not casual trash talk."

"See, that's what I mean. I've heard you say that exact word, but now it's like you take it personal. Kevin doesn't know you're bisexual."

"I've said 'fag' in reference to myself and *maybe* a few times when I was in my teens as a synonym for gay men. Not as a slur and not to mean 'weak.' It's not the same thing for a grown-ass straight man tossing it out there as an insult on a basketball court. Don't twist it."

He huffed. "You even sound like him."

If that was supposed to be an insult, it didn't work on me. "Jesse's smart about these things. He thinks about inclusivity, racial sensitivity, and diversity. Every student that walks into his classroom has free rein to express themselves. I don't think sounding like him is a bad thing."

Zach's jaw snapped shut, and he scrutinized me so sternly I half expected a flashlight in my face. "This *is* just sex, Brick. Right? Please tell me you're not falling for him and that's why you don't want to talk to those girls."

I didn't answer, but the question made my skin prickle. Our heated voices had drawn the attention of the women. The taller of the two, a pretty redhead, took a sip of her drink, then twirled her straw around the ice with her eyes trained on us like she fully expected I'd offer to buy her another. She had nice legs, full lips, a wide smile. Attractive by any standard. But I didn't want to get into that elevator, let alone push any of the buttons. Not like Jesse. Nothing like Jesse. "There isn't anyone at that bar that interests me."

"Christ Almighty." Zach heaved a sigh. "You said you wanted to explore. See who catches your eye. You said you rushed into things with Jane because they were too easy and now you're doing the exact same thing with Jesse."

"Hey. There is no rushing." I gave up playing coy with the language. Zach was one of my oldest friends and he'd figured it out. I wasn't going to insult his intelligence by pretending otherwise. I'd explain it to Jesse later. "It's a relaxed thing." The words came with a tight squeeze in my chest. They weren't necessarily untrue. Jesse and I had made no promises to each other. Maybe at first I'd been interested in relationship-quality sex far more than a relationship, but we were far past that. I didn't want to leave Zach with the impression we were friends with benefits. "I like him a lot, and it's really good. Honestly, I haven't been tempted to look elsewhere. I've actually been thinking I should probably . . . I don't know what you call it at our age—do adults ask each other to go steady?" I huffed a laugh at how ridiculous that sounded. Ever since our trip, I'd been thinking of a way to tell Jesse how I was feeling without drawing attention to the fact that I had no idea what I wanted. What was the grown-up equivalent of *Please don't date other guys, but let's keep living in our own places, and never talk about the future?*

Zach sat back, speechless. I held his stare until finally he shook his head, disappointment twisting his lips. "Brick, you divorced Jane not even a year ago, man. Please don't rush into a commitment because you're thinking with your dick again."

"That's not fair; this isn't the same as with Jane. Besides, that wasn't only about sex either. I loved her. We had a good run."

"Yeah, until you started screwing other people. Jesse doesn't seem like he's the type to be in an open relationship, my friend."

"Zach," I warned, and he raised his hands up in surrender.

"Fine. I know better than to talk you out of something you've set your mind to, but do me a favor: at least think about pumping the brakes a little. Try taking a sample size of three or four before picking out china patterns again."

I waved my hand dismissively. "No one said anything about china patterns. It's good." Jesse and I could figure it out. There was plenty of middle ground between fucking around and saying *I do.*

Exasperated, Zach's hands flailed. "You can't possibly be this obtuse. If you've been seeing each other exclusively for months, I guarantee you a guy like Jesse is getting ideas."

Zach's views on relationships were a little jaded, but his comment activated a vague memory from the night Jesse and I agreed to explore our mutual attraction. Jesse had said he had goals when it came to relationship stuff and didn't want to waste time being my big gay experiment, but I'd been so focused on reassuring him I was attracted to him, that I'd all but glossed over the "waste time" part.

My stomach turned with the thought, equally upset by the idea of Jesse seeing someone else as I was about Zach being right. Even if there was a hybrid track for us, would it be completely selfish of me to ask Jesse to jump on it?

Chapter Eighteen

Brick

Jesse's leg was shaking as he typed out a message on his phone during our hour-long drive to meet Jane at a steakhouse near the airport. I rested my hand on his thigh, but it didn't settle him. "Is this about meeting Jane or did something happen at school today?"

"I'm crafting an email to Zach. Did you know he gave Emily detention? I'm really surprised she didn't say anything to me about it." He glanced up at me, shook his head, and read as he edited, "'Detention is the epitome of a completely useless excuse for schools—' No, wait. '—school administrators to address a problem without actually doing anything effective. It's lazy . . .'"

I cringed. The last thing I needed was him to fire off a message to Zach before I told him about our conversation and the detention referral for Emily and Peter. I wasn't avoiding it necessarily, but it hadn't really come up, and now that it had, I couldn't risk him overreacting.

I squeezed his knee, partially to stop it from shaking but also because it calmed me to have my hands on him. I wasn't nervous about him meeting Jane, but this was the first chance I'd had to introduce Jesse to someone important to me, and I wanted tonight to go well. I really hoped Jane behaved herself.

"Hey, maybe you should wait before you send that."

His eyes darted up to me with enough fire, I almost regretted saying anything.

"Zach's preoccupied with the TRE going south. Maybe take it easy on him the next couple weeks."

"I don't know about that long, but I suppose it doesn't hurt to calm down before I send it. I'll finish it in the morning." Jesse tried to smile as he patted my hand that was resting on his knee. "At least Sierra is doing better. She looked good, right?"

I exhaled with the short reprieve and the change in subject. We'd joined Sierra and Olivier for Canadian Thanksgiving. It felt all kinds of wrong to celebrate the holiday on a Monday, but, my god, could Olivier roast a turkey. Mouthwateringly moist. "She seemed better," I agreed.

"Is it wrong that I'm disappointed they're not finding out their genders?" Jesse smiled. "I made a whole stink about gender reveal parties, and it shouldn't matter, but I'm secretly obsessed with knowing. I feel like a total hypocrite."

"I think it's fine. As long as parents are cool if their kid turns out different from what they expected. I don't really see the point of trying to raise kids completely gender-neutral."

"You don't think the binary is perpetuated by everyone forcing their kids into the norms?"

"No." I cringed, stealing a quick peek to test his reaction. I didn't want to lie, but I didn't want him to be worked up when meeting Jane. She was exactly the type of person to dig if she suspected tension. "It's kind of the same with sexuality. We start off thinking all kids are straight because most of them are. Genitals will usually match one's gender identity. As long as parents stay open to the idea that that assumption may be wrong and make sure their kids know there is nothing wrong with that, then I don't think we need to bend over backward pretending otherwise."

"Hmmm."

I laughed. "What's that mean?"

"Just absorbing your opinion."

"Do you disagree?"

"Well, I wasn't allowed to play with dolls because it was too gay, so I'm fairly sure my parents didn't pass the second part of your test. But yeah, Sierra and Olivier would probably let their kids play with whatever they liked."

"That explains why you're excited about the twins. Real-life baby dolls for you to play with." I tossed it out, semi-joking, but Jesse turned to me with a sudden seriousness and deep sense of longing in his eyes.

"I can't wait to be an uncle."

My mind flashed back to our earlier conversation about kids, but his wistful expression did not reconcile with the nonchalance I remembered. I racked my brain, trying to recall how the subject had even come up. He'd asked me, I thought. We'd been talking about why Jane and I never had them.

"You okay?" He smiled at me with his head tilted to the side. "You're flushed." He pressed the back of his hand to my forehead. "You don't feel warm."

His concern was touching but a little too on the nose for my current anxiety. Was Zach right? If Jesse's goals involved a husband and kids . . . He was in his early thirties and well established in his career. It was the perfect time for him to settle down, and now his best friend was having her first kids . . . how much stronger would his desire be after he *was* Uncle Jesse?

He grabbed my hand and kept it in his, squeezing my fingers lightly and casting a sweet smile in my direction that had my heart doing cartwheels. I loved how he took care of me, but that's how Jane was in the beginning too.

What would happen if he realized we were on completely different timetables? I pushed those thoughts aside and tried to think of something . . . literally anything else to talk about.

"Uncle Jesse was hot," I said for no other reason than it was the first thing that popped into my brain.

Jesse's brow lifted as though he had no idea what I was talking about, until understanding dawned on his face. "John Stamos?"

I nodded and Jesse tossed his head back. My blood pressure normalized as we made fun of each other's teenage crushes for the rest of the drive. Jesse and I had a great thing going. We had amazing sex and enjoyed each other's company. It was exactly the type of relationship I needed right now. Joking and laughing with him was perfection. Why screw with perfection?

The GPS guided me to a place close to the airport. After parking, I turned to him, noticing his considerably more tense expression. "You ready?" I asked, brushing my hand behind his neck as we sat in the lot, loving the way he pressed into my touch.

"As I'll ever be." He drew in and released a deep breath, before clicking open the door handle. I met him on the sidewalk in front of the car and kissed his temple.

"She's harmless," I reminded him, but the closer we got to the door, the greater my unease. What message was I sending inviting him to meet my ex? *Oh, well.* There wasn't much I could do about it now. I guided Jesse by the lower back inside.

"BB." Jane waved from the booth four back from the hostess stand. Her voice had always carried, and tonight was no exception.

Jesse's eyebrows went up, and he whispered, "Is that short for 'baby boy'?"

I laughed, motioning to her to acknowledge I'd heard her. "No, it's short for 'she was married to me for twenty years and still wasn't allowed to use my actual first name.'"

"Ah." Jesse chuckled. "Got it."

"Janie," I said as she rose to greet us. I hugged her and introduced her to Jesse. She hid her surprise well as she shook his hand. She was well aware of my tendency to pick lovers that resembled me in size, so I'm sure she expected Jesse to be bigger and closer to our age.

"Nice to meet you, Jane," Jesse said, sliding into the booth opposite her. "How was your first flight?"

"Oh, fine. Thanks. Much easier now that I don't have to sit next to this one. He always took half my seat."

I gave her a warning look, and her left eye closed in a teasing wink. "Jane is like one of those velociraptors in the Jurassic Park movie. She's throwing things at the fence to test for weaknesses."

"Oh, stop." Jane swatted my arm. "I am not."

Jesse watched our interaction with a not-quite-authentic smile. I squeezed his leg gently, but even halfway through our meal his shoulders were up and his expression guarded. I did my best to include him in the conversation, but Jane wanted to catch me up on a litany of folks we knew. I cast a silent apology to Jesse. He had to be bored senseless, but there was no stopping Jane when she got like this. Any interruptions would spiral into a dissertation of how I didn't care about what she had to say—a common theme in our bickering. The truth was I cared about the important stuff, but Jane could go on and on, detailing stories of people I had absolutely zero recollection of. If I admitted to not remembering them, I'd be subjected to a detailed recount of every interaction we'd ever had until I pretended one of them triggered my memory. I'd forgotten how grating her habit was.

"Jane's never lost touch with anyone. She's the consummate pen pal."

"Oh, you get used to putting in extra effort to stay connected. Did you hear the Indrises are back from Hawaii? I can't believe they wanted to leave, but Mary's folks are in upstate New York and she hated Oahu. I wish we'd done a stint in Hawaii. That reminds me, Caleb, their oldest, is graduating—"

"Jane," I said to get her attention, then gave her a warning glare that meant *change the subject*. She waved her hand dismissively, but the message was received.

"Well, I'm sure they'd appreciate you sending a card. So, BB. Mom wanted me to ask you about Thanksgiving. Phyllis and her family are coming after all, and she wasn't sure if she needed to save our room or move me to the hide-a-bed."

Jesse's phone dinged, and he lifted it briefly, turned pale, and stiffened.

"I'm not sure of my plans, but let your mom know if I do come, I'll get a hotel room from now on." I rubbed a hand over Jesse's back in silent support of whatever had upset him, but he eased away.

"Oh." Jane blushed. "Sorry, of course. Jesse, I apologize. I didn't mean to insinuate that we—" She gestured between us and rambled through a cringe-worthy explanation until I cut her off.

"I think what Jane is trying to say is even when we were married, the only thing happening in that room was sleep."

"Yes." Jane exhaled. "Yes, precisely."

"Whose Phyllis?"

Jane smiled. "Phyllis is my cousin. You probably met her during that whole petition thing. You got that taken care of, right, BB?"

"Yes, thanks." I wiped my mouth and put my napkin over my plate. "Thank you again."

"What is she talking about?" Jesse trained narrowed, mistrusting eyes on me.

"Jane's cousin helped me petition for the rule change."

Jane nodded. "I still can't believe Zach screwed you over like that. He should know you weren't going to just drop it. I'm glad St. Ursula came through; that was genius to use the all-girls school angle to get them to change the requirement. BB was always a brilliant strategist."

Jesse's eyes darted toward Jane, and as soon as they turned back to me, I realized he wasn't confused, he was pissed. A cold-electric ripple of panic shot through me. "Jesse, it's not what you think."

"What's the matter?" Jane asked.

"Can you excuse me for a minute?" Jesse asked, shifting on the booth toward me with enough determination I knew he'd crawl over me if I didn't move.

"Jesse, I—" I braced a hand on the table for leverage as I attempted to get out of his way.

"Brick, I'm serious. You need to let me up. Now."

"Okay. Okay." I stumbled to my feet, and he nearly knocked me over as he bolted past me. "Jesse . . ." It was too late, he was too far away. I would have caused a scene to yell after him. I would have to let him calm down first and then try to reason with him.

"Thanks a lot, Janie." I slumped back into my seat.

Her face fell. "What'd I say?"

I sighed heavily. "I didn't tell Jesse I wasn't able to use his petition."

"Oh," she said, looking remorseful for a moment. "But why?"

"I was trying to avoid that . . ." I gestured toward where Jesse had stormed off.

She frowned. As much as we'd bickered and fought, Jane loathed a public scene, but I could tell she wasn't impressed with my approach. "You should go talk to him."

"He probably needs a few minutes to cool down."

She nodded. "He's not what I expected."

"I know."

"He's young. Thirty?"

Close enough. I nodded. "Thirty-three."

"Why didn't you tell him? You said he was your assistant coach."

"I figured it was better to handle it on my own. Once I worked it out, there was no sense getting him upset."

"Ah," she said, a small, knowing smile playing over her face. "Still sticking with the 'I alone can fix it' plan."

"I did fix it."

"BB, you always do this. It's the same shit you pulled with your parents. Give everyone happy talk and keep the peace. Sometimes people need a chance to voice their opinions, even if that means there's a fight. The problem is you don't know how to deal with situations when you can't order people around."

"I don't recall not being able to fight a problem of ours. And that's bullshit. I didn't give you orders. Hell, I had enough trouble getting you to follow a polite request."

"There would have been fewer fights if things weren't getting sprung on me after you'd already determined the solution. You knew I didn't want to leave Georgia yet—"

"Jane." I pinched the bridge of my nose, a fresh reminder of how miserable married life had been those last few years. She kept going, recounting a good five years of my mistakes in record time. "Jane." I sighed, exasperated. "We're divorced. There is nothing to fight about anymore."

"Brick, stop being an ass. Go find him and explain the situation. You talking to me is doing no one any good. Tell him again I'm sorry for the bed thing. That was awful. He probably thinks I'm trying to trick you into sleeping with me." Flustered, she gathered her purse and motioned for the check with her other hand. I took out my wallet and dropped cash on the table to more than cover it.

She looked like she wanted to object, but I'd paid for her meals for over twenty years, it hadn't occurred to me I probably didn't have to anymore.

"Thank you for dinner," she said, a genuinely pleased smile on her face. "You're a good man, BB. Just so freaking stubborn."

"You're welcome. Can we try this again sometime?"

I walked Jane out and waited for her to get in her Uber. When I returned to the restaurant, I headed toward the restroom, figuring that's where Jesse had escaped to, but I found him at the bar.

"Hey," I said, watching him stir a cola with his straw. "Buy you a drink?"

He sent a hateful glare my way. "You think this is funny?"

"No, Jesse, I don't. I was only teasing, you know, like I normally do."

"I'm going to call a car to take me home. It's taking a while to find someone to take me that far."

"You're not taking an Uber back to Northridge."

He raised his brow at me, pretty much guaranteeing he would do exactly that just to prove I had no say in the matter. Which, fine. It's not like I could order him into the car with me. Damn it! I hated when Jane was right. "I would strongly prefer if we finished our evening as planned," I said through gritted teeth.

Jesse set his drink down on the bar with a thud. "I'm not going to make a scene in front of your ex."

Too late, I thought, but caught myself. That was definitely pressing a button I didn't want to light up. "Jane left. I'll take you home, and we can talk about this privately." I kept my tone low and even, trying not to hint at how aggravating I found this public negotiation. I brought him here; of course, I was going to make sure he arrived home safely.

"Don't you dare talk to me like that. I'm not a child." Jesse spun on his barstool toward me so quickly I had to leap back to avoid getting hit by his flailing limbs.

My stomach cramped, and my neck muscles tightened as I lifted my hands in surrender. "Jesse, I understand you're upset. Can you at least give me a chance to explain?"

"You want to explain? Okay, maybe you can start with this email I received a few minutes ago from Savannah about Emily's detention. Why didn't you tell me you sent the referral?"

"Oh, come on. That had nothing to do with you. Do you tell me about every referral you send?"

"Did you at least try to talk Zach out of the detention?"

The bartender gave us a dirty look. The manager was now hovering in the corner, seemingly ready to intervene if Jesse got even the slightest bit louder.

"It wasn't my call. Now, will you please lower your voice and come home with me so we can talk?" I begged through gritted teeth.

His lips parted, poised to protest, when his phone screen went blank. He huffed out a breath of frustration. "Great, my phone died. I'm only doing this if we don't talk about it on the way. I can't be trapped in the car with you. I'll hear you out when we get home, not before. That way I can leave if I want."

His demand was drawing additional attention. I glanced around, twirling the coaster as I considered the long painful car ride. I'd been in enough winless battles with Jane to recognize the futility of my situation. No matter how angry I was, there was no set of circumstance where I'd abandon him in Dallas, but I had no doubt he'd do something impulsive like jump out of a moving vehicle if I pushed a conversation on him. Maybe the break would do us good; we both needed time to calm down. "All right. If that's what you need."

Jesse

The tightness strangling my chest refused to relax, but I swallowed the bile licking at the rear of my throat and forced my eyes out the passenger-side window. Somehow the silence made my mind even more cluttered. More confused.

He'd told me he couldn't guarantee me the type of relationship I was after, and after tonight, I should be relieved he hadn't. By the time we pulled into his neighborhood. I was rethinking my offer to listen to him at all. I was tired and in no place to have a rational conversation. But a promise was a promise.

"Jesse." It was the first time Brick had spoken since we got in the car. I looked up as he grabbed the back of his neck. "We're here."

Hands shoved into my pockets, I lagged a few steps behind Brick toward his front door. I stood in the entryway watching as Brick put his keys and contents of his pockets on the table and turned on the lights. While I carelessly toed my shoes off, he sat in the chair specially placed at the entryway, unlaced his shoes and pulled them off one at a time, then, with a quirk of his brow, picked up mine. Silently, he lined up both pairs on the tray inside his front door as though he couldn't fathom why anyone would leave shoes on the floor although we certainly had before plenty of times. I couldn't help wondering if this was what he had been like with Jane. Had he done this little ritual after their fights even when he had clearly been the one who was wrong? If so, why?

"Did you and Jane always have a tray inside your door for shoes?"

Brick frowned. "We lived several places where it snowed. It keeps all the slush from getting on the floor."

"So, yes?"

"Jesse." Brick sighed, pinching the bridge of his nose. "Yes, since I was a small child, we had a mud room and a tray to put shoes. Do you have a point?"

He stared at me a few seconds before I dropped my gaze to the floor. It didn't matter what his rituals were. They weren't ever going to be our rituals.

His tone softened. "Do you want to sit down so we can talk?"

"Just say what you have to say."

"Well, I'm going to sit, at least." He grabbed a beer and popped the cap, taking a long pull before plopping down in his recliner. He had the wary look of a man who'd been through enough domestic arguments to have developed a routine. After seeing him with Jane, I recognized the placating expression.

This is what serious relationships meant to Brick: a series of inconvenient discussions he'd rather not have.

Brick leaned back in his recliner. "As far as the detention goes, I referred Emily and Peter because I caught them in the supply closet when they weren't supposed to be there. A rule, by the way, you insisted on. I thought they both deserved detention, but Zach decided Peter would get a warning since technically he had permission to be in the closet, and Emily didn't. And as for the rule change, I knew it would upset you that Zach wasn't being cooperative, so I explored other ways to accomplish the same thing. Once I found one, I didn't think it mattered."

"Bullshit."

Brick cocked his head, like it surprised him I'd been honest when that was exactly what he said he liked about me. "I'm sorry. What part of that do you think is bullshit?"

"You didn't tell me because you knew I would raise hell and you didn't want to deal with my opinions or have to take them into consideration."

He gave a long-suffering sigh. "I achieved the aim with an economy of effort."

"'Economy of effort'? Who the fuck talks like that? Brick, you lied. Now you're trying to gaslight me."

"I didn't lie. If there is one thing the Army made me proficient at it was problem-solving. I considered all the feasible solutions and made a decision. My decision resulted in our desired objective and, until Jane mentioned it, caused the least amount of conflict. I stand by it."

"Well, good for you. Guess we're back to the supply closet all over again, except this shit mattered."

"Jesse." Brick smiled patiently, placating me the same way I'd witnessed him do with Jane.

"Don't do that."

"What?"

"Don't look at me like I'm being overly dramatic. I brought up Emily's detention, and you didn't even mention you were the one who referred her. I told you I was nervous about Zach following through, and you told me it was taken care of. How do you think that is okay?"

"It was taken care of! I did what I said I was going to do. I just had to do it differently. What difference does it make how it got accomplished?"

"Because having an all-girls school challenge for the right to participate had nothing to do with fairness for Emily, which was the whole reason I participated in the first place."

"I know. And that was good for us. They changed the rule exactly how we wanted and there was no controversy. I don't understand why that upsets you?"

"Because you decided without me."

"Jesse, what would you have done if I had involved you?"

"I would have stood up to Zach."

"And then what?"

"I don't know. I would have sent the petition anyway."

"Exactly. Which might have set off an entire cascade of events. Maybe you lose your job or the superintendent gets pissed and cuts the budget and a whole bunch of folks lose their jobs. People like Olivier. Students would end up with fewer choices. The saga could end up in the paper and taxpayers take it out on the school. Then what?"

"You sound exactly like Zach. Sometimes doing the right thing is worth the consequences. Sometimes you have to stand up for what's right. Have some integrity."

"Christ, Jesse. You're questioning my integrity now? Do you even hear yourself? I'll put up with occasional rants and, okay, maybe I should have told you about the referral, but I've made more important decisions in a month than you've made in a lifetime. Some of my decisions had life-and-death consequences; you are blowing this completely out of proportion."

"I'm not in the goddamn Army, Brick. You aren't my boss. You said you liked my opinions. When I stand up for myself. Well, this is me standing up for myself. You had no right to cut me out of this."

"I didn't need your input, and I was trying to avoid you getting upset over nothing. It's fixed. Does someone have to end up pissed off for you to feel you won?"

"What's that supposed to mean?"

"I mean . . . I don't understand why you're so upset. Academic Olympiad changed their rules. Emily can take part next year with no problems. I don't particularly like Zach's point of view on this either, but in the end, it's his decision. You said yourself the TRE is important, and it's above our pay grade. What difference does it make?"

"'Above our pay grade'?" I repeated incredulously. "I'm a teacher. My students' well-being is never above my pay grade."

Brick sighed, and I could tell by his softer tone he was trying to take the temperature down a notch. "Look, I'm sorry. Okay? I really am. If I'd realized it was going to upset you this much, I would have said something, but I don't know what you expect me to do about it now. It's done."

My lips twisted as I considered it. What did I expect? He wasn't my boyfriend. He'd never promised me anything that entitled me to feel this level of betrayal. I'd done exactly what I said I wouldn't do. I'd given in to magical thinking and fallen in love with someone who was so far from what I wanted he might as well have been on a different planet. I forced myself to take a deep breath, and exhaled slowly. "Fine, I realize your relationship with Zach is more important to you than I am."

"Jesse, Christ Almighty. That's not fair. You make it sound like I chose him over you. Zach knows how I feel about you."

My spine stiffened. It was bad enough that students knew, I absolutely did not want to deal with the faculty and administration gossip. That was a condition of our arrangement I'd made very clear.

But if Brick told his best friend about us . . . then maybe that meant something. "You told him about us?"

"No . . . Well, yes. He figured it out, and I didn't deny it." Concern creased Brick's brow.

"What *exactly* did he figure out, Brick?"

Brick swallowed under my intense glare that asked a very different question.

"How *do* you feel about me?"

A pained expression swept over his face, almost enough to make me abandon my inquiry. Except, I didn't think I could end it not knowing for sure.

"Zach knows we've been spending time together and that I enjoy your company." He avoided my gaze. "We're probably overdue to have this talk, but maybe we should . . . Lately, I'm not sure if we're on the same page."

"Go on." My voice was tight, and my eyes burned as I struggled to keep from crying.

"I guess, if I'm completely honest with myself . . ." he began, then inhaled sharply like there was overwhelming pressure on his chest. "I'm still where I was when this started. I like you and I love spending time together, but this constant bickering and having to justify my every decision and thought process? I can't do this again."

"I see." I studied him for a minute, hoping to see something more. I nodded slowly, resigned to the reality of the situation.

"Tonight was a reminder of the unpleasant end to rushing into things before you're ready. I'm not in the market for something more than what we're doing right now." Brick's tone offered nothing beyond the words themselves. "Are you okay with that?"

"It is what we agreed to," I admitted. I was unable to fully accept he'd given me the answer I asked for. It just wasn't the one I wanted.

A wave of relief swept over his face, and he rose from his chair and stepped toward me. "I'm sorry for not telling you about the referral and the petition. Honestly, I didn't know it would upset you quite this much." He held out his arms to me. "C'mere. Please."

And reluctantly, I went. I needed one last night to say goodbye.

Brick snored softly beside me, and I stared at the wall, wide-awake, unable to get the conversation out of my head, kicking myself for being an idiot. I was angry for all the butterflies I'd allowed to flutter in my stomach the first time we'd met, for laughing at his playful teasing, for telling him about my father. For letting him in. I'd felt closer to Brick than any man I'd ever dated, and clearly he wanted to keep things going exactly as they were. The worst part was, I think I understood why. Tonight had given me the clarity of a slap in the face. Brick might be over his divorce, but he still had a long way to go before he was over his marriage. I couldn't do or say anything that was going to change twenty years of his experience of what it meant to be in a committed relationship. But I sure as hell wasn't going to put myself in a position where I was afraid to speak up for myself because I might reinforce his worst fears.

When we'd gone to bed, I'd left Brick with the impression that I'd forgiven him for not telling me about the Academic Olympiad business and for breaking his promise to me about Zach, but in reality, I didn't harp on it because I knew it didn't matter anymore. To him, we were spending time together and fucking, but without the entanglements that came from an actual relationship. Brick didn't tell me because my opinions might have caused an argument and he didn't want to deal with that. And in the type of relationship he wanted, he didn't have to.

This was exactly the wake-up call I needed. My eyes stung as the bitter truth settled over me. I had no right to be angry, nor did I have anyone but myself to blame. I'd forsaken the carefully placed guardrails meant to keep me on track and skidded into an embankment, and now it was up to me to figure out how the fuck I'd dig myself out.

I couldn't transport us to a magical future where Brick was ready for something serious. If the casual thing was what Brick wanted, then fine . . . but it wasn't what I wanted. No matter how much it hurt, it was time to move on.

Chapter Nineteen

Brick

I woke to find Jesse sitting fully dressed in the living room. Surprised, I leaned down to kiss him good morning, but he turned his head at the last minute so all I got was cheek.

"You're leaving already?" I gazed down at him, concerned by his stiff posture, and tried to make sense of the chilly reception. Jesse didn't look angry exactly, but he didn't look happy either. "Breakfast?" I finally asked.

He shook his head and drew in a long breath. "I, uh, I think we need to talk."

It was the same tone Jane had used after she'd hired the lawyer to pull the trigger on the divorce. I knew he'd let the whole "telling Zach" thing slide a little too easily the night before. "Okay?" I took a seat, preparing to hear him out and to assure him that Zach knowing didn't change things. I'd explain that I really had no choice but to be honest. He'd have to understand. "What's up?"

Jesse shifted uncomfortably. "It's about last night . . ."

I cringed but cleared my throat to hide it. "I figured. I knew you wouldn't let it go so fast."

Jesse glanced out the front window for a minute with tight lips and furrowed brows. I'd never seen him struggle to find words before. Slowly, Jesse pulled in a deep breath and met my eyes. "I think it's best if we stop seeing each other."

A shock wave of nausea turned my stomach. "Because of Zach? I didn't have a choice, Jesse. He guessed—"

Jesse held up a hand and shook his head. "Stop." I'd never expected to have the tone he used to shut down back-talking teenagers turned on me, but it worked. My mouth snapped shut and he continued. "I've been thinking about it all night. I understand why you didn't tell me about Phyllis and Zach. That's not what this is about. I really have enjoyed spending time with you, and you're a good man, but I want something different than you do."

I attempted to swallow the huge lump in my throat, but it wouldn't budge enough for me to mount an argument. Zach's warning was echoing loud and clear in my mind. "Jesse—"

"So," Jesse continued softly, "since this isn't something either of us can change and we work together, I think it's best to end this before things get awkward."

I held his gaze, still not wanting to accept what he was saying. The burning behind my eyes was uncomfortably close to tears. I shouldn't be surprised Jesse was asserting himself. It's what had attracted me to him in the first place. He'd asked me not to waste his time, and promising him an outcome I wasn't sure I was ready for would be unfair to him. Still, I couldn't let him leave without at least trying to negotiate a compromise. "Is this about the guy you were sketching? Are you wanting to see someone else? Because I'm not thrilled by it, but we can make it work. Talk to me. You can't end things and not give me a chance—"

His eyes welled red and his breath stuttered when he opened his mouth to speak. "Let's not do this, okay?" He stiffened his jaw and looked me in the eye. His voice didn't quiver any more when he went on. "I respect where you are in life. Teaching is a second act for you. You've done the marriage thing already, and I know what we agreed to. I've been down this path more times than I can count, and it always leads to the same place—a dead end. This was a mistake. My mistake. You want fun and easy, but I want what Sierra and Olivier have. I want a husband and kids. A family, and I'm never going to get it if I keep dating men who aren't in the same place as me."

"Jesse," I choked out, the lump burned away by a thick rush of stomach acid. "Please—" I clenched the nape of my neck, wincing at the sudden onset of tension pain. This time, Jesse didn't make any moves to comfort me. Instead, he picked up a grocery bag from the floor.

"I'm going to go, okay?"

I stared at him holding the bag full of art supplies and clothes, struggling to comprehend he'd packed up his belongings while I slept. This wasn't a discussion he'd prepared to have, and the outcome wasn't open to debate. He'd stuck around to inform me of his decision. As bad as it hurt to watch him walk away, I knew there was no way to stop him.

Seconds later, the front door shut, and like that, it was over.

I collapsed in my recliner, exhaled a long breath, and tried to catalog what I was feeling. I'd never been through a sudden breakup before. With Jane, we'd dealt with all the bitterness and disappointment of our failing marriage over a long period. We'd agreed on how to split up assets and handle our debts long before she'd found us an attorney to make it official. By then, the only emotion left to experience was relief.

In a lot of ways, this breakup was just as efficient. No drama. No screaming matches. Neither of us had said anything hateful. I tried to tell myself it was for the best. We wanted different things, so it had to end sometime. It was good Jesse hadn't pushed me for something I wasn't ready to give, because if he had given me an ultimatum, I didn't know that I would have turned him down. Perhaps resentment might cause it to fall apart anyway, but at least then there'd be anger and bitterness to dull the pain.

"Lieutenant Colonel," Peter said, an edge of concern in his voice as he stood in the doorway of my office.

"Yes?"

"You asked to see me, sir?"

I glanced around, trying to focus. *Distracted* didn't begin to describe how this week had been. I was a mess as I jostled papers looking for the note I'd left myself. When I found it, I took it off my computer and handed him a list of merits and demerits for the week. He read it, confusion spreading across his face.

"Is there a problem, Lim?"

"Sir, you assigned Gomez twenty-five demerits for not completing the supply closet inventory."

"Yes, it was his week, was it not? I checked the log and it was blank."

"Yes, sir." Peter shifted uncomfortably. "But when he asked me for the key, I told him I no longer had access to one, and he led me to believe when he asked you for it, you told him you no longer trusted students to complete the task. If you'd like to unlock it, I'll stay late to complete the duty, or I'll take the demerits. Respectfully, sir. It doesn't seem fair to punish Gomez for my poor judgment."

I dropped my head and motioned for the paper. Skimming it, I noticed other entries that seemed uncharacteristic for the students and probably needed to be double-checked. I sighed. "You're dismissed, Lim. And you're right. I'll correct this."

Hunching forward, I resumed the work I'd started to distract me from the hollow ache in my heart. Peter's footsteps sounded toward the door, but a few steps later reversed course. "Um, sir?"

I sighed, looking up at him blankly. "Yes?"

"Are you all right?"

That was the question—wasn't it? I wasn't all right. I was numb and exhausted from lack of sleep. The simplest tasks were throwing me for a loop, and I had a fucking basketball game with Zach tonight. "I'm fine, Lim. Thank you. You're free to go."

Alone again, I checked my email, staring at it like it was in a foreign language until it was time to go to the gym. I heard the outside door open and click shut. My heart jumped, thinking maybe it was Jesse. I hadn't seen him once since he'd dumped me. He was no longer parking in front of my building, which seemed intentional, but he couldn't avoid getting supplies forever.

I stood, grabbed the blank inventory sheet, and took several long strides across the hallway toward the supply closet. When I got to the doorway, I saw Marie standing at the table, sorting through a box of watercolor kits. When she saw me, she smiled sympathetically, and I wondered if she knew Jesse and I had broken up.

"Am I in your way, Brick?"

"No. Sorry." I slid the inspection sheet into the metal clip on the wall. "Just needed to hang this. Looks like you're busy." I jutted my chin to her pile of paint kits. "I'll leave you to it."

"Yeah. Wanted to get this ready. Need to go do my civic duty. I hope there isn't a line."

I inclined my head in question, but then it struck me that the TRE was today. Despite all the buzz among the faculty, I'd forgotten. I hoped Zach wouldn't be too much of a mess, because I lacked the mental strength to be his cheerleader right now. "Should be a strong turnout."

"No one wants more cuts. I think it'll pass. Don't you?" Her optimism seemed forced, and I honestly had no idea. Zach had become obsessed with reports of door knockers he'd heard about trying to convince people to vote no.

I knew from Jesse that Marie had the least seniority. If she lost her job because I hadn't changed my voter registration in time, I'd feel terrible. "I hope so."

"Hey, Hausman." Zach's voice echoed down the hallway. "You ready?"

Marie's expression sought an explanation. "Zach and I play in a basketball league together. We have a game tonight."

"Ah," she said. "Well, good luck."

I said my goodbyes and stepped back into the hallway to meet Zach in my classroom. When I cleared the doorway, he spun to face me, a large wolfish smile plastered on his face. I forced back the strike of bitterness, but that fucking shit-eating grin got to me. He should be a wreck. This damn TRE was the reason he couldn't honor his commitment to me. It was what forced me to call Phyllis and what started my argument with Jesse. If it weren't for Zach, Jesse and I would still be together.

"You all right?"

"Peachy," I said and the faintest irritation flickered across Zach's lips, so I cut out the attitude. "I'm fine. Let's go."

By the third quarter, I'd fouled out, and since I scored exactly zero points, my team seemed less upset by that than our competition. The time on the bench only focused my attention on Zach.

When the final buzzer sounded, he grabbed my arm and held me there while the rest of the team disappeared into the locker room.

"Okay. I let the trash-talking and bad passing go." He rubbed his jaw where I'd thrust a basketball at his face when I knew he wasn't looking. "But what the fuck is up with you tonight?"

"Nothing." I massaged the heel of my hand into my neck..

"Bullshit. Is your neck acting up?"

"No," I said sharply, but the wince probably didn't help convince him. "Jesse and I broke up. You were right: he wanted something serious. Happy?"

Zach frowned. "I'm not happy you're throwing basketballs at my head, and I'm sorry you're upset, but yeah, man. It's for the best. You obviously weren't on the same page."

"I know." I sighed and sank to the bench, rolling my neck from side to side.

Zach put his arm on my shoulders and squeezed. "Give it time. Believe me. I dated someone right after Catherine left. It got serious pretty quickly, but I think most people have that rebound. You have exciting sex and a little restored ego, but then it starts to slip into relationship-land and you realize you haven't really let yourself experience freedom yet. Now you can take the time to experience the single life. It's great, man. Do what you want. Fuck who you want. Why would you ever want to go back to having a ball and chain?"

I mulled it over for a minute. Jesse had never once felt like a ball and chain, even when he was blowing up at me. "It wasn't like that. I miss him."

Zach's lips tightened, and he offered a half shrug. "I think it's time I introduce you to the joys of being a single man in this town. You need to meet a divorcee. You won't believe how many single women in their forties are out there waiting—beautiful, smart, successful. They've done the marriage thing, and they want some no-strings-attached fun while their kids are with the ex or at college. It's the perfect arrangement for a guy like you."

A lump grew in my throat, but before I could formulate a response, Zach's phone dinged, and his face went slack. "Oh, fuck." He shook his head in utter dismay.

"What?"

"The TRE. It failed by forty-two votes."

"Shit. Really?"

Zach ran his fingers through his hair repeatedly. I'd only seen him truly wrecked the night Catherine moved out, but this was a close second.

"Now what happens?"

"I don't know, man. The final decisions will be up to the superintendent; we can live without some stuff, but we're not in a position to forgo all the needed repairs, and the student population is going to keep growing. Some of our buildings aren't up to code, and we're out of room to add portables. That money has to come from somewhere. They'll have to roll back the increased tax rate we used in the budget immediately, so this years' shortfall alone is going to be brutal. Maybe they'll finally go nuclear. They've been talking about it for a while."

"What does that mean?"

"Redistricting and merging the two high schools. Northcreek High and Middle School are on the same campus, so they'd combine the high schools and use the middle school for a ninth-grade academy."

"How does that save money? What happens to the middle schoolers?"

"They'd probably push the sixth graders back to the elementary campuses and have the seventh and eighth graders use the newer Northridge buildings."

"It sounds complicated."

"It's a goddamn cluster. We'd have to redo teaching assignments, transportation routes, merge computer systems, everything, really, but on paper, it's huge savings, and that might be all that matters. With a single high school campus, we can eliminate about thirty percent of labor costs while keeping most of the class offerings and extracurriculars. Class sizes would go up, of course, but we'd reduce facilities, maintenance, and administration costs too. Our older campus buildings are terribly inefficient to run."

"Christ, Zach. What happens to you if they merge schools?"

"I'd interview for the principal position and if I didn't get it, I'd leave. You'll be fine. The JROTC program isn't part of the same budget and Northcreek doesn't have one."

"What happens next?"

"I'm sure there'll be an emergency school board meeting. We'll work with them to see if there's a desire to put together another TRE that they think they can pass next year. But in the meantime, they'll ask me to put together a revised budget. Best case, I'm looking at a ten percent across-the-board cut, which is tough, but at least it lets me use a scalpel."

"What if it's more?"

Zach shuddered. "The scalpel is useless. I'll have to pull out the axe."

A lump rose in my throat. "I know you can't say for sure, but Jesse . . . the art program . . . is it in danger?"

Zach frowned. "Let me put it this way, if—and I mean if—I'm asked to hack my way to a twenty percent budget cut, the only things safe are the vital organs."

"And art isn't a vital organ?" I sat straighter, my protective nature rising to the service.

Zach gave a sad laugh. "Ah, no. In this scenario, the entire arts program, particularly the AP art program, is basically a pinky finger. I can't believe the Lims and Armstrongs pulled this off."

Fury rose in my chest, I could barely keep my face even as I stood. "We have to do something."

Zach glanced up at me and rose to meet me, placing a hand on my chest. "Brick, don't."

"What?"

"Don't go all Brick on me. You have that 'I will fix this' look of determination on your face that's going to end up in a brawl at a school board meeting. Let me handle it."

"Well, then you better give me something to do, Zach, because I'm not going to sit back and let you get rid of Jesse."

"That's not what I'm doing."

Jane was right: I'd been giving Zach happy-talk for far too long. He needed to step up and do the right thing for a change. "It certainly doesn't sound like you're planning to fight for him or for your students by hacking the budget. Why don't you get off your ass and do something?"

"This isn't the Army, Brick. I can't act like you and bark orders at the school board or behave like Jesse and go on a tirade to the superintendent until they find more money. I'm not going to sit on my ass, but I don't control how much funding the school gets, only what we do with it. I'm playing the hand I'm dealt."

"Since I've known you, you've always avoided the hard stuff. In school you didn't crack a book and made straight As, but if the class was too hard, you dropped it. You smile and those divorcees come running, but if they want an actual relationship, then no dice."

"What exactly do you expect me to do? Go door to door and beg?"

"Yeah. I mean, if that's what it takes. As it is, you did everything you could to keep parents from getting upset, but it didn't work, so now you've given up, and you're going to wait for orders from the superintendent and try not to piss him off so you keep your job. As long as you come out unscathed, to hell with everyone else."

"Unscathed? Damn, Brick. Tell me how you really feel! You have no clue about the bullshit I deal with. Yesterday, I spent my afternoon calling in favors to make sure the proposal to arm teachers doesn't gain traction. Every week there is a new book some parent is offended by, and the librarians will threaten to quit if I even consider pulling it. You know, I was hoping that I'd finally have someone on my staff who cares about something other than what they're trying to get out of me. Someone I can actually confide in without them worrying about what it means for them. Guess not," Zach spat.

We locked eyes, his shoulders drawn up and his jaw clenched like he was working overtime to hold his emotions at bay. Which emotions, I couldn't say—no one accused Zach of wearing his heart on his sleeve. But thirty-plus years of friendship told me I shouldn't ignore the flare of concern his expression had ignited. "You can confide in me."

"Can I? Or is everything about Jesse now?"

I might not know what was going on with Zach, but I wasn't convinced it was about Jesse. Not completely anyway. "Jesse isn't the bad guy here! He'd be the first to help if there was something that actually impacts the education or well-being of the students. So would I. As our principal keeps reminding us, we are all here for the kids."

Zach gave me a weary half smile and seemed to appreciate the levity. "I know, but you can't fix political problems by picking fights with the wrong people. It just makes the situation worse." His pointed stare implored me to let him handle it his way. "Trust me, please. I'm good at my job."

I relented with a silent shake of my head.

"What about Jesse?" he asked cautiously. "Is he worth fighting for?"

"Yeah. He is." *So, why hadn't I?*

"If you're not ready . . ."

"I think there might be someone else he's interested in. If I wait, I might lose him."

Zach laughed sadly. "Catherine left me because I was riding the fence about having a family. Biggest regret of my life."

My eyes flared and mouth gaped. Zach had said Catherine had left him for another man out of the blue when they were trying to have a family. "I thought you were trying."

He gave a resigned shrug. "We were for a while. When it didn't happen for us naturally, I wouldn't get tested to see if it was my problem. Wouldn't even talk about it. Maybe I did exactly what you said. Marriage got hard, and I couldn't do it. Maybe she was right to leave me."

"Why didn't you tell me?"

"You were getting ready to deploy. It doesn't matter. Catherine got what she wanted."

"She had a baby?" I didn't intend to sound as surprised as I was. But man, I couldn't believe I didn't know that. That he didn't tell me.

He nodded. "Last year. Used my 401K money for in vitro with her new husband too. Can you believe that shit?" The earlier emotions Zach had been fighting to hold off broke through in the form of a tremble of his jaw and unsteady breath. He looked away quickly, swiped his hand across his cheek and sniffled, before dragging his hand over his shorts.

I squeezed his shoulder. After all he'd done to help me, I didn't want him to think he was in it alone. "I'm sorry I wasn't a better friend when you needed it. With the divorce. At school. I'll try to be better about that."

"Me too." The look in his eyes seemed to acknowledge what we hadn't said. Although Zach was my best friend, we'd always avoided being truly vulnerable with each other. When we were younger, it had felt like a necessary boundary to make sure my former feelings toward him would never return, but, after being with Jesse, I knew there was no risk of that. Zach made a pained face as he confessed, "I don't live some sort of charmed life. I may not advertise them, but I have problems like everyone else."

"I hope you know you *can* talk to me. I'm here for you." I hesitated, unsure how best to say the next part. I didn't want to add an exception to acceptable topics, but I needed him to understand, he couldn't put me in the middle. Even if things with Jesse didn't work out, I wouldn't take Zach's side over Jesse's or play into Jesse's worst fears. "But if it's about Jesse . . ."

Zach nodded. "Understood. But did you want to talk about Jesse?"

I hesitated for a beat, but the sincere compassion in Zach's expression changed my mind. I needed a trusted friend to talk to—I'd never felt so conflicted. "I don't know what to do. It's not like I'm afraid of getting serious, but I don't want to make promises I can't keep."

"What exactly is he asking you to promise?"

I stared at Zach; the details were kind of fuzzy. I couldn't be sure what Jesse had actually told me and what I'd inferred from his insistence that we didn't want the same things. "After he said he wanted a husband and kids, I sort of stopped listening."

Zach shook his head and tsked. "Jane always said you were a shitty listener."

"Hey." I punched him in the biceps.

He held up his hands in surrender. "Good that we're both still young enough to change, don't you think, Lieutenant Colonel?" Across the bench, Zach's eyebrows went up and he grew serious. I knew he was calling me out on my bullshit just as I had his earlier.

It was the closest to a heart-to-heart we'd ever had, so I couldn't dismiss it.

My thoughts drifted back to my fight with Jesse, stomach clenching with the realization that I'd treated the most important person in my life like I managed sensitive situations in my previous job. Keeping information "need to know" to not lose control of the narrative. Presenting data to make it seem the only reasonable alternative was the one I wanted. A terrific way to navigate a bureaucracy like the US Army, but not so great when navigating interpersonal relationships.

If I had any shot with Jesse, I at least had to be someone he thought was worth waiting for. Someone that listened to his input even when I had my own ideas. A partner. But was that enough?

Maybe forty-six wasn't too old for a lot of things. But getting remarried? Having kids? I didn't know if I saw that in my future, and was it fair to ask Jesse to wait for me to figure it out if there was a chance it wasn't?

Chapter Twenty

Jesse

The faces of my coworkers were equal parts numb and terrified. Zach tried to sound upbeat as he recounted the latest news from the school board. He fielded questions with an uncommon amount of candor, yet most of the answers boiled down to "I don't know and probably won't until after the holiday break." So, Merry Christmas to everyone wondering if we'd be dealing with steep pay cuts, unemployment, or skyrocketing classroom sizes—everything was on the table.

Brick wasn't at the meeting, probably because it was teachers-only and his classification was a little murky since the JROTC program wasn't funded by the school. It was fine by me. I was doing my best to move on.

Olivier's leg bouncing next to me caught my attention. I cast a sideways glance at him, cringing at the abject fear on his face. Sierra had told me he wasn't sleeping, and the dark circles under his eyes all but confirmed it. I squeezed his shoulder supportively, which he patted in acknowledgment as Zach concluded the meeting.

When it was over, I accompanied Olivier back toward our cars. Neither of us wanted to stick around and listen to the doomsday predictions making the rounds through the faculty.

When I stopped, Olivier leaned against the door and waited for me to find my keys in my bag. "Hey, would you like to come over? Sierra could use your company."

I looked up from my search. "Of course. Is she okay? The babies?"

"Oh, yeah. Babies are good, she's . . . You'll be a better distraction than me," Olivier said. "You can ask Brick to join us. Where was he, anyway?"

Shrugging, I avoiding Olivier's eyes and returned to my quest.

"What did you do?"

My hand met with a metal ring and I pulled the keys from the bag, holding them up. "Found them!"

Olivier shot me a pointed look.

"Why are you assuming I did something?"

His face didn't waiver.

I sighed and unlocked my door, which Olivier promptly blocked me from opening. Stepping back from the car, I met his gaze. "Don't tell Sierra, okay? I ended it. We weren't in the same place."

He muttered something in French I didn't understand and then switched to English. "What does that mean? You two are always together."

I laughed joylessly. Sometimes I swore Oliver used his foreign language skills to be deliberately obtuse. "I want what you and Sierra have. Brick doesn't want to get serious."

"Wait. Weren't you already serious?"

"No, it was casual."

His face screwed up, and he shook his head at me. "I won't say anything, but you're going to want to tell that to Sierra sooner rather than later."

Sooner turned out to be after dinner. Olivier was reading, and as we often did, Sierra and I cuddled up on the couch, watching reruns of *Friends* and sketching side by side. My heart wasn't in it, so I was mostly doodling, half-heartedly reimagining Sierra's fish tank into a New York coffee house à la Central Perk. It was dumb, but I needed to get my mind off of him.

"What do you think of the name Phoebe?" Sierra asked.

I glanced up and shrugged. "Phoebe Lesueur," I said, testing it out. "It's pretty. Do you have a middle name?"

"We talked about using mine. Phoebe Amélie Lesueur."

"Well, it's very French, and her initials would be PAL, that's cute."

"Actually, Phoebe isn't really a French name." Sierra laughed.

"What other names are you considering?"

"We like Bastian for a boy. Or maybe Luke. I don't know about Luke Lesueur, though. Kind of sounds like a soap opera villain. Olivier was pushing for Pierre, but *meh*." She made a funny face. "I've vetoed."

"I like Bastian better than Luke, but don't you want to coordinate their names with the same letter or sounds?"

"No," Sierra said firmly. "Names are too important. I want them to have beautiful names that they don't want to shorten. No terrible nicknames for my kiddos. I'm sure Brick would agree."

My body tensed at the mention of the name I was trying to forget, and Sierra absolutely noticed. Her eyebrows shot up. "Where is he anyway? You two have been inseparable for months."

I reached for my wine and took an overly generous mouthful, then returned the empty wineglass to the kitchen. I dropped to the sofa and leaned my head on her shoulder. She raised her hand and patted the side of my head.

I blew a long breath out of my mouth. "It's over."

"Oh, Jesse," she said, straightening and turning to face me. "Why this time?"

I unloaded all the gory details. I told her about Emily's detention, Phyllis and Zach and how Brick had dismissed my feelings on the matter, then took her through our breakup and my feeble attempts to get over him with a lot of tears and a whole lot of wine.

When I was done, she leaned over and kissed my forehead. "You know I love you, right?"

I nodded. "I love you too."

"Good. So you know I have your absolute best interest at heart when I tell you that you're a complete idiot."

I blinked.

Sierra didn't. She stared at me with narrowed eyes. "I'm serious. You have to stop self-sabotaging every relationship. You can't keep ending things with guys you've barely gotten to know. Brick was crazy about you, and he treats you well."

"Why would I settle for something less than what I want?"

Sierra sighed, obviously exasperated. "But you . . . you loved him, and it's only been a few months. You think you're closer to what you want now than you were last month? Why didn't you give him a chance? You just walked away."

"I did take a chance. He doesn't want me, okay?"

"But *you* walked away from *him*." I winced, but she showed no mercy. "He is perfect for you and you're letting him go. Why? Because he doesn't want to get married after a few months of dating?"

I rolled my eyes. "No one was asking to get married tomorrow."

"Are you sure? Because it sounds like Brick said he wasn't looking for more than what you were doing right now. Not that he was never open to it."

"I want more than what we're doing right now."

"What more do you want?" she cried. "You spend all your time together, he takes you on romantic trips, he invites you to his school shit, he told his friends about you, and introduced you to his ex, which is basically the only family he has. The only things left are moving in together and getting married, which you agree it's too soon for."

"But he didn't consult me after what Zach did. He doesn't want to fight. He wants to keep having fun."

"Oh, he wants to have fun with you? The horror." She clasped her palms to her cheeks. Sierra's sarcasm never did mask her annoyance very well. "Jess, c'mon. Literally no couple wants to fight. Zach's his friend and you're his boyfriend. Or you were. I get it. I hate being in the middle of you and Olivier when you disagree. It sucks. Have you considered he didn't say anything because he didn't want to be forced to choose a side or maybe he really did think it wasn't a big deal, but that's a reason to talk, not a reason to break up."

"I . . ." Fuck, I didn't know what to say. "I can't have the rug pulled out from me again. I can't live everyday wondering when it's going to blow up. What happens in a year? Two years? What happens if I turn forty and I'm still waiting for Brick to want to marry me? I love him, I'll admit that. But it will hurt so much worse if I keep investing in us."

"Yeah, it might blow up in your face. There is no guarantee with any relationship. Could be in a year or two, you realize he's not getting there and you have to make a tough call. Maybe you reach forty and adopt on your own. But what if things continue as they are now?

What if each day that goes by your relationship grows deeper and he falls as madly in love with you as you are with him? Do you really want to miss out on that?"

"If it means I meet someone who is ready now? Then, yes. Besides, he's never been in a relationship with a man. He needs time to figure out what he wants."

"Did he say that, or have you let your overactive imagination run away and take you with it again?"

I bit back my frustration and gnawed the inside of my cheek as the truth sank in. Brick never mentioned wanting to see other people. He'd actually seemed upset that I might be. Yet, he'd been willing to entertain some sort of open arrangement, so that was further proof we weren't looking for the same thing. "Aren't you always telling me I don't need a relationship to be happy. Where is that friend?"

"You don't need one, but you were happy with Brick. I know you were. I just don't understand why you didn't talk to him first. Why you walked away from something great." She paused for me to answer, but I didn't have anything to say. She closed her eyes, clearly struggling to keep from telling me I was an idiot in four hundred different ways. "So what happens now? You go back to your screening interviews and what? Wait for someone who says 'Let's go to Vegas and get married'?"

"It could happen."

"Yeah. It could, but there's no guarantee that works out either, love. Maybe Mr. Vegas is a serial cheater, or you learn about a deal breaker on your first anniversary. Then what? At least with Brick you know he's a good guy. A man whose ex-wife's family still invites him to holidays is a hell of a reference."

I exhaled. "I miss him, but I can't gamble on him. He's going to break my heart."

"So you break it yourself first? I can see it all over your face. The way you talked about him and how fucking happy he made you. This was it, Jesse. You were in the relationship you said you always wanted, you were on the road, cruising along. So what if your destination is a little further away than you hoped? Could be you're on the scenic route. But what good does it do to turn around and go home?"

"Maybe I'm waiting for a faster car."

"Maybe you could have tried to negotiate the route with the other driver first," she shot back, then frowned. "I'm sorry. I worry about you. I know how hard it was for you to lose your mom and not have a relationship with your dad. I don't want you to be alone."

I hugged her. "I get what you're saying, but I don't need him. I have you and Olivier and the babies." I rubbed her bump and glanced up at her face. Her eyes welled red, and I went rigid as I figured out what she was struggling to say. "You're leaving?"

"I'm sorry," she said, tears bubbling over. "We're moving back to Canada after the babies are born."

A sharp stabbing pain stole my breath. "No," I managed to get out, shaking my head.

"I'm sorry. We've run the numbers so many times. Teachers are paid so much better there, and my parents want to help. If we stay here, Olivier has to get a second job, or I'll have to quit painting. That's best-case scenario, where he doesn't get laid off or have to take a pay cut."

"But if they cut the art program, my students are going to need a place to take lessons. Business will get better. I know it will. Can't you rent out your old loft above the Artsy Soul?"

Sierra shook her head. "Not unless we want to do some major renovations. You have to go through the store to get up there. It was fine when it was me, but I don't want a stranger traipsing through at any hour. Besides, it won't matter. Any money I make would go to childcare. Unless we can find someone who's willing to watch the babies for next to nothing, we don't have any other choices, Jesse. I swear, if we did, we would take them. We have time. There's immigration stuff and Olivier is going to finish the school year, and we want the babies to be born in the States. It'll be okay. I promise."

Chapter Twenty-One

Brick

On Thanksgiving Day, I sat on Jane's parents' porch swing, freezing my ass off and regretting my decision to give in to Jane's demand. Her family was nice enough, and her mother made a damn fine meal, but it was weird. The harder her family tried to act like it wasn't weird, the more uncomfortable it became, particularly when Jane announced she'd lost her job.

The front door opened, and Jane stepped out onto the porch.

"You look like you'd rather be gargling glass." She handed me a beer and took a seat next to me, tucking herself against my chest to be protected from the wind and pulling my arm around her. She smiled up at me. "Remember when we used to come out here to fight? Isn't being divorced so much better?"

I laughed. "I'm sorry to hear about your job, Janie."

She shrugged. "It was only a retail gig. I liked the people more than the job. I'll be all right. I need to move, anyway. Maine is too expensive."

The words *Texas is nice* were on my tongue, but even through we'd broken up, the thought of Jesse being upset by Jane living closer held me back. I lifted my arm, and she sat up, turning toward me. "Still, I know you enjoyed it, and it can't be easy for you navigating the job market after all these years."

She laughed sadly. "I should add 'military wife' to my résumé. Want to be a reference?"

"I would, you know. As long as it's for an executive assistant or communications gig and not for a housekeeper. I won't stake my reputation on your ability to make a bed."

She swatted me on my arm. "Very funny. How's your school budget thing? Zach making progress?"

"Yeah. He made a very impassioned pitch to keep Northridge together and to keep program cuts off the table. The school board is working with the community to see if a new package can be put before the voters next year. Too soon to tell."

"Poor Zach."

"Poor everyone. This could really hurt some good teachers and kids."

"I'm surprised you came, then. Not like you to leave when you can be in the thick of it trying to tell people how it ought to be done."

I grimaced hearing her echo Zach's impression of me. My talk with Zach the night of the election, and several more that followed, had underscored some of the changes I needed to make, and staying out of his way on the school bond issue was surprisingly the easiest thing on the list. "Zach asked me to let him handle it. I'm looking for some grants to help bridge funding for some programs. Besides, you all but demanded I be here."

"'Demanded'? That's not how I remember it." She scoffed and winked. "Why should you be alone for a holiday? We're divorced, but we're still family. My folks still love you."

"I know. I love them too, but it doesn't feel right."

"I assume Jesse not being here has something to do with that."

I frowned. "We broke up. I hope it's temporary, but I'm not sure. I'm trying to work on some things."

"I see," Jane said, using her tiptoe to rock us back and forth. "Um, do you want to talk about it? I mean, with me? It's a little odd, but I'm willing to listen."

"Are you sure about that? I don't want to hurt your feelings."

"Why would it hurt my feelings? Did I have something to do with your breakup?"

I laughed sadly. "No. Other than it happened the night of our dinner, pretty sure it's my fault. But I've been doing a lot reflecting lately, so I'm worried you'll think I'm doing things for him that I wouldn't do for you."

"Ah. Well, if it makes it any easier, I don't think there was anything you could have said or done that could have made me change my mind about the divorce. I'm sorry it didn't work out with Jesse, but based on what I saw at the restaurant, I can't say I'm surprised."

"You don't have to tell me. I know I should have told him about Phyllis. I should have told him about a lot of things."

"So you had a fight? Did you try to work it out?"

I shook my head. "I thought we had actually. He accused me of not caring about his feelings and I apologized. But the next morning, he said we wanted different things and ended it. No discussion. Just walked out the door."

She winced. "I'm sorry. That sucks."

I turned, intending to flash a smile of acknowledgment in her direction, when I caught the wistful thousand-yard stare of her profile. The expression of a woman reliving exactly what it felt like to have the rug pulled out from underneath you. The same one she wore all the way to Virginia from the second I told her we'd be leaving Georgia after a few months instead of the three-year stint we'd been expecting. Guilt twisted my gut. *You told her we didn't have a choice.*

It was an unexpected opportunity that eventually led to my promotion, but I could have made a different decision. Hell, I could have involved her in the decision instead of dropping it on her at the last possible minute when it was too late to do anything about it.

"Hey," I said to get her attention. She focused on me, blue eyes peering up. "I . . . There were a lot of times when I wasn't a good husband to you, and I'm sorry."

Jane's expression was guarded, but I didn't miss the brief moment of relief that flashed in her eyes. "I'm not sure how you want me to respond to that." She might have been conflicted about answering, but I could tell she was grateful for the long overdue acknowledgment.

"Sorry. I don't want to drudge up the past. I was thinking about Georgia. You were happy there. That little house. You had your family close by. You were researching schools."

"Yeah. I was," she said quietly.

"That's when it was over, right? When you knew for sure."

She patted my thigh, her lip quivering, and I had my answer. "You had your good points too, BB. It's a holiday. Let's not do this, okay?"

My heart sunk. All this time. I knew we were broken, but I had no idea for how long. She stayed with me for a full seven years after that moment.

I was still reeling from that revelation, wondering what it said about me. For twenty years to never have missed a detail when it came to my work life, but to choose not to see all the ways I was making her miserable.

I pulled her closer into a side hug and kissed the top of her head. "I should have asked you what you wanted more. I'm sorry."

She looked up at me, her eyes softened around the corners as though she'd been waiting years for me to admit what should have been obvious. "It's not all your fault; it's sort of how you were raised. Your dad made decisions and your mom fell in line. I tried really hard to be like your mother, BB. I wanted your happiness to be enough for me. Even back in Georgia, if you'd told me about what it meant for you, I probably would have told you to take it. Eventually, I couldn't do it anymore. That's why I put my foot down about kids. I knew if we had them, I'd be miserable."

"Then I'm glad we didn't. Maybe it's for the best Jesse ended things; I'd hate myself if I made him miserable too."

"Was Jesse right? Do you want different things?"

"That's the part I can't seem to work out. Probably. He's young and wants to start a family. Kids. The whole deal. I can't even get my brain around it. I can barely see a month ahead most days."

She nodded, and we rocked back and forth quietly. I nursed my beer, thinking about Jesse and how much I missed him.

"Why don't you want to have kids anymore?"

I coughed, nearly choking on Jane's question, and instinctively my hand flew to my mouth to stop the liquid from escaping. Using my jacket sleeve to wipe my mouth and hand, I answered, "Probably because I'm forty-six."

She clucked her tongue and slapped me playfully across the chest. "No one's asking you to get pregnant, BB. You wanted kids when we were married. Has that changed?"

"I have no idea. I just retired from the service, divorced, moved across the country, bought a house, began a new career, and started dating again. Isn't that enough life change for one year?"

Her nose wrinkled. "I'm still not clear on what happened. Did he give you an ultimatum?"

"No. Not exactly. He was mad that I told Zach about us. Then, the next thing I know, we're talking about our relationship and what I want. I didn't know what to tell him. I barely know what I'm doing right now, so I said I couldn't do more."

"Yowser. I hope that isn't how you explained it to him." My face fell and Jane's eyes widened. She sat up, twisting to face me. "You did explain that to him, right? You told him you needed time to figure out your future."

I opened and closed my mouth a few times, racking my brain to remember what I'd said. "Not exactly. I don't know."

"BB, what did you say when you were talking about the status of your relationship?"

I replayed the conversation, the parts that I recalled clearly. "That I wanted to keep having fun with him."

Jane's eyes narrowed, concern apparent. "Fun? How did you say 'fun'?"

"What do you mean how did I say fun?" I tossed my hand up.

"Well, did you say fun like 'we have such a good time together and I'd like to keep building on that' or did you use it like as a euphemism for 'don't make me talk about feelings'? What did you tell him you want?"

"What are you talking about? I said I wanted things to stay like they were. I want what we'd been doing. It was perfect."

"Oh, BB," she chastised.

"Don't 'Oh, BB' me. This is what I told him I don't want. I hate this. I don't want to have to justify my every move and decision. This is the opposite of fun."

She pushed a long breath out of her mouth and waited for me with a pointed stare to catch up. When it hit me, the realization was so sharp it stole my breath. *Oh, shit!* "Well, I didn't mean it like that. I only meant I don't want to do what we did. I want to make sure I'm ready this time, that I don't go into a relationship when I'm still trying to figure out myself."

"I know what you meant, but can you see how maybe that wasn't the most articulate way to say 'I love you but want to move slowly because I've had a lot of change in my life recently'?"

I shook my head. No one was better at holding up a mirror to my behavior like she was. "Christ, Jane."

"Oh. You're not in love with him?" she mocked. "Could have fooled me."

I gave her a dirty look, but more for being right than anything else. She tended to gloat. I missed Jesse like crazy, and there was no doubt I wanted to keep seeing him and only him. *Why did I fall in love with such difficult people?*

The only reason I hadn't tried to fix things was because he wanted something that I thought I couldn't give him, and I didn't want to hold him back. "Noble sacrifices." I laughed under my breath.

"Huh?" Jane asked.

"Nothing. Something I said to some students. They kept trying to take the blame for each other when I caught them going at it in a closet."

"Young love." She laughed.

I nodded, but as we rocked back and forth, I fixated on the advice I'd given Peter. Maybe I'd been thinking about this wrong. First, I needed to find out what Jesse really wanted. Did he actually expect an imminent proposal, or did he want to know I was serious about him and open to things moving in that direction?

Then I could determine if we really had different goals or were only on different timetables.

Because those felt like very different conversations.

The Monday morning after Thanksgiving break, I found Emily outside my classroom. She was sitting on the railing, phone in hand, with a smile as she happily tapped away.

"Good morning," I said, summoning enthusiasm I didn't feel in the slightest.

"Hi, Mr. B.," she said cheerfully and slid down, slowly lowering her feet to the ground, then brushed the dust from her denim skirt. "I know I don't have an appointment, but I wanted to talk about my drawing portfolio."

"Sure. I need to run to the supply closet before class"—*before Brick arrives*—"but come on in." I unlocked my door and flipped on the lights.

I set my stuff down on my desk and waited with waning patience as she stopped to respond to a text in the middle of retrieving her portfolio. She giggled briefly before texting back, which only reminded me of the two texts from Brick I'd left on read.

"Emily," I snapped, then reined in my foul mood. It wasn't Emily's fault I was avoiding Brick. "Let's put the phone down for a second."

"Oh, sorry." She slid her phone into her pocket, pulled out her sketch pad, then flipped it open and handed it over. I studied the drawing: a simple four quadrant layout with a hyper-realistic flower in various stages of opening. It was well done, but not what I'd expected for the project we agreed to, which was a series on gender fluidity.

"The detail work is fantastic. Tell me about it."

"Well, my concentration is fluidity. I know we talked about the body-parts composition, which I liked but didn't love, so I started playing around, and I realized lots of things take different fluid shapes—water, flowers, animals, humans . . . love. I want to do each in this same layout. I'm still going to use the one of my eye, showing the evolution of my brow line. Do you think that's too simple?"

"As an AP submission on sustained investigation, it works fine, but you've been working so hard on it, are you sure you want to abandon the original plan?"

"It doesn't matter how long it takes, honestly. I feel like I'm in a different place than the beginning of the year. I incorporated my coming-out experience into my 2-D portfolio, but this one . . . I don't know. I wanted it to be more hopeful."

Her phone dinged, and I could see the struggle in her face as she resisted the temptation to check her screen while I continued talking about the various merits and drawbacks of her idea. Her attention floated to the phone, then she flashed a gigantic smile.

I cleared my throat, and she returned her attention to me.

"Let me guess: Peter?"

She bit her lip and returned the phone to her pocket, nodding. "He came to school early for drill team, but Mr. Hausman isn't here yet, and he doesn't have a key anymore. He wanted to know if I was on campus. We don't get to hang out much except at school. I didn't see him all break."

"I'm sorry his parents are so difficult."

She shrugged. "It's better. We can talk and hang out now. Peter stood up to his parents for me, you know, because of what Mr. Hausman said."

"Oh, what was that?"

"That if he wanted to be with me, he couldn't just take the good stuff and pretend the bad didn't exist. His grandpa was cool; he's helped get his parents to back off. Peter's only allowed to use his car for school now, and my mom doesn't let me go to his house because she doesn't trust his parents, so that still sucks, but at least it's something."

Emily went on about other rules her parents and Peter's had established and how they were making it work and Peter's looming college decision, but I couldn't stop running my mind over Brick's advice. It was exactly the opposite of what Brick and I had done. We'd spent all our time together taking only the good; neither of us had even tried to reconcile our pasts. I'd shared a little about my dad, about as much as Brick had shared about his marriage to Jane, but we'd never talked about it.

"Are you okay?"

"Sorry, Emily." I returned my attention to her, then attempted to rejoin the conversation. "Has Peter decided about West Point?"

Her lips twisted, and I was fairly sure she might have already answered my question, but she didn't call me out on it. "He's not sure, but he might go to UCLA next year. They have a good ROTC program."

"UCLA is a great school, and Los Angeles is an amazing city. Strong art program."

She gave me a half smile. "Mr. Berry, can I ask you a personal question?"

"Sure."

"Did you ever wish you hadn't come out?" Her gaze fell to the floor, and she twisted her fingers into her clothing. I frowned and paused to consider what might have prompted her to ask. Coming out was such a personal journey, one that didn't necessarily offer the same incentives to gay men as to trans women, but I choose to answer honestly.

"No, I can't say that I did. Of course, it was difficult, but I always knew I wanted to live out of the closet." She lifted her head to look at me, the corners of her mouth turned down. "Did something happen?"

"No. But . . . one reason I want to do something different for my portfolio is I realized that so much of my high school experience is going to be about coming out and being trans. My therapist encouraged me to have experiences where I get to be Emily, not Emily the trans girl, that was a big reason I did the Academic Olympiad competition, but then Mr. Nelms was in charge, and this year started off with the whole pronoun thing, and Mr. Hausman wanted to change the rules so I'd get to be registered as a girl, so it kind of became about me being trans too. I realized even when people mean well and are on my side, like you and Mr. Hausman, I'm never going to be just Emily here. So, I asked my dad if I can live with him for my senior year."

My first instinct was to react to losing her as a student, but when she paused to look at me, it was the familiar face of hopeful anticipation—like she was awaiting my critique—that helped me realize what Emily was really seeking from me. She wanted my blessing.

I reconsidered my response, recalling the ways I'd subtly put pressure on her to use her art to speak for others and inspire other trans youth. I swallowed my remorse.

She didn't need my permission, or anyone else's, to be whoever she wanted to be, so instead I accepted her decision as a done deal. "Los Angeles, huh? Nothing to do with Peter?"

A slow smile spread across her face. "Bonus, for sure. But no one knows me from before there. I'll be Emily, and I think I want to keep it that way. When the TRE didn't pass, my mom was worried they'd cut the art program, so she started considering it, then my dad told her over Thanksgiving that he wanted to get to know his daughter before she went to college, and I think that sealed the deal."

"That's amazing. I'm going to miss being your teacher, but I'm thrilled for you and your dad. I know he had a hard time with your transition."

"He did. I always knew he loved me, but he's coming around. You should have read the letter he wrote to Governor Abbott. He actually said that denying transgender youth access to gender-affirming care was the real child abuse and that starting hormones had literally saved my life. He never uses my dead name or brings out old baby pictures anymore. My therapist says most people get where you need them to be eventually; it always takes longer than you want. You have to have faith in people and not give up."

Somehow, the fact that Emily, my sixteen-year-old student, stuck with relationships that seemed fraught with disappointment and heartbreak made what Sierra said sink in that much deeper. A part of me wanted to blame her optimism on lack of life experience. And maybe it was. But even Sierra, who'd experienced plenty of life had told me I'd given up on Brick far too easily. "You know, I had a very close friend tell me something very similar lately."

When her phone *ding*ed again, I gave up and handed back her sketch pad. "Here. Get," I teased. "Go meet your *boyfriend*." I drew out the word, soliciting another laugh from her.

She giggled but wasted no time checking her phone. "You want to come with me? He's with your *boyfriend*," she mimicked me.

The thought of seeing Brick made me flush from head to toe. I wasn't quite ready to handle that conversation, and I certainly didn't want to do an awkward reunion in front of students, but my first period needed supplies and at least at school there'd be a level of enforced distance. "Sure, you mind helping me?"

"No. Can I leave my bag here?"

"Yeah, we'll lock the door."

I followed her outside, and she cast a nervous glance at me that blossomed into a big, toothy smile. "I told Peter you didn't break up."

"What?"

"I called Mr. Hausman your boyfriend and you didn't correct me. Peter said he's been grouchy and distracted, so he thinks you broke up with him. You didn't, did you? Because it will devastate Blake and Jazmin."

"Oh, um ..." *Why hadn't I corrected her?* "When have I ever shared personal information with students?"

Emily frowned. "But you know a ton of personal stuff about me."

Fair. "It's complicated, okay?"

She huffed incredulously. "It can't be any more complicated than what Peter dealt with, but he pulled his head out of his ass and figured it out. You should too. Mr. Hausman is great."

I laughed despite myself. "Don't swear. I'm still your teacher."

"Sorry." She flashed a very non-contrite smile. "You know why I like Mr. Hausman?"

"No. Why?"

"Because he deals with me like he does everyone else. Most teachers aren't as bad as Mr. Nelms, but I can tell they're totally transphobic and, like, even if they don't say things, they think I'm a freak. Then there are lots of teachers like you, who know what I went through and, don't get me wrong, I appreciate that you treat me like a girl, but sometimes I feel like you think I'm weak and delicate. I don't want to be constantly protected. Mr. Hausman doesn't do that. When he came to talk to me about AO, he put it out there. 'Here's what the rules say, and it sucks.' Then he changed the rules *without* putting me in the spotlight, which was awesome."

That stung.

Brick was right. I'd been so worked up about being cut out of the process, I hadn't truly considered that Emily might have preferred it not be about her. "I'm sorry if I treated you like you were delicate. I think you're very brave."

"Thank you. You've been really cool with letting me hang out in the mornings and leaving early to change when the school year started."

"So you still want to show up without appointments and get special privileges? Perhaps I've been too lax with you," I teased. I had a reputation of being pretty flexible on those matters with all my students. "Maybe I should have been sending in referrals, instead?"

She cringed. "Let's not go crazy or anything. But, you know, when I got the detention, Mr. Hausman didn't care that I was making out with Peter, only that I broke a school rule."

She made good points. If anything, Brick tried to be fair and consistent in his approach to everything—students, Zach, Jane, me.

We made our way to the supply closet. Peter was inside, and he smiled widely as Emily came into his view, then hugged her. As much as Emily and Peter needed supervision, I was rethinking my plan to hang out with two teenagers who were exchanging enough sugary, lovey-dovey looks to send a diabetic into a coma.

"Hi, Mr. Berry," Peter greeted me.

I returned his greeting and pulled the box down I needed. "Emily, do you think you can count out twenty-two of these for me? I'll be back shortly."

She readily agreed, and as soon as I left, I knew where I was going.

I needed to see him and make sure he was okay. Maybe clear the air and tell him there were no hard feelings. Admit he'd been right to keep me out of the rule-change petition. I would have only made it worse, while he did what was best for Emily.

With a goal in mind, I took a deep breath, rounded the corner, and headed toward Brick's classroom. As I neared the open door, I stopped short at the sound of Zach's voice saying my name.

Chapter Twenty-Two

Brick

"What is this?" Zach asked as I handed over a stack of papers.

"It's the grant."

"You wrote a grant?"

"No, I found the grant. I can't write the grant for you."

He skimmed it and frowned. "Brick, this would be a drop in the bucket. The community meeting went well. The board is confident we can get the money to repair the buildings."

"But it's not nothing."

"I don't think this is necessary." He flipped through the material. "Oh. This could support fine art programs not otherwise covered in the school budget." He rolled his eyes. "This is for Jesse."

"It's a possible source of revenue. Don't dismiss it." Zach had come a long way, but he still didn't quite get survivability operations. We needed to use dispersion to limit the damage done. "I've told you. Enemy forces should never be able to use a single attack to take you out."

"Don't put all my eggs in one basket. Got it. Thanks, Sun Tzu," Zach deadpanned.

"Anytime."

"Speaking of eggs in one basket, I can introduce you—"

I chastised him with a look. I'd made it more than clear I wasn't interested in jumping into a new anything, particularly with a woman. Not that I still didn't appreciate the ladies, but my experience with Jesse had proven to me I wanted to be with a man. Scratch that—I wanted to be with Jesse, but since I'd gotten no response to my *Happy Thanksgiving* text nor the one asking to speak to him yesterday, I wasn't feeling optimistic. I was trying to be patient and follow his lead, which didn't come naturally to me at all, but that was sort of the point. "You know my position on that matter."

Zach nodded, but his attention was behind me, on the doorway of my classroom, a small, resigned smile on his face.

"I'd like to hear your position on that matter."

The sound of Jesse's voice sent me whirling. I stared open-mouthed as he leaned in my doorway. The air pressure shifted, and I couldn't take my eyes off of him.

He looked good. Really good. If not a little sad. I battled with myself to keep things professional because there were students around somewhere and Zach, whose presence I probably needed to explain.

"Or, you know, I could just assume." Jesse's tongue peeked out and tracked his upper lip and his mouth curled into an almost teasing smile.

Was he? Was this . . . All I wanted to say got stuck in a traffic jam, so the awkward silence stretched on.

Zach cleared his throat. "Okay, well, I'm gonna . . ." He motioned to the door, and Jesse stepped forward so Zach could escape. On his way out, Zach stopped next to him and clamped a hand to his shoulder. "Love what you've done with your classroom, Mr. Berry. The floral walls were impressive."

Jesse's gaze jolted to Zach, but instead of getting defensive, he smiled. "I wasn't aware you'd seen it."

"Mr. Samuel suggested I check it out when the semester started. Certainly offers more inspiration than the drab walls. As always, I appreciate your going above and beyond to help our students be successful."

"Well, that *is* who I'm here for," Jesse quipped.

"Seems we have something else in common, then." Zach shot me his signature smirk over his shoulder and exchanged a nod with Jesse that felt like a peace offering. I bit the edge of my lip, willing myself to not get my hopes up.

When we were alone, Jesse pinned me with his stare, his head tilted slightly, like he was considering what he wanted to say. It was new territory for sure; we'd never both been unsure of what to say simultaneously. "It's called communication, Brick. You know, I say a few words, you say a few words."

"Um, I may have missed the question."

"Your position on meeting whoever Zach has in mind. You want me to guess or should we try words?"

"I'm opposed." I arched an eyebrow, not sure where this was headed. Jesse had clearly overheard our conversation, but he hadn't jumped to conclusions. He'd stayed and initiated a conversation. That had to mean something, but to be crystal clear that I wasn't interested in anyone else I added, "Vehemently opposed."

Jesse shifted his weight. "Because you don't want to date a woman?"

"Because I'm not interested in dating anyone but you."

Jesse's lips parted as he digested that fact, but the rest of his face was doing little to hide how much that pleased him.

Hope blossomed in me. "You're all I want."

Jesse gnawed on his lip, looking uncertain.

"I know this might be a shock to you, but I think I fucked up."

"How so?" he asked.

"When I said I wanted to keep having fun, I didn't mean I *only* wanted to have fun. I should have said we began this relationship wanting to see where it goes, and I really loved where it was going."

Jesse's lips twitched in what might have been an aborted smile. "Is that all?"

"No. I didn't tell you about things that had to do with Zach because I didn't want to fight, but with some reflection, I realized we probably wouldn't have fought if I had actually talked to you about it, and, I don't know, maybe we still would've fought, but it would have been better than losing you or letting you think I don't care about you, because I do."

Jesse bit his lip. "I care about you too," he said softly, his eyes aimed down at the floor.

"I miss you."

He lifted his gaze and finally a real smile. My heart surged with optimism.

"If you missed me too, then maybe there's a way to—" I was interrupted by the first bell and the clang of the exterior door opening. He cast a nervous glance to the students flowing through the hallway.

"I do." Jesse's words came out rushed, but he turned back to me, eyes uncertain. "I miss you too."

"Yeah?"

A few students entered the classroom, pausing with curious looks, as I forcefully guided Jesse into my office and shut the door. "We can't talk now," I admitted, since we only had about three minutes and Jesse was at least a five-minute walk from the portables. "But come over tonight, okay? Please."

Jesse hesitated but slowly met my gaze. "Yeah. Okay. I'll text you when I'm ready to leave."

I'd been on the receiving end of some highly anticipated communications—PCS, TDY, deployment. I'd spent a long three hours waiting for word on my father's condition following news of his heart attack. Waiting for Jesse's text that day felt just as consequential.

I did my level best to move through my schedule without getting my hopes up. Fundamentally, I wasn't sure our positions had changed that much. All I knew was my email inbox was clean, my classroom was spotless, and I'd pretty much decided I would do anything short of outright lie to him to get him back.

I'm ready.

I released a breath as I read his text, nearly dropping my phone as I scrambled to my feet. I grabbed my bag and double-timed it toward his classroom, only to run into him a few paces out of the front door.

"Sorry." A shy smile played on Jesse's lips. "My meeting with Marie and Tessa about the art show ran long."

"It's okay." I closed the space between us, fighting the urge to touch him.

He peeked up at me, eyes blazing with desire, and I lost the battle. I reached for his cheek, and his hand rose to cover mine, his fingers warm. "Losing you has been . . ." My voice choked off as the emotions threatened to turn liquid.

Jesse patted my hand. "I know. Me too. Um . . . I'm parked over there, but I kind of wanted to take you somewhere. Would you mind driving?"

"Not at all."

Jesse settled into my car, and we were quiet as he navigated us about thirty minutes to a nearby town full of older neighborhoods and shuttered businesses.

"Turn left." Jesse pointed to a road I would have missed if he hadn't told me to slow down. "It's about two miles."

I drove straight, slowing to navigate the pothole-ridden street until we arrived at a rundown house flanked by boarded-up properties that backed up to a wooded area. "Stop here."

Jesse leaned forward, glancing out the driver's-side window with an apprehensive expression that made my stomach flip. The home was one story, small and boxy. It had what appeared to be at one time white siding and an overgrown yard, with weeds nearly as tall as the picket fence it was propping up. "Park there." He pointed to a gravel area two lots over.

"I don't understand. What are we doing here?"

"This is where I grew up."

I glanced at the house, then back to him. "Here?"

Jesse shrugged. "It's a little worse now since they closed the paper mill, but yeah. My dad still lives here as far as I know."

He exited the car, but instead of walking to the house, Jesse started toward the rear of the vacant lot at the edge of a poorly maintained wooded area. Tree limbs were broken and falling over, like it'd been through a severe storm, although I didn't recall any. My gaze dropped to the ground, keeping an eye out for snakes and other creatures I didn't want to think about.

"Look around, Brick. It's ugly as far as the eye can see and inside, it's even uglier."

I worried this was a kind of a test, but if it was, I didn't have the answer. All I had to offer was a hug, and I wasn't confident that he would welcome it. Jesse toed his foot in the dirt and took a glance around.

"I don't know what to say."

He flashed a brief smile at me, enough to say he appreciated my honesty. "It's okay. I don't need you to feel sorry for me or anything, but I wanted you to understand. My default setting is this. Anything I have that's not this, I had to create myself. It's one of the reasons I was so attracted to art. I was dying for something pretty to look at."

"You've come a long way."

"I have, but there's always been one thing missing. I want to show you."

"Okay."

Jesse led me into the dense foliage behind his house, and we walked what had to be a half mile until it opened up on the other side to what felt like another world. The alternating dark and lighter green mowing lines of a perfectly manicured suburban yard stretched up a small slope to the back of a large two-story white house. One of those fancy playground sets and a multiple-level deck with doors leading to what appeared to be a walk-out basement. Blackhaw trees and other plants, many of which I recognized as the fully matured version of my flowerbeds, ran parallel to the picket fence that divided the side yard from their neighbors.

Jesse pointed up. "I used to sit there." I followed his finger to the remains of a dilapidated tree house perched in the branches above us. "My grandfather, my mom's father, made that for me. I used to watch the family that lived there every day. My dad would come home and drink, and my mom would tell me to go to my treehouse. The Johnsons: their son, Jacob, was in my grade; his dad, Ryan, worked at the bank; and his mom, Karen was a teacher." He laughed sadly. "My art teacher. I remember she used to sit out on her deck with an easel and paint while Jacob played. They were perfect, I used to fill up notebooks with pictures of them. When I got to be about fifteen, I stopped drawing Karen and started drawing myself, but there is always a Ryan and there is always a son."

"Is that the guy from your drawing? The dream guy?" When he nodded, I moved my gaze away from his. Jesse's liquid blue eyes made it difficult not to say the one thing I knew would bring him back to me. To make promises I wasn't ready to make. Losing him made my chest feel cleaved in half, but I wouldn't get what I wanted by lying. At Jesse's weary-sounding sigh, I faced him again.

"I haven't seen him since I was a teen, but I can't let this dream go, Brick. I can't. I know in my heart I need it to be happy. But since we broke up, I can't seem to let you go either. I love you, and I think maybe I need you too. I don't know how to choose. And I guess what I should have asked you before... What I need to know is..." He wiped away the tears that had bubbled up from nowhere. "Do I have to?"

"I don't need you to give up what you want for me. I would never ask you to." I squeezed his hand, and God, how I hoped he believed me.

He took a stuttering breath, his face falling and tears finally spilling over and streaming down his cheeks. "But it's not what you want, is it?"

"It's not that I *don't* want it. I just..." Jesse looked so heartbroken that the very idea of saying the wrong thing—failing to explain myself—made my stomach churn. I took a quick breath and tried to find the right words to convey my reality.

"When I married Jane, that is what I thought my life was going to be too, but it didn't work out that way. The last year, I've been through so much change—leaving the military isn't like quitting a regular job. Being in the Army is all-consuming. For my entire adult life I've been told where to live, where to go, and what time to be there. There's a very clear chain of command and a very rigid set of rules, and I'm still sorting through not having that structure. In my personal life..." I swallowed. "Look, Jane made a ton of sacrifices for me, and I owed her a lot. It wasn't all bad, parts of marriage were great, but there was also a ton of guilt, frustration, and anger too. I'm forty-six years old, and I've never lived alone before. Ever. I'm still figuring out what this new chapter is for me. I'm having to reimagine everything, but right now my picture is sort of blank."

Jesse's face was equal parts surprise and genuine empathy, but now that I said what I needed to, I was afraid to stop. Afraid to take a breath for fear he'd run the other way.

"I don't know myself anymore, Jesse, but I know I love you, and when I love someone, I'd like to think it's in my nature to want to make them happy, to want to do whatever is in my power to give them what they want. But I've also only recently realized how unhappy Jane was, and I know that relationships don't work if one person has to fit themselves into someone else's life. So, what I guess I'm trying to say . . . What I should have said before is: I need time." I gestured to the house behind us. "I need time to finish my picture, but I know I want to be with you. I want us to keep moving toward a future together, just slowly."

"I'm thirty-three," Jesse said, his voice defiant and certain. "What if I say when I'm thirty-seven, I'm going to adopt a child with or without you?"

I smiled and brushed his cheek. "Baby, you could have already had children and I'd still want to be with you. I love kids; obviously I went into teaching to help mentor kids, but that's not the same thing as committing to be a father."

"But you'd be okay with me adopting?" The words came out choked like he didn't trust himself to say anything more than that.

I'd never seen Jesse so conflicted, and my body moved without thinking to comfort him. My arms closed around him, wishing like hell I could give him everything he wanted. I hated being unable to fix this, but it was his decision. I didn't want anyone, especially someone I loved, gambling their future happiness on me. I wouldn't make the same mistakes with Jesse that I made with Jane. "Yeah, I would, but I hope we'd talk about it when you're ready and see where I am."

Our eyes met, and his expression returned to one of desperation. It killed me not to be able to take the pain from his face and the hurt from his eyes, but words were useless now. He stretched to reach my mouth, and I met him. Soft and uncertain and sad, I tasted the entirety of his dilemma in the brush of his lips, but it was the only thing I'd wanted since he appeared in my doorway that morning. I clung to him, kissing him back because I needed to comfort him.

"I love you," I whispered. Jesse buried his face into my neck. "We should—" Fuck, I couldn't think when he did that. "—finish talking."

"It can wait. Everything else can wait. I want you, Brick. You make me feel . . . I just want to let it be good. Please, I've missed you and I need you to take me somewhere and make me feel good."

Jesse grunted as I swooped him up and hauled him over my shoulder.

"Brick," he screamed, laughing too hard to get out whatever other words of complaint he might have had. I charged through the woods, breathing hard as I double-timed it back to the car. When I finally set him down by the passenger door, I was completely winded.

"Need to get back to the gym," I panted, barely able to speak.

"That was entirely unnecessary," Jesse said, still laughing.

I dipped my head to kiss his forehead, transforming my expression and face so he'd know I was serious. "Your happiness will never be unnecessary to me—both in bed and in life."

Jesse shivered, and a grin returned to his lips that obliterated the last ounce of strength I'd used to hold hope at bay.

"Then take me home."

Jesse

"That's it." I gripped the mattress like it was about to take off. But I didn't hold back. "Like that."

Brick made a low and thready sound as he headed straight for my rim with firm swipes of his tongue. I smiled into the pillowcase, giddy with anticipation. He liked immediate feedback, and I was happy to give it to him. I moaned, whimpered, and cursed as he pulled back and replaced his tongue with slick fingers, stretching and teasing me with deep strokes.

"Fuck," I grunted as he brushed my prostate, my hips lifted from the bed, and Brick laughed.

"Yeah. Push back. Fuck yourself."

I rode back hard, grasping handful of sheets as he worked me mercilessly, going deeper and harder with each stroke.

"I've missed you. Fuck, Jesse. You're so sexy."

"Fuck me," I begged, not even recognizing my voice anymore. There was a rustle of a condom wrapper opening, the *squick* of lube, and then finally the pressure of Brick's cockhead entering me.

"Yes," I keened followed by a long groan. He rocked forward slowly, his closed fists denting the mattress on either side of my head. I let go of the sheet to wrap my hands around his. His skin felt hot and alive. And loving me. *He loved me and it was good. It was perfect.*

"Okay?" Brick sounded breathless as he gave me time to adjust.

I tilted my hips, letting him slide deeper. Breathing through the stretch, I clutched his hand tightly as I waited for pleasure to gather at the base of my spine, then relaxed fully into the sensation. "Yeah. Go."

Two strokes later, and my cock rode the mattress, giving me just enough friction to keep me rock-hard but stop me from coming. Brick's fingertips dug into my hips as he sped up. His sweat rained down my back and mingled with the kisses he dropped along my neck and shoulders.

I closed my eyes, forcing my brain into shut-off mode. I focused on the indistinct mutterings of approval Brick was making and the feel of him moving inside me. I needed to let go of worrying about the future, what came after our orgasms. There was so much good here. So much worth waiting for.

"Come for me," Brick begged, straining hard.

"Not sure . . ." With a grunt, Brick hauled me up, holding me with my back plastered to his chest.

"Stroke yourself." Brick's moans got higher pitched, his movement more forceful as he matched my rhythm. He kept going, grunting desperately in my ear. "Fuck, I love you. I love you so much, Jesse. Come for me, baby. Need to feel you come."

All the sensations in my body intensified—his cock throbbed deep inside me. Knowing that I was giving Brick so much pleasure let my body do what it needed to. I came on a loud shout, spilling over my hand.

Brick held me through the aftershocks. We cleaned up and were lying on his mattress, sprawled out, as though someone had thrown us there. My eyes were closed when a heavy hand found me, landing on my stomach. I gripped it, hauling it up until it rested with mine over my heart.

Despite the blissed-out postcoital feeling, questions and what-if scenarios popped into my mind trying to finish the conversation we'd abandoned. I wasn't sure I needed them all answered, but I had to do something to quiet the voice.

I opened my eyes to study Brick's profile. He wasn't sleeping, but the rhythmic rise and fall of his chest let me know he wasn't fully awake either. I wanted him so badly. Wanted to wake up next to him every day and know he was mine and I was his. *Could this really be my future?*

Suddenly, the hand I was holding moved and his lips curled into a smile. "You're thinking awfully loud about something over there and I have to say that's not really a winning strategy for us."

"What happens if I need to move?"

Brick rolled toward me and I mirrored him. He brushed his lips to my forehead and smiled. "Then you're in luck, because one thing you get in the military is a ton of moving experience."

My mind threatened to rush ahead, but I forced myself not to let it. Not to assume he meant to dodge my question. "I'm serious."

His smile straightened, and he brought his hand up to caress my hip. "I'm sorry. I didn't mean to make light. Why would you need to move?"

"I don't know. For any reason. Maybe I'll want to be closer to Sierra and the babies."

Brick's face tightened in confusion. "Is she going somewhere?"

"They're moving to Montreal after the babies are here. Don't tell Zach, but Olivier is going to resign."

"Oh, no. Are you okay?"

I shrugged. "I understand. It sucks, but they have to do what's best for their family. Sierra needs to be able to paint, and if moving to Canada so Olivier can make more money or her folks can help with the babies lets that happen, then so be it."

"Well, I'm not sure you can immigrate to Canada to be close to a friend, but if it's important for you to move for any reason, then we'll talk about it and make it work. We may have to manage long-distance for a while, but I never want to be the reason you don't do anything you want to do."

I smiled at how sincere his expression was. No smirk. No joking. He wasn't just talking about where I lived.

"You're probably right about Canada. I don't want to live in the cold anyways. But who knows with the budget issues, I could have to move to find another job."

"Hopefully no one is going to lose their job, but *if* you did, then we'd talk about how we'd make that work."

"How can you be so sure we can work it out?"

Brick raked his hand through my hair, and I pressed against his touch. "The thing about military life is there's never any certainty. Deployments, transfers, and injuries—the couples who wanted to be together always found a way to make it work because the alternative wasn't an option. If both people want it, you figure it out."

"You and Jane didn't figure it out."

"That's true," he said, a hint of wistfulness in his voice before he stiffened slightly. "Does the fact that I'm divorced make you nervous about our chance of success?"

"Honestly. Yeah. A little. Like, I don't want to be afraid to speak up for myself or challenge you sometimes because it might start a conflict, you know? If you didn't want it to work with her, why am I different?"

"I don't think it's you being different from Jane that's important. I'm different, that's what matters. I'm going to do my best to not repeat my mistakes. Jane and I married too young. She made a lot of sacrifices for my career; at some point, I started expecting it, then she started resenting me, then I started resenting her. It was a vicious cycle, but we're both much happier now. She's a good person, but we weren't a good match for a lot of reasons." Brick laced his fingers with mine, then lifted our joined hands to his lips and pressed a gentle kiss to the back of my palm. "Speaking of Jane . . . I wanted to tell you that I spent Thanksgiving with her and her family. I stayed at a hotel, but I want to be honest with you."

"I see," I said, processing the news to determine if it bothered me. I wasn't really that surprised by it. He did tell me that he'd been invited, and we weren't together at the time.

"Does that upset you?"

I wrinkled my nose. "No, but is that something you're going to do every year? Like, would you spend Christmas with her too?"

"Jane's always going to invite me for the holidays because since my parents died, her family is my family. I don't have to go if we have other plans, but I would like them to know you."

"You want to introduce me to your family?"

"Yes, and I know Zach isn't your favorite person, but if we're going to be together, then I want you to get to know him as my best friend, not our boss."

"Zach," I whined, half-joking as I attempted to roll away from him and onto my back.

Brick chuckled and wrapped his much longer leg over my thighs, keeping me on my side, tucked against him. "I know it's asking a lot, but yeah. I want us to be in each other's lives, Jesse. No secrets. No keeping it quiet. I want the fact that I'm dating a great guy to be public knowledge."

"Okay. Okay. Yes. Let's do it," I said, laughing as I fully surrendered to our position and his requests. His breath caught, and the brevity slipped away for a moment as we gazed at each other, confidence surging between us.

"Yeah?" He brushed my cheek in an unspoken acknowledgment of the future he was offering and the pace I was agreeing to.

I nodded. "Yeah. I'll give Zach a chance."

He smiled, shaking his head in amusement. "Good. One last thing."

I laughed. "Hey, I didn't know this was a negotiation. When do I get to make my list of demands?"

"Go ahead."

"No, finish your list and then we get to mine."

"I love bantering with you and teasing you about your idiosyncrasies. I need that in my life. I can be serious when you need me to be, and we can talk about the future. You can talk to me about whatever's going on in your head, but no matter what, I don't want to lose the fun. You make me laugh, and one thing I wish I hadn't done in the past was let all the serious, mundane life crap take over and turn me into a cranky bastard."

"Fun, got it." I laughed. "Is it my turn?" I said eagerly.

"Yeah. Let's see, I asked for three things, so hit me with the relationship demands."

I really only had one request, so I thought of the other two on the fly.

"You have to talk to me, even if you don't think I'll be happy about it. My imagination will always be worse than whatever you don't tell me. I promise."

"I get that now."

"I need plenty of creative time."

Brick blew out a breath of relief, since he'd already learned that about me. "Easy. You got it. You can draw me naked as much as you want or, you know, other guys too, if that's what you need."

"You really don't get jealous, huh?"

Brick shook his head emphatically. "Not when I trust someone. I know too many guys who spent their deployments obsessed with what their girl was up to, but I never understood it. Either you trust them or what's the point of being in a relationship?"

"I do trust you and I know you and Jane had an arrangement, but I need monogamy. I can't see myself ever being okay with anything else."

Brick smiled. "Absolutely not a problem."

"Okay, so do we, like, shake on it or something?" I laughed at the relative ease of our conversation. It felt like finally we were on the same page.

"No." Brick rolled onto his back and pulled me on top of him, with a mischievous grin—the same knowing smile and twinkling eyes that said he absolutely thought I'd be putty in his rather large hands. "Oh, I think we can do way better than a handshake."

Chapter Twenty-Three

Jesse

"Hey, Mama." I ushered Sierra into Brick's house, and Olivier trailed behind us with some sort of covered dish. No matter how many times Sierra cautioned me to relax, I was a little nervous for Brick's and my first mutually hosted dinner party.

I helped Sierra settle into the recliner. "Feet up or down?"

Olivier laughed, and Sierra gave him a dirty look before answering, "Definitely up."

"She's been swelling like crazy. Her ankles are the size of grapefruits." Olivier settled the tray on the table and pulled off the cover. "I brought some baked brie in puff pastry. Sierra's been craving it."

I flipped the lever to bring up the ottoman, when the patio opened, and Zach and Brick stepped inside from the deck.

"Wow, Olivier, I didn't know your wife was expecting."

Zach stepped forward, hand outstretched, when Sierra said, "Expecting what?"

Zach stopped dead in his tracks, eyes widened comically and face brightening. Even his ears turned fire engine red.

I stifled a laugh and tapped Sierra lightly on the shoulder, trying not to make eye contact with Brick, who hid his laughter behind a swig of his drink.

Olivier broke first. "Sierra's been getting a lot of mileage out of that one lately. We're expecting twins in March."

The relief on Zach's face almost made me feel sorry for him.

"You're evil," I chastised Sierra.

Sierra flashed a wicked smile and rubbed her bump mischievously. "Sorry, Zach. Pregnant lady prerogative. It's in the handbook."

Zach shook his head, stepping forward to complete the handshake he'd abandoned. "You got me. I was about ready to find a hole to crawl in."

"Drinks?" Brick offered, clamping Zach on the shoulder as they exchanged a look of amusement.

"Beer," Zach and Olivier said simultaneously.

"Water is good," Sierra said.

While he went to fill drink orders, Sierra and Olivier chatted happily with Zach, who visibly relaxed as the conversation moved from school budget worst-case scenarios to Christmas plans.

"Brick and I are thinking of going on a trip," I said.

"Oh, where?" Sierra asked. "Maybe you can finally go to Europe."

Olivier clucked his tongue. "Do not make your first trip to France in the winter. Maybe Germany—the Christmas markets are wonderful."

I laughed. "You do know we're teachers, right? We were thinking of Florida. Europe is going to require planning and some level of confidence I'm going to have a job next fall."

Brick smiled and rested his hand on my shoulder. "I'd love to go to Paris with you."

"Are you crazy? If you take me to Paris, you're going to have to shop."

"I'm aware. Maybe next summer. We'll figure it out." He winked at me.

We kept chatting as Brick went in and out to the grill, and tried not to discuss work, but it seemed to be on everyone's mind, so came up again as we sat down to eat.

"Is there *any* news you can share on the school board meeting?" I asked. "It'd be nice to know if the rumors are true."

Zach sat up straighter. "What are the rumors?"

"That there's going to be a five-hundred-dollar fee for sports and fine arts activities. It's ludicrous."

"I just hope the campus merger doesn't happen. If it does, foreign languages is going to be hit very hard." Olivier frowned.

Zach nodded sympathetically. "I know you're not in a great position if that happens."

"It won't matter," I mumbled and took a bite.

"Why won't it matter?" Zach asked, confused.

The conversation fell silent, as Olivier and Sierra shot me a dirty look, which was when I remembered Olivier hadn't resigned yet. "Shit." I cringed. "I'm sorry." I jokingly scowled at Brick. "This is why you're not supposed to be friends with your boss."

"Um, well," Oliver said nervously. "This isn't exactly how I planned to notify you, and we were waiting for all the immigration stuff to be finalized, but Sierra and I are planning to relocate to Montreal when the school year is over."

"Oh," Zach said. "The merger is really the last resort. I'm optimistic—"

"It's not that. We'd decided to move regardless if the TRE passed. We simply can't afford two babies on our income, and without affordable childcare, Sierra can't run the store and paint."

Sierra started crying.

"Oh, honey." I rushed up to get her a tissue. Standing behind her, I rubbed her back while she gathered herself.

"I'm sorry," Sierra said through the sobs. "It's these damn hormones. I never used to cry at all, but I love the Artsy Soul and I poured my heart into it. I don't want to leave. We asked a contractor for estimates to build a staircase and entrance to the upstairs unit, thinking if we could rent it, it might be enough extra to make it work. It was way out of our budget."

I retook my seat as she calmed down. "Maybe someone at the school needs a place? At least then it wouldn't be a stranger."

"We've asked." Olivier shook his head.

The conversation continued as Zach offered possible solutions that Olivier and Sierra had already considered. I grew increasingly frustrated. There had to be some way. "God, I wish there was something I could do. I'd do anything to keep you guys here."

Brick leaned over and whispered in my ear, "What if there was?"

I twisted to face him. "What?" My question came out louder than I'd intended and the entire table stopped speaking and stared at Brick.

"Um." Brick straightened, seemingly very uncertain. "Maybe we should talk alone, first."

"Brick, c'mon. I'm desperate. If you have an idea, share it."

Brick hesitated, glancing at Zach briefly before answering. "So, it's only an idea. You may hate it, but I think I know someone who can help."

"Who?" Sierra and I shouted in unison.

"Jane. She's been having difficulty finding a job, and she's mentioned she'd like to move. She might be willing to help with the babies for a discount on rent. She did a ton of childcare through the years. She's really good with babies."

Zach laughed. "Oh, Lord."

I snapped my attention to him. "What's that mean?"

Zach's amused expression sobered into concern. "Nothing. It's actually kind of perfect. Jane's great with kids, but I was just picturing her living close to Brick again."

Brick shook his head. "I have no issues with Jane living close by if Jesse doesn't. As long as it's not in my house. She's not exactly the tidiest person," he warned Sierra.

"Would you . . ." Sierra studied me. "Would you be okay with that?"

Olivier rested his hand over Sierra's. "Perhaps we need to let Jesse and Brick talk about that alone."

I glanced at Brick then Zach and back again, my brain searching for hidden subtext before I could stop myself. Until I realized what I was doing. I didn't need to look for ulterior motives. Not with Brick. A sense of calm settled over me. It made sense why he wanted to talk to me alone first, and I appreciated his prioritizing my feelings over his need to fix things. "If this helps Jane and you guys get to stay here, I'm all for it."

Brick's eyes widened. "Are you sure?"

I leaned over to kiss the worry from his face. "We'll figure it out, right?" I winked.

"Yeah," he said with a knowing smile. "We'll always figure it out." Brick kissed me a little too enthusiastically, and I couldn't help the whine of neediness that escaped.

Zach choked on his beer mid-sip. "Damn," he said, reaching for a napkin to clean up.

I returned to my chair, panting to catch my breath. "Hey, Brick had to watch you lose your virginity. You can handle a kiss."

Zach's eyes bugged out as Sierra and Olivier shared an amused chuckle.

"Oh, I need to hear this story," Sierra said.

"No," Brick and Zach reacted in unison. Brick cleared his throat. "No one needs to hear that story. Zach, you never finished telling us about the school board meeting."

"I do actually have news. Among friends, and not faculty, of course."

We all nodded, acknowledging the sensitivity of information.

"Shockingly, the Lims, Armstrongs, and Abbotts are getting some serious social backlash for their efforts to kill the TRE. Apparently, people were not aware that the 'merging schools' option would result in far fewer spots on varsity sports teams. Several of our football parents were very upset."

I rolled my eyes. "As usual, almighty football cannot be touched."

Zach confirmed with a nod. "So, looks like campus merging and rezoning are off the table, and we now have the board votes to raise the debt limit, which doesn't need to go to the voters. That means we can do the repairs, but it's not quite enough to address the overcrowding issue, so that's being coupled with an extra class period for the middle and high school teachers next year."

Brick, Olivier, and I groaned at the mention of longer workdays.

"I know," Zach acknowledged. "But it buys us time, and we can teach more kids with the same number of teachers and not increase class size. Plus it avoids layoffs. Then next year, we're going to try again with a penny swap."

"What's a penny swap?" Sierra asked.

"There's basically two budgets for the district. The operations budget and the budget we use to pay debt. You can't use the debt budget to pay for operations. In a penny swap, we increase the tax rate to the operations budget but offset it by lowering the tax rate from the debt budget. So essentially, we get more money for operations without raising taxes. About the only thing we can't do is build a new math and science building, so everyone is going to stay where they are classroom-wise."

"It sounds like a good plan," I said.

Zach dropped his fork, mouth gaped as he stared at me.

"What?"

"Did Mr. Berry just compliment me on my plans?" Zach teased.

"Oh, shut up. I'm not that bad."

Sierra laughed out loud, and I glowered at her. "What? I'm not. The portables are growing on me. and the closet is working out okay now that I've arranged it properly."

"Whatever you say, love." Brick patted my head playfully. "He's not good with apologies," he stage-whispered to Zach.

"Fine. Yes, I think this is a solid plan. I'll even teach the extra period with a minimum of complaints. You know, 'for the kids.'"

Zach turned to Brick, smirking. "If I only knew regular sex was all it took to make Mr. Berry reasonable, my life would have been so much easier. If you value our friendship, you will never break up with him."

"Well, if you insist."

"Hey," I objected, but it was too late. Sierra and Olivier joined in, each taking a turn to tease us and conjure ever increasingly interesting ways for Brick to deescalate my temper. When Brick's phone rang, he left the table to retrieve it.

"It's Jane," he announced. "Should I mention the thing?"

I glanced over at Sierra, whose hopeful expression gave me a sense of complete confidence I was doing the right thing. "If you're okay with it and Sierra and Olivier are interested, I think we figured it out."

Chapter Twenty-Four

Brick

Eight months later . . .

"*B*onjour, lover." Jesse pulled open the curtain of our flat to reveal a sunny, Parisian summer morning. "It gets me every time," he declared, beaming at the view.

I cast my eyes at him. Sunbeams bathed him in natural light, like the heavens wanted a spotlight on his long, lean torso and the swell of his ample ass. "I agree." I laughed. "The Eiffel Tower isn't too bad either."

Jesse twisted, smiling at me. I pulled back the white duvet and patted the mattress. "Come here."

He crossed the room and put his knee on the bed as his gaze ran down my naked body. Reaching out, he stroked a hand over my chest hair. "You're so freaking sexy like this, but if I get into this bed, we will not make it to the Louvre today, and it's our last full day in Paris."

"We will. I just want to say a proper good morning first . . ." I yanked him down and pulled him on top of me. He pecked my lips with his and laughed when I tickled that little spot behind his ear.

I studied his face and nipped at his plump, pink lips. "The French way." I kissed him, my tongue pressed to the seam of his mouth until he opened for me.

We made out like we had all the time in the world, leisurely and luxuriously. I slid my tongue over his, tracing the contours of his mouth, and retreating to nibble his lips before diving back in. My hands roamed his body. Months of learning how to make him moan and writhe had paid off—I knew his body as well as I knew my own now. Knew exactly what all the buttons did. Which ones to press and which ones to avoid. I'd never know another man like I knew him.

Jesse slid his legs over my thighs until he was kneeling on the mattress. He pressed one hand to my chest for leverage and rocked up, using the other to position my cock to his opening. Panting, he slid down me without warning. I still gasped at the sensation of being inside him with no barrier.

Jesse lifted and rocked his hips, making love to me so passionately my eyes rolled back in my head. "Fuck, baby." I grabbed his cock and gave him my fist to fuck. "Yeah," I moaned. "So perfect." I lassoed my hand around his neck and pulled him down to kiss him but only managed hot panting into his mouth between murmurs of pleasure and whispered curses.

I knew immediately when I struck my favorite button. His eyes lit up and he tipped his head ever so slightly, then pressed up with a palm to my chest and rode me harder. "Faster, Brick. I'm close."

"Yeah. Come with me." I bent my knees and pistoned my hips, thrusting inside him. He met me stroke for stroke, almost violently chasing his release, and mine, since the feel of his throbbing ass usually sent me over the edge. When he let go, it was beautiful. Utterly breathtaking. Afterwards, he flopped onto the sheet beside me, breathing fast, always pleased with himself when we came together, and laughed. "Good morning."

"Just good?"

He tapped my jaw playfully. "A healthy dose of stars were seen." He pinched my cheeks and gave me another hard kiss before he went to clean up. "Don't fall back to sleep, Bainbridge. I mean it."

I scowled, but somehow over the past year, Jesse had joined the club of one who got to use my first name occasionally without penalty. While Jesse was in the shower, I rose from the bed and found the small key ring I'd bought covertly on one of our shopping trips. I fingered it, butterflies swirling inside me.

It'd taken lots of words and late night heart-to-hearts, but Jesse and I had finally found a sweet spot with communication, particularly when it came to our future. I'd committed to always telling him where my head was at so he never had to guess or feel like he was pressuring me into moving faster than I was ready for. He'd committed to telling me when he was anxious about our relationship not progressing so I had a chance to address his fears. It'd been over three months since we'd last discussed moving in together. At that time, I'd told him I wasn't ready and we'd agreed to revisit the decision when his lease was up at the end of the year. But in the weeks leading up to our trip, something had changed for me. Every time he'd mentioned needing to go home to pick something up or wanting to sleep in his bed, I'd felt the sting of regret. I wanted my home to be his home. My bed to be his bed.

I'd decided I wouldn't ask him immediately. I needed to make absolutely sure I was ready. That nothing would arise during our extended trip that would cause me to have any doubts. I'd worried I set the bar too high, but to my surprise, I'd met it. I had zero doubts I wanted to wake up every morning with Jesse. Today, I would make good on my promise.

We finished dressing and strolled arm in arm to a small café we'd discovered earlier in our trip. Olivier would probably be horrified, but while we'd made a healthy dent in the list of must-try restaurants he'd given us, I'd eaten an entire bakery's worth of croissants over the last thirteen days.

We took a seat, and Jesse ordered for me since his French was at least conversational.

"Are you sad we're leaving tomorrow?"

Jesse beamed at me, a knowing smile playing on his lips. "Not at all, two weeks was plenty. I can't wait to get home to see the babies."

It was unexpected, but Bastian and Phoebe's arrival introduced some flexibility to Jesse's stance on future parenthood, almost as much as it helped me wrap my brain around its merits. We agreed the babies were adorable, and while we both loved being around them, Jesse confessed the up-close vantage point of parenthood was a fair bit different from the perspective he'd drawn from his treehouse. Now, the topic was something he went back and forth on, depending on how recently we'd spent time with the twins, which was often. Jesse thought with our lifestyle, maybe skipping the newborn stages and adopting an older child would be a better fit. Lately, he'd been researching the requirements for foster parenting. We talked to one of our colleagues who fostered, and she'd told us with my military background and Jesse's own experiences combined with his gift to help kids express themselves through art, we could be a perfect balance for a child coming from an abuse and neglect situation. It was a lot to think about, but we still had time to figure it out.

"Have you talked to Jane?" he asked.

"Not since last week. Did Sierra say how it's working out?"

"Kind of perfectly it sounds like. Jane's all settled in. Sierra opens at ten or works in the studio in the morning, and when one of the babies needs to nurse, Jane will come downstairs and mind the store for her. Olivier is done with summer school at three, so he picks them up and takes them home. Then Jane helps Sierra close so she can get out of there at a decent hour. She offered to help keep books and do some other administrative tasks too."

"Jane would be great at that. She loves the loft and she was thrilled to not have to pay rent, and with my retirement pay, that's all she really needed. Are you still feeling okay about her living so close?"

"Yes," Jesse answered. "Thank you for asking, but it's good. Really. I'll tell you if I start to have a problem. We'll figure it out, right?"

"Always." I kissed him and flagged the server for our check.

After we'd eaten, we took a taxi to the Louvre; the landmark pyramid entrance was overrun by tourists, but neither of us was bothered. Like all of our explorations, Jesse was excited for the experience and waited in line with the same anticipation of a kid at Disney. His enthusiasm was more than enough to keep me entertained.

We went through the museum at a snail's pace. Jesse preferred to hone in on specific pieces of interest, whereas I liked to peruse the room and read all the descriptions. We'd go room by room, and when we finished each section, he'd tell me about his favorite and help me see it from an artist's perspective, and I'd give him a rundown of any interesting history I'd picked up.

The method had worked well for us the entire trip, and since next year's Academic Olympiad theme was announced to be "Great Civilizations of Antiquity," we'd gathered a ton of pictures and factoids for the team to use.

I found an entirely new appreciation for the city now that I wasn't being dragged through it at breakneck speed because Jane was in a rush to go shopping. That was one thing about being with Jesse I found so perfect. We enjoyed doing things together, but we gave each other space to enjoy our own interests too. He'd sit and draw while I watched football. I'd sit outside on the deck with him, listening to music or reading while he painted. I joined him on some of his shopping trips and did my own thing during others. He never made me feel guilty or acted bored. I loved that. I loved knowing that he'd be by my side but that I had the time to rediscover myself and what I wanted from my second phase of life.

The time went by quickly, but the museum was huge, and our feet wore out before our brains did. When we returned to street level, Jesse started toward the Seine, but I slowed him.

"Aren't you getting hungry?" Jesse asked as he tucked his arm around my waist and smiled up at me. "There's a place on Olivier's list I wanted to try tonight."

"As long as we can take a taxi," I said with a wince.

"Oh, babe. You tired? Should we sit for a minute?"

He pointed to an empty bench, and we plopped down together, people-watching all of the folks taking pictures with the giant glass pyramid in the background. With lazy hands, Jesse started rubbing my nape. He did that all the time now, even when it wasn't hurting. It was how he took care of me. It was why I wanted to take care of him. I peeked over at him and this feeling—every bit as strong as the one I'd had my first deployment and that first day in the classroom.

I was in the future . . .

With my future.

My life fit perfectly with Jesse's because he was my life now. Warmth filled my chest and despite my plans for this to happen over dinner, I couldn't hold it in anymore.

"Hey, Jesse." I took his hand.

"Yeah?"

He glanced over at me, eyes squinting into the sun. I leaned forward so I could see his face. One last check to make certain I wasn't being swept away by the romanticism of Paris. When he turned to me, the warm feeling intensified into longing. A desire to make him mine. In every way that mattered. I had it in my power to make this man's dreams come true and, damn it, I was going to do just that.

"Um . . ." My hands were slippery, and I almost dropped the key as I fished it from my pocket. With a deep breath, I lowered to one knee.

"Brick, what are you—" Jesse's eyes went wide, and he gaped at me, which might have been because he thought I was crazy. His gaze flew to the shiny object in my hand and he gasped, "Oh. My. God."

I laughed, shaking my head. Realizing my rehearsed comments would not work any longer. I grabbed his hand and kept it in mine, then spoke from the heart.

Looking down at where our hands were joined, I explained what I was feeling. "So, I know this isn't a ring. It was supposed to be my way of asking you to move in with me. A symbol of my commitment to you. I didn't want it to be something that only lets you into my home. I wanted you to think of it as the key to my heart because it's already yours, Jesse." I glanced up to see his eyes welling red, brimming with tears. "This trip has shown me I don't know how to be without you anymore. I don't *want* to be without you. Jesse, will you marry me?"

Jesse began sobbing, and for the span of my erratic heartbeat, I worried that not having the ring had spoiled his image of the perfect proposal, but within a few milliseconds, there was a softening in his body and an excited cast in his expression when he nodded and shouted, "Yes! Of course!" and catapulted off the bench and into my arms.

Applause resounded from the crowd we'd attracted, but I blocked them out, focused solely on Jesse and the joy he radiated as he kissed me. A few moments later, the crowd had moved on, leaving us in silence to digest the seismic shift my impulsive move had taken our relationship. I stood, pulled him to his feet, and grabbed his hand, then, turning it palm side up, dropped the small silver key chain and key into it and curled his fingers around it, holding his hand there.

"It's yours. We can find you a ring as soon as we get back. Whatever you need to make it match your picture, okay?"

Jesse held the key to his chest and hugged it over his heart. "I needed you. I love you so much. No one has ever loved me like you do. I . . . We'll figure out the rest. I know we will, but even if it is just us, it's enough. I know this isn't . . . I know you didn't feel the *need* to get married. Thank you for this."

"I didn't only ask for you, Jesse. I *want* to marry you. I want to start a family with you. I'm not sure how many or what ages or when, but this isn't . . . I'm not giving you permission to draw me into the husband placeholder you have in your picture, love. This trip helped me finish *my* picture. I drew you into mine."

Dear Reader,

Thank you for reading Logan Meredith's *Draw Me In*!

We know your time is precious and you have many, many entertainment options, so it means a lot that you've chosen to spend your time reading. We really hope you enjoyed it.

We'd be honored if you'd consider posting a review—good or bad—on sites like **Amazon, Barnes & Noble, Kobo, Goodreads, Twitter, Facebook, Tumblr,** and your blog or website. We'd also be honored if you told your friends and family about this book. Word of mouth is a book's lifeblood!

For more information on upcoming releases, author interviews, blog tours, contests, giveaways, and more, please sign up for our weekly, spam-free newsletter and visit us around the web:

Newsletter: riptidepublishing.com/newsletter
Twitter: twitter.com/RiptideBooks
Facebook: facebook.com/RiptidePublishing
Goodreads: tinyurl.com/RiptideOnGoodreads
Tumblr: riptidepublishing.tumblr.com

Thank you so much for Reading the Rainbow!

RiptidePublishing.com

RIPTIDE
PUBLISHING

Also by Logan Meredith

About the Author

Logan Meredith began writing as a teenager when beautiful boys started keeping her company at night. Unfortunately, the voices she heard were imaginary, and their conversations resulted in horrible insomnia. They only let her sleep when she started typing their words down. Thankfully, being awkward as hell and a head taller than anyone else in school afforded plenty of spare time for writing.

At first, she tried to make them play with characters from her favorite television series or books. She found her lost tribe with a ravenous, crazy group of fan fiction lovers online and started sharing her stories. Then something amazing happened: new characters arrived and demanded their own stories. Only they wanted their own world to play in, and they wanted to find their true loves. So between her day job and making time for her family, she tries to keep up with the requirements of her beautiful men for their happily-ever-afters.

A native of San Antonio, Texas, and a graduate of the University of Texas at San Antonio, Logan is an accomplished cross-country mover having honed her skills bouncing between five states. She currently resides in Houston, Texas. In addition to writing, she spends her time reading and rereading her favorite books, cheering for the San Antonio Spurs, playing Words with Friends, and procrastinating pretty much everything else.

She is a proud member of the LGBTQA community and vocal advocate for mental health awareness, suicide prevention, and equality campaigns.

Logan welcomes the chance to interact with readers.

Twitter: @ll_meredith

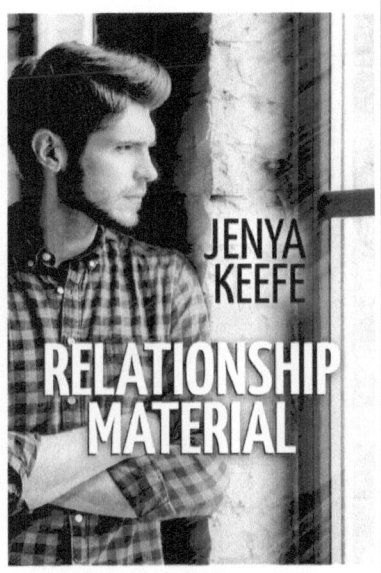